MAGGIE MAY AND MISS FANCYPANTS MYSTERIES

BOOKS 1 – 3

BOOKS BY ALEKSA BAXTER

MAGGIE MAY AND MISS FANCYPANTS MYSTERIES

A DEAD MAN AND DOGGIE DELIGHTS

A CRAZY CAT LADY AND CANINE CRUNCHIES

A BURIED BODY AND BARKERY BITES

A MISSING MOM AND MUTT MUNCHIES

A SABOTAGED CELEBRATION AND SALMON SNAPS

A POISONED PAST AND PUPPERMINTS

A FOULED-UP FOURTH

NOSY NEWFIE HOLIDAY SHORTS

HALLOWEEN AT THE BAKER VALLEY BARKERY & CAFE

A HOUSEBOUND HOLIDAY

TABLE OF CONTENTS

A DEAD MAN
AND DOGGIE DELIGHTS

A MAGGIE MAY AND MISS FANCYPANTS MYSTERY

ALEKSA BAXTER

CHAPTER 1

I hadn't been in the Baker Valley a day before the trouble began.

Fancy—that's my three-year-old Newfoundland, full name Miss Fancypants—and I were sitting out back in the yard at my grandpa's reading a book and minding our own business, enjoying the mid-spring day.

Well, I was reading. Fancy was curled up nearby, her head on her paws, watching the world go by. Not that there was much of a world to see. My grandpa's place is on the edge of town and backs up to a mountainside covered in tall evergreens and aspen trees, so all she really had to see was five hundred feet of trees followed by an incredibly blue sky without a cloud in sight.

Man, I love Colorado.

Anyway. There we were, minding our own business, not bothering a soul, when Fancy jumped up and raced to the fence, barking like a mad woman. And it wasn't her "Hey, is that a dog, can we play?" bark either. It was her, "There's a jerk too close to my home" bark.

I reluctantly set my book aside—I'd just gotten to the good part, too—and dragged myself over to see what was bothering her. She'll usually stop if I just check out whatever it is and tell her she's been a good girl, but as I was walking across the yard I heard someone barking back at her.

That's right. Some jerk on the other side of the fence was *barking* at my dog. Seriously? I mean, what the…? Who does that?

I'd just spent five years living in Washington, DC and not once had someone barked at my dog. They'd stepped away from her like she had the plague, and there'd been an inordinate number of people who thought leaving chicken bones on the sidewalk was just fine and dandy, but none of them had *barked* at my dog.

And, because I was still in big city mode and not "love thy neighbor because you live in a town of a hundred where everyone knows everyone" mode, I stepped up on that little board along the bottom of the fence and told the guy off.

You know what he did? You know what that jerk did then?

He barked at me, too!

He lunged at me like he was going to attack me and barked. Three times. Woof, woof, woof.

I just stared at him like he was crazy. I mean, I'd moved to Baker Valley because it was supposed to be peaceful and nice and this is what I got on my first full day there? Some weird man barking at me? I didn't even know what to do at that point.

Unfortunately, while I was busy trying to figure out if werewolves might actually be real, which would at least explain the man's ridiculous behavior, my grandpa got involved.

With a shotgun.

There I was, hanging onto the fence, Fancy barking her head off at my feet, and my grandpa comes walking around the side of the house to confront the guy, shotgun in hand. At least I was pretty sure it was a shotgun, I'm not a gun person myself, but it had two long barrels that he pointed right at the guy. *After* cocking it or whatever it is you do with a shotgun to let someone know that when you pull that trigger it's gonna hurt.

"Son, you'd best get on your way." He planted his feet and pointed the gun right at the man, steady as steady could be.

I held my breath wondering if the man was stupid enough to bark at him, too. I figured it was a fifty-fifty chance and I really didn't know what my grandpa would do at that point, but I was pretty sure I didn't want to find out.

Fortunately, the guy just backed away, hands up. "Sorry, Mr. Carver. Didn't mean any offense. Just walking by."

"Well walk a little faster." My grandpa followed him with the gun, eyes flinty and jaw clenched tight. "And next time you leave my granddaughter alone or I'll put you in the ground where you belong, you hear me?"

"Grandpa," I hissed. "You can't say things like that."

This was exactly the type of thing I'd moved to Baker Valley to prevent. Well, okay, I'd had no idea before I moved that my grandpa was capable of pointing a gun at someone and threatening to put them in the ground where they belonged, but he had been slipping lately, and I'd been worried about him all alone now that my grandma was gone.

Barking guy muttered something under his breath as he hiked a slim trail up the mountainside, but at least he was smart enough to keep going and not say it loud enough for my grandpa to hear.

My grandpa followed him with the gun until he finally disappeared from sight, and then returned to the front of the house without another word, waving a hand at our neighbor, Mr. Jackson, on the way. Mr. Jackson nodded back at him and returned to tending his raspberry bushes as if my grandpa threatening someone with a shotgun was a daily occurrence not even worth mentioning.

I hopped off the fence with a loud sigh. Fancy came to check on me and I scratched at her velvety black ears, trying to process what had just happened. "Holy cow, Fancy!" I whispered. "He almost shot that man."

She leaned into my hand with a grumble of pleasure as if to say it was all good now, no harm, no foul.

Was I really the only one that thought it problematic that my grandpa had almost shot someone? I knew I should take the gun away. I mean, you can't have an old man running around pointing a gun at people, no matter how much they might deserve it.

But I was also pretty sure he wasn't just going to hand it over. And I didn't really want the thing. As dangerous as he might be with it, I would be even more so. I'd never handled a gun before and would probably end up shooting myself if I tried. Not to mention, it wasn't the best way to start off my new life living in his house, trying to take his gun away.

Maybe I could skate by with a stern talk this first time around. And take the gun if it happened again? Oh, that was a good plan.

I trudged back towards the house. "Come on, Fancy. Let's see if we can talk some sense into the most stubborn man I've ever met in my life."

She followed along at my side, tail wagging. I paused to grab my book, wishing I could just sit back down and lose myself in its pages, but I couldn't shirk my commitment, not on my first day of self-appointed grandpa duty.

As I led Fancy inside I comforted myself with the thought that at least he hadn't shot the guy.

🐾 🐾 🐾

"Grandpa?" I called as I pushed through the back door and made my way past the laundry room towards the kitchen.

Fancy shoved ahead of me, her tail wagging a mile a minute as she went to find him. I swear, she loves him ten times more than she loves me. She'd spent the entire night before with her head resting against his feet as we caught up. With me she stays nearby but never actually close enough to touch. Him? She was practically in his lap.

Curse of my life, to own a dog that likes any man more than she likes me.

I found them both in the living room. Grandpa was seated on the worn brown couch he'd owned for at least twenty years, small bits of stuffing pushing out of the tears in the seams. Fancy was leaning against his legs moaning happily as he scratched her ears.

"Where is it?" I demanded, crossing my arms for emphasis as I stared him down.

"Where's what?" He glanced up at me, not the least bit intimidated.

If I hadn't know that he was eighty-two-years-old I would've probably put his age around sixty. He was a trim, tough man who looked like he could take on the world without hesitation, a white t-shirt peeking out from behind a short-sleeved plaid shirt that was tucked into his worn Levi's. Part of the looking younger thing came from the fact that his hair had never grayed, just faded from dark brown to a lighter brown.

I exhaled through my nose, my lips pressed tight together in disapproval. "The gun. You know, the one you just pointed at some stranger walking behind our house?"

"That wasn't a stranger. That was Jack Dunner. Kid's been worthless since the day he was born." He reached for his shirt pocket and then let his hand drop when he remembered he'd stopped smoking three years ago. Too late for my grandma's cancer, but better late than never.

"Well you can't just go pointing a gun at someone because you think they're worthless."

"Look, Maggie May…"

"Maggie, please." It's not easy to be named after a Rod Stewart song, especially when your family insists on using the entire name every time they talk to you.

His lips quirked in a small smile. "Fine, *Maggie*, you have to understand that some people need a little bit more than a firm word to keep them in line. And with a kid like Jack Dunner about the only thing he's going to understand is a punch to the jaw or a shotgun pointed between the eyes. Trust me. I've dealt with plenty of Jack Dunners in my day."

I rolled my eyes. I couldn't help it. Here I was, thirty-six-years-old, rolling my eyes at my grandpa. But, really? I mean, come on. Some people are only going to understand a punch to the jaw or a shotgun pointed between the eyes? Who says things like that? And *believes* them? Because he clearly did.

"Don't you roll your eyes at me, Maggie. You didn't grow up around here, you don't know anything about anybody."

I slumped down on the couch opposite him with an exaggerated sigh, trying not to get stuck as it sagged under my weight. It was a hideous goldenrod color that had probably last been popular in the 70's. Based on the springs poking into my thigh, that was probably how old it was, too.

I tried again. "I didn't grow up here, I'll grant you that. But I can't think of anywhere where it's okay to point a shotgun at someone. You're lucky Mr. Jackson didn't call the cops on you. Or this Jack guy—who is not a kid by the way. He looked to be about twenty-five or so."

"He's a kid to me. Wasn't too long ago I was walking him through how to field a grounder."

My grandpa had been the volunteer coach of the town baseball team for forty years or more. He'd coached every boy and girl in town at one point or another.

"Well maybe you should've worked on his attitude while you were helping him with his fielding instead of having to pull a shotgun on him now."

My grandpa shrugged, reaching for his non-existent cigarettes once more. "Some folks are just born bad, Maggie. Nothing to be done for 'em."

"Oh that's ridiculous. No one is born bad, Grandpa."

I stood. I needed some fresh air. It had been my decision to move to Baker Valley, but so far things weren't exactly going to plan.

I grabbed my keys. "Look. I need to swing by the store. See how things are going and check in with Jamie. You going to be okay here?"

He snorted. "I think I can manage for a few hours."

"Well just be sure to put that shotgun away, would ya? And try not to shoot anyone while I'm gone?"

"I'll try, but no promises."

I glared at him, but he just winked back at me.

"Come on, Fancy. Let's go."

She glanced up at him before making her slow way to me, making it abundantly clear she'd prefer to stay with him. "You will actually like this, you know, you purebred mutt," I muttered as I put on her leash and collar.

We walked down the front steps to the beat-up van I'd bought just to make Fancy's life easier. I'd loved my old SUV but even at three Fancy already had bad days where it hurt to jump up. And using a ramp? Yeah, no. She jumped over the ramp every single time, making it even worse. So a van it was. I felt like a PTA mom, except my kid was a large black dog who never listened to me.

As Fancy made herself comfortable on the bed that took up half of the back of the van—I'd removed the seats we didn't need—I glanced towards the house, wondering if I'd made a mistake moving to Baker Valley.

It had seemed like such a good idea at the time. I'd live with my grandpa—who wasn't exactly a spring chicken anymore and who'd been all alone since my grandma died two years before. I'd get away from my miserable corporate job and be able to live in one of the most beautiful places I'd ever seen. And, best of all, I'd finally be able to open a business with my best friend from college, Jamie, who was one of the best bakers I knew.

It also gave me a chance to indulge my love of dogs. We were calling the place The Baker Valley Barkery and Café. Get it? Barkery instead of bakery? Because it's a bakery for dogs? At least, half of it is.

(It's alright. Most people don't get it. They keep telling me there's a typo in our logo. I figure someday we'll be famous enough that everyone will know exactly what a barkery is. Until then I'm doomed to multiple conversations about how, no, that really is not a typo, thank you.)

The other half, the café side, was for people. Assuming we ever actually opened. Jamie had been doing all the heavy lifting on getting the place open while I moved. We were two weeks away from opening day, theoretically, but when I'd talked to her the night before she'd told me there had been some "complications" that might delay our opening but not to worry about it, she had it handled.

I'd trust Jamie with my life, but I also knew her well enough to know that when she said there had been complications that might delay the opening that that was Jamie-speak for all hell had broken loose. I needed to see just how bad things were.

As I pulled out of the driveway I figured at least it wasn't going to be worse than my grandpa pointing a shotgun at someone, right?

Wrong.

CHAPTER 2

By the time I reached the store I'd calmed down enough to see the humor in the whole shotgun situation. It helped that I had a good twenty minute drive to get there. And not through urban sprawl like I was used to, but along a two-lane highway that wound its way through cattle land that was green with spring and dotted with the occasional red barn or one-story ranch home tucked away half a mile off the highway, usually down some rutted dirt road separated from the rest of the world by a rusted metal gate.

The whole area is called Baker Valley because it's a long narrow valley tucked into the Colorado mountains. For tourist trap purposes the towns in the area all agreed to pool their advertising funds and advertise the whole valley, but there are actually a half dozen small towns spread throughout the area. My grandpa's place is at the west end of the valley in a town creatively named Creek that has two gas stations, one church, the county seat, a funeral home, a pioneer museum, and about forty houses, half of which probably started off as mobile homes until someone built a foundation around them.

About ten minutes from there is the town of Masonville. It's where everyone in the valley goes to school and boasts its own McDonald's and a supermarket. (New additions in the last decade. Prior to that folks would drive the hour and half into Denver to stock up on groceries once a month, assuming they didn't live on the deer they hunted and the vegetables they grew in their backyard.)

Another ten minutes past Masonville is the shining jewel of the valley, Bakerstown. (Someone was being awfully creative when they settled the valley, let me tell you. But that was the Colorado settlers for ya. Take your last name and slap it on everything you could find. If that failed, call a spade a spade. So we got Bakerstown for the Baker family, Masonville for the Mason family, and Creek for, you guessed it, the creek that runs through town.)

Bakerstown is the hub of all activity in the valley because it has the ski slopes. Not that most of the locals ski—they're far more interested in snowmobiling—but everyone knows that the skiers are the ones with the money, so the ski slopes are a necessary evil if you want to live somewhere as beautiful as Baker Valley year-round and not live off the land.

And it is beautiful. Picture a sprawling green expanse surrounded on all sides by towering mountains that are covered in evergreens up to the tree line and have snow on the peaks even at the height of summer. Add to that one of the clearest streams you've ever seen running through the whole area like a silver ribbon. (That stream is Fancy's favorite. She loves to go wading and bark at the fishermen there in search of trout.)

I don't know what it is about Baker Valley, but it's always been magic to me. The sky always seems bluer, the clouds—when there are any—are whiter and softer, the air is cleaner, the people are nicer. (For the most part. Not as nice as when I was a little girl who'd come to visit my grandparents for the summer, but still nicer than most of the world.)

I'd never lived full-time in the valley, but it was always where my heart was. And now it was my home, too. All my worries melted away as I drove towards the store, because I was finally where I wanted to be, doing what I wanted to do.

🐾 🐾 🐾

That soaring happiness lasted right up to the moment I parked outside our store and noticed the boarded up doors and windows and the black scorch marks on the brick façade.

I sat there, not wanting to go inside and find out why our formerly-pristine building looked like it had been hit by a bomb. I would've probably sat there forever, but Fancy started crying her head off at me to get out of the car.

You'd think a hundred-and-forty-pound dog would have a deep, booming bark but nine times out of ten Fancy resorts to a high-pitched cry that's about as painful on the ears as fingernails on a chalkboard.

It's highly effective, I'll give her that. No one wants to sit in a car with a dog making a noise that obnoxious in their ear. So as much as I wanted to bury my head in my hands and ask, "What now?" I scrambled out of the van and let Fancy out.

Sitting in the car wasn't going to make things better anyway. I needed to find out what Jamie had kept from me and hope it wasn't so bad we'd have to delay our opening. All of my plans hinged on being open that first weekend in June.

Something that did not look very likely at that moment.

CHAPTER 3

I walked Fancy to the grass at the far end of the parking lot and turned back to look at the store. The little cartoon Newfie heads on either end of the sign made me smile—they'd been my idea, in honor of Fancy. In between, in the curly script the sign guy hadn't wanted to use, it proclaimed this as the home of the Baker Valley Barkery and Café.

(I'll admit, it was a little hard to read, but I thought it had flare. Better than using Helvetica like he'd suggested. How boring would that have been?)

The café was on the left, the barkery on the right, each with their own door and large picture window that would give guests a great view of the mountains—once the cheap plywood that was currently covering them was removed, that is. If I hadn't known better, I would've thought a hurricane was coming, the way the windows were boarded over. But this was Colorado, so clearly something else had happened since my last visit.

Inside there should be tables set up on both sides with a pass-through that would allow someone on the café side to access the barkery side and vice versa. There was a lot less seating on the barkery side than the café side because we wanted to leave enough room for dogs as well as humans to sit comfortably.

We'd also added little cubbies surrounded by half-walls on the barkery side where people could leave their dogs safely for a few minutes while they ran to the restroom. (I've been that person traveling cross-country with their dog who just needs to pee real quick but doesn't want to leave their dog in a hot car while they do, so I can appreciate the need to have a safe space like that.)

My space—the service counter of the barkery—was at the far back on the right-hand side. We had one of those glass display cases like any good bakery would, but all of the treats were going to be for dogs instead of humans. Fancy's favorite were the Doggie Delights—which were basically balls of peanut butter with other yummy stuff added in—but she was only allowed one per day. Those calories add up fast, and a big girl like her needs to watch the stress she puts on her joints.

Fancy's personal cubby—which was big enough for an extra-large dog bed and her food and water bowls—was in the far corner behind the barkery counter.

Opposite that was our dogphenalia section that included Baker Valley leashes and collars, mugs with a circular version of our logo, those dog window stickers everyone loves, and whatever other kitschy items I thought might sell to a dog-loving tourist crowd.

There were also some pre-packaged treat bags I'd had manufactured so people could take them home as gifts for their furry friends who hadn't made the trip. (If you ever want to know how private label packaging works, just ask. I know more about it now than I ever wanted to.) And just in case we didn't attract enough visitors to the store, I was also planning on offering everything via our website, too.

I wanted to make it as easy for people to give me their money as I could.

The opposite side of the store was Jamie's side. It was a regular café that was going to serve things like coffee and cinnamon rolls. (Jamie makes the best cinnamon rolls in the world. I kid you not. They are better than any cinnamon roll I have ever tasted and I have made it my life's mission to try cinnamon rolls everywhere I go.) The café side included a full kitchen and a small office that were kept completely separate from the barkery side.

Let me tell you, negotiating everything with the local zoning inspector had been a challenge. He was full of what-if scenarios. What if two dogs were seated too close to each other and got in a fight? What if someone tripped over a dog trying to get to their table? What if dog hair made its way into the human food? What if, what if, what if.

We'd met every single objection and then some, and I was proud of what we'd built, but now, looking at the scorch marks on the bricks around the windows and doors, I was a little scared to step through that door.

No point in delaying, though. Best to see what had happened and figure out how to deal with it. I led Fancy across the lot, forcing myself to take deep, calming breaths. Jamie was alive and well. We still had two weeks. It was going to be okay.

🐾 🐾 🐾

Jamie met me at the door, wiping the sweat from her face with a hand still covered in a thick leather workman's glove. She'd braided her long brown hair back, but little tendrils had escaped and were fuzzed around her face.

As she pulled the gloves off her slender fingers and tucked them into the back pocket of her jeans, I asked, "Do I want to know what happened here?"

"It's fine. Nothing to worry about. I've got it under control."

I've never seen Jamie ruffled. You could put her in the middle of a total apocalypse and she'd look around with a shrug and say, "Well, best get to it. Things aren't going to fix themselves." It's what makes her such a great business partner. Always dependable, competent as all get out, and never willing to admit defeat.

But this time I had to wonder if she'd lost her connection to reality. There were black soot marks on the ceiling on the café side and it was clear that all of the glass in the windows and doors had been violently removed by a significant amount of force. A sooty smell hung in the air and Fancy sneezed twice, shaking her head.

I glanced towards the kitchen which was a soot-stained mess from the little bit I could see. "It's fine?"

"A minor setback, that's all." Jamie bent down to say hi to Fancy while I pressed my lips together and counted to ten, reminding myself that if Jamie said she had it handled, she probably did.

We'd known each other since we were babies and I'd come to the valley to visit my grandparents, but we hadn't become life-long friends until freshman year of college at CU when we found ourselves on a volunteer project to repaint a local elementary school. The thing was a disaster. There was paint, thankfully, but that was about it. No paintbrushes. No drop cloths. No one who knew a thing about anything.

Jamie and I both stepped up at the same moment to take things in hand. Within an hour we had all the supplies we needed and four teams hard at work. We'd been best friends ever since. And after years of complaining to one another about how miserable we were working for people who didn't see what we could and commiserating over how much we missed the valley, we'd decided enough was enough, pooled our savings, and decided to open the barkery and cafe.

Things *had* been going well.

"So?" I asked.

Jamie shrugged one shoulder. "We didn't get the gas on the stove in the café hooked up the way it should've been and there was a bit of an explosion."

"A bit of an explosion? Was anyone hurt?"

"No. It was just Katie and me working at the time." She nodded towards a young woman with bright red hair pulled back in a ponytail and the most flawless porcelain skin I'd ever seen in my life who was hard at work scrubbing down the floor. "Luckily the gas buildup wasn't near as bad as it could've been because I'd propped open the front door to let in some fresh air, so the explosion took out all the glass and knocked me for a loop, but that was it."

"Jamie! Why didn't you tell me?"

"Because I had it under control and there was nothing you could do about it from wherever you were that day. Would you have really left Fancy and your U-Haul truck in Lexington, Kentucky so you could fly back</p>

here and check on me? No. And I wouldn't have wanted you to. I knew you'd be here in a few days and I could tell you then."

I eyed her up and down. "No broken bones?"

"No."

The way she answered made me narrow my eyes and study her more closely. "Concussion?"

"Just a minor one. I'll have a few extra headaches for a while, that's it."

I glanced towards the girl scrubbing the floor who was now trying to keep Fancy at bay. Clearly not a dog person the way she was grimacing and shoving at Fancy. "And Katie?"

"She was outside when it happened, so no injuries there, thankfully. Kitchen took the brunt of it."

"Fancy, leave the girl alone," I called as I headed for the kitchen. Fancy came to join me, Jamie trailing along behind us.

I stopped at the entrance to the kitchen. The walls and the ceiling were almost completely black and what looked like part of the stove was still embedded in the wall to my left. The burnt smell was almost overpowering and Fancy backed away pawing at her nose.

"Here, Fancy." I opened the door next to the kitchen and let her out into the dog run we'd had built out back. She went eagerly, but then turned back to stare at me plaintively when I didn't follow her outside.

I turned back to Jamie. "It could've killed you."

"But it didn't." She flashed me one of her signature smiles. "I'm lucky. You know that."

I shook my head. She was lucky—as this incident proved yet again—but still. That didn't mean she had to be cavalier about it. What if she'd been in the kitchen when this happened? What if she hadn't propped the door open?

I shivered, trying not to think about it. "Are you going to sue the idiot who messed the gas line up?"

"No. And neither are you. It was just a freak accident. No one needs to be sued over it. Everything's going to be fixed in time for our launch and that's all that matters."

I glanced back at the kitchen. "We're launching in two weeks and that's going to be fixed in time?"

"Luke promised me he'll take care of it and I trust he will."

"Luke, huh?" I stepped closer, holding her gaze. "Is this the same Luke who broke your heart at least once a year from third grade through high school and then at least twice in college? Mr. Honeyed Words and Hollow Promises?"

She crossed her arms and glared me down. "He's the best general contractor in the area. He'll get it done. Trust me."

I wanted to argue—the fact that Luke was involved did not bode well—but I bit my tongue and let it go. Jamie was blind where Luke was concerned and the last thing I needed was a big blow up fight with my best friend and business partner two weeks before our launch.

I just hoped she was right about him getting everything done in time. There was a big dog show that was going to be held at the local convention center in two weeks, and if we weren't open in time for that I wasn't sure how the barkery was going to get the word of mouth buzz it needed to succeed. The café side would probably survive a late opening, but the barkery? I didn't think it would.

While Jamie and I had been talking, Fancy had wandered back over to Katie, muddy paw prints showing her wandering trail from the back door to Katie's side.

"Sorry about Fancy," I called to her. "I'll clean that up in a minute. By the way, I'm Maggie." I leaned across the counter and held out my hand.

She stood, clearly not wanting to, and took my hand. "Katie."

Her handshake was about as warm as her non-existent smile and she barely made eye contact before looking away. I studied her as she made her way behind the counter and into the kitchen area, face completely blank of emotion. It's always fascinated me when I meet a really attractive person who's like that. I always wonder how someone can get such positive attention from the world—because with skin like that *and* red hair you know men had to bow and scrape around her all the time—and yet come out so…meh.

My own looks—tall, blonde, and curvy enough to get some attention—had certainly made my life easier. Maybe I could see being shut down with men, because it could be too much sometimes, but all the time? It was just weird.

Jamie, knowing this particular fascination of mine, distracted me by handing me a Coke from the little mini fridge under the counter. "Katie is Georgia's daughter. You remember, Georgia, right?"

"The one who liked to eat mud?" I whispered.

"That's the one."

I gave Jamie my "what were you thinking?" look but she just shrugged. She loves to collect strays and help "fix" them. I figure that's what explains her lifelong fascination with Luke.

"Katie will be with us through next summer and then it's off to college. Right, Katie?" she asked as Katie returned, a mop in hand.

Katie faced off against Fancy, the mop gripped in her hands like a bat. "That's my mother's plan."

I stepped between them and waved a treat under Fancy's nose, luring her to her cubbie behind the barkery counter so I could lock her out of Katie's way before something bad happened. Fancy hesitated for a second—she didn't want to leave the action—but treats always win with her, even when they're the size of a peanut.

You'd think a dog her size would need big treats, but nope, not at all. She'll follow you anywhere for a crumb of a crumb of a crumb.

I settled Fancy down and returned to the café counter, careful to keep out of Katie's way. "And what do you want, Katie?" I asked, genuinely curious and determined to break through that cold exterior. I figured she had to have some hidden passion, right? Everyone does, even if it's stamp collecting.

"I don't know." The way she said it made it pretty clear she was done talking to me. And the abuse she was inflicting on that mop and floor were enough for me to just leave her to it. She didn't want to talk, fine with me.

I turned back to Jamie. "You would not believe what my grandpa did this morning…"

I walked her through the whole crazy incident while

Katie worked around us, violently cleaning the floor until it shone. Jamie laughed so hard when I told her about my grandpa pulling his shotgun, I thought she was going to hurt herself.

I grinned. "It was pretty funny, wasn't it?"

"Oh yeah. And your grandpa's right, you know. There isn't much that will get through to a man like Jack Dunner, but I bet that shotgun woke him up and made him pay attention."

"It certainly woke me up, I'll tell you that."

"Can I go?" Katie interrupted us.

Jamie blinked at her, clearly surprised, but then nodded. "Sure. See you tomorrow?"

"Yeah." She dumped the mop in the kitchen and left without so much as a smile or wave.

"That is one odd girl," I muttered as she revved the engine on an old blue pickup truck and backed out of her parking spot.

"Yeah, well, her mom keeps her on a pretty tight leash. Doesn't want Katie to end up like her, you know."

"How old was she when she had her first kid?"

"Fifteen."

"And how old is Katie?"

"Seventeen."

I shrugged. "She's already done better than her mom then, yeah?"

"Yeah, tell that to Georgia. She wants Katie to avoid all boys until she's at college and maybe even after that."

I winced. "That's not going to work out well…"

"No, it's not. So when Katie asks to leave a little early or come in a little late every once in a while, I let her. Kid's gotta be a kid, you know."

"Hm. Well, when that backfires, you can deal with Georgia. Woman scares me. Always has." I went to let Fancy out of her cubbie, but she was sound asleep, sprawled on her back, her right paw sticking straight up in the air. Goofy girl.

"It's just a half hour here or there. No big deal." Jamie looked at Fancy and shook her head, smiling.

"A person can do a lot in half an hour, you know." We walked back to the café side and I grabbed a wash rag to start wiping down the tables that all had a fine layer of soot on them. "By the way, does Katie get friendlier the more you know her?"

Jamie smacked me in the arm. "Be nice, Maggie. It's hard to be a teenager."

I guessed, but I sure hoped she'd warm up soon, because she was not my idea of the ideal café employee. I'd have to stash her in the back and help all the customers myself if she didn't warm up, which sort of defeated the whole purpose of having her around.

Ah well. I glanced at the burned out kitchen. One disgruntled unfriendly teenager was the least of my worries.

CHAPTER 4

The day before the store opening dawned blue and beautiful, like most days in spring in the Colorado mountains. Fortunately for me, the last two weeks had passed without any exploding stoves or reports of my grandpa pointing a shotgun at someone new. I'd spent most of the time with Fancy, Jamie, and Katie Cross—who'd grown on me some, but not much—getting the store ready for our opening.

Luke had come through for us, just like Jamie said he would. He was still an over-the-top flirtatious sleazeball who was going to break my best friend's heart—again—but at least by the day before the opening we had a fully-functional store that didn't show a single sign of fire damage.

I had plans that day to go into the store and make sure everything was perfect for our launch, but not until after noon. Poor Fancy had put up with a lot of long hours sleeping in her nook at the store and I figured she'd earned a little hike in the woods before opening day.

Not that I really thought she minded all that time snoring away in the corner. She is a Newfie after all and

Newfs aren't exactly the most energetic of breeds. But I knew she also liked to get out and smell new things and we really hadn't had a chance to do so since our arrival.

So after I fed her breakfast at five-thirty in the morning—an unfortunate side effect of living those first crucial months of her life in an apartment with a neighbor who had a loud alarm and liked to get up at that time every morning of every day—we headed up the mountain behind my grandpa's house.

Most of the mountainside was covered not only with big evergreens and tightly-clustered aspens, but with juniper bushes and long grass that you wouldn't want to try to walk through. Fortunately for us, there was a nice little trail I'd seen Mr. Jackson tending the day of our arrival that was just wide enough for me and Fancy to walk side-by-side. Mr. Jackson had done a good job of cutting back the branches, because not one slapped me in the face as we made our way towards the ridgeline about five hundred feet above my grandpa's house.

Fancy's a good girl so she didn't pull on her leash at all, just stopped to sniff and pee on things every few feet. She sometimes became a little too focused on one spot or another and I had to tell her to leave it and give a slight tug to move along, but usually I just let her do her thing. The walk was as much for her as it was for me, after all.

It was a gorgeous late spring morning. Birds were singing in the trees, bees were buzzing around on the early wildflowers scattered along the mountainside, and everything smelled fresh and clean and alive.

I was winded within five minutes because I wasn't used to hiking up mountainsides, and certainly not at seven thousand feet, but that was okay. It was worth it to feel like no one else in the world existed for just a little bit, especially knowing how stressful things would be once the store actually opened.

I probably should've thought about bears or mountain lions or criminals living in caves, but I didn't. I'd always thought of the mountain as part of my grandpa's home. Hardly anybody went there so it was easy to think of it as an extension of his backyard.

I took a break on a large rock slab most of the way up the mountainside. It was big enough it created a perfect space for sitting and watching the sleepy little town below us. I could just barely hear the freight train that passed through town down by the creek on its way to some unknown destination. When we were little, Jamie and I would go up there to watch the trains while we munched on peach slices sprinkled with sugar that her mom had put in a plastic baggie for us.

(It's a wonder neither one of us has diabetes or serious weight issues, the way we used to eat.)

Fancy sprawled out on the ground next to the rock, content to let me have my moment. She was snoring away within moments.

I took a deep breath. Tomorrow was the day. Tomorrow we'd open the Barkery and Café and see if this crazy little dream of ours had any hope of succeeding.

I was scared. Scared that I'd finally chosen to risk everything and pursue my dream and that I'd fail. Scared that I'd have to go back to living in the city, driving an hour each way to work, spending all day everyday inside while the sun shone outside, arguing with people about things that probably didn't matter to anyone but us.

I'd never held it against the folks that liked that sort of thing, but for me that rock in the middle of a mountainside had always been where I'd wanted to be. Right there, looking down at the peaceful little town that was my home, my dog at my side.

It had taken longer to get there than I'd wanted, but I was finally making it happen.

I just hoped it would work out…

🐾 🐾 🐾

After a while, Fancy got restless. Or at least her version of restless, which involved her giving me what I like to call her puppy side-eye where she looks at me out of the corner of her eye like, "Are we done yet? Can we go do something interesting now?" and cries really softly.

If I ignore her, she'll stop. She's good that way. She's learned over the years that sometimes I just have to do my work and she has to be patient until I'm done. But if I show the slightest weakness, she won't let up.

Since the hike was as much for her as for me, we moved on after her first little cry. We continued to the ridgeline where we could see a gorgeous valley nestled between four separate mountain peaks. I'd always loved that valley as a kid; it was so pristine and untouched, nestled there where no one could find it, a secret little hideaway.

I narrowed my eyes at the small wooden cabin that now stood at one end of the valley, rows of something growing nearby. We were too far away for me to tell what was being grown down there, but I figured I had a pretty good idea. Just because Colorado had legalized pot didn't mean that private grow operations had gone away. It wasn't my scene, as a user or a grower, but I'd heard that some folks still grew their own despite the laws.

I turned away from the valley, disappointed to see a treasured childhood memory tarnished that way, even though I'd known it was inevitable. Everything beautiful and private is eventually discovered and destroyed. Still makes me sad when it happens, though.

Reminding myself that the forest around me was still a thousand times more beautiful than the concrete streets of most major cities, I nudged Fancy farther along the ridgeline, determined to enjoy it while I could.

Fancy tugged at her leash and glanced back at me, pleading silently for me to let her run free. I debated doing it. She's good at staying nearby, so I didn't figure she'd run away or anything. But I still remembered that one time at Elk Meadow when she'd seen a couple elk and left me for a good ten minutes while she chased them. I'd been convinced that was the end until I heard her crying her little heart out trying to find me.

I wasn't going to take that kind of risk again, no matter how much she wanted to go exploring. Instead I let her tug me along the trail, her nose pressed tight to the ground as she followed some scent I couldn't detect.

Not until the end that is. Dead things have a certain common stench all their own. Not that I'd known that before I had a dog. But once I got Fancy and we started going to big outdoor dog parks I'd soon learned all about the smell of dead things.

She loves them. We'll be walking along just fine and then there she'll go, off into the bushes, and I'll come up to find her peeing on something that reeks of death. A badger, a squirrel, a rabbit. You name it, she's peed on it.

That's nature for you. Things die, and when they do, they stink. And when they stink, dogs like to pee on them. It's the circle of life. Or so I tell myself.

And trying to keep Fancy from a dead thing once she's found it is almost impossible. I'm not a small woman—about five-eight, one-sixty—but there's no way I can hold back a hundred-and-forty-pound dog who's built for pulling things when she's determined to go somewhere.

So I turned my face away as we got close and let her do her peeing thing. (Thankfully, she's only tried to roll in dead things twice and both times they were fish, so no worries she'd do that this time.)

When she'd finished, I tugged on her leash. "Come on, Fancy, let's go."

She wouldn't budge. I started to worry maybe she really was going to roll in this one and pulled harder. "Come on, Fancy."

I grabbed her collar and pulled her back, but she fought me for every step. "Darn it, Fancy. What's so special about this one?" I demanded.

I almost fell on my butt in surprise when I looked past her and saw what she'd been peeing on. Because it wasn't a badger or a squirrel or a rabbit.

It was a man. And not just any man, but that crazy man who'd barked at me the day after I arrived. At least, I thought it was. Maybe. Stupid ballcap was the same. Hair color looked to be, too.

I stepped closer to take another look, burying my nose in my elbow to try to mask the scent. Somehow I'd been fine when I thought it was a small rodent I was smelling, but now that I knew it was dead human I wanted nothing to do with it.

Of course, Fancy thought my stepping closer was an invitation to pee on him again…Sigh.

It was a little hard to tell if it was him, because the body was mostly buried under some old leaves, but it certainly looked like him. I was tempted, just for a moment, to move the leaves out of the way to check. Call it morbid curiosity—I'd never seen a dead person who hadn't died in a hospital before. I knew these kinds of things happened, but never in my world.

Fortunately, I'd watched enough crime scene shows on television to know I didn't want to mess with the scene or get my DNA all mixed up with his, so I dragged Fancy far enough along the trail to get away from the immediate smell of him while I tried to figure out what to do next.

CHAPTER 5

The obvious choice when you find a dead body is to call the cops. Maybe the guy had just been mauled by a bear or something and that's all there'd be to it. Just a "Howdya do, there's a dead body on that trail up there that someone needs to take care of" and I could be on my merry way.

But…

My grandpa *had* threatened him with a shotgun. Not that I really thought my grandpa was capable of tracking a man up a mountainside, gunning him down, and burying his body under dead leaves.

Not really.

I mean…No. He'd had a rough early life, but he was past all that now.

At least, I thought he was.

But what if he wasn't? What if he really had followed this guy up the mountain and gunned him down? Sure, I believed that murder was wrong and people should do their time and all that. But my grandpa? He was old. He didn't deserve to go to prison. (Again.) Not at his age.

So letting a little more time pass until someone else

discovered the body made a certain amount of sense to me. Maybe by then Mr. Jackson would've forgotten the little confrontation he'd witnessed or at least be a little more fuzzy on the details.

I know. I'm a horrible person. But this was family we were talking about.

There was also the hassle factor. Did I really want to call the cops and get all mixed up in them finding a dead body the day before I was supposed to open my new store? They'd probably want to question me. And who knew how long that would take.

Everything at the store was ready to go—Jamie and I weren't the kind of people to leave things to the last minute—but still. I didn't want to spend most of my last day of freedom in an interview room waiting to be questioned about the death of some jerk who'd barked at me.

Not to mention the gossip factor. This was a small town. People would know I'd found the body and that's all they'd want to talk about. I didn't want to ruin our opening with thoughts of dead people under bushes. Talk about unappetizing.

(I really am a horrible person, aren't I?)

But then I figured he probably had a mother who was missing him by now and who deserved to know that he wouldn't be home for Christmas. And what if he had kids? Didn't they deserve to know where their daddy was?

While I debated and thought things through, Fancy lay down on the path. (She's not one for standing if she doesn't have to.) As I processed all the pros and cons she rested her head on her paws and watched me with her steady amber gaze, her mind already made up.

"Fine," I sighed and reached for my phone. "See? Happy now?"

She closed her eyes while I dialed 9-1-1.

Luckily for the dead guy, I had enough of a signal to complete the call, because if I'd had to walk back down the mountain first, I probably would've rethought my decision. But no, the call went through just fine. I explained to the very sweet and patient woman who answered exactly what I'd found.

I'm not sure she believed me—Creek isn't exactly a hotbed of criminal activity—but she took down my information and told me an officer would be by my grandpa's to talk to me after they'd checked out my story.

Good enough. I'd done my civic duty. If they decided it was a prank call, fine by me, I'd just be sure not to let Fancy close enough to pee on the body next time we were in the area.

I stomped my way back down the mountainside to my grandpa's, Fancy trotting along in front of me happily sniffing anything and everything, tail wagging with joy.

At least one of us was having a good day.

🐾 🐾 🐾

When I got back home I told my grandpa what had happened, watching his face for any sign he already knew. His only reaction was to reach for his non-existent cigarettes and say, "Someone was going to shoot that man sooner or later. Only question was who," and then turn his attention back to the daily crossword.

I didn't want to freak Jamie out the day before the opening so I just texted her that something had come up and I'd try to be in later but didn't know when. She immediately thought something had happened to my grandpa and I had to text her back to let her know no one was hurt or injured. Or at least, no one that mattered. When she texted a "???" to that, I just let her know that I'd give her the full story once I got there.

Whenever that was.

And then I waited. And waited. And waited.

I had a book I'd been enjoying, but my mind was so distracted I stopped trying to read it after I read the same paragraph ten times and still couldn't remember what it said.

I tried grilling my grandpa about the dead guy, but he told me to leave him alone. (He takes his crossword puzzles very seriously. Even has a crossword dictionary he carries around like other people carry a bible. And doesn't appreciate if you look over his shoulder while trying to find something to do and solve one of the answers for him either, let me tell you.)

I was tempted to start looking the dead guy up on the internet but then decided that probably wasn't the best of ideas. What if the cops seized my computer and saw all those searches? What would they think?

(Probably nothing, I know. But you try finding a dead body behind your house and then waiting for the cops to come by and see what you come up with to entertain yourself while you're waiting.)

Finally, when I was about at my wit's end and ready to just head out to the store for something to do, there was a knock at our front door.

"I've got it." I raced to answer the door while my grandpa grunted a reply without even bothering to look up from his crossword. Fancy lifted her head halfway from where she was lying at his feet and then dropped back to the ground with a loud sigh. (She's not the best of guard dogs...)

I yanked open the front door—it sticks but I maybe gave it a little more force than it needed in my excitement—to find a very good-looking man in a cop's uniform, hand raised to knock again. He was tall, dark hair, blue eyes, and filled out his uniform in a very pleasing sort of way.

I gave myself two seconds to appreciate an example of the beauty this world has to offer and then I shut all that nonsense down, because I had a business to start up, a grandpa to take care of, and a dead body to discuss.

"Bout time you got here," I said. I knew I was being rude, but he'd made me wait a long time. Plus good-looking men make me cranky. I don't like being distracted.

He grinned at me in that way overly-confident men sometimes have. "Maggie May. It's been a long time."

I glared at him. I'd remember knowing a man who looked like that. And I didn't. "I'm sorry, am I supposed to know you?"

My grandpa, who'd finally bothered to join us, squeezed my shoulder. "Now, Maggie May, is that any way to treat your first love?" He shook the man's hand. "Women. How quickly they forget. How've you been, Matt?"

Matt—whoever that was—shook my grandpa's hand with a firm grip and slight nod. "Good, Mr. Carver. I'm at my dad's old place. Getting all his stuff sorted and taken care of."

"And the new job? You're liking it?"

He shrugged one shoulder. "It's not as exciting as Iraq."

"Not much is, I'm sure. That a good thing or a bad thing?"

He thought for a moment. "Both."

My grandpa laughed and I crossed my arms, glaring at both of them. "If you two are done catching up? I assume you're here about the dead body?"

"I am." He grinned at me, the smile wrinkles in the corners of his eyes giving him a mischievous look that was a little too appealing.

"Let me get my shoes and I'll show you where it is."

"No need. We already found him. I left Sue up there doing her thing so I could come down, welcome you to the neighborhood, and get your statement."

"Who's Sue? And why do you think you know me? I'd…remember if we'd met."

He laughed. He had a good laugh, but I shoved that thought away as fast as it occurred to me.

"Sue is the coroner. She's taking her pictures and seeing to the body. And we have met. Many, many years ago. I lived in Creek before my mom moved us to Bakerstown. According to her, you and I were inseparable."

My grandpa chuckled. "You two *were* adorable together. Of course, I can't say I appreciated how Maggie chose to demonstrate her affection for you." He pointed at the wall behind me where the word Matt was scrawled in permanent black marker, twelve-inches high, the letters poorly-formed and wobbly. "Thirty years and I've never been able to remove that no matter how hard I try."

I flushed scarlet. "You're *that* Matt?"

"Yep. Sure am."

My grandpa laughed. "You want me to drag out the photo of the two of you cuddled together in my armchair reading a book? It really is a great picture."

Fortunately, Fancy chose that moment to introduce herself. She nudged Matt's hand with her nose, demanding his attention.

"Hey, there, who do we have here?" he asked as he knelt down and started rubbing her ears. She groaned in pleasure and practically knocked him over as she leaned into him, eyes closed in ecstasy. I was grateful for the save, but disgusted by how easily she let him win her over. Sellout.

I headed for the kitchen, desperately in need of a Coke. This day was not going at all the way I'd planned it. At least Fancy redeemed herself when Officer Handsome tried to follow me to the kitchen. She wove her way between his legs like an oversized cat and almost tripped him. I smiled. Something needed to bring that man down a notch or ten. He was far too confident for his own good.

Of course, he just laughed. Points to him for being a dog person, but a man who was handsome *and* a dog person was so not what I needed right then.

CHAPTER 6

The three of us settled at the kitchen table, a small metal table shoved up against the wall, leaving only three possible places to sit. My grandpa picked up his crossword and pretended to be working on it, but I knew he was listening to every word we said.

Matt opened the Coke I'd given him, the sound of its fizzing filling the air between us. He said there was no need for a formal interview down at the station. Unless I'd killed the guy, that is.

After confirming that no, I had not killed the man, left his body there to rot, and then gone back to report it later, we got started. The first few questions were simple enough. Name. Address. Age. Marital Status. I raised an eyebrow at that last one but answered Single and moved on like it was nothing worth noting.

Then he asked me how I'd found the body.

I'd debated this one while I was waiting for him to arrive. Should I tell the cop my dog peed on the dead body before I realized what it was? Or should I just keep that to myself and let him assume any pee on the body was from wild animals? Because they'd have to notice, right? I mean, that kind of thing leaves something behind. And on all those cop shows they always are able to tell who the pee belonged to.

I mean, okay, not like they're going around testing pee all the time on those shows. But often enough that it's come up as the one little thing that gets the killer busted in the end at least once or twice. I wouldn't want them going down the wrong path only to find out it was my dog that had done it.

So after taking an extra swallow of Coke, I told him what Fancy had done. Both he and my grandpa stared at me.

"What?" I said, defensively. "Don't look at me like that. She likes to pee on dead things. She's a dog."

Matt glanced at Fancy who was sound asleep under the table, her head nestled against his foot, traitor that she was. "You don't look like you like to pee on dead things," he told her.

"She has hidden depths."

He laughed softly. "So I see. You didn't know she was peeing on a body?"

"No. I wasn't looking. I could smell it, but I don't like to look too closely at the dead things she pees on."

He scrawled a series of notes on his notepad. I tried to see what he was writing—I'm pretty good at reading upside down—but his handwriting was completely illegible.

He noticed and turned his notes towards me. "Short hand. My grandma taught me. You'd be amazed how much knowing it has come in handy over the years."

Ah. That explained it. He was cheating. I made a mental note to learn short hand. I don't like not knowing what someone is writing about me. Not that we were ever going to cross paths again, not if I could help it.

"That all you need?" I asked, ready for him to leave and never come back.

"Almost. Did you know him?"

I bounced my Coke can against the table, trying to figure out how to answer his question. "You mean, had we been introduced?"

He narrowed his eyes. "Sure. Let's start there."

"No, we had not." I beamed at him, pretty pleased with how I'd side-stepped that landmine.

He leaned closer and I felt like the overhead kitchen light had suddenly been transformed into one of those police interrogation lamps. "Did you know who he was when you found the body?"

"I had my suspicions." I held his intense blue gaze, refusing to crack.

"How so? If you hadn't been introduced?"

I bit my lip, trying to figure out how to step around the question. The only sound in the kitchen was the tap, tap, tap of my Coke can on the tabletop as I tried to find an answer that wouldn't implicate my grandpa.

Unfortunately, he did it for me.

"Oh for heaven's sake, Maggie May, just tell the man." He turned to Matt. "The day after Maggie arrived, Jack went walking up the trail behind our house, and when Fancy here barked at him he barked back at her. So Maggie told him what for and he barked at her, too."

Matt nodded. "Okay. What was so hard about that?"

"Because Maggie probably thinks I shot him."

"Grandpa!" I pressed my lips together and bugged

my eyes out in the universal sign for keep your mouth shut, but he wasn't even looking at me.

"And why would she think that, Mr. Carver?"

My grandpa reached for his non-existent cigarettes and cussed softly when he remembered he didn't smoke anymore.

"Sir?"

"Because I threatened him with my shotgun. You know how that boy was, words were never enough."

"Grandpa," I hissed. "You didn't have to tell him that."

Matt raised an eyebrow at me and I sat back in my chair, feeling only slightly guilty for encouraging my grandpa to lie to the police.

My grandpa looked right at me as he added, "I didn't shoot him, by the way. Not worth the lead. Especially when someone else was going to do it sooner rather than later."

Matt tapped his pen on his paper. "I believe you, sir, but that puts me in an awfully awkward position."

"Why's that?"

"Because it looks like Jack was shot with a shotgun. At least that's Sue's preliminary."

"Well, I didn't do it. Lots of people in this town own shotguns. Now, if you'd found the body on my front yard, maybe you could think it was me. But not halfway up the mountainside. I'm too old to go tracking someone down like that."

Matt pinched the bridge of his nose. It was clear he believed my grandpa but he was also a man of the law and he couldn't just ignore such a likely suspect. "Do you have the gun, sir?"

"Of course I do." My grandpa crossed his arms and

glared at Matt like he'd just proven himself to be a little low in the intelligence department.

Matt didn't even flinch. "Is it locked up tight in a gun safe?"

My grandpa snorted. "What good would that do me? Take me ten minutes to get the stupid thing out and by then I'd be dead or the trouble would be gone."

I winced. I wasn't surprised, but I really, really wished he hadn't said that.

Matt made a note on his notepad. "So your shotgun, which you swear you did not use to kill Jack Dunner, is somewhere in this house but not locked up?"

"No. It's in my truck."

I almost fell out of my chair. Seriously? He'd left a shotgun in his truck?

"Is the truck locked?" Matt asked, his tone making it clear he already knew what the answer to that was going to be.

"No. This is Creek, not some big fancy city. I don't need to lock my truck."

"Grandpa…" I buried my face in my hands. Did he honestly not understand how problematic it was that he was carrying a loaded gun around in an unlocked truck? Set aside the fact that a man had been murdered with a weapon just like that, he had to know it was never a good idea to leave a loaded gun just lying around.

Didn't he?

Matt nodded once. "Okay. I'm going to need to see that gun, sir."

"See it or take it?" My grandpa leveled a look at Matt that had backed down more than one dangerous man over the years.

"Both." Matt met him glare for glare, which I had to reluctantly admit was pretty impressive. "If you'd had it locked in your gun safe, maybe I could've left it with you. But you're telling me that you had an unsecured firearm sitting in a vehicle anyone could've accessed within the vicinity of a murder. I have to consider that your gun, whether you shot it or not, was the murder weapon."

My grandpa huffed a laugh. "Fine. Take it. But you better bring it back to me as soon as you're done with it."

"So you can point it at someone else who upsets you?" Matt asked with a smile.

"Now you listen here, Matthew Allen Barnes, I knew you before you could toddle. And you will not make smart aleck comments to me like that. I am a responsible gun owner and I want my gun back once you see that I didn't use it to kill someone. Got it?"

"Yes, sir." Matt downed the rest of his Coke and set it back on the table. There was still a faint smile on his lips. "Maggie, it was nice to see you again after all these years. Mr. Carver, if you'll lead me to the gun?"

As they walked to the door I hoped that would be the last of it. Unfortunately, the way things had been going so far, I suspected Officer Barnes would be back sooner rather than later.

Just what I needed.

CHAPTER 7

It was almost a relief to go to the barkery after that morning's excitement. Jamie had brought in her golden retriever puppy, Lulu, and we let Fancy and Lulu run around in the dog run out back while I filled her in on all the details.

"You don't think he really did it, do you?" she asked.

"No. He couldn't have. I mean, okay, he probably *could* have, but he wouldn't have. Like he told the cop, waste of lead."

Luke, general contractor and all around pain in my, well, you know, poked his head out the barkery door. "Hey, Beautiful. Hey, Sunshine. How are you ladies doing today?"

I rolled my eyes and ignored him. I'd learned long ago that any man who calls all women by little names like that all the time is a player. You don't have to keep track of who you're flirting with if every woman is Beautiful or Sunshine.

Unfortunately, Jamie had never learned the same lesson. (As her string of unfortunate boyfriends showed.) "Hey, Luke," she simpered at him. "I thought you guys were done with all your work."

As he stepped onto the back patio I caught a peek of Katie staring forlornly at him before the door closed. Not her, too. What was it about the man? Sure, he was good-looking in that rugged cowboy/bad boy sort of way. You just knew he'd suggest going skinny dipping in some private pond tucked away on a bit of property he didn't own given even a little bit of encouragement. But, really. Couldn't they see through his crap?

He leaned against the wall and leered down at us. (Okay, I call it leering. Jamie would've called it smiling and wouldn't have noticed the way he angled himself for the best view down her shirt.)

"I figured I'd drop by, give things one last look, and maybe give my ladies a little kiss on the cheek for good luck." He had the audacity to wink at us.

Jamie giggled. I stood up. "I'm good, thanks. And you just remember that that red-headed beauty inside is too young for you to be giving kisses to, you hear me?" I glared at him.

"Who, Katie? She's seventeen. That's not too young."

"Yes, it is. You go anywhere near that girl in that way and you will answer to me. Got it?"

He shrugged me off. "You don't have to be such a buzzkill, Maggie. She'll be eighteen in two more months."

I glared him down. I hadn't missed the fact that he knew exactly how old she was and exactly when he could make a move on her without repercussions.

Jamie looked up at him, a slight frown on her face. "Are you attracted to Katie?" Her voice trembled. Great, just what I needed. A love triangle between my best friend, the resident sleaze, and our shop assistant.

Luke leaned in and brushed his hand down the side of Jamie's face. "She's a pretty girl, that's all. Not a beautiful woman like you are. You're so beautiful I sometimes forget to breathe when you're around."

Jamie swooned. I made gagging noises. "Come on, Jamie, you're better than this."

I shook my head in disgust, but there's no stopping a woman who's fallen for the wrong guy. "I need to do a final inspection. I'll leave you two to whatever this is. Fancy, come on, girl." I whistled and she came trotting to me, Lulu trailing along behind.

As I pushed my way past Luke and back inside I told myself I should be grateful Luke had taken such an interest in the store. Without him we would've never recovered from the fire in time to meet our grand opening date. But I wasn't so sure the tradeoff of having him around was worth it.

I found Katie in the café's kitchen, her nose pressed to the glass as she watched Luke and Jamie.

"He isn't worth it, you know."

She flinched back and pretended to be wiping down the counter. "I don't know what you're talking about."

"Look, I was seventeen once, too. And when I was I thought it was so cool how these older men found me attractive. Like, wow. A man not a boy and he wants *me*. But I'll tell you something…You get to be that man's age and you think about being attracted to a seventeen-year-old and then you realize how downright skeevy that really is. Jamie and I grew up with Luke. He's old enough to be your father."

She threw the washrag in the sink. "I said I don't know what you're talking about. Just leave me alone, would you?" She stomped past me. "Tell Jamie I had to go, but I'll be here tomorrow."

She strode across the seating area and yanked the front door open, setting all the bells along the top jangling. I had to lunge for Lulu's collar to keep her from following Katie outside. Did the girl have no sense for anyone but herself? Geez.

I muttered curses as I turned to inspect the store one last time, telling myself I had better things to do than try to protect one seventeen-year-old girl from getting her heart broken by a loser. That was just part and parcel of growing up—letting some guy sucker you into thinking he was more than he was. She'd learn.

CHAPTER 8

The next day dawned clear and blue and perfect. Fancy and I left for a quick walk around the neighborhood—not up the mountain, one dead body was enough for us, thank you very much—as the sun was just starting to rise, coloring the sky all pink and orange.

I took a deep breath as I watched the colors spread along the horizon, reminding myself that no matter what happened from this moment onward at least I'd tried.

I could've easily stayed in DC and kept making good money while being silently miserable, but I hadn't. I'd taken the chance to get what I wanted. And even if I failed, even if I had to go back there some day to put a roof over my head, at least I'd know I'd tried. And the time I was getting with my grandpa—as long as I left his crosswords alone and kept him from shooting someone—was invaluable.

If I'd waited another ten years, it might've been too late. For all of it. It would've certainly been too late to spend quality time with Fancy.

As we reached the corner and passed by Luke's rundown house, I stuck my tongue out. You'd think for someone who billed himself out as a construction contractor that he'd make a little bit of effort to keep his house from looking like a derelict dump. But no.

When we'd been up on the mountainside the day before I'd been able to see into his backyard. It was a mess, full of rusted and rotted metal. I was surprised someone hadn't called him in as a health hazard yet. Maybe if he kept playing with Jamie the way he was, I would.

Serve him right.

As I glanced up the mountainside I saw Mr. Jackson headed towards the ridgeline, a pack on his back. Interesting. I hadn't figured he kept that path tended as a hobby. Maybe the extracurricular product that I'd spied down in the valley belonged to him.

Could he have killed Jack? A little drug dispute gone bad? Maybe Jack had tried to steal his product and he'd put an end to it the best way he knew how. He certainly knew his way around a gun—he always had extra deer or elk meat to offer the neighbors and had served in 'Nam. Maybe he was even trying to frame my grandpa by using a shotgun. He had seen that fight after all.

I pondered the thought as I walked along, liking it more and more as I thought it through. But then I shrugged it off. If Mr. Jackson had killed Jack, Officer Handsome would figure it out soon enough; he didn't strike me as the type to miss something so obvious. And, really, it wasn't my business. Let the cops handle it. I had a business to run.

Personally, I didn't care if they ever caught the killer. I was just glad Jack Dunner wasn't going to be around to bark at me and my dog anymore.

About half a block later I saw Katie running towards

me on the other side of the street, her long red ponytail swinging back and forth with every step, headphones snaking up to her ears, her arms moving with such perfect precision I wondered for a split second if she was actually a robot.

I waved, but she didn't so much as flinch, even though she had to have seen me. Not a ton of people out that early after all.

I entertained myself the rest of the walk around town trying to figure out what career Katie would excel at. Fashion CEO a la *The Devil Wears Prada*? CIA operative tasked with seducing Russian oligarchs? Prison warden? Nah, a prison warden would need to be friendlier than that. Maybe headmistress of a military school. That had possibilities.

I know. It wasn't very nice of me—I told you before I'm a horrible person—but I just don't understand people who don't like dogs. I mean, it was bad enough when she snubbed Fancy that first day—broke her little heart—but Katie didn't even like Lulu. Who doesn't like a golden retriever puppy? And even more than that, who takes a job at a *dog barkery* if they don't like *dogs*?

I didn't get it. Any of it.

Ah well. She was a hard worker at least.

When she was there. She certainly needed to duck out early quite a lot. But now that we were opening that was going to stop or she was going to find somewhere new to work. Jamie would object—she's nice that way—but eventually she'd see that you can't run a business if no one's there to serve the customers.

With that cheery reminder, I headed back home to change and get to the store. It was show time.

🐾 🐾 🐾

I was so scared I was trembling as I pulled up outside. I knew the café side would do well—people need their coffee and cinnamon rolls—but it was the barkery side I worried about. It wasn't exactly a small-town concept, so I'd be relying on tourists to find and like it. Not the easiest audience to court. A loyal customer is gold that keeps paying day after day, but I'd be trying to run a business based on drawing in new customers week after week. Not the best strategy.

At least we'd planned for all outcomes. If the barkery did fail, we'd just expand the café into the barkery side and I could still bring Fancy to work.

It just wouldn't be the same, that's all. Plus, I don't like to fail. It's not me.

Fancy cried in my ear, reminding me that we couldn't sit in the car all day, we had to get inside and get open. Jamie was already there—probably had been since four or five—baking up all her daily goodies. I was lucky enough that all the dog treats could be made a day or two before, so I got to "sleep in" as much as Fancy ever allowed me to.

(You should know that as much as I make little comments here or there about Fancy, that I adore her more than the world. So don't for one minute think that I don't happily roll out of bed at an ungodly hour and schedule my entire day around my dog with anything less than absolute gratitude that I have her in my life. Truth be told, if it weren't for Jamie and my grandpa I could honestly say that I like Fancy more than anyone in the world. But that crying to get out of the car thing? Pure misery.)

I led Fancy inside, flipped on the lights on my side of the store, let her out the back to run around in the dog run with Lulu, and then snuck across to see how Jamie was doing. She was elbow-deep in dough and I could see what looked like muffins baking in the nearest oven. A tray of cinnamon rolls was cooling on a tall rack nearby, the scent heavenly.

"You need me to do some taste testing?" I asked. "First day of business and all. We don't want to put out an inferior product."

She laughed. "I set one aside for you. Right there. Have at it."

I took a bite and sighed in pleasure. It was still warm, the frosting all soft and gooey, melting on my tongue in that perfect way good cinnamon rolls have, the cinnamon blending with the sugar in a perfect ratio of spicy and sweet.

I would've been best friends with Jamie even if she couldn't cook, but it certainly didn't hurt things that she was magic when it came to baking. "I'm going to get so fat working here."

"Haha. Hardly. You know all the running around we've been doing getting this place ready? Just wait until we're open."

"I hope you're right." I polished off the last of the cinnamon roll and stared out the back window where I could see trees swaying in a slight breeze as Lulu and Fancy rolled around on the grass. "Do you think we did the right thing, coming back to the valley and opening this store?"

"Yes. Without a doubt. And, remember, I'm the one who grew up here so I had no illusions about it being some idyllic mountain paradise."

I threw a hand towel at her. "It is an idyllic mountain paradise."

"You keep telling yourself that, Ms. I Found a Dead Body." She threw the towel back at me with a laugh. "Something doesn't have to be perfect to be worthwhile, you know."

I narrowed my eyes. "Are you talking about Luke?"

"And what if I am?"

"He's a player, Jamie. You have to see that."

"Just because a man flirts doesn't make him a player. He makes me laugh. You should be glad I'm getting out there again."

I sighed. Jamie had been through a really ugly breakup six months ago and I'd worried about her. She's a person who isn't happy outside of a relationship. (Unlike me. Give me a good book and I'm just fine all alone, thank you very much.)

"Promise me two things," I said.

"What's that?"

"One, you won't fall for him. You'll keep in mind what I've told you about him and assume that he is probably flirting up half the county."

She pursed her lips, but nodded. "Okay, fine. And two?"

"Two, you'll keep an open mind about other men and try to find someone a little more worth your time."

She grimaced.

"Jamie, please." I heard the front door jangle and glanced out front to see Katie walking towards us. I turned back to Jamie. "Promise? That you'll look for someone better than Luke?"

She shrugged one shoulder.

"Promise?"

"Promise."

I grinned at Katie as she joined us. "And you can help, Katie."

"Help with what?" She glanced at us, emotionless as always.

"Help me find Jamie someone better to like than Lucas Dean."

Katie stared at me like a deer caught in headlights.

"Maggie! You are not going to start enlisting people to find me someone better to like. If someone comes along, fine. Until then, I am just fine with Luke, thank you very much. Katie, can you get started putting out the fruit cups? I hadn't had a chance to do that yet."

"Sure." Katie pushed past me towards the big walk-in, her steps stiff and robotic.

Resisting the urge to check her neck for an off switch, I left them to their prep work. I'd have enough time later to keep working on Jamie. I just wanted to see my best friend happy, that's all.

CHAPTER 9

The weekend went by in a whirl. We'd planned the grand opening to coincide with a big dog show that was being held in the resort event center nearby so we'd had non-stop customers in both the barkery and the café from when we opened on Friday all the way through Monday.

It was great. And exhausting. So I was very happy to have my day off on Tuesday. We'd agreed when we opened the store that as much as it might be good for the business for us to both work seven days a week that that just wasn't sustainable. No point in opening your dream store and burning out in the first six months.

We wanted to love what we were doing, not hate it. And anyone who tells you that when you really love something it isn't work hasn't had to be on their feet for ten hours straight while keeping a smile on their face under all circumstances.

So Tuesday morning—after a nice walk around the neighborhood where I saw Katie doing her running thing once more, but no sign of Mr. Jackson hiking up the mountain—I settled down in the backyard for a little peace and quiet. At least I knew I wasn't going to have some weird man barking at me or Fancy this time.

(I know. A man was dead. I should be more respectful. But he barked at me. I mean, really. How torn up was I supposed to be over a man like that?)

We stayed out there until the sun was high enough in the sky to take away all the good shade spots. I love that space, but there are no trees, so after about 10 am it's not a pleasant place to sit. Walking back into the house, I heard my grandpa talking softly and paused by the laundry room, wondering if he was so far gone already that he was talking to himself.

I crept forward, trying to figure out what he was saying—to see just how crazy he'd become—when a woman's laughter rang out. I let out the breath I'd been holding and walked down the rest of the hall towards the kitchen.

A woman I didn't recognize was sitting at the kitchen table with my grandpa. She was well put together, her white hair tied back in a bun, her clothes neatly pressed and tidy, earrings on her ears, rings on her fingers (lots of rings), and bright red lipstick. I looked her up and down with a touch of disapproval. My grandparents had been married forty years and would've stayed married forever if my grandma hadn't died. I wasn't sure I liked the thought of some well-put-together woman honing in on my vulnerable widower of a grandpa.

I stepped forward. "Hi. I'm Maggie. Lou's granddaughter. Who are you?"

It's possible I was a little forceful with my question, because she laughed. "I'm Lesley Pope. But we've met before."

"When?"

"At the library. Your grandparents used to bring you in when you were visiting. Always had a book in hand. Some things never change." She nodded towards the book I was currently holding.

I'll admit that hearing that she was or had been a librarian made me soften towards her. Just a bit, though. She was still honing in on my grandma's turf.

"Are you still a librarian? Don't you need to get to work?" I set my book down on the table so I could cross my arms as I glared down at her.

"Maggie May. You leave Lesley alone. I had friends before you decided to become my live-in nursemaid, and if I have to choose between those friends and having you stay here, I'll choose them. So scoot along now."

I looked back and forth between them. "Is that all you are? Friends?"

"Maggie May. I am eighty-two-years-old. My mother has been gone a long, long time and I don't need you stepping up to take her place. Now if you don't mind?" He nodded towards the living room.

"Fine. Nice to meet you Lesley." I stomped away, noting that he hadn't actually answered my question.

"And you, Maggie," Lesley called after me. She actually meant it, too.

I didn't. I was too busy wondering if she was taking advantage of my poor, bereaved grandfather.

As I walked across the living room I heard her say, "24 Down is INGRATE. I-N-G-R-A-T-E." My grandpa thanked her, his voice soft and warm.

So *she* could help with his crosswords, could she? Harrumph.

🐾 🐾 🐾

I couldn't figure out what to do with myself while she was there. Lock myself away in my bedroom like I was twelve? Sit in the living room and pretend I couldn't hear them talking softly in the kitchen? I'd already taken Fancy for her walk, and I was forbidden to set foot in the barkery on my day off.

Fortunately, she didn't stay for much longer. I wandered into the kitchen to make Fancy's lunch and casually said, "Lesley seems nice" as I wet and microwaved Fancy's food for her.

"Mmhm. She is." My grandpa didn't even look up from his paper. Stubborn old man.

"How do you know her?" I asked, leaning against the counter in as unassuming a pose as I could manage.

He chuckled. "Maggie May."

"Maggie."

"*Maggie.* I have lived in this town for forty-one years. I know everyone who lives in Creek who's over the age of twenty."

I set Fancy's food in her bowl and turned to look at him. "You loved Grandma."

"I did."

"But…"

He leaned his elbows on the table. "But your grandma is gone. And I've been alone. And it's nice to have an attractive woman who knows crosswords to talk to on occasion. She also plays a mean game of Scrabble if you're ever up for it."

I frowned. "Do you think…I mean, would you ever…I don't know, get married again?"

He shook his head. "Lesley's already married."

"What? Grandpa!"

"It's not like that, Maggie. We enjoy each other's company and her husband…well, he's…he's not well. He's still at home, but he needs a lot of care. And sometimes Lesley just needs to get away from it all for a bit. So she comes here and we talk. That's all we do. Talk. And I'd appreciate it if you kept that to yourself. No one else knows and no one needs to know."

"I'm sorry. I'm just worried about you, that's all. I don't want her taking advantage of you when you're vulnerable."

He snorted. "I've never been vulnerable a day in my life. You should worry more about yourself and less about me. What did you think of Matt? He's grown into a good man despite some hard times. Found himself in the military. It's good to see."

I gave Fancy her after-lunch treat and sat down across from him. "I have big plans, Grandpa. And they don't involve falling in love. Not now. Maybe not ever."

He pressed his lips together and looked at me for a long, long moment. "I'm sorry to hear that, Maggie. I can't imagine what my life would've been like without your grandma. I hope you find what we had someday. And I hope when you do, you don't let it pass you by because of those plans of yours."

I grimaced. Just like he didn't want to have to explain Lesley to me, I didn't want to have to explain all my twisted feelings around what he'd just said to him. "Love you, Grandpa. You up for a game of Scrabble? Or you only play when Lesley's around?"

"I think I have time for a game or two. But you better be prepared to be beat. I don't lose, even when my opponents are pretty."

I laughed. "That sounds like a challenge. And I'll have you know I don't lose even when my opponents are old and crafty."

CHAPTER 10

I'd just played a seven-letter word on a triple word score when someone banged on the front door loud enough to send Fancy into a barking frenzy. "You get the door, I'll shoo Fancy outside," I told my grandpa and ran to herd her out the back.

She doesn't wear a collar at home and is too big to grab and move, but I can usually step in front of her until I get her going in the right direction. Plus, a good treat or two works wonders once she's calmed down enough to realize what I'm holding.

So while Fancy and I did the treat and two-step shuffle out the back door, my grandpa answered the front door. "Matt, good to see you again. You got my gun?"

I could just barely hear them from the laundry room as I blocked Fancy outside.

"I'm afraid it has to be Office Barnes today, Mr. Carver."

Hearing that, I ran back to the front of the house as Fancy howled in protest—I almost never lock her out alone—but I couldn't worry about her right then.

"Why? And who's this?" my grandpa demanded as I slid around the corner and ran through the kitchen.

"This is Officer Clark. He's here to…well, to help me if you decide not to cooperate."

"Cooperate? That's all I've done so far. What's this about, Matt?" My grandpa was almost shouting.

I put a hand on his elbow to calm him down, silently hoping he'd let me step in before he said something he shouldn't. "Officer Barnes. If you could just explain what's going on, I think we'd both really appreciate it."

Matt nodded, lips pressed tight. This wasn't the warm man I'd met the other day, but someone doing a duty he didn't like. "Ballistics on the gun came back. It *was* the one used to kill Jack Dunner. And all the prints we could find on it came back to you, sir."

"Well it's my gun, ain't it? It should have my prints. That all you're going on?"

Officer Clark moved his tobacco around in his mouth as he leaned forward. "There's also the fact that you're a known killer. Did it before, why wouldn't you do it again."

"That doesn't count."

I stared at my grandpa. "What's he talking about? I thought you'd done time for robbing banks not murder."

"It wasn't murder, it was manslaughter. And if I hadn't shot the man he would've shot his wife and who knew who else. If I had it to do all over again, I would, but that doesn't mean I killed Jack Dunner."

"Grandpa," I muttered. "You're not helping things."

He held my gaze. "Maggie May, I've done a lot wrong in my life, but the one thing I haven't done is lied to people about who I was or why I did it. Was robbing those banks a mistake? Yes, it was. But when you're young and poor it's hard to see other paths you can take. I broke the law and I did my time, but I ain't never been a liar and I ain't going to start being one now. That man I shot was like a rabid dog and he needed to be put down. If I hadn't done it, he'da hurt a lot of people that day."

He turned back to the officers. "I'm telling you, Matt, I didn't do this."

Matt nodded. "I hear what you're saying, sir. I do. But I need you to come in for questioning. You're not under arrest. Not…yet. And hopefully we can clear all this right up and you can be home in just an hour or two. But I do have to take you in. This is my job, sir. Somedays I don't like to do it, but it has to be done."

My grandpa thought about it for a long moment and then nodded. "Fine. Let me get my hat."

"I'll come with you," I said. Fancy could handle herself for an hour or two just fine.

Matt stopped me. "Sorry, Maggie, but you might as well stay here. You won't be allowed into the interrogation room with him."

"Should I call him a lawyer?"

My grandpa came back, settling a stained old ballcap with a John Deere logo onto his head. "I don't need no lawyer, Maggie. We'll sit down, we'll talk this through, and we'll get it all cleared up in no time. You just stay here and enjoy your day off."

He gave me a kiss on the cheek before stepping out the door, Officer Clark following after, his hand on his gun like he really believed my grandpa was going to make a run for it.

I looked at Matt. "Should I call him a lawyer?"

He shrugged one shoulder. "I hope it doesn't come to that. If…If we end up arresting him, I'll let you know. And if we're gone more than two hours, swing by the station, that'll mean we weren't able to clear things up easily."

"Okay. Thank you."

I watched him walk down the path and slide into the driver's seat of his police cruiser, my grandpa seated in the back like a common criminal.

Only after they'd pulled away did I step back into the house. I had a lot to think about. Not the least of which was the fact that my grandpa had actually killed someone and I'd never even known about it.

🐾 🐾 🐾

I texted Jamie to ask how busy the store was, desperate to tell her what had happened and get her advice, but she didn't even text me back for ten minutes and when she did it was a one-word text.

Slammed.

So I paced the house, tried to read my book, watched some horrible reality dating show that made me cringe so much I finally had to turn it off, and then paced some more. I finally got so desperate I started cleaning. I dusted all the bookshelves in the front room, washed all the dishes that were in the sink even though I could've just thrown them in the dishwasher, and even mopped the kitchen floor.

When my grandpa still wasn't back after all that, I turned my attention to poor Fancy. "You know who could use a bath," I told her.

She immediately ran out the back door and to the far corner of the yard, staring back at me with those big sad eyes of hers like I'd just committed the ultimate betrayal by even mentioning the b word.

"Come on now. You know you could use one." I approached her with a handful of treats, hoping to lure her inside.

She took the treats, but stayed right where she was.

"Fancy…Look at your paws. Don't you think you'd like to wash that dirt off?"

When it comes to baths, logic doesn't really work with Fancy, but persistence does. I kept at her until she finally ducked her head and slunk into the house. When she was younger I'd had to herd her through the house, closing one door at a time until we finally reached the tub, but now she just resigns herself to her fate and goes straight to the bathroom like she's going to her execution.

What's crazy is she'll happily splash around in even the smallest of puddles but call it a bath and she suddenly hates water.

I closed the bathroom door—just to be safe, we didn't need her running through the house shaking water all over everything—and started the water running.

Fancy buried her face against my chest in sheer misery as I soaked her down and soaped her up. At least she didn't fight me. I'm not sure what I'd do if she ever did. Probably just let her be very, very dirty for the rest of her life.

It was all over in ten minutes. I toweled Fancy down as best I could—not easy with a dog that has a double coat like hers—and then let her loose. Looking at how black the water that drained out of the tub was I knew she'd definitely needed it.

Now you'd think that a dog that hates baths as much

as she does would immediately flee once the bath was over. Not Fancy. She'll run out of the bathroom shaking herself all over anything she can find, but then she'll come back and hang around while I'm cleaning up. I'm not sure what she's thinking when she does that, but she does it every single time.

Crazy girl, but I love her.

Anyway. When I'd finished wiping down the tub—I get a lot of hair off of her during a bath—and went out to the kitchen for a Coke I found my grandpa at the kitchen table working on a crossword puzzle like nothing had happened.

"You're back," I said, sitting down across from him.

"I am."

"Did they clear you? Is it okay?"

He shook his head. His hand trembled as he tried to fill in his crossword. I reached out to put my hand on his forearm where his *Born to Lose* tattoo was, the faded green snake wrapped around a dagger a reminder that his life hadn't always been coaching baseball and going to church in a small town.

"So what happened? What did they say? What now?"

He set the pen down. "They said Jack was probably killed sometime the afternoon of the sixteenth."

"The day after I arrived then. So the same day you threatened him."

He nodded.

"While I was at the store with Jamie."

He shrugged. "That's what it looks like."

"What did you do after I left that day?"

He reached for his non-existent cigarettes and cussed, slapping the table in frustration. "I'll tell you what I didn't do. I didn't track that man up the side of a mountain and gun him down with my shotgun."

"Grandpa. I wasn't saying you had. Was Lesley here that day?"

"You're not bringing her into this, Maggie May."

I was too going to bring her into it if they arrested him, but for the time being I let it go. "So what now?"

"Matt said they don't have enough to arrest me just yet, but that I should stick around town."

"Do they have any other suspects?"

"I don't know. Why should they keep looking? It was my gun and the man was shot behind my house. I suspect it's only a matter of time before they make it official."

"Grandpa, if Lesley was here you have to tell them."

He shoved away from the table. "No, I don't."

"But you could go to jail."

He stared out the kitchen window for a long moment. "I've done time before, I can do it again."

"Grandpa! You're eighty-two-years-old, you can't go to prison."

But he wasn't listening. He'd already turned his back and headed to his room. Stubborn old man. I glared after him for a long moment before making up my mind. If he wasn't going to give the police his alibi, then I was.

CHAPTER 11

The library was at the edge of town in a shiny new brick and glass building that didn't really fit the rest of the town. When I was little the library had been housed in two connected rooms at the top corner of the courthouse, books crammed into every nook and cranny from floor to ceiling, the smell of stone dust and books hanging in the air.

I'd loved that place. The intimacy of being surrounded on all sides by books had called to my soul even if the lighting was horrid and actually moving around those two rooms had posed a significant health hazard.

The new place was fine. It had a large central area with comfy couches, four computers along the wall that anyone could use, two large meeting rooms, and a series of individual study rooms as well. I wasn't sure the actual book collection was any bigger than it had been, but I'm sure the airy space appealed to…someone. Just not me.

Lesley, who'd been manning the check-out desk, saw me as soon as I arrived. "A big change, isn't it?"

"Yeah. It's definitely different."

She laughed, the deep smile lines on her face showing that she'd always been a happy woman. "I miss the old place, too. It was my own personal hideaway—just me and the books stashed away in those little rooms. I read every book in there at least once."

"Really?"

She shrugged, laughing softly again. "Really. Can't say I'd ever want to re-read the book on the different makes of Chevy vehicles through the years, but I wanted to know what we had in our collection for when someone needed a book on a specific subject. And you'd be surprised how often that particular book was needed."

I couldn't help but match her smile even though it felt unfair to my grandma's memory. Darn Lesley Pope for being so nice and likable.

I glanced around. There was one little girl at the computer; her mother was seated in the corner flipping through a magazine, but paying more attention to us than whatever was on the page in front of her.

"Do you think we could talk? Privately?"

Lesley pursed her lips but nodded. "Give me a minute." She went to the back and returned trailing a young man with pock marks all over his cheeks. "Ron, Maggie. Maggie, Ron. Ron's the new librarian. Took over after I retired. Maggie used to visit her grandparents each summer and was one of my best customers when she was around. We're just going to catch up, but if you need me, knock."

"Alright, Mrs. Pope."

We chose the meeting room farthest from the bored mother. As we stepped inside I told Lesley, "The first library book I ever remember reading was *A Wrinkle in Time*. Were you the one that recommended it to me?"

"I am. I thought you'd like the main character. And for more than just a similar name."

I chuckled. "You know, I made people call me Meg for the next six months after I read that book. Until a couple of boys at school started calling me Meg the Hag, that is."

"Kids can be cruel."

I settled into a seat while Lesley closed the door.

"Eh. A few well-placed kicks and they stopped. Too bad I have to resort to words and reason these days…"

Lesley laughed as she sat down across from me, but then her face stilled and she looked right at me. "Are you here to tell me to leave your grandfather alone?"

The chair squeaked under me as I lurched forward. "No. Oh, gosh. You probably don't even know yet."

"Know what?"

"After you left, the police came by and took Grandpa in for questioning. The gun that killed Jack Dunner was his. And his are the only prints they could find on it. Also, I wasn't home at the time they think Jack was shot, so Grandpa's their prime suspect since he doesn't have an alibi." I watched her carefully as I added, "Not to mention, he's killed a man before."

Lesley didn't even flinch at my mention of how Grandpa had killed before. "Oh, poor Lou. He's worked so hard to put his past in the past."

"So you knew about that? About him killing someone?"

She looked at me with a twinkle in her eye. "You kids are so funny. You all think that your grandparents have always been the way they were and never stop to think that they had a whole lifetime they lived before you ever came along. Of course, I knew about it. It was my sister's husband he shot."

"Really?" I leaned forward. "Was he…a bad man like my grandpa said he was?"

She nodded, the color leaching away from her face. "He was. Beat my sister every time he got drunk, which was at least two or three times a week. But she wouldn't leave him. Not until she had her son and he went after the boy. Finally she saw some sense. That night she waited until he passed out, packed up whatever she could find, and came to me."

She ran her fingers along the edge of the table, not looking at me as she continued. "Lou and I were seeing each other at the time. He said she could stay with us and he'd protect her until things blew over."

"Wait? You and my grandpa dated?" I'd known my grandparents hadn't gotten together until my grandpa was out of prison and already in his forties, but it had never occurred to me my grandpa could've dated someone else before he met my grandma.

"We did." She smiled looking back at the past. "We'd been together about ten months when this all happened. Were talking marriage but hadn't made it there yet. And never did, because two nights after my sister came to stay with us, her husband showed up with a gun."

I gripped the edge of the table, trying to picture it.

"There were about eight of us there at the time—including your grandma and her boyfriend, Gene. My sister's husband kicked in the door, screaming about how he was going to kill my sister and anyone who kept him from her, and pointed his gun right at me." Her hands started to shake so she clasped them tight together and held them in her lap. Her smile was gone. "I refused to tell him where she was, so he cocked the gun."

She met my gaze. "That's when your grandfather shot him. Saved my life that day. Probably saved my sister's, too."

I sat there, stunned. How had I never known this story? What else didn't I know about my grandparents? Or my parents for that matter.

She twisted her wedding ring around and around as she continued. "I told your grandfather I'd wait for him to get out of prison, but he wasn't having it. He told me that he loved me more than anyone in the world but he wanted me to be happy and he'd understand if I moved on." She glanced at the ring and shook her head. "I didn't want to. I loved him. I held out for two years, but then I met Bill, my husband, and there was something special there. Something worth pursuing."

She looked me in the eye. "Still is. I love my husband to this day. Bill and I got married a few months later and then, the day after I found out I was pregnant with my first child, your grandfather found out he was being released from prison five years early due to overcrowding."

"Ooh." I winced, thinking what that must've been like for her. To wait for the man she loved, finally give up on him and move on, and then, just when it's too late to turn back, find out he was free. "Was this before the armed robberies then?"

She nodded. "Yes. Your grandfather moved in with Gene after he was released, but Gene had taken up with some bad folks by then and…Well, I'm not sure your grandfather cared much about anything at that point."

"Wait. Is this the same Gene my grandma was dating when that man got shot?"

She laughed. "Of course. Gene was your grandfather's brother. Didn't you know that he'd dated Marie before he was killed in that robbery?"

"I'd never heard his name before. My grandpa doesn't talk about these things much."

"He's worked hard to put it all behind him." She twisted her wedding ring around and studied the small diamond in a simple setting for a long moment. "He was out for less than a year before he was arrested for those robberies. By the time he was released the second time, Gene was dead and Lou had nowhere to go. My husband hired him on at the mine, Lou started spending time with your grandma, they fell in love, and the rest is history."

"Wow. How did I not know any of this?" I shook my head, trying to make sense of all the crazy connections I'd never known about. "My grandpa said your husband's sick?"

She folded her hands in her lap and looked at me, sorrow shining in her eyes. "He's in the final stages of Parkinson's. I care for him as best I can, but it's not easy. Sometimes I just need a break from it all and that's what your grandfather gives me." She held my gaze. "I love my husband, Maggie. And I will stay with him and stay faithful to him until the end. But I love your grandfather, too. Always have, always will."

I didn't know what to say to that. It wasn't at all what I'd expected to hear, but I suspected that if I asked my grandpa his feelings on the matter he might say he loved her, too, which was something I wasn't quite ready to think about.

So I changed the subject. "Do you always go to my grandpa's before you volunteer at the library?"

She nodded. "Every Tuesday and Wednesday."

"Which means you saw my grandpa the day after I arrived. The day Jack Dunner died."

"I did. I wasn't planning on it, but he called after you headed out to the store, so I dropped by for lunch and a quick game of Scrabble."

"You can tell the police. Give him an alibi."

She laid her hands flat on the table. "It won't help, Maggie. I was only there an hour. He had the entire afternoon to still shoot Jack. And…" She held my gaze. "Think of all the pain it would cause if people found out about Lou and me."

"But you said you just talk. That there's nothing more to it."

"We do. But do you think the town gossips will believe that? Do you think that, given my history with Lou and how sick my husband is that they'll really believe that all we do is talk? Do you think they'll ever let it drop? We'll be ten years in our graves and they'll still be talking about how I seduced poor old Lou while my husband was at home dying."

I bit my lip. She was right. I knew she was. Even though I hadn't grown up here, I'd heard enough over the years. In a small town it's almost impossible to escape who people think you are, no matter what proof you give them.

I drummed my fingers on the tabletop. "Do you think he did it?"

"No. Of course, not."

"Are you sure? I mean, he did point that shotgun at him."

She reached across the table and took my hand. "Maggie, your grandfather did not shoot Jack Dunner. He told me what had happened that morning, but he was laughing about it. He wasn't angry."

There was a part of me that wanted nothing more than to drag her straight to the police station so she could tell Matt and clear my grandpa's name. But she didn't deserve what would happen next. Neither did my grandpa.

Which meant I had to find another way to clear him. I had to find the real killer.

"Okay." I stood up, needing fresh air and movement, needing to think.

Lesley didn't move. She was still sitting there, turning her wedding ring around and around on her finger.

"Thank you," I mumbled. "For…for being there for him now that my grandma is gone. I think…He needs that. So I'm…I'm glad he has you." It was hard for me to say, but it needed to be said.

She dabbed at her eyes with a small monogrammed handkerchief and then stood up and straightened her clothes and hair, looking impeccable once more. "Thank you for that. I appreciate it. And I hope we get the chance to know one another better, Maggie."

"Me too."

She left without looking back.

I took a moment to get myself together, wondering where to now. I couldn't clear my grandpa by providing his alibi, so now I had to find the killer. But who could it be? Who would've wanted Jack Dunner dead so bad that they'd follow him up a mountainside and shoot him? And who would know about my grandpa's gun? And the argument they'd had that day?

I didn't know, but I was determined to find out.

CHAPTER 12

Deciding to solve a murder and actually doing so are two completely different things when you're not a cop. You know how they say that determination and hard work can overcome any obstacle? Yeah, they're lying.

Good access to information, others who know what you don't, and the authority to investigate where you're not really wanted are much more helpful. All determination will get you is frustration when you refuse to quit. But it's all I had.

So I figured if I didn't have the information and authority, I'd go to the man who did. Officer Handsome. Matt.

The police station was only a few blocks away. As I walked there, I enjoyed the crisp spring air and tried to let my thoughts cool down a bit. I cut across the parking lot towards the single-story yellow sandstone building that housed the jail and main police station for the county.

It wasn't very impressive inside. It was newly-built, but small, with a central reception desk and four desks behind that, two on each side of the room, facing one another. Behind those were two offices with glass panes that faced the reception area, each holding one more desk. I assumed somewhere down the hallway were the interrogation rooms and jail.

This building was officially the main location for police in the county, but most of the time officers were out on patrol or at the auxiliary office in Bakerstown, so I guess they didn't need a big space. Like I said, Creek wasn't exactly a hotbed of criminal activity. Most of the time the cops were just dealing with out-of-town speeders or the same handful of drunks and domestics week after week.

Matt was the only one there, seated at one of the desks on the left. "Hey, Maggie." He waved me over.

I sat down across from him. "How bad is it?"

He studied me for a long moment, clearly trying to make a decision.

I waited, knowing that most people have a need to fill silence and that the more he said the more I'd be able to help my grandpa.

He rubbed at his chin where some late afternoon stubble had appeared. "You know, after my mom and I moved to Bakerstown I got into a lot of trouble. I was headed down a real bad path. Even landed in jail a couple times. Finally, my parents gave up on talking sense into me and my dad dragged me over to your grandpa's house. Seems your grandpa had sat him down when he was younger and out of control and helped him turn things around."

"I could see him doing that."

"Yeah, he's good that way. Your grandpa gave me some hard truths that day. Made me realize I didn't want to end up in jail or dead before I was thirty. So I enlisted. I needed the discipline and to get out of here for a while. Sometimes you don't appreciate what you have until you lose it."

That hit a little too close to home for me, but I shoved the thought aside. I was here about my grandpa, not to remember my own mistakes and hurts, so I just nodded. And waited, hoping he'd get to the point soon before someone walked in.

He sighed and rubbed at his chin again. "Which is all to say, I owe your grandpa. But I don't know how to help him. Ben—Officer Clark—is so fixated on your grandpa for this that he's not even willing to consider other suspects."

"Maybe I can help."

"How?"

I jerked back in offense and he held out a hand to calm me. "I'm sorry, Maggie. I'm not saying you can't help, I just…How?"

"Let me see what you have. Maybe there's something there you missed."

"Are you a trained detective? A forensics expert?"

I counted to five, not wanting to say the first thing that came to mind. When I felt calm enough, I said, "No. But I'm someone else who wants to see the real killer caught as much as you do. And since Officer Clark doesn't, you should be grateful for any other set of eyes. Even those of a rank amateur whose only exposure to law enforcement has been watching the Justice Channel."

I couldn't help but add that last bit. He was right. I'm not a trained detective or forensics expert. But I am smart. And observant. And, most importantly, I cared enough to keep pursuing this to the end.

"Okay." Matt opened a folder on his desk and turned it towards me. "This is what we have. Your grandpa and Jack had a disagreement the morning of the sixteenth. Your grandpa threatened to shoot him. The weapon used was your grandpa's, and the only prints on the weapon are his."

Before I could argue all the reasons that didn't mean my grandpa had shot Jack Dunner, Matt raised his hand and added, "But…Your grandpa could've shot Jack when they had that disagreement and he didn't. That makes it far less likely that your grandpa tracked him down later and shot him. Only your grandpa's prints were on the gun, but there weren't fingerprints on the barrel or the trigger, which means somebody probably wiped the gun down after using it. Also, the gun was stored in an unlocked location where anyone who knew about it could've found it and used it. We also found various shoe and boot prints along the trail, none of which matched your grandpa's shoe size."

"Okay. So you could argue it either way." I nodded, thinking. "Would it help to know that my grandpa spoke to someone else that day and told them about what had happened with Jack and that he was laughing and not angry when he did so?"

"Yes. Absolutely. Who was it?"

"I can't tell you."

"Maggie…" He leaned forward, fixing me with an intense blue gaze that made my thoughts skitter.

I shook my head. "I can't. I promised. But suffice it to say that he talked to someone about it later that day and that he was not the least bit angry."

"He could've already shot him by then."

"No. This would've been before that."

Matt narrowed his eyes at me, but I refused to let him rattle me.

I leaned forward, resting my elbows on the desk. "Okay, then. So we throw in this conversation with this other person and it's clear it wasn't my grandpa. Who else could it be? Do you have any other suspects?"

He shook his head. "Plenty of people hated Dunner—you saw what he could be like. But I haven't found anyone who hated him enough to kill him."

"Any signs he was caught up in drugs?"

"He definitely used them. But on a larger scale? Not that I found. I could ask around, see if he was making any moves in that direction. Why?"

It sounded silly now that I was about to say it out loud, but it was the only lead we had. "Well…I was thinking that maybe Mr. Jackson shot him. Over drugs."

"Your neighbor, Mr. Jackson? The old man with the raspberry bushes? Why would he shoot Jack Dunner?" He closed the folder and pushed it aside, not even reaching for a pen.

"First, he knows how to use a gun, right? He served in 'Nam and hunts regularly, even off-season. So we know he's willing to break rules he doesn't agree with."

"Hunting deer is not the same as killing someone."

"I know. I'm just saying. Also, the day I arrived, I saw him maintaining that path. He was up there trimming back tree branches to keep it clear, so there's something up that way that matters to him. Another day when I was out walking Fancy in the early morning I saw him headed up the trail with a pack."

"Okay. So the man likes to hike in the mountains and keeps a trail clear so it's easier to do so. Doesn't make him a murderer."

"He should've found the body before I did, though, if he uses that path regularly."

Matt thought about it, but shook his head. "Still not seeing it."

"Also, someone's growing something down in the valley behind Harm's Ridge. If it's Mr. Jackson and what he's growing is illegal and Jack Dunner found out about it and tried to steal it…"

He grimaced. "Then that might be motive for murder. But that's a lot of ifs."

"It has to at least be worth investigating, right? I mean, Mr. Jackson also knew about the argument. And I assume he knew about the gun."

"True. He's really the only other person who knew about the argument, isn't he? Hm." Matt rubbed at his neck, thinking. "Well, it is better than what I have right now, which is nothing. I guess I could check it out."

"Can I come with you?"

Just then Officer Clark came in through the front door, slurping from a McDonald's cup. He tossed a bag that smelled of grease onto Matt's desk and glared me down until I stood up and stepped out of his way. The seat groaned under his weight as he sat down.

"Interviewing a witness without me, Matt?"

"Nah. Maggie and I go way back. We were just getting caught up." He opened the bag and laid out a Big Mac and fries in the middle of the desk. "Thanks for this, man. I owe you."

"Yeah, sure, no problem."

I looked at Matt's pathetic excuse for a dinner and shook my head. "Is that how you eat all the time?"

"Not a lot of fast food options around here, you know."

"You could cook."

Matt laughed. "You don't want to see me try to cook. I can burn water."

I bit my lip. Which was more important to me? Keeping my distance from Officer Handsome or saving my grandpa from jail time?

"How about you come around for dinner tomorrow night? We can finish catching up and you can have at least one meal that isn't a heart attack in a sack."

"Really?" He grinned at me, his eyes twinkling. I instantly regretted inviting him over. But done was done.

"Really. Six o'clock. Don't be late. My grandpa's a stickler for timeliness."

I left before I could change my mind, but that twinkle in Matt's eyes followed me all the way home.

CHAPTER 13

By the time I closed up shop and drove home the next night I was already regretting my dinner invite to Officer Handsome. I could've just called the station to see what he'd found, but no, I had to go invite Mr. Distraction to dinner. I swear, sometimes I'm my own worst enemy.

My grandpa made it worse when he insisted that I set the table in the dining room. And not with normal plates, but with my grandma's china instead. And wine glasses. I stared in shock as he set a bottle of merlot on the table.

"Wine? China? You do know it's just Matt coming over for dinner, right?"

"Company is company, Maggie May. You think your grandma would've let us have guests over and sit on the couches with TV trays?"

"Well, no. But…"

"Just because she's gone does not mean I'm going to devolve into some sort of savage."

I shook my head as I finished setting the table. "Grandpa, Matt's probably used to living on MREs and eating off of dirt floors. And I'm not talking about his time in Iraq either."

"All the same."

I continued to grumble as my grandpa sliced up the roast from the slow cooker while I whipped up gravy to go over the top and put the vegetables into a separate serving bowl. The last thing I needed was for Officer Handsome to go getting any sort of *ideas.*

When Matt arrived he was freshly showered and smelled like some sort of very pleasant cologne. He also had a small bouquet of flowers in his hand that my grandpa insisted I place in a vase and put on the table. I studied both of them, but from what I could tell they'd each come up with their part of things independently.

Still. I wasn't going to let this sort of thing continue. China and wine and flowers…What was this? Didn't they realize we had a murder to solve?

"So, what did you find out? Was Dunner getting into dealing drugs? Is that what someone's growing in the valley? What did Mr. Jackson have to say?"

My grandpa leaned out of the kitchen. "Maggie May, that is no way to treat a dinner guest. You want to talk business, you can wait until after the meal. Talk about something else."

That meant small talk. I hate small talk.

Matt and I stood there awkwardly, staring around for something, anything to say that wasn't connected to the investigation.

"So, Iraq…" I said at the same time he said, "I can't believe that's still here," and gestured to where I'd scrawled his name on the wall all those years ago.

Since he'd knelt down to run a finger over the shaky letters, I was stuck with his chosen line of conversation. I knelt down next to him. "My grandpa claims nothing will take it off. I suspect he just likes to leave it there so he can tease me about it."

"He teases you about it still? How?"

I had to look away before I drowned in those blue eyes of his. "Every single time I start dating someone new, he makes a joke about hiding the permanent markers. Or asks me if I scrawled the guy's name on my walls yet. Every. Single. Time."

My grandpa came out of the kitchen, Fancy trailing along at his side, her nose in the air to smell the roast. "That's why Maggie's stopped telling me when she starts dating someone new."

"No, I've just stopped dating, thank you very much." Before either of them could pursue that one further, I stepped into the kitchen and grabbed a plate for Fancy. As I took my seat, I set the plate on the floor next to me.

My grandpa glared at me, but I chose to ignore him. We might have guests, but too bad, Fancy deserved to be a part of the meal, too. Matt looked at the plate on the floor and then back at me. "Dare I ask what that's for?"

"It's a sharing plate. For Fancy."

"A sharing plate." I could see him struggling to keep a straight face, but I ignored him as Fancy settled down next to me, her paws on either side of the plate, a thin line of drool falling from her left jowl in anticipation of the yummy meal to come.

"Yes, Maggie May. Why don't you explain to our guest what a sharing plate is." My grandpa eyed me from across the table, but I chose to ignore him, too.

"It's very simple. I like to feed Fancy scraps when I eat, and I don't want to just throw the food on the floor, that would be messy. Or get my fingers all slobbery, either. So I set down a plate for her. Simple as that."

I placed a small piece of roast on Fancy's plate. She gobbled it up and immediately looked to me for more, silent and waiting.

Matt smirked. "You set down a plate for your dog? At every meal?"

"Every meal." My grandpa nodded, his face grim, as he served himself vegetables.

Matt and my grandpa both tried to keep straight faces but failed miserably.

"You know, there are reasons I like living alone. Like not having someone sit there and judge me all day every day."

"You're welcome to live alone if you want to, Maggie May," my grandpa said as he covered his roast and vegetables with a thick layer of gravy followed by a healthy amount of ketchup.

"But then I couldn't help you out, Grandpa."

"Like I said."

I dropped a piece of carrot onto Fancy's plate and then served myself as my grandpa proceeded to tell Matt how I'd decided I needed to move in with him because he was so old and helpless. Except, somehow when my grandpa said it, it sounded like the most absurd idea in the world.

I glared across the table at him. "Need I remind you that the first day I was here you pulled a shotgun on someone and are now the prime suspect in that man's murder?"

He shoved a potato in his mouth and chewed, glaring right back at me. "Need I remind you that that happened even though you were standing right there?"

Matt held up his wine glass. "A toast."

We both glared at him.

"To old friends," he lifted the glass in my direction, "men of wisdom", he lifted the glass in my grandpa's direction, "lovable balls of fur that eat off plates like dainty old ladies", he nodded to Fancy, "and a meal that isn't a heart attack in a sack."

"Cheers." I clinked glasses with Matt and my grandpa and let the conversation drift towards less weighted topics, trying not to think about how easily Matt had managed to charm both Fancy and my grandpa.

And me.

CHAPTER 14

After dinner my grandpa pulled out the Scrabble board.

"I thought we were going to talk about the case now," I muttered. That was the whole reason I'd invited Matt over after all, not...this.

He handed me the tile bag. "No reason we can't play and talk at the same time."

I sighed and drew an H. Matt drew an A and pumped his fist in victory. My grandpa drew a Z and handed the bag back to him to let him draw his tiles. "Competitive a bit?"

"There's nothing wrong with wanting to win." Matt laid out his tiles and handed my grandpa the bag next.

I laughed. "Oh, you're going to do well here. But don't think that because you drew that A that you'll actually win. We're serious Scrabble players in this family."

"Bring it on." He grinned at me and I couldn't help but grin right back.

We settled into an intense, but fun game of Scrabble. Matt tended towards longer words and trying to hit as many double-letter or triple-letter scores as he could while my grandpa focused on making multiple words in one play. Me, I just held in there and tried whatever I could that would earn me enough points to keep up with them.

As we played, Matt updated us on the case. He'd checked out the valley, but it was a bust for now. The cabin was still there, but the plants were gone. Whoever had been using the valley wasn't anymore. Whether that was Mr. Jackson and he'd become spooked by the police investigation or whether it was someone else, Matt couldn't say. And without a good reason to do so he couldn't order the lab techs in to take fingerprints or soil samples. A county like ours didn't have unlimited resources.

He'd also swung by Mr. Jackson's house to talk to him, but Mr. Jackson wasn't answering his phone or his door.

"You know," my grandpa said. "I haven't seen Roy in a couple days. We don't talk much, but usually I see him out back or up the hill at least once a day. Didn't think much of it before, but if you couldn't get ahold of him…"

"Does he have any family around here?" I asked.

"No. He has a daughter back east, but they only talk on major holidays. I have her number somewhere around here. Let me see if I can find it."

While my grandpa searched through his old address book, I traded in all my tiles. I hate when I have only vowels to play. My grandpa wrote down the number of Roy Jackson's daughter—it was a New York zip code— while Matt played off a triple word score. I might've called him a bad word for that, but let's just pretend I didn't.

My grandpa chuckled as he counted up Matt's points. "Hm, Maggie. Looks like you've met your match."

I chose to ignore that little comment. "Maybe Mr. Jackson skipped town."

"What for?" My grandpa asked.

"Killing a man and getting caught growing illegal marijuana?"

Matt shook his head. "Too early for that. We hadn't even questioned him. As far as anyone else in this town is concerned, your grandpa is the killer."

"Thanks for that," my grandpa said.

Matt shrugged one shoulder. "It's true."

I sat back, thinking. "Fine, so Mr. Jackson is a dead end. Who else could've done it?"

Matt rearranged his tiles, studying the board intently. "I don't know. A lot of people didn't like Jack, but most felt the way your grandpa here did. That there was no point in wasting a bullet on a man who was going to find a bad end all on his own. He had no money for anyone to inherit. He had an ex-wife and two kids, but he stayed away from them and that's all they wanted from him. He probably had his hands in some petty crimes, but nothing I could find that was serious enough to warrant killing him. If you hadn't found that body, no one would've even cared that he was gone."

"Not even his mother?" I asked.

"Definitely not his mother."

I glanced over at Fancy who was asleep against the wall, snoring up a storm, and wished I could take back my moment of good citizenship. If I hadn't called the cops about the body, it would probably still be up there and my grandpa wouldn't be in danger of going to jail for a murder he hadn't committed.

Darned conscience.

I swore to myself that next time I found a dead body I was going to leave it right where it was. I needed to start keeping out of other people's business.

Yeah, like that was going to happen.

🐾 🐾 🐾

We wrapped up our Scrabble game and Matt left, no closer to finding the murderer than we'd been when he arrived. But I had to admit, it had been a fun night if nothing else. Wine, china, Officer Handsome, and all.

CHAPTER 15

The next day was Jamie's day off at the store and I didn't want to ask her to cancel it our first week of live operations, especially after she'd done most of the work getting the store up and running, so I dragged Fancy out of bed and we made it to the store by four o'clock to get started on all the café prep. As I sprinkled cinnamon on the dough for the cinnamon rolls I thought about how lucky I was that I only had to do this once a week.

I am not a morning person.

By the time Katie came in at seven I was ready for my first Coke of the day which would certainly not be my last.

(Don't judge. I don't drink coffee and I don't do crack, so if I want to have a Coke first thing in the morning and another one at noon and another one with dinner, then I think I should be allowed to do so without judgment. Sorry, but I'm a little sensitive around the issue given the number of people over the years who've told me about how you can dissolve a penny in Coke. The day I stop drinking Coke will probably be the day I get hit by a bus, so I'll enjoy my little addiction while I'm alive to do so, thank you very much.)

Anyway.

Katie and I made it through the morning rush without a single complaint about the food. Jamie *is* magic in the kitchen but I can hold my own, especially when I have her recipes to work with.

Katie and I were wiping down the tables on the barkery side when Lucas Dean walked in, grinning from ear to ear. "How are my beautiful ladies today?" he asked as he swaggered towards us.

I glared at him. "I realize it's probably a bit confusing for you, Luke, but the barkery is for canine dogs not human dogs."

"Haha. Funny." He gave Katie a kiss on the cheek and wink before turning towards me.

Katie blushed and gazed up at him, her eyes full of adoration. Seems my little "old guys wanting seventeen-year-olds is creepy" speech hadn't had much of an effect.

He took a step towards me and I twisted the dirty dish rag in my hand into a rope and held it out, ready to smack him if he came any closer.

"You wound me, Maggie. What can I do to convince you I'm a good man?"

"How about stop hitting on teenagers and leave my best friend alone? That'd be a good start."

He shook his head slightly. "Speaking of your best friend, she around?"

"No. It's her day off. Now, can I get you something or did you just come by to cause trouble?"

"As a matter of fact, if you still have any left, I'll take one of those delicious cinnamon rolls of yours and a coffee to go."

I started to walk towards the café side, but Katie

rushed past me, red ponytail swishing behind her. "I've got it."

"Probably for the best," Luke told me, watching her go. "This way I'll know no one spat in my coffee."

I stared him down. Spitting in his coffee was the least of the torments he deserved, the way he was playing Katie and Jamie and who knew who else. He pretended to ignore me, but I could tell by the way he fiddled with the salt and pepper shakers on the nearest table that he was well aware of my death stare.

Katie came back with the coffee and a to-go bag, staring up at him all gooey-eyed. He winked at her. "Thanks, doll."

"Make sure he pays with more than a kiss, please," I said, trying not to groan in disgust.

He handed over a bill I couldn't see and kissed Katie on the cheek. "Keep the change."

I mimed throwing up as he sauntered out the door in his tight jeans. Watching how Katie stared after him I wondered whether I could get away with permanently banning him from the store. That man was bad, bad news.

Unfortunately, I was pretty sure Jamie would never speak to me again if I did. Not to mention how much Katie might sulk. Broken-hearted teenagers are the worst.

🐾 🐾 🐾

The rest of the day was pretty uneventful. Matt stopped by right before we were supposed to close to tell me he still hadn't been able to reach Mr. Jackson and that his daughter didn't know where he was either.

When I got home I grilled my grandpa on who else

in town might be capable of murder. He raised his eyebrows at the "who else" portion of that question, but we walked through a list of about five people he figured were capable of killing someone under the right circumstances, but then eliminated them just as fast for various reasons.

One would probably shoot any police officer who stepped foot on his property, but would otherwise keep to himself. Another would shoot anybody who crossed him in business, but Jack had stayed far away from him and for good reason. There was one woman on the list who would likely put any woman who came too close to her husband in the ground, but since Jack wasn't a sleazy young woman intent on seducing someone else's husband, we were able to eliminate her. And, of course, there was the man so gun-happy it was a miracle he hadn't shot himself yet, but he only used his guns on his home-built shooting range.

Crazy to realize how many people are probably capable of killing someone when you really stop to think about it, but none were the one we were looking for.

Frustrated and in need of some sign of progress, I snuck over to the Jackson house to see what I could see, but that was a bust, too. The shades were drawn, so I couldn't see inside. All I succeeded in doing was leaving footprints around the sides of the house.

I tried the back door—just in case, since my grandpa hadn't locked his front or back doors in forty years—but Mr. Jackson was a less trusting soul than my grandpa. The house was locked up tight. I wanted to try the front door, too, but didn't know how I could without someone seeing me and calling the cops.

I debated researching how to jimmy a lock online and getting in that way, but I decided that as much as I loved my grandpa I had to draw the line at committing a felony. He hadn't been arrested yet. If he ever was, then maybe I'd reconsider.

Disappointed in my progress, I trudged back home. It didn't help that things weren't going well at the barkery either. After that first big week with the dog show things had slowed down a ton, and I didn't feel like I was pulling my weight. Unfortunately, I wasn't sure what to do to fix things. I'd always known the locals weren't going to be my target customer, but I'd hoped the local business owners might chat us up to their customers a bit more than they were.

Frustrated by a lack of suspects, no Mr. Jackson, and disappointing barkery sales, I decided it was time to go on the offensive.

CHAPTER 16

I spent most of the next day in the barkery kitchen putting together sample treat bags. I couldn't use the Barkery Bites because they have to stay refrigerated, but I also make a great Peanut Butter Crunch Cookie that Fancy loves.

(Of course, Fancy loves anything that remotely looks like food, even bugs if they get too close to her out in the yard. She's not the most discerning of customers. Luckily for me, other dogs liked the cookies, too.)

So I cooked up a couple hundred cookies, bagged them up in cute little paw-print baggies with our logo on the side, tied them off with a 50% off coupon, and—as soon as the lunch rush was over—made the rounds of all the local businesses.

You would've thought I was running for mayor the way I shook hands and kissed puppies. I made sure to take time at each establishment—the resort, the local fishing guide's office, each of the fifteen restaurants in town, the five hotels, the three motels, the hunting lodge, the visitor's bureau, the rafting company, the realty company, and the two gas stations—to explain that I was new in town and that I'd just opened up a gourmet dog bakery.

I also just happened to let it slip that I'd been the one that found the body of Jack Dunner. I lost count of the number of times I said, "That was certainly a welcome to the valley I wasn't expecting." Fortunately, no one knew that my grandpa had threatened him with a shotgun the day he went missing—I'd have to thank Matt and Officer Clark for keeping quiet about that— but they all knew about Jack. Each and every one had a story about what a degenerate the man was.

By the time I finished my rounds I wasn't the least bit sad that he was dead. He'd lied, he'd cheated, he'd slept with other men's wives…But. Everyone also agreed that he'd never upset someone so much they would've bothered shooting him.

I pouted the whole way home. I'd spent an entire day baking, an entire afternoon schmoozing the locals, and I was no closer to finding who had actually killed Jack Dunner than I'd been the day before.

All I could hope was that my goodwill campaign would drive a little business my way.

🐾 🐾 🐾

The next morning I opened up the store and prayed that I'd have at least a few customers as a result of my efforts.

I did. But not the way I'd hoped…

🐾 🐾 🐾

By the next afternoon it was pretty clear that my efforts to make nice with the locals had worked, but that those efforts had had an unintended consequence I wasn't quite sure how to deal with. As I rang up an order of Doggie Delights I looked at the line of remaining customers and frowned.

First in line was Russell, owner of the local Big R and forty-year-old widower. He had a bit of a paunch but kind eyes.

Next was Dean, manager of the local resort and resident Lothario. Rumor had it he'd been making his way through every single woman between the age of twenty and fifty since arriving in town three months ago.

Behind him was James, one of the local fishing guides, originally from Australia. He was hilarious as could be but I was pretty sure he didn't even own a dog. He was also a bit short for my taste.

(Not to mention, I was busy operating a business, taking care of my grandpa, and tracking down a killer…)

After that was Martin, the sixty-year-old *married* man who ran the local specialty pizza restaurant.

Finally, at the very end of the line, were Evan and Abe, the only two I figured were legitimate customers. They owned the old historic Creek Inn and had a St. Bernard they'd named Lucy Carrots—Lucy for Abe's mom and carrots for the vegetable of the day the day they got her. No one had confirmed it for me, but I was pretty sure they had more of an interest in one another than they'd ever have in me.

I bit my lip as Russell leaned against the counter and asked me to walk him through the display case selections the same way he had the day before. If he was flirting with me, he wasn't very good at it. He basically just grinned at me the whole time before finally pointing at the second-cheapest item in the display case with a soft grunt.

As I was ringing him up, Matt came in. He glanced down the line of men and smirked before going over to say hi to Fancy who'd jumped up and started wagging her tail the minute he walked in.

No sooner had the door closed than it opened again and Martin's wife, Gloria, stormed in. She marched right up to the front of the line and threw a bag of sample treats down on the counter. "How dare you," she cried.

"I'm sorry. What did I do?" I asked, genuinely perplexed. Did her dog have allergies? Did she not think I should be asking local businesses to help us promote our business? What had I done?

"Like you don't know. Going around town handing out your free goodies to every man in sight." She glared in the direction of her husband who turned bright red and took a step backward.

Matt managed to stifle his laugh. I wasn't so lucky.

I know I shouldn't have laughed at her—she really was genuinely upset with me—but if you could've seen the men lined up behind that counter…To think that I was trying to seduce any one of them was just absurd.

Her face turned almost purple and her eyes bulged out. I swear I thought she was going to collapse right there and then and that I'd have to call an ambulance and we'd forever more be known as the store where Gloria Parks had died of an aneurysm. "You…you…you temptress, you. How dare you laugh at me you…you *homewrecker*."

I held my hands out to calm her. "Gloria, please. I'm sorry I laughed. I know this is very serious to you, but I'm not trying to tempt anyone with my…"

Matt leaned in. "With your *free goodies*. I believe that was the description she used." He was grinning from ear to ear.

I seriously wanted to slap him, but I was too busy trying to get Gloria to calm down enough to breathe.

Gloria gestured to the line of men, almost taking out Russell's eye in the process. "You think I'm going to believe you when I can see the proof of it before my very eyes? Look at them. Lured in here like flies to your honey trap."

It was all I could do not to laugh again, but I managed. Barely.

"Pick one," she demanded, waving her hand again.

"Excuse me?"

"Pick one."

"Pick one what?" I stared at the line of my customers as they all shuffled nervously and refused to make eye contact with me.

"Pick a man. I don't care who, but pick one. You pick a man and settle down and quit trying to cause trouble around here with your big city ways."

She stared at me like she actually expected me to just point at a man right then and there and settle myself down. Had she not noticed that her husband was one of my so-called choices? Or that the last two men in line had very likely picked one another already and had no interest in me?

I couldn't help but glance at Matt, but he was studiously looking at the ground not wanting to have any part of things now. (Figured the only man in the room I might want to pick was also the only man in the room who didn't want to be picked. Story of my life.)

I shook my head. "I'm sorry to disappoint you, Gloria, but I will not be picking a man today or any other day. I have my grandpa to see to and this business to run and I am not going to go off and settle down until those things are well under control. But I thank you for your concern."

I glanced to the side where Jamie had come to watch events unfold. "And I believe, Gloria, that if you go over to Jamie there that she'd be happy to give you one of her famous cinnamon rolls as a thank you for coming in here today. On the house."

I'm not sure that actually satisfied Gloria, but at that point her husband stepped forward and led her away. I let out a big sigh and turned back to Russell. "Sorry about that, Russell. That'll be $2.95."

🐾 🐾 🐾

All of my former admirers couldn't get out of there fast enough after that. At least they all bought something, even if it was the cheapest item available. Only Evan and Abe lingered to talk about the different products and what I thought Lucy Carrots might enjoy. They left with a whole assortment of treats, including a four-pack of the Doggie Delights.

Once the door closed behind the last of them, Matt stepped forward. "Maggie May, resident temptress who hands out her free goodies to every man she meets."

"Shut up. That was not funny."

He leaned his hip on the counter. "Maybe not for you. But it was certainly entertaining for me."

I straightened the counter even though it didn't really need it. "What are you doing here anyway? You don't have a dog, do you?"

"No, not yet. Someday, though." He scratched Fancy's ears as she shamelessly grumbled with pleasure.

I glared at her, but she didn't care. "So? Why are you here?"

The door opened and Darryl, a local hunting guide, came in. He saw Matt and frowned.

"How can I help you, Darryl?" I waved him forward.

"I was looking for more of those treats you dropped off by the office. Angus really liked them."

"Ah, perfect. Here. This should hold him over for a week or so. And half price since you're a new customer."

The way he kept glancing at Matt he was obviously another one who'd come by hoping for more than just dog treats to take home. I managed not to roll my eyes or acknowledge Matt's smirk as I rang him up and hustled him out the door.

"What did you do, hand out dog treats at the Creek Inn Friday night?"

"No. I just went around town handing out baggies of free dog treats at all the local businesses." I showed him the baggie Gloria had thrown at me. "I hoped it would prompt people to send tourists our way, not…this."

"Don't worry. Word that you only care about your work will spread like wildfire when they all meet up at the Inn tonight for drinks. Poor guys. I'm sure there'll be more than one drowning his sorrows."

I crossed my arms. "It's not just my work. It's also my grandpa. And the little matter of a dead body without a killer, although I wasn't going to tell them that. Plus, there's nothing wrong with wanting something more from life than to be someone's wife."

"Spoken like the big city girl you are." He winked to

take the sting out of his words, but I wasn't having it. I glared him down until he leaned closer and added, "Look. You think I don't get the same pressures you do? Good-looking hometown boy back from military service and with a good job? I must be looking to settle down and start a family, right?" He shook his head. "All I'm trying to do is figure out if I can stay here long-term or not, but every time I turn around someone wants me to meet their daughter or niece or neighbor."

"Good-looking, huh?" I teased.

"Compared to the competition. Or so I'm told." He adjusted the gun belt at his waist, not meeting my eye. "I'm actually here on official business. Sort of."

"Why? What happened?"

"Mr. Jackson's daughter was worried about not being able to reach him after I called. They didn't talk often, but that was on her not him. He always returned her calls within a day. So when she couldn't get ahold of him, she got worried and flew out here."

"And? Did he split town? Do you think he's the one who murdered Jack?"

Matt shook his head. "Definitely not."

"How can you be sure?"

"Well, because odds are two people didn't suddenly snap at the same time and decide to kill someone."

"He's dead?" I glanced around to see if anyone had heard me, but Jamie had made herself scarce. Not surprising since she was as bad as Gloria when it came to wanting to see me settled down. "Where did you find him?"

"His daughter found him. In the kitchen. She had a spare key."

I winced, remembering how I'd tried to open the back door. At least I'd used my sleeve so I hadn't left any prints, but that might've wiped away someone else's prints…And I had left a bunch of muddy shoe prints all around the perimeter…

Looked like this was going to be another dog-peeing-on-a-dead-body moment.

"Was he shot, too?" I asked.

"No. Baseball bat. That's actually why I'm here." He glanced around. "We're going to have to take your grandpa in for questioning again. I wanted to tell you before we did because it would be a really good time for that alibi of his to come forward."

"Why do you have to question him again? It's not like my grandpa's the only one with a baseball bat in town."

He winced. "No. But he's the only one with a bat engraved with his name and 'Thanks for 25 Years of Service' on it."

I buried my face in my hands. "Let me guess. He kept his baseball bats in his unlocked truck, too?"

"That's what I'm assuming."

What was I going to do now? My grandpa wasn't just the suspect in one murder, he was the suspect in two. And I could see the rationale as clearly as anyone. That he killed Jack out of anger and then Mr. Jackson because he'd seen something he shouldn't.

"This just keeps getting worse," I muttered.

"I know. I'll also need to talk to you at some point about the last time you saw Mr. Jackson. We're trying to figure out exactly when he might've been killed. It's been at least a few days."

"Okay. Yeah. Sure." I shook myself, trying to get my

mind moving again. "Does my grandpa know? About Mr. Jackson? And the bat?"

Matt shrugged one shoulder. "A little hard to miss the coroner's van and the three police cars out front. But he doesn't know about the bat. And I'd appreciate it if you didn't tell him. Only reason I'm here instead of there is because I figured you'd have enough sense to call him a lawyer instead of letting him rely on the truth to save him."

"So he needs a lawyer now?"

"It'd be a good idea. Mason Maxwell is the best one in the county and he lives just outside of Creek. Here's his cell. If I drive slow enough you should be able to get ahold of him and get him to your grandpa's house before I get there."

I took the card he handed me, flipping it over and over as I thought through everything that had to happen now. I hated being powerless, but so much of this was out of my control.

Matt clearly wanted to leave, but he hesitated, looking back at me.

"Thank you. For everything," I told him.

"Anytime. I'll do what I can for him, Maggie. If it weren't for your grandpa I probably wouldn't be alive today. And if I were, I'd probably be behind bars."

I nodded as he gave Fancy one last pat on the head and left. He really was a good man. And a good-looking one, too. How inconvenient.

CHAPTER 17

I called the lawyer. He was sharp. I could tell just from the three minutes we spent on the phone. No fluff, no dithering, just what happened, who's involved, where do I need to go, I'm on my way now, goodbye.

Then I called my grandpa. I'd promised Matt I wouldn't tell him anything about the details of the murder, but I figured he better know that a lawyer was headed to his house and why.

To say he was not happy with the fact that I'd called a lawyer is an understatement. He used a few words I'd never heard before—and I've heard quite a few colorful words over the years; my first job was at a skydiving center with a lot of sports jumpers from all over the world passing through. It was an interesting education in multi-lingual cusswords. Among other things.

I finally had to play the worried granddaughter card on him to get him to calm down and agree to let the man represent him. (First, though, I had to acknowledge— three times—that after forty-plus years living in Creek it was absolutely ridiculous that anyone could believe my grandpa capable of killing not just one man, but two.)

After that, I didn't know what to do with myself.

There was no point going home since my grandpa would be at the jail with Matt and the lawyer. Fortunately, things at the barkery picked up just enough that I couldn't leave Jamie alone, so I tried to put thoughts of what was happening back in Creek aside as I smiled and helped each customer who came through the door.

Fancy knew something was off, though. She kept standing up and crying at me until I finally had to put her out back in the dog run. Poor girl. She was just trying to help, but the crying got on my last nerve and I didn't want to take my fear out on her.

(I felt so guilty I ended up sneaking her three Doggie Delights before closing time finally rolled around.)

🐾 🐾 🐾

As soon as the clock struck four I locked the doors with a firm thunk and turned to Jamie. "You have time for a beer? It's been a day."

"Of course." She wiped down the counter on the café side as she answered, never one to stop unless she had to.

"Don't 'of course' me. When you get going with a guy you can sometimes disappear for months." I opened the small fridge I kept for personal beverages and grabbed two Wooly Boogers—sounds disgusting but they're a yummy nut brown ale made by Grand Lake Brewing Company—and headed out back, Jamie following along behind me with the bottle opener.

She opened the beers while I sat on the ground with Fancy for a minute and apologized for having to lock her outside. Fortunately, Fancy's idea of being mad at me involved barking a little lecture and then licking my face and stepping all over me until I'd petted her enough to show that I really was sorry.

After that was done I joined Jamie on the bench and took a long sip of my beer. I savored the taste as I looked at the tops of the trees swaying in a slight breeze, the mountains looming behind them on the horizon. As bad as things were, at least I had this moment, sitting outside after work with my best friend and my dog, a good beer in hand, surrounded by the beauty of the valley.

"I don't always disappear into relationships," Jamie finally said when it was clear I wasn't going to say anything.

"No? Tell me the last one where that didn't happen. Where you weren't practically living with the guy by the end of the first month of dating him."

She thought about it for a minute. "There was Neal."

"Neal? The guy from France that you dated for two weeks before he had to go back home?"

"Yeah. See, I didn't lose myself in a relationship with him." She took a sip of her beer as I shook my head.

"No, but you did talk about what it would be like to live in Paris. You even looked at one-way airfares, if I recall correctly. Probably would've gone if I hadn't pulled you back from the ledge."

Fancy came over and lay down so close her foot was touching mine. Poor girl. I really must've stressed her out. She likes to stay close, but never that close. I rubbed her back for a second, listening to birds singing somewhere nearby.

Jamie elbowed me. "Speaking of men...Was that Matt Barnes I saw in the barkery today? Looks pretty good in a uniform if it was, but he just moved back to town from overseas. He doesn't own a dog, does he?"

I took a long swig of beer. Jamie and my grandpa should form a club. The Busybodies Club. "He was here on business." Because I wasn't quite ready to tell her what business, I added, "You know, he's single. And a helluva lot better man than Luke."

"Are you seriously trying to set me up with him?"

"Sure. Why not? He's good-looking, he's smart, he's kind, he's…"

"Yours."

I lurched to the side, scaring Fancy to her feet. "What?"

Fancy settled a few feet away with a huff of annoyance.

Jamie laughed. "Matt's been yours since we were kids."

"No he hasn't. We hardly know each other." I crossed my arms and glared at the mountains, thinking darkly about the disadvantages of living in a small town.

"You wrote his name on your wall when you were five."

"What does that have to do with anything?" I swore to myself I was going to go home as soon as I finished my beer and remove that name from the wall once and for all; I didn't care if I had to burn down my grandpa's house to make it happen.

"You used permanent marker."

"So? I was five. Do you think that was some sort of deliberate choice I made? Please."

Jamie laughed. "Do you know that my mom told me that when we were all babies. Not even talking yet, I mean, barely crawling. That our mothers put us all down to play and I crawled over to Matt and you crawled over there right away and shoved yourself between us? You couldn't even speak yet, but you'd already claimed him."

"And because *over thirty years ago*, when I was *a baby*, I pushed you out of the way, you won't go near him now? That's ridiculous. I've always hated girl dibs. You know that. He's yours if you want him. Go for him."

She laughed. "No point. He only has eyes for you, Maggie."

I choked on my beer. "Don't be absurd. There's nothing like that there. The only reason we're talking at all is because he has two murders to investigate. Plus, you know me. I don't do relationships well."

"That's because you've always been in love with Matt." She tapped her beer against mine. "And when you finally give up and acknowledge that fact I am not going to be the one standing between you."

She downed the last of her beer with a smug smile as I brooded. Rather than continue what had become a completely ridiculous conversation, I finally told her why Matt had been there that day.

"Oh your poor grandpa. At least you got Mason Maxwell to represent him. That man is amazing. I don't know why he lives up here and isn't dominating the courtrooms of some big city, but if anyone can get your grandpa out of this mess, it's Maxwell."

"He did seem pretty sharp when I talked to him, but if they don't have any other suspects I don't know what he can actually do. I mean, the bat and the gun were both my grandpa's. If it wasn't him, who hates him enough to frame him like that?"

"Didn't you say he had a secret lady friend? With a husband?"

"Who killed two men just to get back at my grandpa? Wouldn't it be easier to just shoot my grandpa instead? I mean, granted, the guy would've known about my grandpa doing prison time. But he's also really ill. I doubt he's physically capable of killing two people."

"So if your grandpa's not the target, then the two men who were killed were. What do they have in common?"

"Nothing except proximity to my grandpa. And maybe pot."

"Pot? That's legal now. Why bother killing someone over it?"

I told her everything I knew, because whether she wanted to admit it or not she had been a little caught up in Luke lately and we really hadn't had a chance to talk about any of this. But even after we'd talked through it we were no closer to finding a suspect to give the police.

As we sat there and watched the sun sink behind the mountains, Jamie asked, "Do you remember when we were little and they found that escaped criminal living in that cave up the mountain behind your grandpa's house?"

I nodded. Before the cops had found him, the local kids had. We'd snuck up to the cave and looked at the stacks of canned food and the dirty sleeping bag spread on the ground, daring one another to go inside until we heard a branch break in the woods somewhere nearby and ran away screaming.

"You think that's what it could be? Some weird survivalist living up in the woods who didn't want anyone to get too close? I mean, it's possible that whatever was being grown down in that valley wasn't pot after all. And that whoever was living down there in that cabin really didn't like being bothered by anyone…"

Jamie ran to grab us each another beer while I thought about it. If that's who it was, then there was really only one way to know…

She handed me a beer and the opener. "Don't you even think about it."

"About what?"

"About going to check that cave. If there really is some crazy psycho running around up there, the last thing you need to do is to cross paths with him. You're smarter than that."

I bit my lip. "He probably wouldn't shoot a woman. And he probably doesn't have his own weapons since the gun and the bat came from my grandpa's truck."

"You going to bet your life on that? And what if he decided to kidnap you instead of shoot you?"

I laughed. "Please. Last time some weird mountain man kidnapped a random girl in the forest was something like thirty years ago."

"That you know about. Just because they don't make TV movies about it anymore doesn't mean it doesn't happen."

I took a sip of my beer.

"Don't be stupid, Maggie."

"I'd have Fancy with me. She's like…a bear."

Jamie snorted as we both looked down at Fancy who'd rolled over on her back and had her front two paws thrust into the sky as she snored away. "Somehow I can't picture the Fanster doing much more than licking the guy to death."

"She might bark at him first. Make him run away."

"What if he shot her instead? You don't want that."

I chewed on my thumbnail as I thought about it. As much as I hated to admit it, Jamie was right. But someone had to find this killer. And soon.

CHAPTER 18

My grandpa still wasn't home by the time I left the barkery and drove to Creek. It was weird to step into that dark, empty house. I'd never been there alone before. And it had never felt so cold and abandoned. There was a roast chicken going in the slow cooker, but I didn't know whether to go ahead and eat or to wait for him.

I was starving, but if he was going to be back soon then I'd wait. But the only way to know that was to call the jail and ask. And who was going to tell me the truth? Matt was probably interrogating my grandpa and no one else would have a reason to let me know anything about anything, especially if it was Officer Clark who answered.

I was just about to leave Fancy to walk down to the jail and see what I could see when the front door opened and my grandpa came in, muttering to himself as he disappeared down the hallway. He was followed by a man who was immaculately dressed in what I like to think of as country club casual—nicely pressed slacks and what was probably a very expensive cashmere sweater. He had salt and pepper hair and a fierce intelligence that evaluated me and Fancy in the space of a few seconds.

Fancy, who normally would've seen a new man in the doorway and gone over to say hi, stayed right where she was, frozen by the warning look he gave her.

"That's an impressive trick," I told him as I walked over, nodding towards where she watched him, still unmoving.

"You just have to show them who's the alpha. Dogs are pack animals."

I raised an eyebrow at that, but didn't say anything more about it. "You must be Mason Maxwell. I'm Maggie Carver. Nice to meet you."

"And you." His handshake was firm, almost aggressive, but not quite.

"Would you care to join us for dinner? I'm sure my grandpa's as starved as I am and there's a chicken ready in the slow cooker."

"You two go ahead and eat. I'll eat at home. But I would like to talk about a few items with you before I leave."

I studied him for a moment, trying to read what was going on behind that chiseled exterior, but I drew a blank. The man was completely unreadable. How odd.

My grandpa returned, still muttering to himself. "I'm hungry. Mason, you staying or going?" He walked right past us into the kitchen and started throwing down plates for all three of us. (Not the china, though. And not in the dining room, but at the small table in the kitchen.)

"He's not eating with us, Grandpa. But he did want to talk to us about a few things."

My grandpa grumbled to himself as he put back one

of the plates. "You going to at least let me give you something to drink?" he demanded. "I'm not much of a drinker anymore, but I've still got a nice bottle of scotch around here if you're interested."

I silently prayed that Maxwell would at least accept the scotch. I was afraid that if he said he was fine or that he just wanted a water that my grandpa would direct all the stress and anxiety of the day at the one person he probably needed most to help him make it through this mess.

But Maxwell must have sensed that, too, because he inclined his head towards my grandpa and said, "I'd like that very much. Thank you, Mr. Carver."

I finished getting the carrots, potatoes, and onions out of the slow cooker and into a serving bowl and then joined the men at the table. I was so famished I didn't even wait to start serving myself.

"So?" I finally asked after I'd taken a couple of bites and seen that my grandpa had served himself, too. "What happened?"

"What happened?" my grandpa muttered, glaring at Maxwell. "This friend of yours showed up at my house, told me to let him do all the talking, and then proceeded to remind me that I was supposed to let him do all the talking for the next two hours while the cops tried to ask me perfectly innocuous questions."

"There is nothing innocuous about being questioned in the matter of two separate murders, Mr. Carver." Maxwell took a slow sip of his scotch and tilted his head to the side, clearly pleasantly surprised by the taste.

"I didn't kill either of those men. And I would've liked to be able to tell the cops that."

"You already did for the first one, yes?"

"Yes."

"And yet you were still the first person they suspected when they found the second body."

My grandpa harrumphed at that and shoved more food into his mouth.

"So where do we go from here?" I asked, sneaking Fancy a piece of chicken under the table. I wasn't comfortable putting down a sharing plate with Mason Maxwell in the room.

"I don't know. If they'd had enough evidence they would've arrested your grandfather instead of just bringing him in for questioning. But from what I can see they're not looking at anyone else for this. So one more piece of evidence and they'll probably arrest him. But until they do that…We just have to wait."

"I didn't kill anyone." My grandpa slammed his hand down on the table, making our plates jump and Fancy run outside barking. "I told them that. They should believe me and find the real killer."

"Mr. Carver, I wish the justice system were as efficient as that. It's not. You should know that given your history."

My grandpa stabbed at a piece of chicken. "I shouldn't need a lawyer to defend myself for something I didn't do."

"When it comes to matters of the law, Mr. Carver, we can all use a lawyer. Take for example the sentence you served for killing that man. He was in your home, with a gun, about to shoot someone. If that isn't justified homicide, I don't know what is. If I had been your attorney, you wouldn't have done time for what you did. You saved the life of an innocent woman and I would've made sure the judge and the jury saw that. You relied on the truth to protect you. It didn't. So if you don't want to repeat the mistakes you made back then and end up back in prison when you don't deserve to be, you need to listen to me. Do not say anything to the cops. Officially or unofficially."

My grandpa glared at him, but Mason Maxwell stared right back. I watched the two men lock their wills and worried that something in the room was going to break from all the energy they were directing towards one another.

Finally, my grandpa bowed his head. "Fine. I won't speak to the cops, officially or unofficially."

Mason Maxwell turned to me. "Same goes for you, Ms. Carver."

"But Matt's the one who gave me the heads up about the cops coming to question my grandpa again. If I hadn't been speaking to the cops, and if he hadn't given me your number, my grandpa would've been all alone there today."

"It doesn't matter. They are not your friends right now."

"But Matt gave me your phone number."

"Still doesn't matter. Do you want your grandfather to go to jail?"

"No." I fought the urge to pout. How did this man make me feel like a little kid caught with her hand in the cookie jar?

"Then don't speak to the cops until this is over. Not even so much as a how do you do."

I pressed my lips together. I knew that he was giving us the best advice he could. It was what I would've probably told any stranger in the same situation. But…

Matt was on our side.

Maxwell tried his glare on me, but I just ignored him. I could still feel it burning into me, though.

"Ms. Carver?"

"I heard you." I stabbed at a carrot with my fork as I tried to figure out how I could save my grandpa if I couldn't work with Matt. I'd be flying blind. Maybe it was time to go back up that mountain and see what I could find. I seriously doubted there was actually a killer lurking up there. I mean, how likely was that?

Of course if there was, it would be a really stupid thing to do to go up there.

But this was my grandpa we were talking about. I had to do *something*. Something more than wait around for them to find enough evidence to arrest him.

CHAPTER 19

The next day at the store I was distracted, trying to figure out what to do. Jamie had told me not to go back up the mountain, and I knew Matt and my grandpa would both tell me the same.

And yet…

I was going to need to take some sort of risk if I wanted to save my grandpa.

Jamie and I talked about it that afternoon while Katie cleaned up after the lunch time rush. (On the café side we had a panini and soup option that was really popular with both the locals and the tourists. I'd also started putting some of the barkery packaged items on the café counter and those at least were selling well now that my local admiration society had disappeared.)

"You can't put yourself in danger, Maggie. If you think there's something to be found up that mountain, then let Matt be the one who does it. That's his job."

"But Mason Maxwell told me not to talk to him. Plus, he's not going to take the time to look over every little inch for clues like I would. I mean, yes, he owes my grandpa for getting him on the right path, but he's still not family, you know?"

Jamie shook her head. "I'm telling you, it's a fool's errand to go back up that mountain."

"Do you honestly think there's some crazed killer hanging out on the mountain behind my house? Really?"

"No. But that doesn't mean there isn't one." She started to refill the napkin dispensers.

I joined in to help out, the clanging metal sound as I shoved napkins into each one suiting my mood. "Tomorrow's my one day off for the entire week. It's my only chance to find something to clear my grandpa's name. I'm out of options, Jamie. What else can I do?"

"I suppose relax in the backyard and read a good book isn't an option?"

"No."

"Maybe you should ask around to see who might've wanted to kill Mr. Jackson? You haven't done that yet, have you?"

As I considered the possibility, Lucas Dean strolled through the front door. (On the café side this time. Ever since my little comment about him being a dog he'd made sure to use the café-side door, which was just fine with me.)

I glared at him as he passed by Katie, just daring him to kiss her on the cheek like he had the last time he'd been in the store. If he did I was going to take all my pent up frustrations out on him and kick him out the door so fast his head spun. I was done with him and his hijinks.

But that's the thing about Luke. He's good at reading women. So he didn't stop to kiss Katie on the cheek (although she did stare after him adoringly) and he also didn't kiss Jamie on the cheek when he reached us (although she also gazed at him like a love-struck teenager).

"Ladies. Is it too late for lunch?"

"Not at all," Jamie answered, smiling, even though I knew she'd already packed the leftover sandwiches up and stored away the soup in the walk-in. "What would you like?"

"You know what I like. Surprise me."

Jamie dimpled up at that while I rolled my eyes and resisted my childish urge to cough out a less than flattering description of him.

As Jamie went to the back to prepare his lunch, Luke turned so he was leaning with his elbows on the counter next to me, which allowed him to watch Katie who was wiping down the same table over and over again while glancing up at him every few seconds through lowered lashes.

I really hoped he'd do something horrible before that girl turned eighteen, because he was going to crush her like a bug when he got his hands on her.

To pull his attention away from Katie, I forced myself to talk to him. "How are you, Luke? What are you up to these days now that you're not working on the café?"

"This and that. Some fancy rich man's wife is moving in for a long stay in that mansion up on the hill, so I've been doing work for her. She has some interesting needs, including an entire room devoted to her Irish Wolfhound. You want to give me one of those little goodie bags of yours, I could leave it for her."

The last thing I wanted was to be indebted to Luke for anything, but business is business and if some rich socialite decided the barkery was worth patronizing that could turn everything around. So I gave him three of them. "For her and her friends."

"How generous." He leaned closer. "How come you can't be that generous with me, huh, Maggie? I remember you were much more generous when we were little."

I laughed. I couldn't help it. "Are you seriously referring to that one time we played 'show me yours I'll show you mine' from fifty feet away when we were, what, six or seven years old?"

"I'm just saying you used to be a little more open to adventure. Now you're…frigid."

If my grandpa hadn't already been under suspicion of murder, I might've taken Lucas Dean out for good right then and there. Frigid? Frigid? Because I didn't want to get involved with some cad who played on the emotions of every woman he met? Or because I had priorities in my life that didn't involve bedding the nearest man I could find?

Fortunately for Lucas I believed a family should only have one person under suspicion of murder at any given time.

Jamie returned with Luke's lunch and I took the opportunity to take Fancy and Lulu outside for a bit of play time. We all needed the diversion and I couldn't stand watching Katie and Jamie get all gooey over him for another moment.

🐾 🐾 🐾

Jamie joined me after Luke was gone. "Katie's watching the shop. You okay? What did Luke say to you that had you giving him the death stare?"

"It doesn't matter. I'm not wasting my breath on that

man. I need to figure out what to do to help my grandpa."

I laughed as Lulu took a flying leap at Fancy, knocking her to the side. Fancy stared back at her as if asking, "What on earth was that about?"

Jamie laughed, too. "How about just spend some time with your grandpa tomorrow? If he does get arrested won't you want to have spent as much time with him as you could?"

"But if I can find out who really did this I'll get that much more time with him."

Fancy, not to be outdone by Lulu's acrobatics, took one large paw and pinned Lulu on the ground. Lulu squirmed free and ran to a safe distance before turning to bark at her.

"Leave it to the police, Maggie."

I pressed my lips together. I was never going to convince Jamie that my stepping in and trying to solve the murders was anything other than a foolish mistake that was probably going to get me hurt or killed. And sometimes the best way to keep a friendship going is to just agree to disagree without ever actually saying you've done so.

"Online sales have started to pick up," I said, changing the subject.

"Really?"

"Yeah. Maybe it's all the dog show folks ordering online to replace what their dogs have already eaten. I don't know. I'm just glad to see at least someone somewhere likes my barkery idea."

"Ah, Maggie. Success doesn't happen overnight."

Fancy came over to me and leaned against the side of

the bench, keeping a wary eye on Lulu. I scratched behind Fancy's ears as Lulu grabbed her chew toy and started running around the yard, throwing it for herself. "Easy for you to say. The café's been humming along since day one."

"That's because people know what a café is. And if you give them good food at good prices, don't have too much competition, and have enough people with income in the area that can afford to eat out, you can succeed."

"Oh, is that all it takes?"

We both laughed because we were intimately familiar with all the statistics on how many restaurant businesses fail. Every single person we'd told about our plan trotted out some version of the number whether they knew what it actually was or not. The general consensus had been that we were doomed, doomed, doomed and would be crawling back to our old jobs within a year.

Jamie shook her head as Fancy decided it was time to take that chew toy from Lulu and raced after her, but Lulu easily kept head of her. "All I'm saying is that people need to get used to the idea of a barkery. And once you start drawing in the tourists you'll be fine. People who didn't bring their dog this time around will next time. And then you'll be turning customers away at the door."

"I hope not. Those poor dogs."

Jamie laughed.

After a second, I joined her. "If it isn't one problem, it's another, isn't it?"

Fancy gave up on chasing Lulu and collapsed into a heap on the grass. She only has about five minutes of good playtime in her at any given point in time. Lulu, fortunately, was about the same. She collapsed at Fancy's side.

"Ain't that the truth," Jamie answered me. "But I'd rather be so busy I had to take reservations than so dead I could sit outside here with you and the pups and not worry that Katie was going to get overwhelmed. Although it is pretty nice."

"That it is."

We both looked at the dogs, just in time to see Lulu open an eye and oh-so-casually scooch herself forward until she could chomp on Fancy's tail. Fancy shot to her feet with a yelp and turned to glare at Lulu who looked up at her, the picture of innocence, long strands of black hair hanging out of her mouth.

"I think that's my cue to take Fancy back inside before she decides to eat Lulu." I jumped to my feet and dragged Fancy away. I didn't really think she'd eat Lulu, but I wouldn't have put it past her to pin Lulu on her back and growl a very strong opinion about what could happen to puppies that bite other dogs' tails.

None of us needed to see that even if Lulu *had* earned it.

Meanwhile, Jamie went to remove the hair from Lulu's mouth and give her a small lecture about not biting Fancy. Given the tone of the words I was pretty sure it just sounded like praise to Lulu. That dog was going to be a hellion when she was full grown...

Unless I could tame her wild puppy ways first. As I led Fancy inside I brainstormed all the ways I could help with Lulu's training without Jamie noticing. What can I say? It's not in my nature to leave things be when I can do something about them.

Which brought me back to how to help my grandpa.

CHAPTER 20

I tried to talk to my grandpa about everything that night, but he didn't want to talk. He told me that he'd said his piece and now it was up to the law to figure out the truth of the situation and that there was nothing to be done until they did.

I brooded as we sat side-by-side on the couch and watched old episodes of *Frasier*. I wasn't in the mood for humor, not when a killer was on the loose and my grandpa was still the only real suspect. The only thing that kept me sane was playing Sliding Tiles on my laptop. Unfortunately, unlike the game—where if you slide all the pieces around enough you eventually get to the end—I couldn't see a way forward with the murder investigation unless I either risked my life or risked the anger of Mason Maxwell.

I didn't sleep well that night trying to figure out what to do next. I really, really wanted to go up that mountain. But I also knew that if there was actually something to be found up there that I'd be a fool to do so. One, because of the possible risk to my life. Two, because if there was forensic evidence then the cops should really be the ones to find and process it.

I was still law-abiding enough to think they were the best ones to find any evidence, although it was a close call.

When I took Fancy out for her walk the next morning she really wanted to go up the mountain. In her case, though, I knew it was because she'd found something smelly that one time and was hoping to find something equally smelly again. I resisted the urge to let her lead us with her nose and pulled her towards the street instead.

We passed Katie out for her normal morning run. She was as friendly as always—running past without even glancing our way. Weeks of working together and I still hadn't figured out what made that girl tick.

I decided to walk Fancy down to the ballpark and let her run around for a bit. It was a gorgeous morning and she'd earned it. Of course, her version of running around is to sink into the soft green grass of the ball field and watch the birds fly by.

Don't get me wrong, that's just fine with me. I knew a woman when I was in DC who had a Vizsla. She would run that dog a mile to the dog park, let it play for forty-five minutes, run it the mile back home, and that dog would still want to play more. I am far too lazy for a dog like that. Fancy fits me perfectly—one walk a day with the rest of the time spent sleeping or eating.

I sat down next to her and tried to enjoy the morning, but I just couldn't stop thinking about my grandpa and what I could do to save him. I looked towards the mountain where they'd found Jack Dunner's body—I couldn't see my grandpa's house from there, but I could see the ridgeline—but it was just a mountain like any of the other ten I could see from where I was sitting.

I wished I was up on my rock looking down on everything instead of down at the ballpark feeling lost, but I made the best of it by pulling out my phone and surfing Facebook to see what perfect lives people were pretending to have now. Like the friend who'd just posted all her photos of her amazing vacation in Mexico that I knew had involved spending three out of five days sick with Montezuma's Revenge.

I debated adding my own life-is-perfect photo, but I knew I couldn't do it. I'd add some silly caption like, "Gorgeous morning, too bad the cops still think my grandpa killed two men," and then I'd have to spend the rest of the day explaining and calming folks down.

Finally Fancy had had enough and we headed back. We passed Katie about a block and a half from home. I swear there wasn't a drop of sweat on her, which made me reconsider that robot hypothesis. I ticked all the clues off. Cold handshake, minimal smile, no acknowledgement of people she knew when she saw them on the street even though she lived in a small town, and now no sweating after what must've been at least a forty-five minute run.

At least her cheeks were a little flushed, but I bet a good roboticist could pull that off. Sweating, though? They probably weren't there yet. And women do sweat. I played sports in high school; I know. Or—for those ladies who claim not to do something as crass as sweating—women most definitely glisten. A lot.

Not Katie, though.

Muttering about the unfairness of life, I returned home, still not sure what I was going to do.

🐾 🐾 🐾

I finally settled for the sensible option. I called Matt at the station and reminded him that there was that robber's cave hidden away up the mountain and suggested that maybe if he checked there he'd find some additional clues about the murders.

He, of course, wanted to know if I had any specific reason for believing that the robber's cave held clues to the murders. I assured him that no, I did not have any specific reason for believing what I did and told him I would've been happy to investigate myself except for the danger of getting shot and all.

He laughed. "Oh, I see. You won't go check because of how dangerous it could be, but you're just fine with me getting shot?"

"No. I didn't say that. But as Jamie pointed out to me, that's *your* job, not mine."

"Is it now?"

I could almost picture him smiling on the other end of the phone and glared at the wall where I'd written his name all those years ago. I was not flirting, I swear.

"Alright," he said. "I'll check it out and then drop by after to let you know what I found."

"Um, maybe call. Grandpa's lawyer told me not to talk to you." I bit my thumbnail and turned away so I couldn't see his name anymore.

"And yet here you are… Just can't stay away…"

"Would you please just check out the cave and let me know what you found?"

"Yes, ma'am," he said, the laughter evident in his voice as he ended the call. Men. Can't live with 'em and you just can't shoot 'em.

🐾 🐾 🐾

That left me with nothing better to do but wait. I stationed myself in the backyard with Fancy and a book, but I wasn't really reading it. I was too busy watching for signs of Matt heading up the mountainside.

He and Officer Clark passed by around nine o'clock. Matt waved as Fancy ran up and down the fence barking at him, but Officer Clark didn't even look in our direction. I waved back and then settled in to wait for their return. But instead of either one coming back down the mountain, a police four-wheeler headed up the path about an hour later, an older woman behind the wheel.

I wanted to stay out there and see what happened next, but by then the sun was shining right down on me and Fancy was crying to be fed, so I reluctantly dragged myself inside. At least they'd found something. I just hoped it was the clue that would clear my grandpa's name.

CHAPTER 21

Thirty minutes later there was a booming knock at our door, like a battering ram. When I ran to answer, hoping to see Matt standing there with a smile on his face, I instead found Officer Clark. He had on those mirrored sunglasses that wouldn't let me see his eyes, but his hands kept opening and closing like he wanted to hit something and his jaw was clenched tight.

"Where's Lou Carver?" he demanded, looming over me, his hand moving towards his gun.

"Why do you want him?" I asked, moving to block him from coming into our home. I know I should've been nicer, but the way he was acting scared me.

"None of your business. Is he here?"

I looked past him, hoping to see Matt coming up the drive, but it was just me and Officer Nasty in a showdown on my front porch. I was willing to poke the bear a little, but not enough to get arrested.

"Yes. He's here." I wanted to reach for my cellphone which was stashed in the pocket of my sweatshirt, but I suspected he'd draw his gun on me if I did. I needed Mason Maxwell there to run interference before something bad happened.

Officer Clark put his hand on the door and moved towards me, but I held my ground, trembling with fear, but determined to keep him away from my grandpa until I knew what was going on. "I'm sorry, but I did not give you permission to enter my house. Why are you here? Do you have a warrant?"

I know. Stupid. But Fancy had started barking in the background and I didn't know what Officer Clark would do next. The last thing I wanted was for him to shoot her.

"Ma'am. I need to see Mr. Carver. Now." His voice lashed at me and I knew he was about a second from shoving me out of the way.

"Okay." I tried my best soothing the beast tone and held up my hands to calm him. "Let me just put the dog out back so she's not in the way and then I'll get him for you. Please wait here."

He clearly wasn't happy, but at least he took a step back instead of another step forward. I carefully closed the wooden door to a crack, wishing we had a screen door. The way Officer Clark was acting I wasn't sure what he'd do when I opened the door next. I wouldn't have been surprised to see him draw that gun of his.

First thing I did was block Fancy in the backyard. She did not want to go, but I wasn't going to risk her being shot. Second thing I did was call Mason Maxwell and tell him what was happening. He advised me to cooperate and keep calm and said he'd meet my grandpa at the jail. I wanted to ask why he thought they were going to take my grandpa in again, but given Office Clark's behavior it was pretty clear that's where things were headed.

I just didn't know why. What had they found in the old robber's cave?

Finally, I went to find my grandpa in his workroom at the back of the house. He was in the midst of assembling one of his miniature planes. It amazed me he could still do such fine work at his age. I chalked it up to stubbornness. I'd seen him take five minutes to attach one piece because his hand was shaking too badly to place it. Fortunately, he was just sitting there, staring off into space. I didn't think Officer Clark would wait five minutes.

"Grandpa. Officer Clark is here. He wants to see you. I think he's going to arrest you."

He nodded once, but didn't look at me.

"Grandpa?" I glanced towards the front of the house, sure Officer Clark was going to break down the door at any moment.

He wiped his hands on his jeans and reached for his non-existent pack of cigarettes. When he didn't find them he walked over to a locked cabinet in the corner, unlocked it, reached inside, and pulled out a fresh pack of cigarettes and a lighter.

"Grandpa! What are you doing?"

"If this is my last moment of freedom I'm going to smoke a cigarette by God." He started to unwrap the package but I stepped across the room and put my hand on his.

"Please don't do this, Grandpa. I know how hard it was for you to quit. And…Well, you won't have the same motivation to quit again this time. Don't let this set you back that way."

He glared at me, his hand shaking, tears in his eyes, before pulling his hand away and flinging the pack of cigarettes on the table. The only other time I'd seen him cry was when my grandma was dying. It shook me to my core to see him like that.

He pushed past me and stomped down the hall towards where Officer Clark was waiting. I ran after him and stopped him before he could open the door, sure that if he flung it open the way I suspected he was going to that Officer Clark would shoot him.

"Let me, Grandpa. Officer Clark isn't in a good place right now. I don't know what they found up in that cave, but whatever it is, it's convinced him you must be the killer."

My grandpa stared me down and I shrank back. "Maggie May, how do you know where they were looking this morning?"

I bit my lip, finally realizing what I'd done. "I told Matt to look there. I didn't know…I just…I thought maybe they'd find evidence of the real killer. I didn't know it would come back to you…"

His look was cold as ice as he stepped back and smoothed a hand over his hair. "Open the door, Maggie."

I grabbed the doorknob and slowly eased the door open, making sure to keep my body between Officer Clark and my grandpa.

"Here he is, Officer Clark," I said in my calmest voice even though I was trembling from head to toe.

Officer Clark focused on my grandpa, his body rigid with anger. "Lou Carver. You are under arrest for the murders of Jack Dunner and Roy Jackson. Please step out onto the porch. And keep your hands where I can see them." His hand dropped down to rest on his gun.

"He didn't do this. He's not a killer," I cried.

My grandpa stepped past me, slowly, calmly, staring off into the distance like a man walking to the gallows who knew there was no rescue in sight, his hands held up for Officer Clark to see.

"Grandpa!"

"Stay out of this, Maggie. You've done enough." He stepped onto the porch next to Officer Clark, never once looking back at me.

🐾 🐾 🐾

"He didn't do this," I cried again as Officer Clark wrenched my grandpa's hands behind his back. "Where's Matt?"

Officer Clark ignored me as he turned my grandpa and pushed him towards the squad car in our driveway.

"Does he know you did this?" I shouted.

But Officer Clark just kept on walking.

I dashed at the tears that filled my eyes as Officer Clark opened the back door of the car and pushed my grandpa inside, not treating him with the care you'd expect for an eighty-two-year-old man.

"I called his attorney," I shouted at him. "You speak to my grandpa before he arrives, I'll sue your asses to the end of time."

(Yes, I did use that language with that man. No, I'm not sorry about it. You see your grandpa put in cuffs and shoved into a squad car and tell me what you'd want to say to the person doing it.)

I turned my attention to my grandpa even though he probably couldn't hear me through the car window and still wasn't looking at me. "Grandpa, wait for your attorney. You do not speak to them until he's there, you hear me?"

Neither man acknowledged me as the cruiser backed out of our driveway and headed for the police station. I watched them go, my chest tight.

This did not look good. What had they found up there?

CHAPTER 22

I didn't know what to do. I didn't know why they'd arrested my grandpa. I called the station and asked for Matt, but they said he wasn't in. I figured he must still be up the mountain with whatever they'd found there. But what was it?

Only one way to find out.

I threw on my hiking boots, leashed up Fancy, and headed up the mountain to confront the man who'd said he was on my grandpa's side but had just let him be arrested and was too coward to even be there when it happened.

I was full of righteous anger, rehearsing over and over again exactly what I was going to say to Mr. Matthew Allen Barnes, betrayer that he was. How dare he sit at my grandpa's table and tell us how much my grandpa had done for him and then turn around and do this? What kind of man does that? Certainly not the kind of man I'd thought he was.

Fancy wasn't too happy with me because I only let her stop to smell things when I had to stop to catch my breath. Hiking at seven thousand feet is no joke. I finally had to slow down both for my sake and Fancy's. It's a good thing I have her around. She keeps me healthy in more ways than one.

I didn't want to. I didn't want to think. I just wanted to be angry and yell at someone, because I was scared. My grandpa didn't deserve this. He'd turned his life around. He'd been a vital part of this community for forty years.

But unless a miracle happened he was going to go back to spending his life in a cramped space with a bunch of dangerous men. At eighty-two-years-old. He couldn't do it. He'd die.

I pushed forward, scared and furious, my free hand clenching and unclenching, my calves aching, my lungs burning. Fancy kept looking at me, the worry clear in her eyes, but I couldn't calm myself, not even for her.

I found Matt outside the cave, flipping through a plastic file box full of folders. I could see the four-wheeler parked nearby and a woman I didn't know inside the cave taking pictures.

"How could you?" I shouted as soon as I was close enough for him to hear me

"Maggie! What are you doing? You shouldn't be here." He snapped the lid closed on the file box and stepped towards me, hands out to restrain me.

I glared him down. What did he think I was going to do? Make a mad dash for the stupid box and run away with it?

"How could you?" I screamed at him again, Fancy whining at my side.

"How could I what, Maggie? What are you talking about?"

Like he didn't know. I started to cry. I hate when I get angry and cry. I hate it. Which just makes me cry more. But I wanted so badly to hurt someone and I had no one to hurt. My grandpa had just been arrested and now Matt was standing there like he didn't know or didn't care?

"Don't pull that dumb act with me. You had him arrested. Officer Clark just dragged him away from our home in handcuffs."

Matt's first reaction was confusion, but that was quickly followed by a dawning realization of what must have happened, which was just as quickly replaced with an anger that matched my own. He pressed the button on his radio and said, "This is Officer Barnes. Get me Officer Clark. Now."

I crossed my arms, realizing I should've brought a coat with me. Even in early summer it can be chilly once you get into the higher elevations. I focused on taking deep breaths, trying to calm myself enough to make the tears go away. The area around the cave had an earthy, decayed smell that was almost but not quite unpleasant.

A woman replied over the radio, "Sorry, Officer Barnes, but Officer Clark is with a suspect. He said not to disturb him."

Matt swore and glanced back at the cave and the file box. "Sue, you okay if I take the four-wheeler for a bit?"

The woman in the cave nodded. "Yeah. Actually, if you take the boxes down with you, I can just walk back down on my own."

"Thanks." He strapped three boxes onto the back of the four-wheeler with bungie cords, his movements quick and efficient, those of a soldier in battle.

"What's going on, Matt?" I pulled Fancy closer when she tried to sniff at the boxes.

He jumped like he'd forgotten I was even there. "I can't tell you that, Maggie, I'm sorry."

He started to get on the four-wheeler and then turned back to me, his jaw tight as he flicked a glance at the woman in the cave. "There were photos, Maggie. Photos of your grandpa and Lesley Pope. Together."

"Together together? Or just sitting on the couch holding hands together?" Had Lesley lied to me? Were she and my grandpa having a full-blown affair?

"Sitting on the couch. Nothing…intimate. But for Officer Clark that was the motive he needed. I told him to wait. That your grandpa wasn't going anywhere. But…" He cussed. "I should've known. I don't know what his issue with your grandpa is, but he's had it in for him since day one."

He was standing so close I could smell his aftershave. "I'm sorry, Maggie. I'll do what I can, but it doesn't look good right now."

"Thank you." As he turned away, I glanced at the file boxes. Three of them. All of my grandpa and Lesley? "Wait."

Matt was already on the four-wheeler, ready to leave.

"Are those all of my grandpa and Lesley Pope?"

He shook his head. "There are photos in there of pretty much every single person in town. You were right about Mr. Jackson and the pot, by the way." He glanced at the boxes. "Anyone who thinks people in small towns don't cheat or lie should look through those boxes. But I gotta go, Maggie. Before Ben does something we all regret."

A Dead Man and Doggie Delights

I pulled Fancy out of his way and watched as he drove down the mountainside. Now that my grandpa had been arrested and they'd found a motive for why he'd killed Jack Dunner, I wasn't sure what Matt *could* do. But I was glad he was still willing to try.

CHAPTER 23

I couldn't go home. I was too upset. So I headed to the big rock and sat cross-legged at the edge, looking down at the town I'd always thought of as a perfect haven from the real world.

How wrong I'd been. Creek was just like anywhere else in the world, a bubbling pot of conflicting needs and wants that occasionally boiled over into the worst sort of things people could do to one another.

What they'd found in the cave made a lot of sense. In our one brief meeting Jack Dunner had struck me as the type of man who wouldn't hesitate to blackmail his own mother if he thought there was profit in it. (Disagree if you want, but I think the fact that a man is willing to bark at a complete stranger shows a lot about his character and does in fact call into question his loyalty to his mother.)

I didn't want to believe my grandpa had killed Dunner. He'd told me he hadn't and I'd never had cause to doubt him before.

But…

It was his gun. And he had threatened the man. He

had also made it quite clear he thought the world would be a better place without a man like Jack Dunner around. And he'd also made it more than clear to me that he'd do almost anything, including go back to prison, to protect Lesley Pope's reputation.

So which was I supposed to believe? The word of my grandpa, a man I'd know my entire life but not grown up around, who had had some tough times when he was younger, but who I'd never seen lie in over thirty years? Or the cold, hard evidence?

I tucked my knees up against my chest and rested my chin on them as I thought. Fancy looked up at me with those amber eyes of hers and cried softly.

I ran my fingers along one of her ears, letting the velvety feel of it calm and center me.

Gut or facts? Which to believe?

I stared at Fancy for a long moment and she stared right back at me, steady as the rock on which I was sitting.

Gut.

I didn't care what the evidence said. I knew *who* my grandpa was. And so did Fancy. He hadn't done this, which meant someone else had.

But who?

I didn't know. But I did know that it was time for my grandpa's alibi to come forward. No secret to protect there anymore. I needed to talk to Lesley Pope. Now.

🐾 🐾 🐾

I dragged Fancy home—poor girl was having a bad day between being locked out back, not being allowed to enjoy her walk up the mountainside, and then being dragged back home. Well, at least she hadn't been arrested and thrown into jail like my grandpa. It's never easy when you have to choose between those you love, but I knew she'd recover. She's a forgiving kind of girl.

She curled up on the goldenrod couch with a loud sigh while I rooted around for my grandpa's address book—I'd seen where he kept it when he gave Matt Mr. Jackson's daughter's number. Lesley's number was easy enough to find, the digits in my grandma's handwriting. I shoved the hurt of that to the side as I dialed her number.

"Hello? Lou?" she answered, clearly surprised to be receiving a call from my grandpa's number.

"Lesley, it's Maggie."

"Maggie, what's wrong? Is your grandfather okay?" I could hear the tension in her voice, but I wasn't sure if it was concern for my grandpa, worry that her husband would overhear her on the phone, or both.

I took a deep breath to keep from crying. "They arrested him for the murders."

"Oh no. When? Why? I thought they didn't have enough evidence?"

"This morning. Officer Clark came for him. He was so angry I thought he was going to shoot him. I don't know why that man has it in for my grandpa, but he does. Matt said he hasn't wanted to even consider another suspect ever since he heard my grandpa was involved."

Lesley sighed. "I know why."

"You do?"

"The past just won't stay in the past, will it? The man your grandfather shot was Ben's grandfather. Ben's father, Mark, was the man's son from his first marriage and Mark has always questioned whether he was really abusive like everyone said or whether your grandfather shot him for the money. My sister inherited fifty thousand when he died."

"So Officer Clark grew up believing my grandpa had murdered his in cold blood."

"Yes. And…My husband is Ben's mother's uncle, so he knows that my husband is sick." I could hear the tears in her voice. "Well, no reason to withhold that alibi now, is there?"

I spared a moment to feel sorry for this woman whose entire world was about to be destroyed. Because there was no way this was going to stay within the walls of the precinct if Officer Clark knew about her and my grandpa. By tomorrow everyone in town would know that my grandpa and Lesley were "close". Within a week that would be twisted by rumor into something more than just two people who cared for one another spending time together. This would haunt her—and my grandpa—the rest of her life.

I still loved Creek, but in that moment I really hated the way small towns can burn like wildfire with a juicy bit of gossip. I thought back to the three boxes full of photos and hoped there was something in there even more juicy than my grandpa and Lesley. Not that their lives would ever be the same after this, no matter what else the police found…

"Can I help?" I asked, not sure what to do now.

"No. Best if I handle this alone. Thank you for letting me know, Maggie. Hopefully your grandfather will be home to you soon."

I hoped so, too.

CHAPTER 24

I called Jamie next—fortunately it was late afternoon by then and the store was slow—and told her everything that had happened, including the fact that it was my fault my grandpa had been arrested. Why had I thought it made sense to tell Matt about the robber's cave before I checked it myself?

"Don't be ridiculous, Maggie. You know you couldn't go up there yourself, not with a murderer running around."

"But if I'd found the boxes…"

"What? What would you have done? Hidden the photos of your grandpa and Lesley? You're not like that, Mags. You might be able to not tell someone something you knew, but you'd never destroy evidence."

I stared out the back window. She was right, but I didn't want to hear it.

"I could've snooped through all the other photos and found a suspect."

I sank down on the couch next to Fancy who gave me a glare and hopped down to go sleep on her bed in the corner, her back to me. Great, I'd gotten my grandpa arrested and my dog was mad at me, too.

I had to fix this. Somehow.

"So what now?" Jamie asked.

"I don't know. Hopefully when they talk to Lesley they'll realize my grandpa didn't do this. But…" I bit my lip. The only way to be sure my grandpa wasn't going to be charged with murder was to find the real killer, which meant I needed time to investigate. I didn't trust that the cops were going to look for anyone else.

But Jamie was my friend and she'd risked everything to open this business with me. I couldn't bring myself to ask her for what I needed most. Fortunately, there's a reason Jamie's my best friend.

"Take tomorrow off. I'll cover for you," she said.

"Are you sure?" I protested while secretly thanking my lucky stars that she'd made the offer.

"Positive. You'll owe me one, though."

I wanted to hug her, but settled for, "Thank you, Jamie. You're the best."

"I am. And don't you forget it."

We both laughed.

"You have any idea who else could've done it?" she asked.

I shook my head, even though she couldn't see me. "No. But I bet the answer is in those boxes the cops found. Only question is, how am I going to get a peek at them?"

"Just remember, you won't be doing your grandpa any favors if you get arrested, too."

I shrugged that off. "I'm not going to get arrested. I'm just going to snoop around a bit, that's all."

"Maggie…"

"What?"

"Please be careful."

"I will. And thank you again for agreeing to watch the store." I hung up, the beginnings of a plan starting to form.

🐾 🐾 🐾

That plan solidified into something real when Mason Maxwell called me half an hour later. "They're going to keep your grandfather overnight," he said, not beating around the bush.

"But he's an old man. He can't be in jail overnight." I thought of all the pills he took each day. He couldn't live without them. He was innocent but before I could prove it they were going to kill him with their stupidity.

"He's tough. He'll be fine. It's just a tactic to get him to break, but they don't understand that with a man like your grandfather the harder they push, the harder he'll fight them. I should be able to get him released tomorrow."

"Did they already question him? What did they say? What did they have? Is he still their only suspect?"

"They had some photos of him and Lesley Pope that Officer Clark thought meant something. The worst of the photos showed them sitting on the couch holding hands, though. I can't imagine a man committing two murders to keep it secret that he was holding a married woman's hand."

"Well, there is some history there." I told him what Lesley had told me about their past and Officer Clark's grudge.

"Ah. I didn't know that part. Your grandfather isn't the most forthcoming client I've ever had. Thank you."

"Does it change things?"

"No."

"Did Lesley come by? Did she give her alibi for him?" Fancy had finally forgiven me and she came to sit next to me with a loud huff. She's not a fan of my being on the phone.

"She did, but it's not enough to change things at this point. Too much time that day of the first murder that's still unaccounted for. And with the photos, the police can allege she made it all up to protect him."

Fancy groaned and rolled onto her back demanding a belly rub. I tried to silently shush her, but wasn't very successful.

"So what now?" I asked.

I could almost see him shaking his head on the other end of the line. "Best thing that can happen now is the killer slips up and kills someone else while your grandfather is in custody."

"Oh, that's horrible!"

"Horrible, maybe, but still the truth. Two murder weapons, both your grandfather's. Two dead men, both men your grandfather had a motive to murder. Your grandfather's history as a felon. And no other suspects."

Disgusted by my lack of attention, Fancy jumped off the couch and went outside to bark at the sky. Poor girl, but she had to understand that sometimes other people took priority.

"But what about the photos? There have to be other people in there who also have a motive to kill Jack Dunner."

"Maybe. But that doesn't change the fact that the murder weapons belonged to your grandfather or that he's a felon."

"The weapons were in his truck. Anyone could've taken them from there."

"But who would know that? And who would be bold enough to come into your grandfather's driveway to take them?"

I sighed. "That's the million dollar question, isn't it? Thank you, Mr. Maxwell. I appreciate everything you've been able to do for my grandpa."

"You're welcome. I'm sorry I couldn't do more."

After I ended the call, I cooked up a grilled peanut butter and jelly sandwich—my personal version of comfort food—while I thought through my plan. Fancy, seeing that melted peanut butter was on the menu, decided to forgive me for once and for all and joined me at the table, drool spooling from her jaws as she watched me tear off a gooey bit of peanut-butter coated bread.

If only every problem were so easy to solve.

CHAPTER 25

I spent the next two hours putting my plan into motion, my eye on the clock as I whipped up a batch of homemade split pea soup and fresh bread from the bread maker. (I'm so glad they have that Express Bake setting, because I never think to make a loaf of bread in time to use the normal setting.) While those were cooking I gathered up everything I thought an old man might need for a night spent in jail.

It was weird to step into my grandpa's bedroom and then into his bathroom and to riffle through his things trying to figure out what he used on a daily basis. He had one of those little day-of-the-week plastic pill holders and it was still half-full, which at least saved me having to read all of his medicines and decipher which ones he was supposed to take when.

I still loaded up all the pill bottles, too, just in case someone accused me of trying to sneak recreational drugs to my eighty-two-year-old grandfather during his stint in jail. I was careful not read any of the labels, not wanting to know if he had any embarrassing prescriptions. Just my luck my grandpa would be on Viagra or something.

When the soup and bread were done, I packed them up along with some trusty little cheese sticks and all the necessities I'd put together for my grandpa and headed for the door.

Fancy had her saddest of sad faces on as she watched me leave without her. That's what happens when you pretty much take your dog with you everywhere. When you can't take her with you, she acts like the world has ended and her heart is broken. Poor girl was having a rough day of it.

"Fine. You're getting fat, you know, but…" I ran to the kitchen and grabbed a puppy ice cream out of the freezer. "Here. I'll be back in an hour or so, okay?"

She daintily took the container from my hand and immediately went out back, her mind now on more important things. Dogs are wonderful, aren't they?

Humans, not so much.

I walked towards the police station through the chill early evening air, a large King Soopers reusable grocery bag slung over my shoulder, bumping my hip with each step. What if this didn't work? What if Matt wasn't there? What if he saw right through my ploy? And what if they wouldn't let me leave my grandpa's meds for him? Was he going to be okay until they released him?

Each step and each thump of the bag against my hip all I could think was what if, what if, what if.

But I'm good at what ifs, so for every single one I thought up, I thought of an answer too. If A then B. If C then D. On and on I thought through all the alternatives until I was as prepared as I could be.

That didn't keep away the clenching in my gut as I grasped the handle to the station door and stepped inside. The place felt even smaller at night with half the overheard lights turned off. There was a desk lamp on at Matt's desk, though, so I had hope.

He wasn't there. No one was. There'd been a soft chime as I walked in, so I was sure someone would be there soon, but I couldn't let this chance that I'd been given pass by. I carefully stepped towards Matt's desk. I knew I was taking a risk by not shouting out my presence, but if I was any judge of character—which was sorely in question these days—I knew that if I asked, Matt wouldn't let me rifle through the secrets of every person in town just to help my grandpa. I suspected that would be a line he wasn't willing to cross. Which meant I was going to have to sneak the information.

I quickly scanned the papers on his and Officer Clark's desks. There was a notepad right there in the middle of Matt's desk, covered in writing, but unfortunately it was in short hand. I'd tried to find a book or website that would let me learn it and had perused a few sites I'd found, but it still looked like gibberish to me.

Thankfully, Officer Clark did not use shorthand. There was a printed list in the center of his desk that looked very much like a high-level inventory of what they'd found in the boxes. I scanned it quickly, not sure what good it would do me. Matt was right. Pretty much everyone in town *was* on the list. It also didn't tell me *what* the folders included, just that they existed.

I took a long moment to study the list, trying to memorize what I saw, asking myself if anyone on there was a likely suspect. Four of the five people we'd thought capable of killing someone were on there, so that was one place to start.

"Found what you were looking for?" Matt asked from the hallway.

I swear, I jumped a foot at the sound of his voice. I might've squeaked loudly, too. I looked up to see him leaning against the wall, his arms crossed, like he'd been there all day.

"How long have you been there?" I asked.

"Long enough. I could arrest you for poking around a police station, you know."

I tensed for a second—I believe anything anyone says for at least one or two seconds before questioning it—but the tone of his voice said he was just teasing.

He walked towards me, slower than normal, exhaustion in every line of his body. There were dark bags under his eyes, too.

"Mason Maxwell said you're keeping my grandpa overnight," I said, more harshly than I'd planned, but there was a part of me that saw him looking so exhausted and wanted to take care of him, which was not what I needed. I was there to save my grandpa, not…I shook my head. "You said you'd try to help him."

"And I am. Why do you think I'm still here even though my shift ended two hours ago and I don't get paid for overtime?" He flung a hand at the notes on his desk. "I've looked through every single file Jack Dunner had, Maggie. None of it's worth killing over."

"To you, maybe. But for some people…" I glanced back at the list. "Like a reverend."

He rubbed at his face. "I'm just not seeing it, Maggie. But I'll look again. And I'll keep looking until I've exhausted every angle."

I nodded. It was all he could offer, after all. "I

brought you and my grandpa soup. And my grandpa's medicine. He needs that, Matt. If you're going to hold an old man with a heart condition overnight, you need to let him have his pills. No point killing an innocent man."

"You know we have rules about these things…"

I didn't answer, just waited.

He sighed. "What else do you have in there?"

"Pajamas, toothbrush, toothpaste, hairbrush."

He started shaking his head as soon as the first word was out of my mouth. "The pills I'll let you leave. And, even though it's against the rules, I'll bring him out to the interrogation room for dinner—he's the only prisoner we have right now. But the rest? This is jail, Maggie, not the Ritz Carlton. The county provides all the rest of that."

I pressed my lips tight together. "Fine. Are you going to eat with us? I brought enough for three."

"You're something else, you know that?" He ran his hands through his hair. "Yeah, I'll eat with you. But no discussing the case. Agreed?"

"Agreed."

It wasn't exactly what I'd hoped for, but it was better than nothing.

🐾 🐾 🐾

I almost cried when I saw my grandpa come down the hall in an orange jumpsuit. He looked so old and frail out of his Levi's and flannel, his shoulders slumped.

"It's going to be okay," I told him as I gave him a hard hug.

He sank into the seat Matt gestured him towards, shaking his head. "No, it's not. The damage is already done, Maggie. Poor Lesley. Why'd you tell her?"

"Because she deserved to know. Because I thought the secret was already out and that her coming forward might save you a night in jail. Or more. I was just trying to help."

He grunted as he took his first spoonful of soup, back to ignoring me. It hurt to have him angry at me, but I'd had to do what I'd done. I hadn't had another choice.

"Wow, this is really good, Maggie," Matt said, taking another bite of soup.

My grandma always said the best way to a man's heart was through his stomach, I was hoping that the best way to his mind was, too. "Thanks. So…" I started, all casual-like.

"Don't you even try to use your feminine wiles on me Miss Maggie May Carver." He tore off a hunk of bread and dunked it in his soup before taking a large enough bite to fill his mouth completely.

"Feminine wiles? What are you talking about?"

"I'm talking about you coming down here with a nice home-cooked meal and a smile and trying to get my secrets out of me. You can stop the seduction now. It's not going to work."

"Please." I opened my cheese stick. "I wouldn't know how to seduce a man if I tried. The first time I tried batting my eyes at him he'd probably ask if I had something stuck in my eye. If I'd wanted to seduce your secrets out of you, I would've sent Jamie down here instead."

My grandpa smiled slightly. "She's not trying to lie, you know. It's just that Maggie May has always underestimated the effect she has on men."

"Oh, enough. I try to do something nice by bringing both of you a real meal and this is the thanks I get?

Meanwhile, poor Fancy is at home alone probably thinking she's been abandoned." I chomped into the cheese stick and glared at both of them, but neither one was the list bit rattled.

I fixed my glare on Matt. "Are you going to release my grandpa tomorrow? He doesn't deserve to be sitting in jail like this, even if you are going to charge him with murder."

"Yes. He should be out by noon. I wanted to get him processed and through today, but Officer Clark is convinced your grandpa is the worst sort of person imaginable."

"You know why, right?"

He shook his head. "No. Why?"

"I thought all small towners knew all the gossip." I glanced at my grandpa. "You knew, didn't you?"

"That his granddaddy is the one I shot? Yeah, I knew."

Matt stared at my grandpa. "The abuser you did time for killing was Ben's grandfather?"

"Yep."

"Figures. I knew there was something more there than a normal case, but I couldn't put a finger on it." He nodded to himself like a bunch of little things were suddenly clicking into place.

"So does this mean you'll let me help solve this case?" I asked. "Tell me what you know, I'll help you brainstorm other suspects."

My grandpa snorted. "You keep helping with this case, Maggie, I'm liable to find myself in the electric chair."

"Grandpa!"

Matt shook his head. "Sorry, Maggie. I can't do it. I'd love to, but…Too many people involved now. It'd cost me my badge if I let you look through those files, and rightly so."

Ah, well. It was worth a try. And at least he'd confirmed my assessment of his character. Not that that was going to help me clear my grandpa. At least it made me confident that my grandpa really was innocent, though.

(Not that I hadn't thought he was before. But, you know, there was a lot piled up against him—not least of which was the fact that he probably *was* perfectly capable of killing a person if he saw the need for it.)

CHAPTER 26

The next morning I was no closer to figuring out who the real killer was than I'd been the night before. I'd snuck one more look at the list on Officer Clark's desk while Matt was taking my grandpa back to his cell, but without knowing what the files contained and how important each secret was to the person being blackmailed—because I assumed that's what the files were for—there was nothing there for me to work with.

Still, something about the list kept bugging me and my mind kept going back to it over and over again. There's only one thing for me to do when that happens— go for a hike. The physical movement somehow focuses my brain in a way that sitting and thinking doesn't.

So as soon as it was light enough out, I leashed up Fancy and headed for the mountain. I figured it was safe now since the cops had been all over it the day before.

I let Fancy have her way, sniffing this and that for as long as she wanted to. Part of it was guilt over how badly I'd treated her the last few days, but I'll admit I was also secretly hoping she'd find a fresh dead body that had been killed in the last twelve hours.

(Not really. I mean, okay, maybe a little? I didn't want anyone else to die, but it was the easiest way to clear my grandpa's name.)

Sadly, all she found was a dead squirrel. I made sure that's all it was before letting her do her thing since I was pretty sure the cops wouldn't be so forgiving if I let her pee on another dead body.

Eventually, we made our way up to the robber's cave, but the cops had cleared the place out. I could see from the clear space on the ground where the containers with all the blackmail information had been, but that was it. No incriminating footprints or signs that said, "The real killer is Joe Bob Smith."

So that was a bust.

I went back to my rock and sat there, looking down on the sleepy little town of Creek, counting the train cars as an early morning freight train passed through town. This one had forty-two cars, not even close to my personal record count of ninety-nine.

I could see Katie on her normal morning run, arms moving with precision, red hair swishing from side to side with each step. My grandpa said she was actually pretty good with young kids—she'd helped with the t-ball team the summer before—but I couldn't picture it. (Creek was too small for boy's teams and girl's teams, so boys and girls played together all the way until middle school when they started playing for their school teams.)

Then again, my grandpa had also said that Luke was an excellent coach, too, so maybe he wasn't the best judge of character. I couldn't picture Luke having the patience to work with little kids. He was too much of a cad for that.

Although…Coaching was probably a prime opportunity to meet all the single moms of a certain age in town. That I could see; Luke was good with the kids because he wanted an in with the moms. Now it all made sense.

I glanced back down at Katie just in time to see her abruptly turn off the street and dash to Luke's gate. I sat forward. What the…?

She opened the gate and closed it, glancing around to make sure no one had seen her and then strode across his cluttered and cramped backyard and opened the sliding glass door.

No hesitation. Like she'd done it before.

A lot of things crashed into place in that moment. The way Luke always made sure to wink at her or kiss her cheek or flirt with her. The way she was always leaving early, usually after Luke had been by. Jamie's comment that her parents were strict and kept her on a tight leash. The flushed cheeks but no sweat when I'd seen her returning from her jog that day I'd gone down to the ballpark.

I stared intently at Luke's house, waiting for confirmation of what I now suspected—he and Katie were having an affair. That lying, no good, dirty dog. Actually, calling him a dog was an insult to all the wonderful canines of the world.

I should've known. I'd figured he'd make a move on her once she was eighteen, but before? It must've started when they were coaching together last summer…

The curtains on Luke's windows were all drawn tight so I couldn't see anything inside the house, but after about twenty minutes Luke and Katie reappeared at the sliding glass door, sharing a last passionate kiss. He didn't even have his shirt on, the creep.

I shook my head, wanting to run down that hill and pummel him into little pieces for hurting my best friend like this. Once again he'd played her for a fool. Not to mention how he was messing with Katie's head, too.

"That…"

I used a word I won't use here. And a few other words on top of that. I'd known he was a jerk. I'd known it. But I hadn't realized he was the type of guy to break the law and mess around with a seventeen-year-old girl. And he had broken the law, hadn't he?

What he was doing with Katie was illegal. There was way too much of an age difference between them for it not to be. Which meant…

Luke could be the killer.

That's what had been bugging me since I'd seen that list on Officer Clark's desk. It wasn't the names that were *on* the list, it was one of the few names that *wasn't* on the list. Lucas Dean. There should've been a folder an inch thick on him and his shenanigans, but there was nothing. Not one photo.

Because he'd killed Jack Dunner and then taken the evidence before anyone could find it.

He knew about my grandpa keeping his gun in his truck. He knew about the bat. He lived just a couple houses down from the crime scenes, so they were in his backyard, too. And he had motive.

It all fit. Lucas Dean was the killer.

I pumped my arm in the air. "I did it, Fancy. I found him."

She looked at me with one eyebrow raised, not the

least bit impressed. Probably had known all along, smart girl that she was.

But I was thrilled. I could free my grandpa now. "Come on, Fancy. Let's go."

I practically dragged her down the mountainside, skipping over every root and rock in my way. It was all going to be okay now. My grandpa wasn't going to go to prison. I'd found the murderer.

CHAPTER 27

I dropped Fancy off at home, my hands shaking in excitement. A small part of me wanted to run straight to Luke's door and confront him with what I'd seen and what I knew. That man deserved a good what for for what'd he done to Jamie, let alone Katie and who knew who else. I bet his blackmail file was *two* inches thick.

But…

Prudence won out. If I was right, Lucas Dean had killed an old man with a baseball bat and hadn't hesitated to frame my grandpa, a man he'd worked with. Confronting someone like that was a darned good way to end up victim number three. And the only good that would come of that is they'd stop suspecting my grandpa of murder since he couldn't possibly kill me while in jail.

I decided I'd rather live through the day, thank you very much.

I headed to the police station instead, almost jogging I was so excited. I passed right by Luke's house on the way and made a point of not looking in his direction. He'd get his soon enough and I didn't want to tip him off, not when we were so close.

Matt was already in and looked to be the only one there. I wondered if he'd ever left given the way his hair was slightly mussed and his eyes were bloodshot. He waved in my direction, but didn't move to meet me. "If you're here for your grandpa, it's going to be another hour or two before he's fully processed for release."

"No. I'm here to tell you who the real killer is." I was practically bouncing up and down.

"I've been up all night pouring over these files and you solved it? Without any evidence at all? Just thought it through, did you?"

I came around the counter and grabbed the list off of Officer Clark's desk. "Look at the list."

"I've looked at that list a hundred times, Maggie. What am I supposed to see?"

"It's not what you're supposed to see. It's what you *don't* see." I grinned at him, too excited to contain myself.

He took the list from me and looked at it once more, rubbing at his face, the scritch-scritch of his fingers rubbing against stubble the only sound in the room.

"Think about it. Who should be on that list, but isn't?" I asked.

He sighed. "I don't know. Probably a few people."

"How about Lucas Dean?"

"Luke?" He shook his head, but did scan the list to confirm his name wasn't there. He set the list down and leaned against the desk, arms crossed. "I've known Luke since we were kids. He doesn't have it in him to kill someone."

I pressed my lips together, deflating like a popped balloon. He was supposed to believe me, not question me like this. "You know him so well, do you?"

"Maggie…"

"Do you think he has it in him to take up with a seventeen-year-old girl?"

Matt opened his mouth and then shut it again. He frowned. "Katie?"

"Yep. I just saw them together. I was up the mountain behind his house and saw her sneak in through his backyard. They came back maybe twenty minutes later, shared a passionate kiss—him without his shirt on—and then she left."

He grunted.

"Did you see that in him?" I asked.

He shrugged one shoulder. "No. But I can see that before I can see murder."

"But don't you get it? If Jack Dunner found out about him and Katie and tried to blackmail him…Maybe Luke decided it was safer to just eliminate Dunner rather than pay him."

"And Roy Jackson?"

"Maybe he saw them together, too. He was certainly on that path often enough. I know there was the one morning when I took Fancy out for a walk that I saw Katie running—towards Luke's house, obviously— around the same time I saw Mr. Jackson headed up the mountain. If he saw what Luke was doing and confronted him about it…"

Matt thought about it for a long moment.

I wanted to grab him and shake him. It was so obvious. Finally, he pushed off of the desk. "You're right. It all does fit. I'll bring him in."

I whooped and Matt leveled a steady stare at me. "He may not be the killer, Maggie. I'll grant you he's the best alternate suspect we've had so far, but it might not be him."

I waved his concern away. I knew it was Luke. I knew it. It all fit together perfectly. And Matt would see it, too. He just needed a little time, that's all.

Luke was going to be arrested for murder. Today. Which meant I needed to go see Jamie. She deserved to hear about this from me instead of from some gossipy busybody who happened to visit the café after word got out.

"So you're going to bring him in?" I confirmed.

"Yes. As soon as Marlene arrives, I'll go get him." He glanced at the clock on the wall. "Should be about fifteen minutes from now."

I flashed him a smile. "Thank you," I shouted as I ran out the door.

Finally, everything was falling into place.

🐾 🐾 🐾

I was so excited, I ran the whole way back to my grandpa's place. Not the best of ideas since I never run. I had to stop on the front porch and gasp for breath as I held my side against the sharp pain I felt there. I could've sworn I'd developed shin splints, too, but I was pretty sure that was just my middle-aged body being overly dramatic.

Fancy cried at me through the doorway until I let myself inside. As I waited for Matt to arrest Luke, I debated calling Jamie to tell her what had happened, but I knew this was the kind of news that was best delivered in person. I quickly changed instead, so I'd be ready to go as soon as it happened.

When eight o'clock rolled around I stationed myself at

the kitchen window and watched for any sign of Matt or Luke. A few minutes later I saw Matt walk out of the police station—at least it looked like him, I was just far enough away to not be positive. Whoever it was walked down the street to Luke's house and disappeared from view.

I braced myself, wondering just how dangerous Luke was. What if he tried to run? What if he pulled a gun on Matt? Or a baseball bat?

But, no. I could see him killing when trapped in a corner like he had with Jack Dunner, but killing someone he'd known since he could walk? Nah. Lucas Dean was bad, but he wasn't that bad.

And I was right. Because a few minutes later I saw two men leave Luke's house and walk towards the police station, chatting casually. The one that must be Luke had his hands in his pockets, completely at ease as he walked next to the officer.

Honestly, I think Matt should've hauled Luke in in cuffs for the Katie thing, but I was starting to realize that just wasn't his style. It must be hard to be a cop in a small town where you know everyone. You aren't just arresting a perp, you're arresting someone you played football with or whose dad coached you in baseball. I had to feel for the guy. But not too much. Not if that got in the way of him finding the real killer.

I waited until they made it back to the station and then leashed up Fancy and headed for the barkery.

CHAPTER 28

The whole drive I was fidgety, going over things again and again and again. It had to be Luke. It had to be. It made so much sense. There was no blackmail file on him. He knew about the bat and the gun. He lived right there. He had a secret to hide. And it was a big enough one that people would kill for it.

But…

He was Luke. Worthless cad and flirt who'd probably sleep with anyone he could, but was he really a killer? Would he really take a *baseball bat* to someone?

Eh.

Maybe?

But if it wasn't Luke then I was back at square one and my grandpa was back to being the one and only real suspect.

I so wanted it to be Luke, but the closer I got to the barkery the more I wondered if it really was. I still needed to tell Jamie about Luke and Katie, because he was going to go to jail for that…Maybe. Except the pictures were gone if they'd ever existed. And I was the only one who'd seen them together. And all I'd seen was them kissing, which I was pretty sure was not illegal.

I felt nauseous thinking that Luke might get away with that. Especially knowing Jamie and her never-ending ability to forgive people for their flaws. It wasn't that I didn't have flaws of my own—I had plenty—it was just that I didn't see the point of letting anyone off the hook for it. If you were mean, you should admit you were mean. If you used others, you should admit that, too. And you should be told it was wrong and to try better next time. Not forgiven every frickin' time.

Of course, one of the reasons Jamie and I were such good friends was that very capacity of hers to forgive people when they messed up and to not hold a grudge. See, I could be friends with Jamie because she was just a genuinely good person who didn't hurt others. She could be friends with me because she forgave and forgot when I was prickly and rude.

I pulled up outside the store, all of my earlier excitement gone. Sure, it was possible Luke was still the killer, but Matt's words had wiggled their way into my brain and made me doubt it. And I just knew in my gut of guts that Luke was going to get a pass for the Katie thing. Because what love-struck seventeen-year-old is willing to turn on her older boyfriend? None.

Ugh.

As usual, Fancy didn't let me sit and brood, barking her head off and demanding to be let out of the van as soon as we were parked. She dragged me right for the entrance, too, probably eager to see Lulu. Jamie didn't bring Lulu in every single day the way I did Fancy, but she'd started bringing her in more and more.

Fancy and Lulu were double trouble. They adored

each other, but had their moments of insanity, too. Puppy teeth are sharp and Fancy's paw of doom was not to be underestimated. I let Fancy drag me towards the door, trying to figure out what I was going to say to Jamie.

Should I tell her anything at all?

🐾 🐾 🐾

The breakfast rush had just about ended. Katie was wiping down the tables and taking dishes to the kitchen while Jamie rang up the last customer. I glanced towards the barkery side, trying not to feel sad at how quiet it looked. At least online sales were ticking along nicely…

As soon as the last customer left—a man I didn't recognize who had the definite look of a tourist with his fancy sunglasses—I let Fancy off her leash. She immediately ran to the cubby where Lulu had been sleeping and the two proceeded to cry and lick and bite at each other.

I almost laughed at the way Fancy's tail swished back and forth, but instead I turned my attention to Jamie. And Katie; I'd forgotten she'd be there.

Jamie tilted her head to the side. "Hey, Maggie. I thought I told you to stay at home today. How's your grandpa?"

"They should be releasing him in an hour or so. At least Matt, Officer Barnes, let me bring him his meds last night. Who knows what shape he'd be in otherwise."

"So they really think he did it, huh? Your grandpa? That just doesn't fit, does it?"

Katie walked back out of the kitchen. "Yes, it does. That man is definitely capable of killing someone."

I blinked slowly, stunned by her words. My grandpa actually liked her. I couldn't believe she'd just said that about him. I mean, granted, I'd thought it a time or two myself. And it was probably true, but…Who says that kind of thing?

"He didn't kill anyone," I said, lashing out. "It was Lucas Dean."

Katie dropped the plate she'd been holding and it shattered on the floor just as I realized what I'd said. "Jamie…"

I stepped toward her.

"What are you talking about?" she asked, her hands shaking as she tried to figure out what to do with them. "Luke? He's not a killer. Why would he…? It can't be Luke."

"It wasn't Luke." Katie was there next to me, her eyes flashing with anger—the first time I'd seen real emotion from her. She'd picked up a piece of the shattered plate and it must've cut her because blood was dripping from her hand onto the floor.

"It wasn't Luke!" she screeched.

I stepped back from her, finally seeing what I'd missed. She was right. It wasn't Luke. It was her. It was Katie.

Katie had known about the gun. And the bat. She'd been there when I told Jamie about my grandpa threatening Jack Dunner and about the robber's cave. She had the same secret to hide. It wouldn't put her in jail, but if she was in love with Luke…

"You're right. It wasn't Luke, was it, Katie?" I took another step back.

Jamie was frozen behind the counter.

"It was you, wasn't it, Katie?" I asked. "Why did you do it? Why did you kill those two men?"

She tightened her grip on the broken plate and it sliced deeper into her palm, blood flowing in a steady stream to the floor. Part of me wanted to take the plate away from her before she hurt herself worse, but another part of me was sort of hoping she'd lose enough blood to faint because I wasn't too interested in fighting a teenaged murderess who'd already killed two people.

Jamie started to come around the counter, but I waved her back. "Stay back, Jamie. She's dangerous. She killed Jack Dunner and Mr. Jackson."

"Did you? Katie? Why?"

Katie wasn't looking at anything we could see, but she nodded slowly. "I was going to lose Luke…He said we had to stop…"

She shook her head, like she was trying to clear it of something.

I slowly reached for the cellphone in the outer pocket of my purse, hoping she wouldn't see it, but she dropped the plate and grabbed a steak knife off a nearby table, lunging at me with it, her eyes wild. "Don't. Put it away. Over there." She gestured towards the corner.

I threw the phone away from me, risking a glance towards Jamie who'd started inching her way towards the store phone. All she had to do was get it off the hook and dial 9-1-1. That's all she had to do. But as she took a step towards the phone, Katie screeched at her and sliced her knife through the air.

"And you!" She swiped at Jamie again. "You were going to take him from me. He loved *me* until *you* showed up." She swiped at Jamie again and I started to back towards where I'd tossed my phone, but Fancy chose that moment to notice what was going on and came running, barking her head off.

I lunged for her collar and pulled her back just as Katie swept her knife towards Fancy. That awoke a fury in me that I could barely contain. "What is wrong with you," I screamed at her.

I know—this girl had already killed two people and was looking like she was going to try to kill me or Jamie, too, but I didn't lose it until she threatened my dog. What can I say? I have some very skewed priorities. Plus, Jamie and I could handle ourselves. Fancy…

Well, it turned out Fancy could handle herself, too.

She tore free of my grip and ran right at Katie, snarling. I'd never seen her do that before, but let me tell you that when a hundred-and-forty-pound dog comes at you, teeth bared, it can be downright scary. Scary enough that Katie shrieked, dropped her knife, and ran towards the corner of the store.

Fancy cornered her there, barking her head off in her "you've really upset me and I want you to know it" bark. I raced to my cellphone and hit Emergency, but hung up a moment later.

Because pulling into the parking lot outside was Officer Matthew Allen Barnes. My white knight—if he'd been about five minutes earlier, and hadn't had Lucas Dean with him.

CHAPTER 29

"Fancy. Enough," I said, cutting through her barking, as Matt and Luke came inside. She glanced back at me, clearly not ready to let it go, but when she saw Matt she wagged her tail and ran over to him. Traitor.

Luke stepped past Matt and Fancy and headed for Katie.

"Luke? What are you doing here?" she asked, her voice trembling as she swayed on her feet, her hand still dripping blood all over the floor.

I almost felt sorry for her then. Almost.

"Katie, what have you done?" He stepped closer, hands held up to calm her.

"I just wanted us to be together…" she whispered. "I just…We were going to go to Mexico when I turned eighteen. Remember? I…" She started weeping. "I just wanted us to be together. I just wanted us to be together."

"Oh, Katie." He pulled her close as she sobbed into his shoulder. "I'm so sorry."

I glanced at Jamie. She was watching them with a frown, her arms crossed. I realized she still didn't know about Luke and Katie. I stepped closer. "I saw them together this morning. At Luke's house. I thought that meant Luke was the murderer. I came here to tell you."

Jamie looked at me, dazed. "But…He and I…"

I shrugged, not wanting to remind her in that moment that Luke was a cheaty cheat cheater and was never going to change.

Fancy finally ambled over to my side and I put her back on her leash. The store was a mess, blood all over the floor, tracked there by her giant paws, but I didn't care. I was just glad to have her back by my side.

I heard sirens and glanced up to see an ambulance pulling up outside. I guess Katie did need it, although honestly I was okay with her bleeding out a little bit more first. (She'd threatened my dog and my best friend. You don't do that and expect me to care one whit about you.)

Matt saw my look and gave me a half grin and shake of the head as another officer arrived. He turned to brief him, pointing towards Katie and then the ambulance. The officer went over to Luke and Katie and they slowly walked out to the ambulance as Matt came over to join me and Jamie.

"I told you it wasn't Luke." He leaned against the counter like he owned it.

I gave him my death stare, but it didn't faze him one bit. He glanced at the bloody floor. "What exactly happened here?"

I met his unflappable look with one of my own. "Katie didn't like it either when I said Luke was the killer. That's when I realized who the killer really was. She grabbed a knife and I think would've hurt one of us, but then Fancy came to the rescue."

I scratched at Fancy's ears. "Who knew you had it in you, girl?"

She just groaned and leaned into my hand, all signs of her ferocious snarl long gone.

"So Fancy's the hero of the day, is she?" Matt walked over to the barkery side and grabbed a Doggie Delight out of the case. "I think your mother would agree that you've earned a special treat, young lady."

Fancy sat, waiting for him to give it to her, patient as patient could be, drool forming a puddle at her feet, but Lulu started barking up a storm, not wanting to be left out if treats were on offer.

I shook my head and grabbed her one, too. Dogs. Gotta love 'em.

CHAPTER 30

I shooed both of the dogs out back into the dog run, figuring we had enough bloody paw prints already, we didn't need to add to the count. When I came back inside Matt and Jamie were talking quietly, leaning close to one another across the counter. For a brief moment I felt almost jealous, but then I remembered that I was the one who'd told Jamie to go for him. I reminded myself that if Jamie ended up with a guy like Matt that would be the best thing in the world.

Far better than her ending up with Luke. I let them have a moment and then joined them. "So I assume you're done with Luke now, yes?"

Jamie grabbed a rag from the bleach bucket under the counter and started scrubbing at the blood stains. "Nobody's perfect, Maggie."

I didn't want to argue with her. Not today. Not when so much ugliness had already happened. She'd come around eventually, once she really thought about what he'd done, she just needed time to see it.

Instead I turned back to Matt. "By the way, you better make sure to charge Katie with two counts of murder and one count of attempted murder."

"For what happened here, today? Wouldn't that be two counts of attempted murder? And it's not like she really wanted to kill you guys, she was just upset that her whole world was unraveling."

"No. Not for today." I glanced at Jamie. "For the explosion. In the kitchen. I'm pretty sure that was Katie's fault, too. It was just her and Jamie here that day and she was conveniently outside when it happened."

Jamie turned back to me, mouth hanging open. "Do you really think…?"

I nodded. "Yeah. I do. I think she was crazy in love with Luke and that when you showed up and he started showing you attention that she wanted you gone so she could have him all to herself again. Jealousy of you was probably what made her snap in the first place. Jack Dunner and Mr. Jackson happened after that."

Jamie sank into a chair and buried her face in her hands. "How did I not see it?"

Matt squeezed my hand before stepping back. "How about I get your statements later."

"Thanks. Appreciate it."

I locked the door after him, flipped the café sign to closed, and grabbed us two beers from the mini fridge. "Come on, Jamie. Let's go outside with the pups."

She glanced at the beers in my hand. "It's not even noon, Maggie."

"Eh. It's five o'clock somewhere. And if the last hour didn't make you want to have a drink, I don't know what would. Now come on. Let's go."

We spent the next hour sitting outside on a gorgeous early summer day, the wind blowing through the trees, trying to make sense of the last few weeks as our dogs slept in the shade nearby. Neither one of us wanted to deal with the mess inside, although we knew we'd have to eventually.

For the time being it was just enough to know that we were both safe and that my grandpa was going to be freed. Jamie still couldn't wrap her mind around the whole Luke and Katie thing—any of it—and I sort of doubted she ever would. She's one of those rare people who sees the good in everyone, even the murderers, liars, and cheats. Part of me was glad this hadn't ruined her. Part of me wished she'd wisen up a bit.

I did at least manage to convince her to let me ban him from the store for life. It wasn't much, but it was progress.

As I sat there drinking a beer with my best friend way too early in the morning, I took a deep breath.

My move to Creek hadn't turned out at all the way I'd thought it would. My grandpa wasn't the feeble, needy old man I'd believed him to be, but was instead spry, stubborn, and, most surprising of all, in love. The valley wasn't the haven from the real world I'd always imagined, either. I knew now that people there were full of the same wants and needs, hatreds and loves as anywhere else.

The barkery wasn't yet the raging success I'd hoped for. There was an annoyingly handsome cop I couldn't stop thinking about. We were down one shop assistant. Our store was covered in blood. Jamie was probably still in love with Luke…

Despite all that, it was still the best decision I'd ever made to move to the valley. I was glad that my grandpa was probably going to be around a lot longer than I'd thought. And that I lived somewhere with people as real and flawed as I was.

And I was still living in one of the most gorgeous places in the world, running a business I loved, with my best friend in the world and Miss Fancypants at my side. Life wasn't perfect, but I couldn't imagine it being much better.

A CRAZY CAT LADY
AND CANINE CRUNCHIES

A MAGGIE MAY AND MISS FANCYPANTS MYSTERY

ALEKSA BAXTER

CHAPTER 1

I was peacefully sleeping, snuggled under my comforter, all nice and warm when I heard the small little cry from the end of the bed. It was a tiny little sound, not the loud bark my Newfoundland, Miss Fancypants—Fancy for short—could've made. I mean, when you're a hundred and forty pounds you can make an awful lot of noise if you want to.

But Fancy's not like that. Our time living in an apartment when she was little had two main effects. First, she loved to wake up at the unholy hour of five-thirty every morning, rain or shine, no matter the day of the week. And, second, she was quiet but insistent.

I knew from experience that she'd make that tiny little whining sound every few seconds until I dragged myself out of bed and fed her. So even though it was my day off, it was time to get up.

I crawled out of bed and sat on the floor next to her giant dog bed. She nestled her nose against my foot and rolled on her back for a good belly rub before violently sneezing and jumping to her feet.

Time for food. (Believe it or not, that was our

morning routine, sneeze and all. Not sure what it was about my foot or rolling over onto her back, but nine mornings out of ten she'd sneeze and jump to her feet within a minute of my sitting down next to her.)

I grumbled as I followed her down the hall to the kitchen. I was only thirty-six years old but after a full week of working at the barkery I felt like a little old lady. I was not used to being on my feet that much. You'd be surprised how much your body can ache after an entire day of cooking food. Standing does in fact take a lot of effort.

I'd moved to Creek, Colorado just a few weeks before to take care of my grandpa—who it turned out didn't need my help—and to open a business with my best friend Jamie. I'd known Jamie since I was little and I'd spend a month each summer with my grandparents, but she and I hadn't become best friends until we went to CU together. We bonded over a shared practicality and appreciation for people who get things done.

It had taken over a decade but we'd both finally grown tired of the corporate grind in a big city and decided to move "home" to start our own business: The Baker Valley Barkery and Café. (And no, that is not a typo. It's part bakery for dogs. Get it? Barkery? The café side serves the needs of humans. That's Jamie's side. The barkery side is for the dogs. That's my little brain child.)

And at that point, well…

Jamie makes the best cinnamon rolls in the world, so the café was doing amazing. The barkery…not so much. I was slowly building a group of steady customers like Abe and Evan at the Creek Inn, but it was slow going. If it wasn't for online sales it would have been very sad indeed.

But how many businesses are a success from day one, right? Not many. Or at least that's what I kept telling myself.

All I could do was show up each day, give it my all, and hope that things slowly trended upward.

In the meantime I finally got to work somewhere I could bring Fancy. But not that morning. It was my day off. Which meant, feed Fancy, take her for a long walk before it got too hot, and then cuddle up on the couch with a good book. My idea of a perfect day.

🐾 🐾 🐾

Of course, Fancy likes to keep me on my toes, so that's not exactly what happened.

As we set out for our morning walk, I took a deep breath of the clean mountain air. It was early summer and the sun was already up above the mountains to the east. The sky was completely clear of clouds and a gorgeous shade of blue that made me smile. There was a slight chill to the air—it was still the mountains after all—but nothing a light wind breaker couldn't handle. I'd tied my long blonde hair into a jaunty ponytail that swished back and forth with each step.

Creek was small—it had about forty houses in the town proper and maybe another couple dozen scattered through the mountains to either side—but it was mighty, too. It was the county seat and also housed the main jail, so there were a couple new buildings at the center of town in addition to the ultra-modern library at the edge of town. (A sad disappointment for me. I'd preferred when the library was in a cramped space on the third floor of the courthouse with books piled from floor to ceiling.)

We were surrounded by mountains on all sides, but not the huge towering kind you might imagine. These ones stretched just a few thousand feet above us. Easily hikeable for those who could handle the altitude.

At the end of town was a mile-or-so-wide gap where the highway led into the rest of the Baker Valley with a stream and train tracks running alongside.

I could hear a freight train passing by as we left the house, but couldn't see it from where we were. Up on the mountainside behind my grandpa's house was a large slab of rock that I'd sat on when I was a little girl, watching the trains that passed through. It didn't matter that I'd never lived in Creek full-time, this little sleepy Colorado town was where my heart had always lived.

Fancy and I walked a loop around the entire town, swinging down by the baseball park where she decided to take a bit of a breather and laid down in the grass, rolling on her back with contented grunts while I looked on in bemused annoyance. That early in the morning it was just us. Creek was never what I'd call a busy place, but before the courthouse opened it was practically dead.

That's okay. I kind of enjoyed the peace after living in DC where there was always someone watching us no matter the hour.

We were headed back home—just in sight of Lucas Dean's house (the jerk)—when Fancy stopped in her tracks.

"Come on, Fancy. We're almost there." I tried to pull her forward, but she jumped backward instead.

Now, I am not a small woman—about five-eight, one-sixty—but when a dog the size of Fancy decides she doesn't want to go somewhere, there's not much to be done about it. And when she decides to start jumping backward a foot at a time, well...*I* at least am hard pressed to stay on my feet. Not to mention the danger that she'd jump right out of her collar, something she was very much trying to do.

(That happened to us once next to a very busy street and scared the living daylights out of me.)

As soon as Fancy jumped backwards the second time, I followed her and crouched down.

"What's wrong, girl? You okay?"

She was shaking like a leaf, her whole body trembling as she stared in the direction of Lucas Dean's house. Not that I thought he was the cause for her distress. I didn't like him, but he wasn't the type to send my dog into fits of terror.

"It's okay. You're fine," I soothed, speaking in that calming sing-song voice that's universally effective with kids and dogs. She burrowed her nose into my shoulder and I leaned my face against the top of her head, petting her back as I continued to calm her.

Eventually she relaxed and the trembles disappeared.

"See? It's okay. Come on now. Let's go home." I stood and tried to lead her that last crucial block towards home, but she was not having it. As soon as I started in that direction she stiffened her legs and pulled backward, all the hair bunching up around her face as her eyes bulged.

She'd go back the way we'd come, no problem. But try to move forward? Nope. Not happening.

I figured I had two choices at that point. First, I could sit on the side of the road—there wasn't a sidewalk anywhere around—and wait for her to settle down enough to move forward. Past experience told me that would take anywhere from five minutes to thirty. And that was only going to work if the cause of her distress wasn't a bear or mountain lion that decided to hang around for a while.

My second option was to try to lead her around the block and come at my grandpa's house from the other side.

(Problem with my grandpa's place is that it's at the edge of town and backed up against a mountain. So there were only two ways to get there that didn't involve climbing said mountain. One was the road we were on and the other was the road that dead-ended into that road. To get to that other road was going to require walking around a very long block.)

Since I'm not one for sitting around and hoping things will work out, I chose the second option.

Fancy was great. She walked along in front of me, doing her little Newfie sashay, happy as could be as we turned towards the highway and then walked along it. She was even great as we turned up that other road. But then she froze again.

We were within sight of my grandpa's place. It was right there. Half a block away. I thought we were gonna make it, but then she jumped backward again and sat on her butt, refusing to go one step farther.

"Come on, Fancy. Please." I held out a fistful of treats to lure her forward, but she was so scared she wouldn't even eat one. (Which for Fancy was a big, big deal. Food is Fancy's lifeblood. I remember after she was spayed the vet said she might not want to eat for a day or so, but that girl was all about her dinner that night. To the point that I was worried I might be feeding her too much so close to her surgery. She was fine, though.)

"What is wrong?" I asked, exasperated.

Of course, she couldn't tell me. She's a dog. But that doesn't keep me from making up what I think she's thinking. And from what I could tell, she was scared of something around the vicinity of my grandpa's house. Something that hadn't been there before. Which probably meant a mountain lion? Or a bear? Maybe even a coyote, although I wasn't sure they lived as high as seven thousand feet. Something was scaring her. And it was something that hadn't been there when we left the house.

I sat down cross-legged on the ground and let her sit on my lap. (No, she didn't fit. But you try telling her that when she was as upset as she was.)

I'd pretty much resigned myself to just waiting her out when a cop car turned up the street.

I buried my face in her fur. "Fancy, I swear…If that's Matt Barnes and I'm forced to talk to him because you pulled this little stunt…"

I'd done a very good job of avoiding Officer Matthew Barnes, a/k/a Officer Handsome Distraction, since he'd tried to arrest my grandpa for murder. (He hadn't wanted to. He liked my grandpa, but the evidence was pretty incriminating.) It wasn't that I disliked him. Or that I found him unappealing. He was actually mighty fine looking, especially in a cop's uniform—the epitome of tall, dark, and handsome and with blue eyes to boot.

It was just that I had better things to do with my time than pine after some hot guy. I was starting a new business. And taking care of Fancy. And my grandpa. And I'd just moved there. Last thing I needed was to get all caught up with someone.

Better to avoid him than to let myself get distracted at such a crucial time in my life.

(Of course, both Jamie and my grandpa would point out that I always thought it was a crucial time to avoid distraction. Whatever. I had plans, so sue me.)

CHAPTER 2

The car pulled up next to us and the driver rolled the window down. Sure enough. It was Matt.

"Taking a little break?" He grinned down at us.

Fancy leapt to her feet, wagging her tail in giddy excitement at the sound of his voice. She's such a traitor. I swear, she loves every man more than she loves me, although Matt is a particular favorite. Her tail slapped me in the face a few times before I managed to stand up myself.

I walked over to the car and before I could stop her, Fancy had jumped up and shoved her head through the window and licked his face. Rather than recoil in disgust like most people would, he just laughed and rubbed at her ears until she was groaning in pleasure.

"How's my girl?" he asked, kissing her on the nose.

"If something ever happens to me, at least I know she'll have a good home," I muttered.

He laughed. "Not me. Your grandpa would never let her go."

It was probably true. My grandpa tried to play it cool when it came to Fancy, but it was pretty clear he adored her as much as she adored him.

"Good point."

"So? You guys were just taking a break on the side of the road?"

(It wasn't unheard of for me to do that. When we still lived in an apartment and Fancy was a puppy she'd want to stay outside forever and so I'd sit on the sidewalk while she sat on the grass and watched the world go by. I'm sure people thought I was nuts, especially in Crystal City. And *especially* when I threw leaves for her to catch. That's okay. I kind of am.)

I told him about my failed attempts to lead Fancy home. "I'm kind of outta options at this point. So I figured we'd sit here until she calmed down enough to make it the last little bit."

"That might take a while depending on what's spooking her."

"I know. But what other choice do I have?"

"You could let me give you a ride."

I shoved my immediate thought about that little comment aside and nodded. "That could work."

And it did. At first. Fancy jumped into the back of the car without any hesitation whatsoever. (It was weird back there. You'd think they'd have upholstered seats, but they don't. It's this strange hard plastic. I guess that makes it easier to clean up whatever fluids people might bring with them. I know. Ew. But when people are drunk or in fights, I'm sure they're not exactly clean by the time the cops show up.)

I sat next to her, but she still slid around a bit as we drove to my grandpa's house. At least it wasn't far; just half a block. Where we had the real problem was when it came time to get out of the car.

Fancy was not having it. And she made her opinion known with a lot of loud barking at both of us. Not her angry bark. This was her "why would you do this horrible thing to me?" bark that's loud and whiny all at the same time.

"Fancy! Matt needs to get to work. Get out of that car right now."

She, of course, ignored me. That's the problem with governing through bribery. When your dog is too upset to be bribed, it all falls apart.

Finally, Matt just grabbed her by the collar and dragged her out of the car. With that crazy plastic all over the place she scrambled to resist him, but couldn't. He didn't hurt her, but it surprised me nonetheless. I would've never even considered doing that.

As soon as Fancy's feet touched the ground and she realized she no longer had access to the safety of the car, she ducked her head down, hunched her shoulders, and raced for the front door. I chased after her, kind of glad for the excuse to get away from Officer Handsome.

"Thank you," I shouted back at him as I caught up with Fancy at the front door.

"You're welcome. I'd say you owe me a dinner for that one."

I pretended not to hear him. Matt is a horrible cook, at least from what he's said, but the last thing I needed was for him to come over for dinner.

My grandpa stepped outside as I let Fancy in. He was wearing his normal outfit of a short-sleeved plaid shirt over a plain white t-shirt and faded Levi's. For a man of eighty-two he looks at least a decade younger if not more, probably thanks to the fact that his hair is just a faded brown instead of white or gray. "You say something about dinner, Matt?"

I ducked inside as he walked towards Matt's car, knowing there was no point in trying to stop him. I wondered where Fancy had gone to. She'd disappeared around the corner as soon as I set her free, but I didn't know where she'd gone from there.

Finally, I found her. She was curled up in the far corner of my bedroom—a place she never goes during the day—her big amber eyes staring up at me.

I sat down next to her, careful not to sit too close because then she'd just run away. "It's okay, kiddo. You're safe now." I pet her soft black head and gave her a little kiss between the eyes. She stared up at me, her eyes full of love and trust.

I sighed. "You know I love you, but you did not do me any favors just now."

Dogs and men…I tell ya.

CHAPTER 3

The next day at the barkery started off well. I actually had a few customers and my newest treat—Canine Crunchies—seemed to be a hit with its target audience. I'd needed some sort of treat that would hold up well and was large enough that I could offer it to unknown dogs without the risk of losing a finger. So far, so good.

But then Janice Fletcher walked in the door. Janice was an older woman who never got the memo that it's bad for the environment to use that much hairspray. And that mustard-colored polyester slacks went out of style at least a few decades ago.

Trailing behind her was her best friend, Patsy Blackstone, who had the unfortunate habit of trying to match her clothes to her hair color. Seeing as her hair was some unfortunate shade of orange that was probably supposed to be red, it was not a good look.

I could've forgiven their unfortunate sartorial choices. (See eleventh grade English teacher, I knew someday I'd make that worthless vocabulary word work for me.) A customer is a customer after all, and I certainly needed more of them.

But Janice came in with a carrycase in hand—the plastic kind you see people use to take their pets on a plane. Again, not necessarily a problem. We were a bakery for dogs after all.

It was when she headed right for the center table with a defiant glare in my direction, set the case on the table, and opened it up that the trouble began. She pulled a large, furry white cat out while it meowed in protest at being taken from its comfortable bed. I immediately sneezed because I am very, very allergic to cats, especially big, fluffy white ones.

"Janice." I smiled as politely as I could. "This is a *dog* bakery. Cats aren't allowed. It says it right there on the door."

She set the cat on the table and let go of him. (Or her, who can tell.) "My Pookums has as much right to be here as any dog."

"Well, no. Actually that's not true." I moved closer, not wanting to antagonize her, but also wanting to keep that cat away from the dog treat counter. I was just glad no one was there other than Fancy who was snoring away in her cubby.

(If you'll recall the café and barkery is set up with two separate sides that have an area to pass through right by the back counter. On the barkery side there are some smaller nooks along the far wall for dogs that need to be left for a minute or two as well as well-spaced tables throughout the rest of the space that allow plenty of room for canine companions to join their owners while at the same time minimizing the possibility of any fights or someone tripping over a paw. Fancy has her very own cubby in the back corner with an extra-large dog bed where she spends most of the day snoring away. In the area between the café counter and the barkery counter there's also a little shop area with touristy items like mugs with our logo on them and pre-packaged dog treats. On the other side of that is the café counter.)

Janice stood up straighter, a wicked gleam in her eye. "Are you saying that cats aren't allowed here?"

"Yes. I am."

Pookums chose that moment to jump down and run across the floor towards the bright and shiny items on sale in the touristy area. Within seconds he'd managed to swat down a handful of keychains and knock a mug to the floor where it shattered loudly, forcing Fancy to jump to her feet and bark in fright.

"Jamie," I shouted. "I need your help. Now!" I glared at Janice. "*That* is why cats are not allowed in here. If you can't keep control of your pet, you can't be in here."

"A dog would do the same thing," Janice spat back at me.

"Well none has. We have a strict leash rule here. You're paying for that mug, by the way." I turned to quiet Fancy.

"I am not. How can you run an establishment like this and expect to leave breakable goods just lying around like that? It's not my fault the mug broke."

I waved a treat under Fancy's nose, but she'd spotted the cat and was not in the mood to quiet down. "Get your frickin' cat and get out of here," I hissed at Janice

(I know. Not the best example of customer service. And especially not in a small town and with a witness who was on the other person's side. But honestly…)

Jamie scooped Pookums up and smiled at both of us. He batted at her brunette braid as she cooed at him and walked towards Janice. "Here. Let me help you put him back in his case," she said, doing so before anyone could stop her.

"You can't expect me to keep Pookums locked up the whole time I'm here," Janice huffed.

I glared at her. "Actually, I don't. I expect you to take him home. Now."

I sneezed. Crazy cat lady and her frickin' white-haired ball of allergies. If that cat was around for much longer I was going to need a shower or have to risk my throat swelling shut.

🐾 🐾 🐾

Now, before we continue, I feel I need to say a few things because you may be a cat lover and I don't want you to get the wrong idea here. I have nothing against cat lovers in general. I think anyone who can love any animal, be it a dog, cat, or rhinoceros, is a good person.

And as a crazy dog lady myself I understand how someone can love their cat to the point of dressing it in costumes and talking to it in a baby voice. Only reason I don't do that with Fancy is she'd probably sit on me the first time I tried to put her in some weird outfit.

So I have nothing against cat people. Or cats for that matter. (Other than the fact that I am insanely allergic to them and that, somehow psychically knowing this, they all try to rub up against my legs or sit on my face. True story: I once woke up to find my friend's kitten curled in a little ball on my throat.)

So when I call her a crazy cat lady it has nothing to do with any other cat owner on this planet. I just wanted Janice Fletcher and her sneeze-inducing feline friend to leave.

🐾 🐾 🐾

"This isn't fair." Janice glared at me as Patsy crowded up behind her nodding in agreement.

"Life isn't fair. Now please leave my establishment. Do not make me call the cops." I'd finally gotten Fancy calmed down by throwing a handful of canine crunchies into her cubby, so walked back to Janice, ready to throw her out on her ear if I had to.

"The cops!" Janice's face turned a violent shade of red. "You wouldn't dare!"

I opened my mouth to say I would, too, but Jamie gently pushed me backward and stepped between us. "Ms. Fletcher, there really are a number of reasons we can't have cats here in the barkery. You have to see that. It's just not safe. And not hygienic to have a cat, or any animal really, running loose in a food establishment."

She handed the carrier to Ms. Fletcher and gently guided her towards the door, Patsy trailing along uncertainly behind them.

"I'm sorry we couldn't accommodate you and your cat." Jamie held the door open for them, smiling in such a way that she was impossible to refuse. "But if you ladies want to come back sometime *without* the cat, I'd be more than happy to give you each a free cinnamon roll."

Before they even knew what was happening, Janice, Patsy, and Pookums were outside and Jamie was closing the door in their face, calmly but firmly.

(Somedays I wish I were her. I'm a little too fiery to pull something like that off as you might have noticed.)

"Well." She pretended to dust her hands off. "Hopefully that's the last of that."

"Hopefully. Thanks for the assist." I turned to Fancy.

"And, you, young lady…You can't bark at customers like that."

Jamie laughed and patted me on the shoulder. "I'd say that's the pot calling the kettle black, wouldn't you?"

"Hey!"

"It's true. You also can't be barking at customers. Not if you want us to be open six months from now."

"I know, but…Seriously. She was looking for a fight."

"Doesn't mean you needed to give her one."

Jamie was right, but I didn't have to like it.

CHAPTER 4

At least one good thing happened that day, even if it came with an unpleasant surprise.

Around one o'clock the barkery door chimed and I looked up to see who was there. The first person through the door was an attractive woman who was probably slightly older than I am. She wore slim slacks, a brightly colored top, and a tasteful, but expensive amount of jewelry. (All except her wedding ring which was visible from across the room.) Her pale blonde hair and skin told me she was probably from or descended from a long line of people from Sweden, Norway, Iceland, Germany, etc.

She also had a dog with her. (Well, two, but we'll get to that in a moment.)

The first dog, the real one, was an Irish wolfhound. He was tall—his head easily reached above her waist— but slim and wiry. I figured he and Fancy were about the same height but she probably had at least twenty pounds on him, if not more. Not that I thought she'd win in a fight. He looked nice enough, but there was a coiled energy to him that made me very glad his owner seemed to be in such firm control of him.

Holding the door open for this intriguing pair of guests was none other than Lucas Dean—a man who should've been in jail if the world were in any way fair. (That would be the second dog I mentioned above.) He grinned at me from behind the woman with that cock-sure smile of his that charmed everyone but me.

Don't get me wrong, I could acknowledge that Luke was a good-looking man in a "convince you to sneak out of your house at midnight and spend a few hours in the bed of his truck" sort of way. I just knew he was a lying, cheating jerk, too. And one that had broken Jamie's heart at least a half dozen times over the years. She kept going back to him, which was the worst of it.

For a smart woman, she was horrible at choosing men.

I gritted my teeth and forced a smile, focusing my attention on the woman. Luke I'd deal with later. He knew darned well he wasn't supposed to set foot in the barkery or the café ever again.

"Welcome to the Baker Valley Barkery and Café," I said. "May I?" I gestured towards the dog as I came around the counter with a canine crunchy in hand.

"Yes. Hans loves a good treat." The woman barked some command in what sounded like German and Hans immediately sat. (I bet *she* wouldn't have had a problem getting Fancy to go home…)

"Nice to meet you, Hans." I held my empty hand out to him to smell and then offered him the treat. He took it with what I can only call an extreme amount of class.

"Hi. I'm Maggie." I held out my hand to his owner.

The woman took it with a surprisingly firm grip. I was expecting some sort of limp squeeze and release, but she shook hands like a businesswoman. "Greta Van-Veldenstein. I have moved here but construction continues on my home. Lucas says this is an excellent place to bring Hans for a break from the noise. He gave me samples of your treats. Hans likes them very much." Her accent was slightly Germanic, but not terribly strong.

"Oh, wonderful. Welcome. I'm sure you'll love it here. Baker Valley is certainly one of my favorite places in the world. May I ask? Where are you originally from?"

"Ah, the accent, yes? Germany. Although I have not been back since the death of my second husband." She smoothed a hand through her hair and turned towards the café side. "Lucas tells me you also have coffee and food?"

Lucas stepped forward. "I'll get something for you, Mrs. VanVeldenstein. Why don't you and Hans make yourselves comfortable. A soup and panini with a black coffee, perhaps?"

She nodded. "Yes. Perfect. Thank you."

Lucas shot me a grin as he dashed towards the café side. (And Jamie.) I wanted to grab him by the ear, drag him to the door, and throw him out, but I couldn't in front of my newest customer and he knew it.

I smiled at Greta. "Well, as you can see, it's pretty quiet right now. So feel free to choose any table you want and let me know if there's anything else I can do for you."

"Will you join me? For lunch? I have a book, but I prefer company over a meal."

"Um, sure. I can do that." I glanced towards where Lucas was leaning against the counter making Jamie laugh.

"He will not join us. I promise."

I winced. "That obvious, am I?"

She shrugged one shoulder. "You will tell me why sometime. But not today. I do not think he is an ex?"

"Oh no. Not mine at least."

She looked more carefully towards the counter. "Ah, yes. I see now. Your friend. The other owner?"

I nodded.

"Then she must join us, too. And Lucas will go back to work."

"I like that plan. Just give me a moment to get the rest of the food arranged and we'll be back to join you."

As I raced to break up Luke and Jamie, and also prepare myself some soup and panini, Greta chose the table in the center of the picture window, Hans settling down comfortably at her feet. Despite her unfortunate association with Lucas Dean, I was giddy with excitement.

I had my first real customer!

CHAPTER 5

Greta turned out to be delightful. It was clear from a few things she said here or there that she was not only wealthy but obscenely rich. I didn't mind, though, because she didn't look down her nose at either of us. She was just sweet and charming. A little odd, I'll give you that. She told us Hans was named for one of her husbands, but she wasn't quite sure which one he'd been. Probably number five or six; definitely not numbers one through four.

"How many times have you been married?" I asked her, laughing.

"It is so hard to remember. Some were very short. And some I think I married but maybe I did not. I believe Friedrich, my current husband, is number nine. Or ten? Maybe number eleven."

Jamie laughed. "Why so many?"

She shrugged a shoulder. "This is a good question. The first marriage was for love. I was young. He was handsome. That was all it took. The second marriage was for money. I was young. I was beautiful. He was not. But he was kind. And wealthy. And then...I do not know. I thought marriage was what you do, yes? Now? Perhaps not." She looked back and forth between us. "And you? You have been married, yes?"

"No." I shook my head in horror. "I don't have time for any of that."

Greta laughed. "You say this because you have not been married. The right husband can be very good for a woman." She narrowed her eyes at me. "But it is best that the first husband be for money. That is the mistake I made when young."

I didn't even know what to say to that. "Ah…"

"Oh, you think you marry for love?" She laughed. "This will disappoint you. He will be human. And you will be sad. Money is better. I will find you someone. My husband has a friend. He would make a good first husband. He is very old and very rich."

I shook my head in horror. "Really, it's…"

"No, no, no. I insist." She turned to Jamie. "And you, Jamie? Have you been married?"

"No." Jamie looked away.

"But you would like to be."

"Um, yeah, I think so." She fiddled with her coffee spoon in a very un-Jamie-like way.

I stared at her. Since when? Please tell me she wasn't thinking of marrying Lucas Dean.

Greta nodded. "Then I will find you a rich man, too."

Jamie started to open her mouth to object, but Greta patted her hand. "This Lucas is a fun man, yes? But he is not a man you marry."

"I don't know about that. I mean he's…"

"No. Listen to me. I have been married many, many times. I know what makes a good husband and Lucas…No.

He does not." She patted Jamie's hand again. "We will find you a good husband. I think you would not want to be a mistress?"

I almost spit out my Coke at that one. "No, Greta. Neither of us would like to be a mistress."

She shrugged and sat back. "It would be easier if you would. More choices. But I understand. I too am not a good mistress."

We were saved from the rest of that conversation by the jangle of the door as someone came in on the café side. "Be right there," Jamie called as she hustled away more quickly than was absolutely necessary.

I gathered up the dishes from lunch. "I should probably get back to work myself. But I really hope you'll come back."

"I will. The construction in my home is very loud. Hans and I need a break. May we stay?"

"Of course. Stay as long as you'd like." I winced as I glanced around at all the empty tables. "Not like we're hurting for space right now."

"It is a nice place you have here, Maggie. Give it time."

"Thank you."

I walked away buoyed by the thought of a new customer and perhaps a new friend. No doubt, Greta was half off her rocker, but sometimes those are the best sorts of friends to have.

🐾 🐾 🐾

And Greta was true to her word. She was there at one o'clock every day for the rest of the week, with her laptop or her book to entertain her, and usually stayed until we closed at four. Hans just slept at her feet the whole time, ten times more well-behaved than Fancy. She's good—don't get me wrong—but Fancy does need to be let into the dog run out back every couple of hours and will definitely make it known when that needs to happen.

Things were finally looking up. I had my first regular customer, some of the local businesses were stocking my dog treats for their customers to buy, and online sales had picked up, too. I was happy.

Until Janice Fletcher returned.

🐾 🐾 🐾

Fortunately, Jamie was able to catch me before I left the house. (She's always in earlier because she does all the baking in the morning.)

"Hey, Jamie, what's up?" I asked as I pulled on my second tennis shoe, my phone cradled between my ear and shoulder.

"You better leave Fancy at home today."

"What? Why?" I glanced at Fancy who was already standing by the door staring at her leash and collar like they might run away and escape if she didn't keep a good eye on them.

"Janice Fletcher is back. And she's not alone."

"You're not even open yet. What's she doing?"

"She's gathered a little group of friends from what I can tell. And they all have signs." She sighed. "I think she's going to picket us."

"Picket? What for?"

"Not allowing her cat, I'd assume."

"Oh that's ridiculous."

My grandpa raised an eyebrow as he walked past me headed for the kitchen and his first cup of coffee. He's not much of a talker until he's had his morning caffeine.

Jamie sighed again. "Ridiculous or not, I think it's best not to bring Fancy through this mess. All we need is for someone to crowd too close and she barks at them and then it's all over the news. Janice's nephew, Peter Nielsen, runs the local paper, remember? I'm sure he'll be here, too, before long."

"That twerp is her nephew?" (I didn't like him much. I'd tried to get him to cover our grand opening and he'd made some nasty comment to me about how a two-bit café that'd be closed in less than a year wasn't news.)

"Yep. So leave Fancy at home."

"Okay. Will do." I hung up and looked to Fancy. She'd lain down in front of the door, staring at me. She may not be able to talk, but that girl can figure things out better than most people.

"Fancy…"

She didn't move, just stared at me with those big amber eyes of hers.

"I'm going to have to leave you at home today. But you get to hang out with Grandpa. You'll like that won't you?"

She harrumphed and laid her head on her paws.

"I can't do anything about this, Fancy. So don't look at me that way. Now move. I need to get your bed from the van."

She scrambled to her feet as I opened the door, but then tried to go outside with me when I opened it. I barely blocked her with my leg. "I'm sorry, Fancy. You have to stay behind."

I snuck past her and closed the door firmly behind me, feeling like the most horrible human being on the planet. But if Jamie was right about what Janice Fletcher had planned, then I really did need to leave Fancy at home. For her sake. Plus, she loved my grandpa. She might be acting all hurt and disappointed now, but she'd probably forget all about me once I was gone. Or so I told myself.

(Just like I'd told myself how much she loved daycare when I was living in DC. She did, but it was no substitute for time in the park with me.)

I lugged the extra-large dog bed back to the house.

"What's that for?" my grandpa muttered, taking a long sip of his coffee. "That dog has enough dog beds already."

I handed him the morning paper that I'd snagged while I was outside. "It's for your workroom."

I dragged the bed down the hall and wedged it into the far corner of the room before he could object. He loves to work on miniatures even though his hands tremble so bad some days it takes him five minutes to place one little piece. And I figured if Fancy was going to be home with him all day she'd want a comfy spot to keep him company while he worked.

"What do you mean, it's for my workroom?" he asked when I returned.

I flashed him my best smile. "Fancy has to stay here today."

"Doesn't mean she needs a bed in my workroom."

"Well she's going to want to stay close to you. And lying on the floor can hurt her joints."

"She has a bed in the living room. She has a bed in your room. She has a bed in my room. She has a bed in the office. And now you think she needs a bed in my workroom, too?"

"I don't have time to argue about this. I'm running late. Fancy needs to stay here today. Please look after her. And please, let the bed stay?"

He muttered something under his breath before taking a long sip of his coffee, but at least he didn't continue the argument.

I turned to Fancy who was now leaning against the wall watching me. "I'm sorry, girl. I have to go. You have to stay here."

She ran to the door and looked back at me, eyes wide.

"No. You have to stay here."

She sank onto her haunches, every line of her body full of hurt and rejection.

I closed my eyes for a moment and took a deep breath. Disappointing a dog is never easy.

Fortunately, Fancy is easily distracted. I ran into the kitchen and grabbed her a doggie ice cream from the freezer. She immediately perked up when she saw what I had in my hand.

"I will have you know that it is way too early in the day for you to be eating something like this," I told her.

She didn't care. I'm not even sure she was hearing what I said at that point. All of her attention was focused on the ice cream treat in my hand.

"Be good for Grandpa. I'll be home in…ten hours." (I knew that wouldn't mean anything to her. She's actually pretty good at telling time, but anything past about five hours is just "a long frickin' time" in Fancyworld.)

I handed her the container and she immediately raced out back to eat her ice cream while I made a quick exit. "Love you, Grandpa."

"Love you, too."

CHAPTER 6

I drove towards the barkery wondering just how bad this little protest demonstration was going to be. I mean, how many crazy cat ladies can one town have? One? Two? Three at most, I'd think.

Turns out the answer was ten. Which seriously surprised me. Who knew there were ten women in the Baker Valley who were so passionate about bringing their cats out to lunch with them that they'd gather to protest our store at seven in the morning?

But there they were. Janice was brandishing a hand-made sign that read "Cats Need Love Too" with little cat paw prints painted on it. Next to her Patsy Blackstone had a sign that read "Cat Hater!" written in a color that looked very much like fresh blood but clearly was not since it was still bright, bright red. The other signs were just as absurd. And the other women looked to have dressed themselves out of the same out-of-date, over-the-top fashion magazine as Janice and Patsy.

Wow. Just…wow.

As I approached the front of the store they converged on me, waving their signs and shouting out little phrases about what a horrible, cat-hating person I was. I'll give them this, they were all in with their protest. But I am not a morning person at the best of times. And when you make me leave my dog at home and then surround me with bad perfume and loud shouting, well, you get the worst of me.

"Back off!" I snapped.

(There may have been two more words in the middle of that sentence, but let's just go with back off for the sake of politeness.)

They gasped and stared at me in horror, moving like some sort of twisted version of the Stepford Brides.

"Did you hear what she said?" one of the ladies said to another.

This after waving a sign in my face and shouting at me?

I glared them down. "Leave now or I'm calling the cops."

"We have every right to protest an unfair establishment." Janice planted herself directly in front of me, the ladies arraying themselves behind her.

"You may in fact have every right to protest the fact that we don't allow cats. But you do not have the right to threaten me or anyone else who wants to enter my establishment. So back off."

(Once more, there might have been a couple extra words thrown in there.)

Janice stepped closer. "Or what?"

Fortunately for me, I heard the little chirp of a cop car trying to clear a crowd and the sound of tires on gravel behind me. The cavalry had arrived.

The ladies all backed up an extra step, but they didn't disperse. I was tempted to turn around and see who it might be, but Janice and I were locked in the midst of an intense staredown and I wasn't going to be the one to blink first.

She needed to know who she was dealing with.

I heard the car door slam and the sound of the cop's feet on the pavement as he approached. "What seems to be the problem here?" he asked.

I winced. It was Officer Clark—the man who'd dragged my eighty-two-year-old grandpa out of his home in handcuffs and who would probably arrest him again given half the chance.

"Officer Clark. These women are disrupting my business."

He crossed his arms and pursed his lips, looking back and forth between the women and the front of our store.

Janice turned to him. "We have every right to protest."

I took a deep breath. Being angry and irrational wasn't going to help any. "I realize that they probably do have the right to protest, but I would ask that they do so somewhere that doesn't threaten or intimidate our customers."

He smirked at me. "They're little old ladies. They're not threatening anyone."

"Do not call me a little old lady."

I thought for a second Janice was going to whap him with her sign, but she stopped herself just in time.

"See?" I said. "When I arrived all ten of them converged on me. I'd really appreciate it if you could keep them from doing that to my customers."

I was pretty sure he was going to ignore me and let them continue their protests. And then I didn't know what I was going to do. If the cops won't help you, what other options do you have?

But another cop car pulled into the parking lot. It was Matt. I'd never been so happy to see him in my life. (Not that I let myself feel that for more than a split second, because…reasons.)

He stepped out of his car with a nod and smile for all of the ladies.

"Hi, Officer Barnes," one of the ladies called. "You never have said whether you'd like to come over for Sunday dinner. My niece would love to meet you."

"I'm sure she would, Ms. Highsmith, but I'm still pretty tied up with taking care of my father's house and starting the new job and all."

Liar. I was pretty sure he spent most of his free time crashed out on his couch watching TV.

"What seems to be the problem," he asked, joining us and looking pointedly at Officer Clark.

"These ladies are protesting the fact that the owners of this establishment won't allow cats."

"They swarmed me when I arrived," I added.

Officer Clark glared at me, but I didn't care. It was true.

"Janice," Matt turned his charming smile her way. "We've been through this before. You can't obstruct a business this way."

She glared at him, but didn't answer.

He turned and scanned the parking lot. "You and your ladies can protest, but you will have to do it over there." He pointed to a grassy area at the far end of the parking lot, at least a hundred feet from the entrance. "No shouting at customers either, even if they park right by you."

"No one will see us over there."

"They'll see you just fine, Janice. Look, Peter Nielsen just pulled in. I'm sure you'll be on the front page of the paper tomorrow. If that doesn't make your point for you, I don't know what will. Now go."

"Before he can take his pictures?"

"Yes. Now."

Janice looked like she was going to argue her point further, but when Matt wants to be intimidating he's very good at it. She stormed away in a huff, her ladies following after like a gaggle of geese.

Jamie came out as soon as they started to walk away, a coffee in each hand. "Can I offer you gentlemen a drink?"

Officer Clark turned to snarl at her, but stopped himself when he saw the attractive woman holding a cup of coffee for him. Jamie flashed him a dimpled smile with a head tilt.

I felt ill. Not Officer Clark, please. I'd rather she kept seeing Lucas Dean.

"Officer Barnes?" She held out the other cup of coffee.

"Best not. Wouldn't want to be seen playing favorites." He winked at me before returning to his patrol car.

Whatever that was about.

"Well, then. Now that that's over." I rushed into the barkery as fast as I could. I was not going to think about Matthew Barnes one moment longer than I had to.

(Even though I was extremely grateful he'd saved us from the cadre of crazy cat ladies outside.)

🐾 🐾 🐾

The rest of the day was fairly uneventful although I was not amused by the pictures and article that Peter Nielsen posted to his website for the noon edition of the *Baker Valley Gazette*. It accused us of being elitist snobs from the big city who didn't want the scummy locals messing up our place. The fact that the protest was about cats was barely even mentioned.

I had to give the man credit. He knew how to stir up controversy.

We spent the afternoon dealing with angry locals who stormed into the store to tell us they had as much of a right to frequent our establishment as some hoity-toity tourist. (Having poor Greta sitting in the front window of the barkery certainly didn't help, but I didn't have the heart to tell her to leave. She was my only regular customer after all.)

Jamie handled it with aplomb. Each time someone stormed through the door Jamie greeted them with a big smile, a coffee, and a cinnamon roll. On the house. By three o'clock we were getting freebie seekers who could barely pretend to be angry, but she treated them all the same.

Chalk it up as a business expense. Like I've said before, Jamie makes the best cinnamon rolls in the world. By the end of the day, thanks to Janice Fletcher, everyone in the county knew it.

Victory snatched from the jaws of defeat. Take that, Janice.

🐾 🐾 🐾

Even though the day had turned out well, I'd missed Fancy. She may spend most of every day snoring in her cubby, but it's still nice to have her around. So when I returned home I was more than happy to sit down on the floor and let her crawl all over me and lick my face for a good five minutes.

My grandpa said she'd spent most of the day lying five feet from the door waiting for me to come home. Poor girl. Seems she'd missed me as much as I'd missed her. Too bad I was going to have to leave her at home another day. No telling what Janice was going to pull next.

CHAPTER 7

You're probably wondering at this point why I'm telling you all of this and no one's shown up dead yet. Don't worry, it's coming. But I felt I needed to get all the pieces in place first so you'd understand how it was I ended up in jail for murder.

Yep, me.

But first…

After Janice's failed attempt to boycott our business things actually settled down for a few days. Other than a nice little bump in sales of cinnamon rolls, it was like it had never happened. We actually had to hire in some temporary counter staff so Jamie could spend more time in the kitchen preparing four-packs of cinnamon rolls that we sold throughout the day. It was beautiful.

To tell you the truth, I almost wanted to kiss Janice and Peter Nielsen for their brilliance in driving so many new customers our way.

I should've known it wouldn't last.

Janice and Patsy barged through the barkery door at two o'clock one afternoon, cat carriers in hand. That's right. Carriers plural. Each of them had one.

I took a deep, deep breath. Jamie was in the back and I knew the elderly woman working the café counter would be no help in banishing these women for once and for all.

"Janice. Please leave my store. I have told you repeatedly that cats are not allowed here."

I glanced towards Greta who'd put down her book and was watching us with interest. Hans was still his usual calm and collected self, but there was no doubt he was focused on the two carriers and what they might contain.

I did not need this. If they let those cats out and Hans wasn't good around cats…

Janice shoved a piece of paper in my face. "It doesn't matter what you want. You can't make me leave. Pookums has every right to be here. I need him."

I scanned the paper. "Are you serious?"

She stood up straighter. "Of course I am."

"You had Pookums declared an emotional support cat?"

"Yes."

I glanced at the date. "You only got this letter yesterday."

"I was just making official what's always been true. I need my Pookums with me."

I pressed my lips together, hard.

CHAPTER 8

Yet again, I feel I have to take a moment and explain something here. I have nothing against emotional support animals. I've met a number of wonderful support animals over the years—ones that allowed people with anxiety to experience the world and ones that could detect potential seizures. I am all for emotional support animals. And if someone had walked into my store with a cat as a legitimate emotional support animal, I would've made it work.

I assume they would've kept that cat close, though. And that they would've understood that taking a cat into a dog barkery wasn't going to be the best idea. But if they'd insisted on being there, I would've respected that.

But this?

This was not legitimate. And Janice Fletcher knew that as well as I did. Which is why I went from calm to trembling with rage in about ten seconds. Not only was this woman trying everything she could to mess with my business but she was taking advantage of something that should be respected.

🐾 🐾 🐾

"Jamie," I shouted.

She came out of the kitchen, her smock covered in baking flour and a small smudge on the side of her nose. "What? What's wrong?"

"You need to deal with this." I shoved the letter into her hands, glared at Janice and Patsy for a long moment, and then retreated to the barkery counter. I literally felt like breaking something in that moment, but I knew I couldn't. Not without making things worse.

As I stood there I fantasized about taking up a sport like taekwondo that would let me break boards. I could keep a stack out in the dog run and go back there and shatter them into little pieces whenever I needed a release. (It's possible customer service is not exactly my forte.)

I spent the next few minutes while Jamie dealt with Janice Fletcher and Patsy Blackstone, mentally breaking boards. Finally, Jamie had it settled. "Please follow me."

She turned towards the café side.

"Where are you taking us?" Janice demanded.

"I appreciate that you have an emotional support animal, but in the interest of safety and health, I have to ask that you come sit on the café side away from any dogs. You'll receive the same level of service and have the same menu of options to order from, but I can't let you sit on this side."

"I'll sue you."

Jamie stared her down. "For what? We're letting you stay here."

"It's discrimination."

"No. It's not. Now, please. Follow me." There was steel behind her words.

Janice and Patsy reluctantly followed her to the other side of the store, glaring back at me with each step. I knew this wasn't over. I knew they'd be back, demanding to sit on the barkery side. I didn't know why, but that woman had it in for me.

I grabbed a cleaning rag and wiped down all of the tables even though they were already clean.

Greta called me over. "What is this that happened just now?"

I explained to her about the cat issue and how now Janice had found a way around my ban by having her cat declared an emotional support animal. Greta found the whole concept very confusing but admitted she had heard some of the same news stories I had about emotional support peacocks and fish.

She shook her head. "This woman, she is wrong. She must be dealt with."

"Agreed. I'm just not sure how."

CHAPTER 9

About twenty minutes later Jamie came to join us. "They're gone. Thankfully. I managed to convince them to keep the cats in their carriers this time, but that won't work next time."

"You're a saint, Jamie. I was ready to kill that woman."

"I know." She chuckled. "Your face was very, very red when I came over."

"So what do we do now?"

"Already done." She waved her phone at me. "I took a copy of the letters and called Mason Maxwell. He'll be by in an hour or so."

"Mason Maxwell? Really?"

He was an amazing attorney. The best in the county. But he also intimidated the heck out of me and was not cheap. I should know. He'd helped us out with my grandpa's little murder charge.

"He's the best. Aaand…It turns out his family and Janice's hate each other."

"I didn't realize there was a big Maxwell contingent in Baker Valley. Or Fletcher for that matter."

"Oh, Mason Maxwell is a Mason. When his mother married out of the family, she gave him Mason as a first name so he'd still carry the family legacy."

"You mean Mason as in Masonville, the town? One of the founding families of the valley?"

"Yep. And Janice Fletcher was a Baker before she got married. One of the other founding families of the valley. They've hated each other since day one."

"This Mason, he is rich?" Greta asked. "And single?"

We both looked at her. What did that have to do with anything?

"I have no idea, Greta," I said. She was certainly an odd one at times.

"Why don't you ask him when he gets here," Jamie suggested, trying not to smile. She pushed herself to her feet. "In the meantime, I'm going to finish up this last batch of cinnamon rolls for the day." She glanced towards the kitchen. "Who knew I'd come to hate baking cinnamon rolls as much as I did drafting analysis reports?"

"I can do some of the baking tomorrow if you want," I offered.

"I might just take you up on that."

Jamie was a genius in the kitchen, but I could hold my own when I wanted to, especially if I was working from one of her recipes. I put that aside for the time being, though. Mason Maxwell was headed our way and for some reason I felt that warranted a tidying up binge. He wasn't exactly condescending, but he was very clearly a man with standards that most people didn't meet.

If he was going to be our attorney in this, I wanted to make the best impression possible.

🐾 🐾 🐾

Mason Maxwell walked through the door exactly an hour later. With his salt and pepper hair and country club attire (nice slacks and a polo shirt this time), he looked very out of place in our cutesy kitschy little café. I felt like he weighed and judged the entire place with that steely gaze of his.

Greta was still there and she watched him with a studied bemusement. Given the amount of money she had some mere millionaire wasn't going to phase her one bit.

"Mr. Maxwell," I said. "Thank you for coming out on such short notice."

"It is the nature of my business," he replied. "How is your grandfather?"

"He's well, thank you. No more cops showing up to arrest him certainly helps." I smiled, but he didn't match my smile. Maybe because I'd sort of kind of ignored his advice when he was representing my grandpa and had ended up getting my grandpa arrested because of it. Or maybe that's just how he was.

Jamie came out from the kitchen to join us, rebraiding her long brown hair as she did so. She had a smudge of flour on her cheek and another one on the tip of her nose making her look impossibly adorable. "Mr. Maxwell? Jamie Green. Nice to meet you."

He actually smiled at her.

(I figured that was a good thing. It helps when your attorney actually likes you, but I still felt a little bitter that he hadn't smiled at me when I said hi.)

He glanced around, pausing pointedly on Greta. "It would be best if we could have this conversation in private."

"I can leave." Greta closed her laptop. "But first I would like to meet this man." She came over to us, hand extended. "Greta VanVeldenstein."

"Mason Maxwell. I believe I've dealt with your nephew and your husband a few times on the land development deal they're planning."

"Ah, yes. Wilhelm has dreams. But not much else, sadly to say. My husband hopes to save him from certain failure."

I stared at her. Even if that was true, who says that to a stranger?

Mason Maxwell took it in stride. "Well, hopefully between your husband and myself we can make that happen."

She nodded, but it was clear she didn't believe it. "You should come for dinner. My husband would like that." She glanced at Jamie and me before adding, "You and your wife?"

"No wife. Just me."

She smiled. "This is sad. But you would like a wife someday?"

If she hadn't kept looking at us I would have almost enjoyed seeing how uncomfortable her questions made him. Who knew that someone could ruffle Mason Maxwell?

"I…Yes. Someday. I just haven't met the right woman yet."

That was a good excuse. I'd have to use that one myself. (Except it was a lie, of course.)

"Good. Then I will find you a wife." As Greta patted his arm he flinched, but I wasn't sure if it was because of her intent to find him a wife or her touching him so casually.

I stepped forward and gently steered her away. "Well then, Greta. Now that you have your latest matchmaking assignment, we better get started with our meeting. See you tomorrow?"

She nodded. "Yes. I will see you tomorrow."

CHAPTER 10

I walked her to the door and locked it while Jamie locked the other side. We joined Mason Maxwell at a table in the center of the barkery where there was lots of room.

"Would you like something to eat?" Jamie asked. "I make a really good cinnamon roll. Or we have soup and panini I could heat up for you."

"Actually, lunch would be great. I was caught in meetings earlier and only managed to eat a granola bar for lunch. I have heard good things about this place. Time I tried it out myself."

Jamie beamed at him and hurried to the kitchen to make him up a plate of food.

I stared at him awkwardly, not quite sure what to do. He wasn't exactly the type for small talk. "Um, why don't I get you a copy of the emotional support animal certificate Janice Fletcher provided us. You can look that over while Jamie heats up your lunch."

"Yes. Excellent."

"Okay then."

I ran to the back, grabbed the document, gave it to him, and then hurried back to the kitchen to keep Jamie company. I simply didn't know what to do with a man like Mason Maxwell. He was so…formal. It wasn't his money that put me off, it was the stick up his butt.

(Sorry. I know. That's rude. But someone who always has perfect posture and never has a thing out of place just…It's not natural. It's not human.)

While I waited I heated myself up a cinnamon roll and grabbed a Coke from the mini fridge. What can I say? My version of the four food groups is a little different than the average person's.

I watched Mason Maxwell from the edge of the doorway where I didn't think he could see.

"What are you doing?" Jamie came to stand next to me and peeked over my shoulder.

"He scares me. He's very intense. Do you know when he met Fancy she wouldn't even go near him? He told me that dogs were pack animals and that you just had to show them who was the alpha."

She laughed. "I would've liked to see that. And he's not that bad is he? He seems very smart. And kind."

I frowned at her. "He's definitely smart. Scary smart. And that's definitely what you want in a lawyer. But…" I shivered. "Kind? Where'd you get that from?"

"I don't know. Something in his eyes maybe."

I snorted.

Jamie turned away to remove Mason's sandwich from the sandwich press and put it on a plate, adding a small bowl of tomato soup to go along with it. I grabbed my cinnamon roll and followed her to the table.

Mason Maxwell eyed my food choices with a raised eyebrow, but didn't say anything. Good thing. He might intimidate me, but I would defend my sugary food choices to the grave. (Yeah, yeah, make the funny comment about how someone who eats like me probably *will* die from those choices. I'll wait.)

Jamie ran back to the kitchen for a fresh cup of coffee while Mason took his first bites of food. When she returned he gave her a hundred-watt smile that so surprised me I almost fell out of my chair. "This is delicious. I may have to start coming here every day."

(Unlikely. He lived at least twenty minutes away and worked from home as far as I knew.)

"You'd be welcome, of course." Jamie flashed her dimples at him.

I stared at them, wondering what exactly was going on. Did they *like* each other? And if so, what did I think about that? I mean, Mason Maxwell was certainly better than Lucas Dean, but…he was Mason Maxwell. My light-hearted but fierce friend deserved better than this intense man with his too-perfect shoes. I mean, really, who wears a pair of Italian loafers in a Colorado mountain town. This wasn't Vail or Aspen. This was Bakerstown. Buy a good pair of hiking boots, would ya?

"Before we get too far with using your legal help," I said, "I think I should warn you we're kind of limited in terms of funds. So taking her to court or something like that is probably not an option."

He took another bite of his food and chewed it thoroughly before responding, his enjoyment of the food evident. "We can work something out. Janice Fletcher has created difficulties for me in the past. It would be nice to be able to repay that." He nodded towards his food. "Actually, as long as you are willing to provide me with lunch on a regular basis, I would say that should cover the costs."

I stared at him. I'd seen the bill he sent my grandpa and it was not cheap. We'd be feeding him for years. But that would be a lot easier to cover than a big whopping bill.

"Are you sure?"

"Yes. Consider it pro bono work with a twist."

Jamie flashed him another smile. "You have a deal."

"Good."

🐾 🐾 🐾

It turned out that Janice Fletcher's emotional support cat was not in fact allowed into the café and barkery. Only a legitimate service animal had to be accommodated in a restaurant in Colorado, and only dogs and miniature horses qualified. So no cats.

Maybe Janice could take her little bevy of protestors to the state capitol and leave me alone for a while.

I was so happy I could've kissed Mason Maxwell. (Well, maybe not that happy. I still found him very off-putting. Jamie could've though. She was all googly eyed over him.)

"So that settles it then." I sat back, wondering why he'd driven all this way out here just to tell us that.

"Not exactly."

"What do you mean?"

Mason Maxwell leveled a gaze at me that had me feeling decidedly foolish. "There is the court of law and then there is the court of public opinion. You already saw the damage Ms. Fletcher did with that newspaper article about how you wanted to keep locals out of your store."

"But that turned out fine because Jamie just gave them all free cinnamon rolls, so now we have more customers than ever."

🐾🐾🐾 238 🐾🐾🐾

"You lucked out last time. But will you the next time Janice Fletcher gets her nephew to write a smear article about this place? The woman is relentless. Other women knit, Janice Fletcher makes it her mission to destroy people."

That didn't sound good.

Jamie drummed her fingers on the table. "So she won't back down even though the law is on our side."

"No. I do not believe she will. Once she realizes this attempt failed, she will try to come at you some other way."

"What other way?" I asked. She'd already protested and served us with this fake letter. What was left?

He shook his head. "I don't know. All I know is that Janice Fletcher does not quit. So if there is anything, anything at all that you have been letting slide, now is the time to fix it. You do not want to have any sort of weakness she can exploit."

"What is her deal?" I demanded. "Seriously. It sounds like the world would be a much better place if she'd just drop dead."

Mason Maxwell leveled his gray-eyed stare at me. "Ms. Carver I would suggest that you keep any wishes for someone to drop dead to yourself. Our conversations are protected by attorney-client privilege, but it is simply a good habit to adopt to never publicly wish for the death of another person."

I snorted. "Like I'm going to kill her. Honestly. Plus, she looks perfectly healthy to me. That old bat will be torturing people for decades."

"You saw with your grandfather that perception matters more than reality. Do not make the same mistake he did."

"Fine. I hope she lives a long and healthy life of making everyone around her miserable. And I hope we're still in the midst of cat and dog wars a decade from now. Happy?"

"Maggie." Jamie frowned at me. "He's just trying to help."

I pressed my lips together and nodded. I knew that, but a part of me was very much done with his condescending attitude. "Okay then. We'll make sure everything is buttoned up and perfect. Thank you for coming out here and giving us such useful advice."

I stood up.

Neither Mason Maxwell nor Jamie joined me.

With a small huff I gathered up the empty plates and took them to the kitchen. Let them do whatever they were doing. I needed to look for any signs of weakness that Janice Fletcher could exploit.

CHAPTER 11

The whole way home I tried to figure out exactly what Janice Fletcher's next move was going to be. And just how much of a spark there'd been between Jamie and Mason Maxwell. And how much that did or did not upset me. Of course I wanted my best friend to be happy, but Mason Maxwell?

Only as I opened the front door did I remember that my grandpa had invited Matt over for dinner. There he was, seated on the brown couch in the living room, Fancy curled up at his side. He looked more at home there than I ever did. And worse yet, Fancy didn't even bother to get down to come see me when I walked in. She barely lifted her head off her paws.

You know it's a bad day when even your dog is mad at you.

"Hey, Maggie." Matt toasted me with the beer in his hand.

"Hey. Forgot you were coming over tonight. Sorry I'm so late." My grandpa came out of the kitchen with a big casserole dish in his hands and I gave him a quick kiss on the cheek. "I really am. But this couldn't wait."

He'd set the dining room table with my grandma's best china, but no wine glasses this time. Seems it was going to be a beer kind of night. (Which was honestly just fine with me. I'll drink a glass of wine, no problem, but when given the choice I usually go for a nice porter or brown ale of some sort instead of wine.)

"Can I help?" I asked.

"You can grab the salad from the kitchen," he grumbled, clearly not happy with me.

I grabbed the salad and a bottle of ranch dressing. If Matt wanted something else he was just going to have to suck it up because ranch was the only dressing choice in our household. We didn't even have vinegar around to make oil and vinegar.

By the time I made it to the table they were both seated and waiting for me. So was Fancy. She'd sat herself down by my chair and proceeded to drool a nice little puddle onto the floor. She's not much of a drooler under normal circumstances, but put food near her and she becomes a faucet.

I set the salad and dressing on the table and turned back towards the kitchen. "Start without me."

"What are you doing, Maggie May? Everything's already on the table."

"I forgot Fancy's sharing plate."

"Got one right here," Matt called.

I turned to see him set a small plate in front of her and drop a piece of turkey from the casserole on it. As my heart did a little flip I wondered why he had to be so good with dogs. Or at least with my dog. It wasn't fair.

My grandpa grunted. He did not like the fact that I fed Fancy from the table. In his world dogs were supposed to only eat dog food. And live outside. Or, at most, come into the laundry area. They were most definitely not supposed to have their own plate at meals. Nor were they supposed to sleep on the couch or have five different dog beds. But if I had to choose between making Fancy happy and making my grandpa happy, well, Fancy was going to win out each and every time. At least on the small things.

Matt, ever the diplomat, asked, "So, why were you late tonight? You said it couldn't be helped?"

"Two words. Janice Fletcher. Do you know that woman showed up at the barkery today claiming that her cat Pookums is an emotional support animal?"

Matt and my grandpa both laughed.

"It's not funny. I cannot have cats in that store."

"Why not?" Matt asked. "It's just one cat. And, no offense, but you're pretty slow most of the time. I figure you'd welcome the extra customer."

I glared at him. All I wanted was for one frickin' person to agree with me.

"Just one cat, huh? Did you know she wants to let her cat roam free? That's not even sanitary. And if a dog goes after her cat that could be dangerous. I'd probably get sued. Not to mention I am very, very allergic to cats. It's a dog barkery, for crying out loud, not a cat café."

My grandpa studied me across the table. "So Janice Fletcher has her sights on you, does she?"

"Seems so. And Mason Maxwell said she's not the type to give up until she's ruined us."

"True. She's taken more than one business in this county down. It doesn't help that that nephew of hers is willing to print any slanderous story she asks him to."

He spent the next ten minutes telling us horror stories

about Janice Fletcher. Seems she'd even caused one poor store owner to be beaten by a customer who believed her nephew when he printed a story insinuating the man was a sex trafficker.

A sex trafficker? In Baker Valley, Colorado? Population not big enough for that sort of thing? I don't think so.

"It sounds to me like the world would be a better place if she'd just drop dead and die." I stabbed at a piece of carrot on my plate and sent it shooting across the table. My grandpa caught it and threw it under the table to Fancy.

"That's a little redundant, isn't it?" Matt teased. "I'd figure it would be enough for her to just drop dead."

I shoved a forkful of food into my mouth and glared him down as I chewed on it.

"Ouch. You're in a serious mood tonight."

"I just can't get a break. I mean, I moved up here to take care of him." I nodded towards my grandpa. "And he doesn't want my help."

"That's right." My grandpa nodded.

"I opened a store with my best friend but now she's all caught up in finding someone and getting married. And then every time I think I'm going to make some progress in turning the barkery into a real business something like this happens."

"Jamie's looking to settle down, huh?" Matt looked thoughtful as he took his next bite of food.

"Don't tell her I told you that!"

"She have anyone in mind?"

Was he seriously interested in her? I mean, I wouldn't blame him if he was, but...Ah! Life. It was not being very kind to me.

"I don't know. She doesn't want to talk to me about it."

I glared at the table, not able to look at him as I added, "If you want to throw your hat in the ring, you'd probably have a pretty good shot. You'd certainly be a better match for her than Lucas Dean or Mason Maxwell."

"Mason Maxwell?" My grandpa snorted. "Well, he does have money, I'll give him that."

Fortunately, the conversation turned to just how much of the valley Mason's family controlled compared to how much of the valley Janice Fletcher's family controlled. It seems they were always warring back and forth, one or the other trying to get the upper hand. Had been for close to two hundred years.

After we'd finished up our meal Matt helped me take the dishes into the kitchen while my grandpa went to fetch the Scrabble board. He's obsessed with that game. And last time we'd played Matt had won, which my grandpa could not let stand unchallenged.

I scooped the remaining casserole into a plastic container and handed it to Matt. "Here. Better than whatever awful food you're fixing yourself, I'm sure."

"Hey, now. Canned tuna and potato chips is a perfectly good meal."

I shuddered. "Please tell me you've at least discovered the wonders of microwave meals? A lot of them actually have vegetables in them, you know."

He shrugged one shoulder. "Vegetables are over-rated."

"You do realize that you don't have to live the life of the lonely pathetic bachelor, right? I'd bet that woman the other day isn't the only one trying to fix you up with a daughter or a niece or a granddaughter. Play your cards right you could get a lot of good meals out of it."

"Yeah, but they'd all come with expectations. And awkward conversations." He set the container on the counter. "Only reason I come over here for dinner is because you were so clear about how, what was it? There are more important things in life than being some man's wife?"

I almost softened that statement, but stopped myself in time. "You know, that German woman at the barkery, Greta? She's like Little Miss Matchmaker. I'd be careful you don't let her know you're single or she'll be trying to set you up, too."

"She's going to find you someone?" He leaned against the counter, crossing his arms.

"So she says. Of course, her idea of setting me up is finding me a nice, old man with lots of money who will die soon. She thinks that's the kind of man who makes an ideal *first* husband. I can marry for love later."

He laughed. It was a deep, rich sound that made my toes tingle.

I bit my lip. "So why is it you don't take anyone up on all those other invitations? Not looking to settle down?"

"I can't exactly make plans with a woman when I'm not sure where I want to be a year from now."

"So not planning on sticking around?" My stomach dropped a little at the thought of him moving away.

He rubbed at his chin. "I don't know. I mean, it made sense to come back here after I got out of the service and my dad died. There was a lot to take care of and the valley was really the only place I'd ever called home. Bob offered me the position as a cop and it all just fell into place. Maybe too easily, you know?"

"So if you don't stay here, what would you do?"

"I might re-enlist. They've offered me a pretty good bonus."

It was all I could do not to step forward and grab his arms and tell him not to go, but my grandpa saved me from making a fool of myself when he called for us from the living room.

As Matt went to join him I hung back, trying to control the emotions coursing through me. I knew if I tried to date him it would be a disaster, but I didn't want to lose him either. It wasn't often I felt that little spark with someone. I shook myself. Hard.

I had priorities. And falling in love was not one of them.

"Anyone want ice cream?" I shouted.

"Yeah, give me a bowl," my grandpa shouted back. "Matt? You want some? Maggie May, make it two."

"Alright. Will do."

By the time I'd scooped out three bowls of ice cream and taken them into the dining room, I was back under control. That didn't mean I wasn't thinking about Matt leaving to re-enlist for the rest of the night.

I was.

CHAPTER 12

The next morning I was NOT in a good mood. I wanted Janice Fletcher to die a horrible fiery death and I wanted Officer Matthew Barnes to stay in Baker Valley and smile at me with that great smile of his and come over for dinner with my grandpa and yet not actually ask me to make an emotional commitment I wasn't capable of making.

To make myself feel better I'd decided it was about time Fancy was allowed to come back to work with me, but she was so wound up by the chance to get out of the house and maybe see Lulu—Jamie's golden retriever puppy—that she wouldn't sit down the whole drive to the barkery and kept crying right in my ear.

So when I picked up a copy of the *Baker Valley Gazette* early that morning and saw the headline, *How Clean Is Your Favorite Restaurant?* I was ready to hurt someone. Especially because it was accompanied by a photo of a bakery box with our logo on it sitting on the top of a grimy pile of trash. The article itself toed the line—there was no actual mention of our store—but that photo sure implied a lot of things it shouldn't.

After the third customer walked in and glanced around the place as if looking for a mouse to scurry out from the corner, I'd had it. "Jamie. You're on your own for a bit. I'll be back."

"Wait. Where are you going?"

I waved the paper at her. "To deal with this."

"No! Let Mason Maxwell deal with it. You stay here."

I shook my head. "They had no right."

"And he'll deal with it. There will be a retraction in the paper tomorrow morning and probably one up on the website this afternoon."

"Doesn't matter. The damage is done. We should sue for lost sales."

Jamie shook her head. "We don't need to sue anyone, Maggie."

I started towards the door again. Jamie was my best friend and I loved her to pieces, but sometimes she was just a little too forgiving.

"Maggie. Promise me you won't confront Peter Nielsen. Let Mason handle this."

"Promise." That was easy enough to do. Peter Nielsen wasn't my target. I was going to the source: Janice Fletcher.

I shoved the door open, the bells at the top making a discordant jangle and stormed to my van, muttering to myself about how the world really would be a better place if some people would just up and die already.

I'd never been to Janice Fletcher's house, but that's the interesting thing about living in a small town. (Or in this case a series of small towns.) You pretty much know where all the major players live. And Janice Fletcher's house was hard to miss. It was a tactless monstrosity that dominated the hillside just outside of Bakerstown. She'd cut down all the trees on her lot so that it looked like some sort of blight had hit the area. The house itself was hideous. It was a giant pimple on the face of the world.

Just like its owner.

I banged on her door, not caring that it wasn't even seven in the morning yet. If she could show up to protest my store that early, she could answer her damned door.

She finally answered on the fifth knock. She had her hair up in rollers and a tatty red robe on. Her house slippers were bulky things with little cat's heads on the end. And she had Pookums in her arms. Well, that's what I thought at least. Until I stepped into her house and realized that there were at least five other cats in that house. They meowed at us in some sort of crazy cat cacophony.

"What's up with your cats?"

"It's breakfast time. You interrupted my feeding them."

They wound their way around her legs and mine, crying out for their food. I sneezed. "Well go ahead and feed them then."

"No. You'll be gone soon enough."

I glanced around the place. There was a double-spiral staircase leading to an upstairs balcony. The main entranceway stretched towards an extremely large living room. At the far end of the entryway was an open doorway with what looked to be stairs leading downward. A large dining room was off to my right with a kitchen barely visible at the end.

The house would've been nice inside if it hadn't been forced to suffer from Janice Fletcher's bad taste. Honestly, some colors just do not go together.

The cats continued to cry, growing louder and louder as they wrapped themselves around her feet and mine. I heard a crashing sound from the direction of the kitchen. Yet another cat? How many did one person need?

(I know. Cats are wonderful and lovely and why wouldn't you have ten million of them if you could. Yeah, yeah.)

I was already regretting the anger that had brought me to her door, but it was too late to back down. "That article this morning was you, wasn't it?"

"Of course it was. And the health inspection will be, too." She gave me such a nasty smile I wanted to punch her teeth out.

(I swear I'm not normally violent like that, but that woman just pushed all of my buttons.)

"Jamie and I keep a clean shop. There's nothing for an inspector to find."

She stroked Pookum's back as she stepped closer to me. "I wouldn't be so sure…"

I sneezed and stepped back. "Did you do something to our store?"

She just smiled at me.

"Did you? What did you do? Why do you have it in for us?" I wanted to grab her and shake her. But I didn't. I swear, I did not lay a single hand on her.

"You should leave now. I have to feed the cats."

"You did something. What?"

"Close the door on your way out." She turned and sauntered towards the kitchen.

I'll admit, there was a small part of me that wanted to run after her and beat her sanctimonious brains in. But I didn't.

I swear.

Instead, I raced out the door and ran to my van. I needed to get back to the barkery as soon as possible. I needed to figure out what Janice Fletcher had done to our store before the health inspector arrived, because you just knew after that article that we'd be getting a surprise inspection.

I was driving so fast as I left I almost side-swiped a green sedan that had just turned onto her block. Right after that I had to slam on my brakes as a man jogged in front of my car wearing a hoodie with the hood up and long sweat pants. I wasn't a big fan of being observed when I exercised either, but that man was taking it to an extreme.

CHAPTER 13

I was almost back to the store when I realized I'd handled that all wrong.

(That's my curse. I act in the moment and then think it through later and second-guess everything. There's always a better way things could've gone. Too bad I can never think of the right thing to say or do in the actual moment.)

I whipped a U-turn and headed back to Janice's house, but got stuck behind some touristy RV that was going at least five under the speed limit. As I quietly muttered to myself about what they should really test for on driver's tests and how some people should simply not be allowed to drive, I tried to think of what I was going to say when I got back to Janice's house.

I mean, she clearly had it in for me. How exactly did I expect to convince her to let up? For one horrible moment I wondered if there was someone else I could point her towards. People like that always need someone to go after, so chances are she wasn't going to leave me alone until she'd either destroyed me or found a better target.

But that wasn't nice. No one else deserved to go through what I was.

I sat outside her house for a long, long moment wondering whether it was worth it to even attempt to reason with her. But finally I pulled myself out of the car and walked up her front steps. I had to try. It wasn't just me this was impacting. It was Jamie and our store and Fancy.

For their sakes I had to solve the puzzle of Janice Fletcher.

🐾 🐾 🐾

The front door was slightly ajar when I reached it, but I figured that was my fault. She hadn't walked me out, after all, so I must not have pulled it closed tightly enough.

I pushed the door open and stepped inside. "Janice? Janice, it's Maggie. Can we talk?"

There was a loud crashing sound from the direction of the kitchen. I headed in that direction through the dining room, but all I found was a wet cast iron pan in the sink and a large plate on the counter with cats huddled around it eating. Whoever had put down their food wasn't the most fastidious person in the world, that's for sure. It looked like someone had just opened about five cans of cat food and dumped them in the middle of that plate without any care or concern.

Odd, but who am I to judge how someone else feeds their pets.

"Janice?" I slowly made my way toward the living room, listening for any sign of where she might be. Knowing my luck she was in the bathroom or shower or something equally embarrassing and awkward.

There was a creaking sound from the direction of the doorway to the basement, so I moved in that direction. "Janice? It's Maggie Carver. Remember me? I was just here. Can we talk?"

I walked through the living room, still seeing no sign of her, but when I turned towards the door to the basement, I saw one of her cat slippers in the doorway. I stepped closer. "Janice?"

One of the cats brushed past me and made its way down the stairs. I heard that creaking sound again. Must be a bad step.

I moved to the top of the stairs and looked down into the darkness, but I couldn't see anything. Not really wanting to, but compelled to do so, I turned the light on.

And saw Janice Fletcher at the bottom of the stairs, a cat sitting on her chest meowing loudly.

I knew I should call 9-1-1. Maybe she was still alive. (Although, no. I won't go into details but it was pretty clear she hadn't survived the fall down those steps.) Still, someone should. The woman was dead after all, and she couldn't just stay down there forever.

But…

And this is horrible. And, yes, it was a mistake. But see, the last time I'd called the cops when I found a dead body my grandpa had ended up almost going to prison for a murder he didn't commit. And now there I was, in Janice Fletcher's house, with a reason to want her dead, and absolutely no alibi because I'd been there both right before and right after she died.

And it was probably just a frickin' accident caused by one of those ridiculous cats of hers or those cat slippers she insisted on wearing. And all that would happen if I called the cops was I'd have to explain what I was doing there and they'd be bound to wonder if it was really an accident with me found practically standing over her dead body.

But I figured if someone like a neighbor or her nephew were to drop by later and just find her they'd easily see the truth of the matter, right?

I know. But that's the way I figured it in the moment. I told you—I have my best thoughts after things happen, not during.

I sneezed and heard a loud crash from the basement. Probably another one of her cats—they were all over the place—but that decided me. I needed to just get the heck out of there. I did not want someone coming along and finding me at the top of Janice Fletcher's stairs with her dead body at the bottom. Plus, if I didn't leave soon I was going to be sneezing and sniffling for the rest of the day.

Not to mention, the whole thing was just creeping me out. Big, dark house. Lots of cats. Dead body. It was a good opening scene to a horror movie if you asked me.

I know. I should've called the cops.

And if you ever find a dead body, definitely do so. But I didn't.

CHAPTER 14

I turned the light back off and carefully let myself out the front door, using the bottom of my t-shirt to grip the handle so I wouldn't leave any prints. And this time I made sure it had actually closed properly. Didn't need all of those cats out wandering the neighborhood. (They looked like indoor cats to me, although don't ask me why I thought that about them.)

As I walked towards the van I looked around to see if there was anyone around who could testify that they'd seen me—not that I knew what I'd do if there was, I wasn't a killer after all—but I saw no one.

I drove back to the store, grateful this time to be stuck behind some slow-moving tourist. Halfway there the shakes set in and I wondered if I'd made the right decision. It wasn't too late. I could still call it in, but what would I say?

"Yeah, sorry. Found a dead body. Not the person who killed them. Decided to leave rather than tell you about it. Now I'm feeling a little guilty about that choice, so figured I'd better let you know so you can swing by there before her cats eat her face."

I know, the cats had just been fed, but all those horrible stories of single women who'd died alone at home and been eaten by their cats were running through my head. (Okay, so maybe that's only ever happened to one person, but in my mind there were hundreds of them.)

I chewed on my thumbnail as I wondered if anyone would even miss Janice Fletcher. Would they miss her enough to swing by her house? If they did, would they go in? Would they look in the basement?

I parked in front of the barkery, still not sure what to do. I thought about calling Mason Maxwell. He was my lawyer, after all. But there was a foolish part of me that was just hoping it would all go away. Janice Fletcher was dead, which meant no more harassment. Someone would find her eventually, I was sure. And then it would all be over.

Right?

Yeah, no.

CHAPTER 15

"Where did you go?" Jamie asked as soon as I walked through the door.

"I just drove around a bit." I set my purse down in the office, downed a couple of Benadryl, and snagged a cinnamon roll that was on a cooling tray.

(I know, I lied to her and that wasn't very nice, but Jamie has a moral center that would've demanded calling the cops, so it was better to just not involve her. I don't lie often, if that's any consolation.)

I took a moment to savor the spicy sweet taste of the cinnamon roll while I pondered whether I could convince Jamie to start making chocolate croissants like you find in France and, if I could, whether I would be okay with the twenty-plus pounds I'd put on as a result. I was pretty sure that was an okay tradeoff. Life is meant to be lived after all.

"I've been thinking," I said. "I bet that article triggers a health inspection. We should clean this place. Top to bottom. Inside out."

Jamie glanced towards the front where our latest shop assistant was ringing up a customer. "This is the busiest time of the morning."

"Not at the barkery. You guys keep handling the customers, I'll do the cleaning."

"You? Are you okay? You hate to clean."

"I know. But needs must and all."

I really do hate cleaning, as some of my college roommates learned the hard way. I'm not filthy or anything. I have a very sensitive nose so anything that stinks does not last. But it's just not something I take joy in and I have a high dust tolerance. Or so it would seem given the complaints of those who do seem to enjoy cleaning.

Anyway. I printed out a copy of the health inspection form and got to work. And I almost enjoyed it. It was nice to have some mindless physical activity to distract me from the mess of that morning. Not that I wasn't thinking about it, just that I at least had something to do with my hands while I thought.

About half an hour later Mason Maxwell walked in looking like some big town billionaire instead of the small-town lawyer he really was. I bet the man didn't even own a pair of tennies. Or hiking boots.

Jamie beamed at him from behind the counter. "Hey, Mason. What can I get you?"

Mason, huh? Like they were good buddies or something. I wondered what he'd do if I called him Mason. Probably frown at me like I'd broken some unspoken rule of etiquette. Not that I wanted to be on a first-name basis with him anyway.

He smiled at her. It almost made him approachable. "Let me try one of those cinnamon rolls I've heard so much about."

"Absolutely. And a coffee?"

I knew that tone of voice. My friend was most definitely interested. I sighed. When was she going to date a man who'd actually be a good choice for her?

I scrubbed at the table I was working on a little harder than was necessary as I wondered what had brought him by. Had Jamie called him about the article? Or had he come by on his own?

"Mr. Maxwell." I set my bleach bucket under the counter as Jamie went to the back to specially prepare his cinnamon roll,

"Ms. Carver."

"I was meaning to call you today. Did you see that article in the paper about sanitation issues at local restaurants?"

"No, I hadn't had a chance to read the paper yet this morning."

Jamie handed him his cinnamon roll. "Maggie, why don't you let him eat his breakfast before you start in on that?"

"Because the sooner Peter Nielsen issues a retraction, the better."

"It's not like he named us."

"No. He just included a picture of one of our bakery boxes right next to the headline." I slammed a copy of the paper down on the counter for Mason Maxwell to see.

Jamie's competent as competent can be and completely unruffleable, but she's also not one for open conflict. Even when it's warranted like it was this time.

Mason quickly scanned the text, noted the picture, and nodded. "That is definitely worthy of a retraction. I will give him a visit as soon as I finish here." He took a bite of his cinnamon roll and closed his eyes for a moment in pleasure. "You are an excellent cook, Jamie."

"Thank you." Jamie blushed and ducked her head. I'm pretty sure she even batted her eyelashes at him.

I decided it was time for me to get to work in the kitchen. It's not that I objected to her liking Mason Maxwell. (Although I couldn't really see it myself. He's so…stiff.) But I just hate to see the way women contort themselves around a man they like. All of a sudden it's batted eyes, girly giggles, and ducked heads. I know it's just biology at work, but doesn't mean I have to enjoy watching it.

(And, no, I'm not immune to doing it myself, which kind of makes it worse, really. To hate it and do it anyway and then hate yourself for doing it. Not that I really hate myself ever, but you know what I mean.)

Anyway.

An hour later when I checked back on Jamie, Mason was gone and she was in conversation with some well-dressed man I'd never seen before, both of them leaning on the counter and talking softly. The man was tall, ice-blond, and dressed all in black, right down to his fancy shoes which looked like a black leather version of the ones Mason Maxwell wore.

Ugh. It was contagious. Before I knew it the whole town was going to be overrun by men in pressed slacks, soft sweaters, and fancy shoes. Honestly, what was wrong with blue jeans?

"Maggie, this is Don. Don this is my co-owner Maggie. Don's in town for business for a few days. Said we might see him around since he'll need a place to hang out that isn't a dingy little hotel room."

Like this man was ever going to stay in a dingy little

hotel room. He probably had a suite at the resort. Or an Airbnb rental that was five-hundred a night.

"Nice to meet you, Don. Mind if I steal my business partner away for a minute?"

"No. Not at all."

He made his way to a corner table on the café side as I turned to Jamie. "Is Mr. Maxwell going to talk to Peter Nielsen for us?"

"Of course. He said he would."

"Just making sure."

"Why don't you like him? I mean, he's smart. He's funny. He's good-looking."

Mason Maxwell, funny? And good-looking? I mean, sure, if you like Sean Connery in his older incarnation and it isn't about the accent. But…

"He's a little old, don't you think?"

"He's not even fifty. And aren't you the one always telling me I need to improve my taste in men?"

"Well, yeah." I glanced towards Don who was trying to listen in without listening in. "But someone like that guy over there was more what I had in mind."

She winked at me. "No rule that says I can't date them both. It's just a little crush, after all. No point pinning my hopes on just one guy who may or may not be interested. Speaking of…" She left me to go join Don at his table.

As I watched them laugh and lean close, I wondered what it's like to be that person. The one that can see the whole dating world as a smorgasbord to be sampled from. Someone who doesn't mind when they find that yet another person is not to their liking after all. Or is but isn't interested. Someone who just lets it all roll past them and enjoys it for what it is.

Me, I take all of it far too seriously. Partially because they don't always shake off when I find they're not what I wanted and then it's just awkward and uncomfortable when they keep calling and won't go away. Or worse, just showing up. Only way to avoid that is to date complete strangers which has its own set of risks. (Seriously, I watch way too many true crime shows. And police procedurals. I'm sure the majority of men are not stalkers or crazy rapists, but watch enough of those shows and you start to wonder.)

But enough about my dysfunctions.

By the time the health inspector showed up for his "surprise" inspection a couple hours later—right in the middle of our lunch rush, I might add—we were ready and waiting and passed with flying colors.

It's good to be prepared.

Unfortunately, when the cops showed up two hours after that? I was anything but prepared to see them.

CHAPTER 16

Matt walked through the door first, Officer Clark right behind him. I knew it wasn't a social visit by the way Officer Clark's hand rested on his gun as he glared at me. What did he think I was going to do? Pull a shotgun from under the counter and shout, "You're never going to take me alive?"

Please.

"Ms. Carver." Matt stopped about five feet away. Ouch, that hurt.

"Officer Barnes. Officer Clark. How can I help you?"

"Were you aware that Janice Fletcher is dead?"

Tricky question, that. If I answered yes, then I was admitting I'd been in her house and seen her dead body and done nothing about it. If I answered no and someone had seen me then I would have started off what was clearly a police investigation on a very, very bad foot.

I knew what Mason Maxwell would say: "Shut your mouth and call your lawyer." But since when did I listen to good common sense?

Jamie came over. "What's wrong? What's going on?"

Matt stepped closer. "Ms. Carver. Were you aware

that Janice Fletcher is dead?"

Officer Clark sighed in disgust. "You know she is. The neighbor saw her running out of there."

I met Matt's blue eyes. "I didn't kill her."

"But you knew she was dead?"

I shrugged slightly before turning to Jamie. "I need you to call Mason Maxwell for me." I turned back to Matt. "Am I under arrest? Or do you just need to question me?"

"Maggie…"

Officer Clark stepped forward. "We should put her under arrest."

I ignored him and kept my attention focused on Matt. "I'll meet you at the station in half an hour if I'm not under arrest. I didn't kill her. I'm not sure anyone did. But I'm not going to say more without my lawyer present."

Matt nodded. "We'll meet you at the station."

Officer Clark sent me one last snarly look but at least they both left without handcuffing me and dragging me after them.

Jamie stepped closer. "Maggie, what was that about?"

"You heard him. Janice Fletcher is dead. And they obviously suspect me."

She grabbed my arm as I tried to step past her. "Did you do it?"

"Do you really think I'm capable of that?"

"I think anyone's capable of anything if the circumstances are right. But if you did do it, I don't think you set out to do it."

"Oh that's a comfort." I pushed past her. "For the record, I would never think you could kill someone."

I grabbed my purse and leashed up Fancy. "Call Mason Maxwell. Tell him to meet me at the jail. I'll swing by my house and tell my grandpa what's happening when I drop Fancy off."

🐾 🐾 🐾

My grandpa was none too pleased when I told him what had brought me home so early, but I told him not to worry it would all be cleared up soon enough. I figured Janice Fletcher had just tripped on one of her eight million cats. Only question was, could anyone prove it?

I figured there had to be some difference in the injuries someone would suffer if they'd tripped down a flight of stairs instead of been shoved down them. It always seems to work the opposite way on those crime shows where they eventually determine that the husband's story of his wife's unfortunate fall down the stairs with her laundry basket was just made up crap.

I certainly hoped so. Because if not clearly someone had seen me running from her house. And not like I had an alibi. I'd been there right before she died *and* right after she died, which meant I might as well have been standing over her body the whole time.

I sat on the floor and buried my face in Fancy's fur, but she quickly pulled away. She loves me, but not enough to let me snuggle all over her. (What can I say, we're a lot alike.)

"I have to go." I pushed myself to my feet. "With any luck I'll be home for dinner. If I'm not, you know where to find me."

My grandpa reached for the non-existent pack of cigarettes in his shirt pocket and then cussed when he remembered he no longer smoked. I grabbed his hand.

It was trembling slightly. "Promise me two things. Well, three."

"What?"

"First, you won't smoke because of this." I didn't want to be the cause for him taking it up again, and I still remembered how he'd gone for the pack of cigarettes he kept stashed in his workroom when they came to arrest him.

"Fine. What else?"

"If they do put me in jail, you'll take care of Fancy for me. I'm sure Matt'll help if you need it, but please, take care of her. She's my world."

He nodded. "And three?"

"You'll take care of yourself."

He snorted. "I've been taking care of myself for eighty-two years. I think I can do so for a little while longer."

I gave him a quick, fierce hug. "I hope so."

He grabbed my chin and looked me in the eye. "You better be home for dinner, young lady."

"I'll try." I gave him another hug and rushed out the door before I could start crying.

I'd never messed up that bad in my life and I wasn't sure how I was going to fix it. But I had to somehow, because my grandpa and Fancy needed me, whether either one realized it or not.

CHAPTER 17

Mason Maxwell was waiting for me outside the police station. The station is so close to my grandpa's house I'd decided to walk, so I had a good long time to watch him as I slowly came closer. He was not amused.

"Mr. Maxwell. Jamie reached you I see?"

He nodded. "What is this about?"

"She didn't tell you?"

"I want to hear it from you."

I glanced towards the single-story sandstone building. I could see the receptionist sitting behind her desk, Matt and Officer Clark behind her, watching us through the glass doors.

"Janice Fletcher is dead. I didn't kill her. I honestly think she tripped on one of her cats. But I was in her house this morning around the time of her death."

"Before or after?"

I bit my lip. "Both. But not during."

He stepped closer, his eyes flashing. "What?"

"I went to yell at her about the article in the paper. And then I left. But when I was almost back to the store I decided to go back to her house and see if I could reason with her. She was alive when I left the first time and dead when I returned. Her body was at the bottom of the basement stairs."

"Did you touch the body?"

I shook my head.

"Did you call the cops?"

I shook my head again. "They said a neighbor saw me leaving. I assume that was the first time, when she was still alive."

Mason Maxwell visibly worked to control his anger. It was fascinating to watch, because he was clearly a man of intense passions who managed to rein them in rather than spew them all over the world like I always seem to.

When he was fully under control he held the outer door open for me, ever the gentleman even when he clearly thought his client was a fool. "Best get this over with."

I turned to him before opening the inner door. "Do you want me to answer their questions? Or refuse to speak? What would you like me to do?"

He took a deep, deep breath. "I would like you to not confront people you have publicly stated you wish were dead, but we're past that aren't we?"

"Yes, we are. So what do I do now?"

He pinched the bridge of his nose, clearly thinking through the alternatives. "Officer Barnes likes you?"

"We're friends."

"And they said someone saw you at her house?"

I nodded.

"Then I want you to tell them everything. Be as open and honest as you can be. That may save you from jail, but don't count on it."

A Crazy Cat Lady and Canine Crunchies

With that cheery thought, I opened the inner door and stepped through to begin my very first (but not last, sadly) police interrogation.

❧ ❧ ❧

Matt and Officer Clark led me past the main portion of the police station where four desks were located, two on each side facing each other, and past two offices with windows that looked out on them.

We went down a short hallway and into a small room. I'd been there before when my grandpa was arrested. It's where Matt, my grandpa, and I had eaten dinner. Somehow I hadn't noticed how cold it was that first visit.

Nor had I noticed the pervasive smell of body odor and stale cigarettes that was only faintly masked by some astringent cleaner.

Nor had I noticed how stiff and uncomfortable the plastic chairs were.

You'd think that making someone as relaxed and comfortable as you could get them would make them more forthcoming, but it seems not. Because I don't think I've ever seen an interrogation room that looks welcoming.

Me, if it were my choice, I'd set up a room like a plush therapist's office with a big mirror on the wall facing the suspect and put two comfortable couches across from each other. I'd make the suspect feel like I was there to help them through this ordeal they found themselves in. *Just let it go. Just tell me what you did and you'll feel so much better.*

Guess that's why I'm not a cop. Or a psychiatrist. Or a priest for that matter.

Matt pulled up the chair directly across from me while Officer Clark paced behind him even though there was another seat for him to sit in.

Mason Maxwell wiped his seat off with a real, live handkerchief before he took a seat next to me. He looked like a fish out of water in his fancy clothes and his country-club manners. I wondered if he'd considered refusing to help me, but it didn't matter at that point. He was there and I was his client and he was going to do what he could.

Matt pressed the button to record the conversation and then introduced himself, Officer Clark, Mason Maxwell, and me. He even advised me of my rights. I could see it was killing him to be there. To think that I'd killed this woman. But he was a man of duty. He'd go where the clues led him, even if they led him to me.

"Ms. Carver. You're aware of your rights. Are you willing to proceed with this interview at this time?" He glanced towards Mason Maxwell.

"We can proceed. I have nothing to hide." I met his stare and held it, willing him to believe in my innocence.

Mason Maxwell placed his hand on the table between us. "My client would like to give a full accounting of her actions this morning. I'd ask that you let her do so before you ask any questions." Smart. Otherwise things would probably deteriorate long before I could get it all out.

Officer Clark paced the room like a restless panther, but Matt simply nodded. Clearly no need to ask who was good cop, bad cop here. "Whenever you're ready."

I took a deep breath and closed my eyes for a moment, trying to marshal my thoughts. I was going to tell them the truth and all of it, but I didn't need to make myself look like an incredibly horrible person while I was doing so.

A Crazy Cat Lady and Canine Crunchies

I laced my fingers together and set my hands on the table before I started. "Over the past couple of weeks Janice Fletcher has been targeting my business. She has a cat, Pookums, and she wanted to bring it with her into my barkery, which is a bakery for dogs. I told her she couldn't. It wasn't safe for her cat nor was it sanitary to have her cat running loose in our store. She then led a protest of my business and threatened me and my customers until we had to call the cops."

So far all I was doing was giving the cops about ten different motives for killing her. Not like they didn't know it already, though.

"After her protest failed she obtained a certificate that declared her cat an emotional support animal. She used that to try to force me to allow her and her cat into my store, but my lawyer reviewed the certificate and the law and informed me that it didn't give her the right to be there."

My throat felt dry and I licked my lips wishing someone would offer me a Coke. I'd have even settled for water at that point, but none was forthcoming, so I coughed a little and continued on as best I could.

"Her nephew runs the local paper, and this morning there was an article in there about restaurants with poor sanitation. It included a picture of a bakery box with our logo next to the headline. The article didn't name us specifically, but it was clear we were the target. And it was clear to me who was behind that article."

I paused to gather my thoughts. Matt hadn't taken his eyes off my face the whole time I was speaking. Officer Clark had stopped his pacing and was standing off to the side, arms crossed, glaring me down like I was worse than the scum on the bottom of his shoe. I quickly turned my attention back to Matt.

"I was very upset by the article. I had been told that Janice Fletcher is capable of destroying people when she decides to do so and I believed that article was another attempt by her to attack my business. So I went over to her place to confront her. I'm not sure exactly what time it was, but I remember thinking to myself that if she could protest my store before seven a.m. then she could darn well answer her door at that time, too."

Mason Maxwell coughed slightly and I glanced at him. He pinched his fingers together in what I assumed was his sign for stick to the facts. But I needed Matt to believe me. Which means I needed him to understand what I'd done and why I'd been there.

I told them about that initial confrontation with Janice and about her cat slippers and how hard those things can be to walk in. (I'd know. My mother, bless her, had bought me more than one pair like them over the years.) I also made sure to point out to them how the cats were meowing and hungry and wrapping themselves around her legs and mine. And how that door to the downstairs had been open when I arrived.

Officer Clark interrupted even though he wasn't supposed to. "Let me see your pants."

I lifted my leg above the edge of the table and sneezed. I'm not normally *that* allergic to cats, but Pookums was a Persian and that particular breed just does me in.

"Ha." He said. "Proof you were there."

I stared at him a long, long moment but refrained from pointing out how my confession that I was there was probably even better evidence in that respect.

"So anyway…" I continued.

I told them how I'd left to get back to the barkery and warn Jamie about the pending health inspection but how I'd changed my mind and turned back around to try once more to reason with Ms. Fletcher. And how I'd found the front door slightly ajar when I returned, so had entered the house looking for her.

"I saw one of her slippers at the top of the stairs to the basement and when I turned on the light for the stairs, I saw her at the bottom. One of her cats was down there with her and she was clearly not moving. I…I thought about calling the cops," I glanced at Officer Clark, "but the last time I found a body and did that my grandpa ended up in jail for a murder he didn't commit. Plus, I thought the whole thing was a terrible accident. That she'd tripped on one of her cats and fallen down the stairs and that someone would find her soon enough. So I left."

Officer Clark slammed his hand on the table. "You want us to believe you didn't push her? I bet you did. I bet you pushed her down those stairs and then left her there to die."

"I didn't push her. And I didn't leave her there to die. She was already dead. You saw the body."

"Liar." He leaned forward until I could smell the bologna he'd had for lunch. "You shoved her down those stairs and then you ran from the house, hoping no one would see you."

"I did not kill Janice Fletcher. She was alive the first time I saw her. And dead when I went back."

"I don't believe you."

"Believe me or not, it's the truth." I leaned back and crossed my arms. They were either going to believe me or they weren't, but I'd told them the truth.

Mason Maxwell leaned forward. "You've heard my client's story. She didn't kill Janice Fletcher. Now, is she under arrest? Or not."

"Not."

Officer Clark glared at Matt for a moment and I thought he was going to override him. He was the more senior officer, after all. But instead he jerked open the door. "Sue needs a sample from those pants. Stay here."

I looked to Matt, but he wasn't quite looking at me. "I swear I didn't kill her."

He nodded, but he still wouldn't look at me. He glanced at his notes. "The first time you were there it was sometime before seven?"

"Yes."

"And while you were gone she had time to feed her cats."

"Yes. That's what it looked like to me."

"And to fall down the stairs."

I nodded. He pointed to the recorder, so I added. "Yes. Again, that's what it looked like to me."

"And you didn't check to make sure she was dead?"

What do you say to that? It sounds horrible. To have someone who must've only been dead a few minutes at the base of the stairs and not even check that they're breathing, but…

"You saw the body. Would you have thought there was any possible way she was alive?"

He set his pencil down. "Why didn't you call the cops?"

I knew what he was really asking. Why hadn't I called him? Why hadn't I trusted him enough to let him know I was standing in Janice Fletcher's house with her dead body at the bottom of the stairs and that I hadn't done it?

I looked down. I couldn't stand the betrayal I saw in his eyes. "It was a mistake. I see that now. I just…I knew I hadn't killed her. But I knew it looked bad for me to be there so close to when she'd died. And I figured she'd just fallen down the stairs, so not like there was some killer on the loose. It just…It made more sense at the time for me to let someone else find her."

I drummed my fingers on the table, thinking how to say what I wanted to say next. "If no one had found her body within the next day, I would've called and told you. But I figured a woman like that in a house like that and with that many cats probably had a cleaning lady who came through daily. And that if that wasn't the case then Peter Nielsen would probably be calling or dropping by at some point in the day to gloat about his article. Or the health inspector would be. I didn't expect she'd be there long."

He turned off the recording and stood. He still wouldn't quite look at me. "Wait here until Sue comes back. We'll want to take some samples from your pants."

"I already told you I was there."

He finally did look at me, his gaze nailing me to the seat. I wished he hadn't. "People tend to change their stories once they're charged with murder. So we like to get all the evidence we can."

"Fine. Take all the evidence you want. But my story isn't going to change. I was there, but I didn't kill her."

I could see Mason Maxwell shaking his head out of

the corner of my eye, but I ignored him. All I wanted in that moment was for Matt to believe me.

"We'll see what the autopsy says." He left, slamming the door behind him.

I glanced at Mason Maxwell. "Well, good news. I'm not under arrest."

"Yet." He stood. "Don't say anything to anyone without me present. I need to make some calls."

After he'd left I stared at the far wall wishing I'd brought a book with me to pass the time. I wondered if they would've let me read it. Or if making me sit in that nasty-smelling room in that uncomfortable chair without water for almost an hour was part of their interrogation strategy. Like I'd really break down and confess my sins over an hour of discomfort.

Since I had nothing else to do I spent the time thinking through every single detail of that morning. Had I left the front door slightly ajar when I raced out of there? And if I had, why hadn't Janice closed it? And had that sound I'd heard from the kitchen when I returned been one of the cats? I'd assumed it was, but what if it wasn't. And the sound from the basement?

Could someone else have been there?

No…

At the end I came to the same conclusion as before: Janice Fletcher had tripped on one of her cats and fallen down the stairs. I just needed the autopsy to prove it and then this would all be over.

CHAPTER 18

At least I made it home for dinner. They kept me sitting in that room for a good hour before Sue, the woman who seemed to handle all crime scenes in the county, came in to take samples of the cat hair on my pants and shoes. Honestly, I was glad to have some of it taken away. The Benadryl I'd taken earlier had worn off by then and my eyes were all watery and my throat congested.

First thing I did when I got home was throw everything I was wearing in the wash and take a shower.

Second thing I did was sit down at the kitchen table with my grandpa and walk him through my day.

"What were you thinking, Maggie May? Going to someone's house to confront them like that? And going back into that house after you'd already left? You don't just walk into people's houses. What if she'd shot you?"

That had never occurred to me, but he was right. If Janice Fletcher had chosen to do so she would have been within her rights to shoot me dead that second time I went to her house. Wouldn't that have been ironic?

(Yeah, I'm pretty sure that's the Alanis Morissette version of ironic that I just used. In other words, don't line it up too carefully with the dictionary definition.)

I drank my fourth Coke of the day—one I'd put in the freezer until it was almost frozen but not quite, something I wasn't allowed to do often anymore after forgetting three days in a row that I'd done so and having them explode while I was at work. The first two my grandpa had cleaned up. The third one he'd made me clean up. He'd also made me promise to never put a Coke in the freezer again. Fortunately, he'd made an exception that day. Seems there was at least one perk to being questioned by the police.

"I messed up. I know. I'm sorry. But it'll be okay. I know it will."

He raised one eyebrow at me. "Haven't you learned by now, Maggie May? Things don't always work out."

Coming from the man who'd been in prison twice—once for a very justifiable homicide and once for armed robbery—and who'd almost been sent there a third time, his view on things was justified. But what can I say? Life is never perfect and there are always ways in which I wish it were better than it is, but I still believed that things would work out because things really do work out in my world.

Eventually.

🐾 🐾 🐾

The next day at the café was a busy one, so Jamie was stuck in the kitchen all day leaving me and our new assistant to manage the customers.

Honestly, given my skills at customer service I should've been the one doing the cooking, but thanks to the *Baker Valley Gazette* word had spread that I'd been taken in for questioning in the death of Janice Fletcher and everyone who could manage it had come by to poke and prod and figure out why that might be.

Seeing as I didn't really want to admit that I'd seen someone dead at the bottom of a set of stairs and then walked away, I stuck to no comment as much as I possibly could, but man, people in a small town. News travels fast. They knew about five times what the article said and about twice what the police had.

Martin Parks—the owner of the local pizzeria whose wife Gloria had accused me of trying to tempt the men of the town with my free goodies—leaned against the barkery counter pretending to debate between buying canine crunchies and doggie delights.

"I hear you were in Janice Fletcher's house the morning she died. That true?"

Don—Mr. Fancy Slacks who it seemed had decided to make the café his office while he was in town—came over to join us. "I heard you were there when she died."

I glared at him. He didn't even know her. And he wasn't even from around here. What did he care?

"I was not there when Janice Fletcher died." I stepped back for a moment and sneezed into my elbow. "But I did visit her that morning."

Martin pointed to the canine crunchies. "I think I'll try a few of those. So you were there?"

I bagged up the treats and rang him up. "Yeah. I went over, told her I didn't appreciate how she was harassing us, and she basically told me to stick it so I left."

Don leaned on the display case. "I heard there was more to it. Surely if that's all it was the cops wouldn't have taken you in for questioning."

"Well, whoever told you that was wrong. It's a small

town. The cops just wanted to be thorough."

"How'd she die anyway?" Martin asked as I handed him his receipt and treat bag.

"I'm not sure I'm supposed to say. But I think it was an accident."

"So it wasn't murder?" Don leaned forward, trying to charm me with those green eyes of his. He was handsome, but he was not my type.

I cleared my throat which had gone all dry and scratchy. Seemed I was still recovering from my exposure to so many cats. Usually my allergies don't hit me that bad but usually I don't have a swarm of cats rubbing themselves against my legs either.

"Excuse me for a second." I grabbed a couple Benadryl and downed them. "Neither of you happen to have a cat, do you?"

They shook their heads.

"You avoided my question." Don smiled at me, but I didn't return the smile.

"I didn't avoid your question. I just chose not to answer it." I looked him up and down. "Why do you care? What are you? A reporter?"

"No. Geez. I was just curious. Sorry to disturb you." He walked away in a huff, but I didn't care. I kind of hoped he'd pack up his things and go. Of course, why should he when he had Jamie's attention. She came out of the kitchen for a quick break and sat down at his table, laughing and talking with him like old friends.

Nothing I could do about it except glare daggers his way every chance I got. Unfortunately, that didn't seem to phase him one bit.

🐾 🐾 🐾

Don's presence made the next few days very interesting in a painful dating show sort of way. He was there every single day for both breakfast and lunch, chatting Jamie up every chance he got. And she soaked it up, loving every single over-the-top compliment and little touch on her hand or her arm or her shoulder.

What made it awkward was that Mason Maxwell had started coming into the café every day for lunch, too. He was more reserved in his attentions. No "you have a smile that lights up a room" compliments, but there was definite interest there. And Jamie made time to sit with him and chat for at least a few minutes every single day, too.

I couldn't figure out which one she liked more. And when I asked her about it she just laughed and asked me why she had to like either one. It was just flirting. A little fun. That's all.

We were sitting out back after we'd closed the café watching Fancy and Lulu play while we drank a beer when she said that.

I narrowed my eyes. "You're not still hung up on Lucas Dean, are you?"

"Honestly, Maggie. I don't bug you about your love life—or lack thereof—don't bug me about mine."

"Oh, you are, aren't you? Jamie. He's a cad. He's…ugh."

I laughed as Lulu grabbed hold of Fancy's tail and Fancy turned to stare at her with a look of confusion on her face like, "Why is this little ball of fur hanging off of me?" Fancy spun around and Lulu went flying through the air, but kept hold of Fancy's tail.

Jamie stood. "You're too quick to judge, you know that? You never give people a second chance. One little mess up and that's it. Done. Over. You have to know by now that no one can meet that kind of standard."

I took another sip of my beer. It was true that I held people to a high standard. But it wasn't *that* high a standard. "I don't think refusing to associate with people who should be in jail for their actions is being too picky."

"Lulu. Enough." Jamie grabbed Lulu and gently disengaged her teeth from Fancy's tail. "Look I have to go. I have a date."

"With who?"

She shook her head.

"Jamie!"

"Don. Happy?"

I shrugged. He wasn't my favorite person, but he was certainly better than Lucas Dean.

Jamie leashed up Lulu and led her to the door, but then turned back to me. "You know, Maggie, some of us actually want to find love and happiness, and we can't wait around for Mr. Perfect to stroll through the door. We have to work with what we have."

I would've argued with her that surely she could wait just a few minutes for better choices than a philandering sweet-talker, an out-of-town busybody, and some uptight lawyer, but I just nodded and took another sip of my beer. "It's your life, Jamie. Live it in a way that makes you happy."

"I will." She slammed the door as she left and I sighed and went to sit on the grass next to Fancy.

"Ah, Fancy. Why does life have to be so annoying all the time, huh?"

We were supposed to move to Creek and then everything would go according to plan. I'd take care of my grandpa, walk Fancy through the woods, the barkery would be a booming success, and Jamie and I would get along perfectly all the time.

I laughed. Yeah, I know. Life doesn't work that way, does it?

CHAPTER 19

Things were still pretty chilly between me and Jamie when Matt and Officer Clark returned the next day.

I was having a late lunch with Greta, laughing at a story she was telling about her sixth or seventh husband who'd been a Spanish bull rider when they walked through the door. Matt led the way with Officer Clark at his shoulder glaring at me like I was going to turn into some crazed psycho at any moment.

"Officers." I stood so they weren't behind me. "How can I help you?"

As I spoke I walked deeper into the barkery drawing them away from Greta. We were friends now but she didn't need to hear all the nasty details of whatever was about to happen.

Fancy poked her head over the edge of her cubby and barked at Matt, standing with her paws on the edge and wagging her tail like a crazy woman. (If she weren't so lazy she could easily jump right out of there, but she never has.)

I looked at him, looked at her, and looked at him again as she continued to bark. Was he really not going to say hi?

He shook his head slightly, but walked over to give Fancy a good ear rubbing. She leaned into his leg and sighed in pleasure. He hadn't been into the café since the day they questioned me so she'd been going through withdrawal. (So had I.)

Officer Clark shook his head in disgust and stepped toward me. "Maggie May Carver, you are under arrest for the murder of Janice Fletcher. Turn around and put your hands behind your back."

"Murder? She fell down the stairs. It was an accident."

"I think we'll believe the coroner on this one. Now turn around."

I started to turn, but Matt stepped between us. "That's not necessary, Ben."

"She's a murderer."

I could see Matt still didn't really believe it. (Thankfully.) "Be that as it may. I'm not going to cuff her. And neither are you."

I glanced at Fancy. "Matt? Can we…? I know I shouldn't ask this, but can I please take Fancy home first?"

Officer Clark glared at him. "She's a murderer, Matt. You shouldn't even be on this case you're so blinded."

Matt glared right back. "Shut up, Ben." He nodded to me. "Sure. Get her leashed up."

I ran to grab my purse and Fancy's leash from the office. Jamie was seated at a table talking with Don, their heads close together. They were even holding hands.

I stopped a few feet away. "Jamie."

"What?" She didn't even look at me.

"The police are here. They're arresting me for Janice

Fletcher's murder."

She stood up, staring at me. "What? I thought you said it was an accident. That she wasn't murdered."

"That's what I thought, but seems they have different information now." I was shaking, but I didn't want her to see it. "Can you call Mason Maxwell for me? Please."

She nodded and took my hand. "It's going to be okay, Maggie. I know you didn't do this."

"Thanks."

Matt was waiting for me next to Fancy's cubby. I could see Officer Clark outside.

"Everything okay?"

"Yeah. Ben doesn't appreciate that you should give people the benefit of the doubt."

He waited as I leashed up Fancy. Greta joined us, nodding to Matt. He looked like he wanted to turn her away, but instead he stepped back and let us have a quick moment to talk.

"I know you, Maggie. You are not a killer."

"Thanks, Greta. I appreciate that." Although to be honest, I figured Jamie's assessment that most people were capable of murder in the right circumstances was probably the more accurate one, especially where I was concerned. I mean, I had actually wished for Janice Fletcher's death after all.

"I know a man. He will investigate. He will find the real killer for you."

"Oh, you don't have to do that. I'm sure…" I shook myself. It's so easy to not ask for help even when it's offered, but this time around I really needed any help I could get. "Actually, Greta, I'd really appreciate any help you can give me. Thank you."

She nodded and stepped back as Matt stepped forward. "Let me have your keys."

"What? Why?"

"Because you're still under arrest. I can't just let you drive away in your van. So I'm going to drive you and Fancy home, make sure she's dropped off with your grandpa, and then you and I will walk over to the station. And to make sure you don't overpower me and take off, Ben will follow behind us."

I laughed. "Like I could overpower you."

"Eh. It might be easier than you think. Come on. Don't want to keep him waiting. No telling what he might do."

I leashed up Fancy and we walked towards the door. "You're not going to get in trouble for this, are you?"

"If I do, I do. It's the right thing to do."

I wanted to say more, but then we were outside and the sun was glaring down upon us and Officer Clark was watching us with his hand upon his gun.

I'd never been more scared in my life, but at that point there was only one thing to do. Take the next step and hope it all worked out somehow. At least I knew I was innocent.

🐾 🐾 🐾

As Matt drove my van with Officer Clark trailing along behind us it was clear he didn't want to talk. But I did.

"Matt, you have to know I didn't do this."

He didn't answer, but his grip on the steering wheel tightened until his knuckles turned white.

"If Janice Fletcher really was killed, then someone else had to have been there between the first time I arrived and the second. Did you print the place?"

He glared at me for a second before turning his attention back to the road. "We aren't country bumpkins, Maggie. We know how to do our job."

"I wasn't saying you were. But did you print the cat food cans? Or the plate that was used to feed them?"

"Why would we do that?"

"Because maybe Janice Fletcher died before she could feed those cats. If that's the case, the killer did it instead."

"Why? Why would someone who'd just killed a woman stop long enough to feed her cats?"

"Because they were annoying. The killer might've done it to get the cats to leave them alone. I would've."

I stared out the window as we passed by a lush green field with a worn red barn in the distance. "Did I tell you about the green car? Or the jogger?"

"No. And don't tell me about them now. We'll have to interrogate you again now that you're officially under arrest for the murder."

"You know Mason Maxwell isn't going to let me tell you a thing now."

He banged his hand on the steering wheel. "Why did you have to leave after you found the body, Maggie? Why couldn't you have just called it in?"

"Like that would've helped. You would've just arrested me for murder then instead of now."

"No. I wouldn't have."

"Come on, Matt. Janice Fletcher and I were in the middle of a feud and I just conveniently happen to drop by her house and find her dead body? How could you *not* suspect me of murder?"

"Maggie, if you didn't do this…"

"I didn't."

"If you didn't do this, I don't know how to prove it."

I sank into the seat and crossed my arms. He was right. I'd assumed the autopsy would clear me. That they'd see that she'd tripped and fallen down the stairs and that would be the end of it. But if the autopsy showed murder…

"What did the autopsy show?" I asked. "Why are you so certain she didn't trip and fall down the stairs?"

"I shouldn't tell you that."

"Please. Give me some sort of chance here."

He drove in silence for a long time. It felt like an eternity, but I knew I had to let him come to this on his own.

"Preliminary finding is that she didn't die from falling down the stairs. There was a blow to the side of her head consistent with a cast iron frying pan we found in the kitchen."

"I never set foot in that kitchen. Well, not until after she was dead. I certainly never touched that frying pan."

"According to the fingerprint analysis, no one ever has."

"It was in the sink the second time I was there. Wet." I shivered, suddenly realizing something that hadn't occurred to me before since I'd thought she'd just tripped and fell. "Matt…Whoever the real killer is…They could've been there when I was."

"What do you mean?"

"What if they were still cleaning up when I was there? I heard crashing from the kitchen when I first walked in. What if that was the killer, setting down the frying pan? And when I looked down the stairs, I heard a noise down there, too. I just figured it was a cat. But what if it wasn't?

There was that creaking sound on the steps I'd heard earlier. I thought it was a cat, but maybe…"

I shivered, wondering if the whole time I'd been walking through Janice's house looking for her there'd been some killer hiding out trying to decide whether to bash my brains in, too.

"This killer is calculated," I said.

"How so?"

"I came back and they didn't immediately attack me. Nor did they run out the front door. They waited to see what I'd do. I bet if I had called the cops that they would've either run or attacked me and then run. Because otherwise they would've been stuck in that house and caught. It would've ruined their plan with making it look like an accident, but they would've had no choice."

Matt pulled up in front of my grandpa's house. "Maybe."

"Promise me you'll at least consider the possibility that someone else did this?"

He shook his head. "What do you think I've been doing ever since I heard the autopsy results, Maggie? Come on. Ben's not going to wait forever."

🐾 🐾 🐾

I'd hated the fact that Matt hadn't dragged Lucas Dean into the police station in cuffs over the whole Jack Dunner affair, but I was very grateful as we walked up to the house that he was such a decent, caring human being.

"Okay. Come on, Fancy. Let's get you settled."

She followed me out of the van, clearly confused as to what was going on. That's the hard part about having a dog—there are just some things you can't explain to them and some things they can't explain to you.

I dropped Fancy and my purse off inside, gave my grandpa the two-second explanation of what was going on, and turned to leave. But the look in Fancy's eyes as I closed the door followed me all the way to the police station. More than anything, I hoped things would work out so that I could return to her. She, unlike everyone else in my life, really truly needed me.

CHAPTER 20

What followed after I arrived at the police station was five excruciating hours of interrogation. Not from Matt, at least. It was Officer Clark who stood and paced and yelled at me and demanded that I confess that I'd killed Janice Fletcher. That I'd become enraged and hit her in the head with a frying pan and then shoved her down a flight of stairs to try to cover up what I'd done.

He smacked the table. He got in my face. He shouted until his face turned purple and spit went flying from his mouth. But there was nothing to confess to. I hadn't killed her. So as painful as those five hours were, there wasn't much to be said.

Mason Maxwell sat at my side the entire time, repeatedly telling him that I'd been instructed not to answer his questions. If it hadn't been for Mason Maxwell, I would've said who knows what just to make it end. I would've never confessed, but there were a few times I wanted to shout back at Officer Clark that yes, I absolutely was glad that Janice Fletcher was dead. That I didn't like someone who would try to destroy my business, which she had clearly indicated she was going to do, and that even though I hadn't done it I was glad someone had.

I didn't know where Matt was that whole time. I wondered if he was sitting in some room somewhere watching the interrogation on a video feed like they do in *The Closer*, but there was no way to know.

At times I hated him for not being there to protect me, but I knew he'd made the best choice he could. Because he would've been just as hard on me. He would've had to be. It was his job and he was the kind of man to do his job well.

Finally, Mason Maxwell stood up. "Enough. You've held my client in this room for five hours without food. She has rights."

Officer Clark looked like he was going to refuse to let me eat anything, but finally he nodded. "Fine. I'll bring her lunch."

He left the two of us alone. I glanced at Mason Maxwell and he pointed to the little light on the table that indicated they were still recording us. Wasn't Officer Clark oh so clever?

"Thank you," I said. "For sitting through this. I appreciate it."

"You are my client."

"I know. But…I still appreciate it. I…You're a better man than I gave you credit for."

He raised an eyebrow, but didn't say anything else.

As the silence stretched on between us, I asked, "Do you think they'll let me out of here now that they've asked their questions?"

"No. I think you're going to be here at least overnight while they decide whether or not to charge you."

I sat back. Lovely. Just what I wanted was some night in the local lock-up for a crime I hadn't committed.

"Can you check with Greta? Remember, the woman from the barkery? She said she was going to reach out to an investigator she knows. Maybe he'll have come up with something while we were sitting here. And let her know about the green car I saw. And the jogger. Maybe one of those will turn out to be the killer, although…" I shook my head. "I have to think the killer was in the house when I was there the first time. It's too short a time period."

Mason Maxwell pointed to the light again.

"I know. But I'm not telling you anything I wouldn't tell them."

"You and your grandfather. Cut from the same cloth."

"Only in the best ways." I tried to smile, but I was so tired by then. Five hours of some sweaty angry man shouting at you is not exactly my idea of a fun way to spend an afternoon.

Officer Clark returned with a pair of handcuffs. "Mr. Maxwell, you can leave. We'll take the inmate to her cell now. Don't worry. She'll get food." He walked over to me. "Stand and put your hands behind your back."

I could've made some snide remark about him finally getting his chance to handcuff me and how that must make him feel like a real big man, but I didn't. I just stood and put my hands behind my back.

I could smell the stink of him—he was one of those men who get sour as the day goes on—as he stepped close and placed the cuffs on my hands. His ragged breath moistened my ear and I shuddered. He really needed to hit the gym every once in a while if he was going to work himself up that way during an interrogation.

The metal of the cuffs against my skin made me finally realize just how serious this all was. I knew I hadn't killed Janice Fletcher, but at that moment I knew it was going to be almost impossible to prove it. I had a motive. I'd been there both right before and right after. I hadn't reported her death until the cops came for me. I mean, if I were on a jury and someone presented me with that case, I'd probably convict.

And I was so not going to do well in prison. You might think that for a woman it would be better than for a man, but I was pretty sure that little ol' me, who'd never even been in a physical fight but wasn't exactly the type to cower in the face of conflict, wasn't going to do so well. I'd probably be beat up my first week there.

I wondered if they allowed you books in solitary. If so maybe I could just ask to be put in solitary and spend the next decade reading. Put like that it didn't sound so horrible. But I bet they wouldn't let me choose my reading material. I'd probably be stuck with religious pamphlets and books devoid of any sort of nuance or moral ambiguity because some high and mighty morality police somewhere had decided it wasn't good to "incite the convicts".

Ugh.

Which would I choose? Reading horrible awful stories with a message I didn't want to hear? Or not reading for the next ten to twenty years? And what about music? Would they let me listen to music? How was I going to live without music?

Mason Maxwell gripped my shoulders. "Hold it together, Ms. Carver."

"Please, call me Maggie. After sitting here with me for all that time, we've gotta be on a first-name basis. Or at least, you can certainly use my first name."

"And you can use mine, Maggie." He leaned closer and held my gaze. "Do not talk to anyone without me present. Anyone. I will get you released tomorrow. Until then, behave and stay silent."

"Yes, sir."

Officer Clark steered me down the hall to an area with six narrow cells, three on each side. He stopped at the second cell on the left. There was a toilet in the very middle of the far wall, a small sink on the wall to my right, and a large sleeping shelf on the wall to my left that was a little less than chest-high. A four-inch-thick piece of padded material was folded up on the bunk with two folded sheets on top. Must be what qualified as a mattress and sheets in these parts. Joy.

I glanced across the way to the cell opposite mine. A woman I didn't know was leaning against the back wall, glaring at me, her muscular arms crossed. Some other woman was asleep on one of those mats, this one on the floor under the bunk. That explained why the shelf for the main bed was so high. It was the upper bunk.

As Officer Clark pulled the metal gate closed behind me, I tried to see the positive. At least I didn't have a cell mate.

Yet.

But at some point I was going to have to pee and I didn't see how that was going to be possible without that woman watching me. Honestly, the mere thought of having to pee with an audience made me need to pee, which just made it all that much worse. Have you ever needed to pee and not been able to and then all of a sudden that's all you can think about? That was me.

I swear, in that moment if Janice Fletcher hadn't already been dead, I would've happily taken her out for putting me through that.

I tried to figure out where to go to make myself comfortable, but it's not like the cell was set-up with a desk and chair. I had the sleeping shelf, the floor, or I could lean against the wall and stare back at the scary lady. Knowing my luck I'd end with her as my cellie for my entire prison term and I most definitely did not want to do anything to provoke her. So the shelf it was.

I made up my bed—if you could call it that—and settled in. To think that some people spend decades living like that. To think that my grandpa had. The few comments he'd made about prison had not been good. How had he made it through and turned out such a decent human being after?

(I know. I wasn't even seeing the worst of prison life. I was in my little small town jail holding cell where I knew at least one friendly officer. Ridiculous of me, wasn't it? But when you've never even come close to anything like it, it's a shock to the system. And not a good one.)

Officer Clark brought back a tray and shoved it through the bottom of the barred gate. The "food" was edible, but barely. Think gas-station convenience food. You know, those stale, tasteless cheese sandwiches that come in those little plastic containers and could probably last through a nuclear winter? Ever had one of those? It was like that. Except I couldn't actually tell you what any of it was, just that there was no taste to it and nothing to season it with.

It was like some horrid dystopian future where people live on optimally structured nutrient supplements because they've forgotten the pleasures of a good meal. I choked it down, though. No point in wasting a meal.

(No matter how bad life has gotten, I have never ever taken it out on myself by losing my appetite. Sometimes I wish I were that person. It would be nice to get something positive out of some of the things I've been through, but that is just not me. I go into "I will not let this defeat me" mode and make sure I'm dead-on with health and nutrition and avoiding self-destructive behaviors. The more I want to drink and do other self-destructive things, the less I do them. I guess that's a good thing.)

After the meal, I hopped up on my shelf, curled into a ball with my back against the wall, and tried to sleep. I figured the less I had to actually be awake, the better.

CHAPTER 21

Turns out that I am not capable of just going to sleep while in a jail cell. I wish I were that cool and collected and confident. I'm not.

Instead I lay there with my eyes closed praying that they wouldn't bring someone else into my cell. And that by the time I had to pee there'd be no one there to watch me, although I could hear people in all the other cells around me.

The *sounds* in a place like that are the worst. Human sounds. There had to be at least a half dozen people there, some of them men, and I could hear them coughing and…other things. (Men are far less shy about the whole peeing in front of others thing. Ugh. Sorry. Too much information.)

Let's just say, I admired that woman asleep across from me. She was made of tougher stuff than I was.

I figure it was about six o'clock or so when I heard a lot of commotion. I sat up on my bunk and watched as all of the other inmates were chained up and led away. Seems the other folks there had been there to make a court appearance and were now heading back to the facilities where they were going to serve their real jail time. So, once the business day at the courthouse was over they were all carted away leaving me all alone in my cell.

In some respects, that was even worse. To be all alone, locked in a cell, with no way out and no idea of who was watching. I kept having these visions of the world ending and my not being able to get out. I want to say *Red Dawn*, the original movie (which I loved when I was younger but did not hold up well for me as an adult) was set in the Colorado mountains? Remember that movie? Russians invade and a bunch of school kids take up guns to fight back? I kept thinking, "What if something like that happens right now? What if I'm trapped here as World War III starts?"

Yeah, I know. Good thing I was only in jail that one night, because I was losing it.

🐾 🐾 🐾

I was tempted to cry as I sat there alone with just the buzz of the fluorescent lights to keep me company. If I'd just listened to Jamie and stayed at the café that day…

If I could just rein in my temper. Wouldn't that be great? To be this nice, kind, forgiving person?

I started to laugh. That was so not me and never would be. I actually like myself, you know. Sharp edges and all. And to be the kind of person who didn't run out to confront a nasty woman like Janice Fletcher just wouldn't suit. As much as my impulses might've led me to this unfortunate moment, they'd served me and those around me far more times than they'd hurt me.

The world needs the Jamies, don't get me wrong. The world absolutely needs some Jamies. But it needs the Maggies, too.

I stared at the far wall and tried to figure out how to get out of there. If it was true that Janice Fletcher had been killed—and why doubt that now—then the only way I was going to get out was to figure out who the real killer was.

So who would want her dead?

It was probably easier to put together a list of who wouldn't. But you could probably eliminate anyone she hadn't angered recently. It seemed to me that most people would act in the moment or they wouldn't act at all.

So who had she been harassing right before her death?

Me.

Well, that didn't help.

I wondered if she had any kids. Maybe they wanted her money. She was from a prominent family, but was she actually rich? Was there anything for anyone to inherit?

Maybe she knew some horrible awful secret about someone and was threatening to expose them.

Maybe she'd had a torrid affair and it had ended badly. (Not likely. But it's not like passion is limited to the young and beautiful.)

I thought about the green car and dismissed it. Same with the jogger. They just wouldn't have had enough time to get to her house, do the deed, clean up, and leave in the time I'd been away.

Whoever had done this was already in that house the first time I was there. They had to be.

Did Janice know? Had she tried to signal me in some way that she was in danger?

I tried to remember if she'd glanced in any direction while I was there, like she was looking towards someone else. Whoever it was, the cats certainly hadn't expected to be fed by them. But maybe…

I wondered how many cats she actually owned. I'd counted…five. But if there were more? What if they'd gone after the intruder and were crying to be fed and that's why the person had been discovered? Maybe they hadn't meant to kill Janice at all. Maybe they'd been in her house for some other reason.

Had she known about the basement door being open? Had she opened it? Or had the intruder?

I was still thinking it through when Matt walked up to my cell door.

"Ms. Carver." It hurt a little for him to call me that, but I knew why he had to do it.

I hopped down and walked over to him, so glad for a familiar face. "Officer Barnes."

I wanted to lace my fingers in his, but had to remind myself that he was a cop first and my friend second. For all I knew, he was round two of the interrogation—the good cop to Officer Clark's bad cop.

Plus, Mason Maxwell had told me not to speak to anyone without him present. I should've stayed on my bunk staring off into space.

Matt unlocked the cell and stepped aside. "Come on. Let's go."

I stepped out of the cell, but then hesitated. "Where are we going?"

"Aren't you hungry?"

I nodded.

"Well, then."

I still didn't move. "They brought my lunch to my cell."

Matt stepped closer. "Yeah, they did. Are you telling me you really want another meal like that one? Because if you don't, your grandpa brought you dinner."

"Really?" I glanced towards the front of the jailhouse. It would be so good to see him. "And you're going to let me eat it?"

"No. I thought I'd come here, let you out of your cell, tell you your grandpa had brought you dinner and was waiting for you at my desk, and then laugh in your face and lock you back up."

"I just. You know."

"Yes. I'm breaking about half a dozen rules by doing this. Don't tell anyone. Now come on."

I followed him out to the front, the delicious smell of chicken noodle soup guiding my steps the last little way. My grandpa was sitting at Officer Clark's desk, a chair pulled up next to it.

"Grandpa." I ran over and hugged him and he patted me on the arm.

"Now, now. I just saw you a few hours ago. Don't go making such a fuss."

"How's Fancy?" I sat down in the chair while Matt sat at his desk.

"Confused. She's placed herself across the front door so no one can come in or go out without her knowing about it. But she's okay."

"And you remembered to feed her?"

"Yes."

"And to give her her dental chew?"

"Yes."

"And her peanut butter treat?"

He shook his head. "That dog is more spoiled than most people."

"But you did give it to her?"

"Yes. She is fine. Trust me."

"Thank you."

Only once I was certain Fancy was okay did I take a bite of soup. It was so good, but I wished Fancy were there for me to feed her some carrots and noodles and chicken. "So, why are we eating here instead of the interrogation room?" I asked Matt.

"Did you want to eat in there after the day you had?"

"Not really. But I'm still curious."

"Because I wanted to actually talk to you instead of having you clam up because Mason Maxwell told you not to talk to anyone without him around."

"So you were listening to us after Officer Clark left the room?" I tore off a hunk of homemade bread and dunked it in my soup.

"Not live. I went back to the crime scene with Sue. We tried to figure out what we might've missed the first time around based on what you told me."

I felt a small surge of warmth towards him. He believed me. "And?"

"Maggie May," my grandpa interrupted. "You know how I feel about talking business at dinner."

"Grandpa. I think that rule can be waived when someone is in jail." I flashed him my "don't interrupt a cop who's about to tell you something good" look, but he ignored it.

"So, Matt. You have any free time?" he asked.

"I might. Why?"

"I could use another assistant on the t-ball team. I think you'd be good at it."

My grandpa had been the volunteer baseball coach for forty years, but he'd lost a couple of his assistants with the Jack Dunner affair.

Matt nodded. "Yeah, I could do that. Sure."

They spent the rest of the meal talking baseball and the different families in town, while I ate my food. I wanted to interrupt and ask Matt what he'd found when he and Sue went back to the crime scene, but there was never a good opportunity.

When we finished, my grandpa pulled out the Scrabble board.

"Grandpa. We're in jail. We can't be playing Scrabble."

"That's alright," Matt said. "It's just the three of us until midnight unless something unexpected happens."

I was all for anything that let me stay out of that jail cell for a bit, but I had to ask. "Don't you have a murder to work on?"

"Maggie May." My grandpa glared at me.

Matt just laughed. "I need some time to think through what I know. This'll be good. Distract me while my mind's working."

As I pulled seven tiles and lined them up on the tray before me I said, "You know, three minds are better than one…"

My grandpa grunted, but at least he didn't say anything about not talking about it.

Matt didn't answer. He played first and managed to start with a thirty-six point play. This was going to be an ugly game for me. I had nothing. But if it led him to tell me what he'd found out on his second pass of Janice's house…

Well, I guess I could lose one game of Scrabble for that.

As we played out the game—Matt and my grandpa left me in their dust after the first five rounds of play and probably wouldn't have noticed if I disappeared halfway through—Matt told us what he'd found. Sue hadn't thought to fingerprint the cat food cans or plate, so she'd done that. And Matt had found a footprint outside near the basement window well.

"What kind of footprint?"

"Definitely not a boot. Or a tennis shoe, from what I could tell. Sue will match it up to a database she has access to. It has two round sections that are very unusual. Probably a man's shoe. Looked to be a size 9 or 10."

"So the killer could have entered—or exited—through the basement window? Maybe that was the sound I heard when I saw her body in the basement."

"Maybe."

"Were any files disturbed? Did you see any sign of what the killer might have wanted?"

I explained to him my theory that maybe the killer hadn't been there to kill her, but had instead broken in looking for something she had.

Matt laughed. "These days all that stuff happens on computers."

"Well. Anyone look at her laptop? It was a Mac from what I remember. She had it at the barkery the day she claimed her cat was an emotional support animal."

"We have it, but nothing on there so far."

"So we have a few more finger prints and a shoeprint, but that's it. I'm still pretty much the only person with an immediate motive."

"Yep."

"Great. Just great."

CHAPTER 22

After that we settled into a general conversation about all the horrible things Janice Fletcher had done to people over the years. There were certainly enough people who weren't going to mourn her passing, let me tell you.

My grandpa managed to win at Scrabble, but only by two points. I think both he and Matt were pleased. Not that Matt liked losing, but since he'd only lost because of an unlucky draw of a Z at the very end of the game I think he was satisfied that the only reason he'd lost was due to bad luck.

Matt wanted an immediate rematch but my grandpa begged off, pointing out that Fancy was all alone at home and probably none too happy about it. (Honestly, I think he just wanted to relish the win for a while, but I did appreciate him thinking about Fancy, too.)

After Matt locked the door behind my grandpa he said, "I better take you back to your cell."

The last thing I wanted was to go back there, but I told myself I should be grateful for the couple of hours of freedom he'd given me that he didn't have to.

"Thank you."

He nodded.

"You okay?" I asked.

He shook his head. "People think a small town cop's job is easy, but it's not. Do you know how hard it is to arrest someone you know? To have to think that they might have killed someone?"

"I'm sorry to have put you in this position."

"It's not just you. Last week we got a call about a domestic and when I showed up it was a guy I'd played football with in high school." He shook his head. "He asked me to go easy on him. Said he'd just lost his temper. His girlfriend was hysterical, telling me he'd threatened to kill her. I had to bring him in and lock him up."

"You did the right thing."

"I know. Doesn't make it any easier though."

🐾 🐾 🐾

He let me use a private bathroom before locking me back in my cell. I spent the whole rest of the night staring at the ceiling, not able or willing to sleep.

I thought about Janice Fletcher. And about my grandpa. And Matt. And Fancy. And Jamie.

I swore to myself that if I got out of there I'd control my temper and my curiosity. No more putting myself in positions like this. One night of jail was enough to cure me.

(Haha. I know. That's like telling the sun not to rise each morning. You can do it all you want, but at the end of the day the sun is going to be the sun and I was going to be me.)

🐾 🐾 🐾

I must've finally dozed off at some point, because I awoke to the sound of someone slapping a tray down on the floor of my cell. "Food."

As I stared at what was probably meant to be eggs, I silently hoped that someone else had been murdered overnight and that the murder would be tied to Janice's and clear my name. Because this was not the life I wanted to be living.

(I know, I know. Not a nice thing to do. But I hadn't killed the woman and didn't deserve to be in jail for doing so and at that point I wasn't sure what else was going to save me. Plus, I figured anyone else who did get killed in connection with her murder would be someone who kind of sort of deserved what they got, you know?)

Fortunately, Mason Maxwell managed to get me out of there first thing after I'd had the joy and privilege to plead not guilty on a charge of voluntary manslaughter. Let me tell you, not something you ever want to have to do, but according to Mason I was lucky that was all they'd charged me with.

Yay?

Mason immediately escorted me back to my grandpa's house. We actually walked there, which shocked me, but as he pointed out it was a gorgeous summer morning and why not enjoy it a bit.

I glanced down at his shoes. "Are those things actually comfortable to walk in?"

"Of course. I wouldn't buy them if they weren't."

I wondered if he'd ever tried wearing tennies. Maybe if he had he'd see how much better those were than some fancy-schmancy dress shoes.

When I opened the front door, Fancy scrambled

away. Turns out my grandpa was not kidding when he said she was sleeping across the doorway. She'd literally had her back right up against the door. She went crazy when she saw me, crying and barking her head off.

Man, did she give me a lecture about leaving her alone for the night. But when I sat down for her to climb in my lap and let me pet her, she took one sniff and ran outside.

"Mind if I take a quick shower?" I asked.

Mason and my grandpa eyed one another, neither one happy with the idea of having to make small talk for however long it would take.

"Five minutes. Promise." I decided to just go. Let them sort out what to do with themselves.

"I'll step out and make a call," I heard Mason say as I rounded the corner.

Well, that was one way to handle things. Simply avoid each other. At that point I didn't really care.

🐾 🐾 🐾

The shower probably took me more like seven minutes all told, but that's because I decided to wash my hair, too. I figure that's what Fancy had smelled. It's amazing how much smells can cling to hair and jail smell has its own unique funk I did not need clogging up my nose for the rest of the day.

When I returned from my shower my grandpa had a plateful of scrambled eggs waiting for me with melted cheese, bacon, and spring onions mixed in. Yum. He'd even fried up a potato for me. *And* put a Coke next to my plate. (He hates the fact that I drink so much Coke, so that was an especially endearing thing for him to do.)

I kissed him on the cheek. "You're the best, you know that."

He batted me away and continued to work on his crossword puzzle.

"You are the best." I started eating as Mason came back in and joined us. Fancy did, too. She never misses a chance at human food, although I had to be careful not to give her any of the onions. Those are bad for dogs.

"So, what now?" I asked Mason.

He studied me as I shoveled another forkful of food in my mouth. I suddenly realized that twisting my hair up in a towel and throwing on my most comfortable lounging pajamas was probably not the most appropriate look. For a second there, I almost set my fork down, straightened my posture, and made sure I had a napkin in my lap.

But then I got over it. Let him think what he wanted. This was my home. I'd eat and look how I wanted to.

He carefully pulled the other chair out from the table and sat down. "Now we set a trial date. There'll be discovery and motions. But that's basically where we are. The case they have is largely circumstantial—no one saw you push her down the stairs or hit her in the head with a frying pan—but it's also pretty convincing."

"What do you think my odds are?"

"I don't like to talk odds."

He sounded like one of those cancer doctors who never want to tell you your odds of making it five years because it'll just be too depressing and, hey, you never know.

"Mason."

"If nothing changes? Probably a ninety percent chance you are going to be convicted. If they offer you a plea deal, you should consider it."

I took a bite of bacon and sighed in pleasure. Salty

fat. Just what I'd needed. "If I take a plea deal, I have to say I killed her."

"Yes."

"But I didn't."

He shrugged. "You can take a plea deal and be out in five years. Or you can stick to the truth and serve a twenty-year term. Your choice."

"Or I can find the killer before I go to trial."

My grandpa set his paper down. "Maggie May. You promise me you will not try to find the killer."

"But, Grandpa, that's my only chance of getting out of this."

"No. You promise me."

I ignored them both as I finished up my breakfast and put my plate in the kitchen sink.

"Maggie May…"

"I don't know what to tell you, Grandpa. I am not going to sit here and let a bunch of strangers decide my fate when I can do something about it."

"I did not bail you out so you could go get yourself killed."

Mason set his phone on the table. "For the record, I agree with your grandfather. If there is someone who killed Janice Fletcher running around loose, the last thing you should do is try to find them."

"If? The police said she was hit in the head with a frying pan. The only reason there wouldn't be a killer running around loose is if you think it was me."

"I misspoke. I apologize. Please sit back down."

I sat, crossing my arms and glaring at both of them.

Mason leaned forward. "The best way to address this is by attacking your motive during the trial. There were plenty of other people who wanted Janice Fletcher dead."

"But none of them were seen running away from the crime scene the morning of the crime. I was."

"Nor did anyone else admit to the police that they were there both before and after." He shook his head. "You haven't given me much to work with, Maggie. But I will work with it."

"Fine. Thank you. I should probably get into work."

"I wouldn't do that."

"Why not?"

My grandpa cleared his throat and handed me a copy of the *Baker Valley Gazette*. The headline on the front page read *Bakery Owner Arrested in Murder of Local Icon*.

Local icon? Janice Fletcher? Please.

I scanned the article. He'd really emphasized the fact that I'd just moved to the area from Washington, DC, somehow implying that I'd brought that big city crime with me. You know, like people in DC just walk around murdering one another left and right.

Granted, I'd had a friend who lived in a place in DC where shots were fired on a regular basis to the point that she'd advised me not to walk from the metro to her house. A cabbie had even pointed out bullet holes in the car right ahead of us once while we were parked at a stoplight. But all that aside, DC was not some murder-filled metropolis like the article made it out to be.

And even if it had been, that didn't mean *I* was a murderer.

I threw the paper down in disgust.

My grandpa took it back, stacking it neatly at his elbow. "Give it a day or two. Jamie can handle things."

Mason stood up. "I need to go. Call if anything comes up. And stay out of it. Let the cops do their job."

The cops doing their job is what had landed me in this mess, but I didn't say that. "Thank you for getting me out so quick." I walked him to the door.

"You're welcome. Just try not to do anything that will get you thrown back in before the trial, please."

I smiled and nodded but after I'd closed the door I stuck my tongue out. Who did he think I was? Some rash and uncontrolled criminal who couldn't curb her instincts for mayhem?

Okay. Maybe just a little. Take out the criminal part and it was probably pretty accurate. But if that was the case, telling me not to do anything wasn't going to help. He should've known that.

CHAPTER 23

Two hours later I was going a little stir crazy. I really, really wanted to go talk to that neighbor who'd seen me run from Janice Fletcher's house. Or to Matt. Or to Greta. Or to Greta's investigator. I needed to figure out who had really killed Janice Fletcher. It was my best chance of getting out of this mess. But I knew that if I left the house I'd just be courting trouble.

So instead I built Fancy a staircase.

Yep, you read that right. I built my dog a staircase to make it easier for her to get up on the bed.

She'd been very sad since we'd moved because she couldn't jump high enough to get onto my new bed. In one sense, that was a blessing, because Fancy pretty much takes up the entire queen-size bed, only leaving me about ten inches of space along the very top edge. But I figured I owed it to her. She'd been raised to expect a certain standard of living and she hadn't had it since we'd moved.

So, since I had the free time and my grandpa had the lumber to make it happen, I set out to build her a three-step staircase that would let her just walk right up and onto the bed.

I built it in place, in my room, because the lumber I was using was not light-weight and I wasn't sure the finished product would actually fit through the doorway.

Fancy lay in the hallway watching this desecration of her sacred sleeping place with her head resting on her paws. Usually she sleeps through most of the day, but not this time. She had an eye on me the whole time I worked, silently reproachful.

"This is for you, you know," I told her.

She didn't care. Change is not her thing. And putting in those steps meant moving her bed.

It took me three hours and four failed attempts to get it done. Fortunately I had pre-made risers to work with, so all I had to really do was put boards across them for each step and build a brace so that the stairs could stand alone and not collapse. But that was actually a lot of boards that needed measured and screwed into place.

(I let my grandpa do the cutting. Me and power saws? Not a good mix. I used a jigsaw once. Almost took out my leg. That was all I needed to know about saws.)

The finished product was actually pretty beautiful. The wood I'd used was redwood and it smelled really nice. I was so proud of myself. Until Fancy decided she was having none of it. She put one paw on the first step, slipped just a little bit, and then backed away and refused to go near it.

I tried putting treats on each step, but she wasn't interested. She ate the ones she could reach and then sat down and cried. When I tried putting treats on the bed she sat off to the side away from the steps and stared pitifully until I gave up and retrieved them for her.

So then I spent another hour adding carpet to each of

the steps figuring maybe she was just scared that she'd slip.

But no. She still wasn't having it.

Next I added boards behind the gap between steps thinking maybe that's why she was scared. Still no joy.

So after five hours of effort all I had to show was a monstrosity of a staircase at the base of my bed and a dog that now refused to step foot in my room let alone use the stairs I'd built especially for her.

My grandpa stood in the hallway watching me try to lure Fancy onto the stairs, clearly trying not to laugh.

"Don't say it." I gave up and sat on the stairs myself as Fancy sprawled in the hallway.

"What? That that's what you get for building a staircase for a dog?"

I leaned my elbows on my knees and looked at him. "What am I going to do, Grandpa? I don't know how to get out of this."

He sat down next to me and patted my knee. "You're going to take this one day at a time. Worst comes to worst, you'll serve your time, get out, and get on with your life like I did."

I shivered. "It won't come to that. It can't."

"It could. And you have to accept that."

"But I didn't kill her."

He nodded. "I know."

"Do you? Do you believe me?"

"I do. You're a little wild around the edges and you have a temper, that's for sure, but not that kind of temper."

"But then…"

He rubbed the back of his neck. "Maggie, life isn't always fair. We want it to be one way, but sometimes it just isn't. And when it isn't you have to live with the life you're given instead of hoping for the one you don't have."

I guess in some part of my mind I'd thought that this would all just work itself out. The killer would come forward or Matt would find a fingerprint on a plate or something.

But why? Why should that happen? I mean, it was a pretty slim chance that they'd suddenly discover some other murder suspect, wasn't it, when they had me admitting to being there right before and right after the murder?

"Come on." He patted my knee again and stood. "Let's have dinner. And then you and I need some more Scrabble practice. Can't let Matt keep beating you so badly."

I followed him out to the kitchen, Fancy trailing along behind us. "After this I seriously doubt Matt will ever come over here again."

"Oh, he'll be back. Trust me on that one."

I scratched Fancy's head. "Yeah, I guess someone will have to help you look after Fancy when I'm in prison."

He swatted my arm. "Don't talk like that, Maggie. That may be what happens, but it hasn't happened yet. And there's no sense wasting the good moments anticipating the bad."

He was right. Plus, as long as I was free there was a chance I could find the real killer. (I know. Danger, blah, blah, blah. But really? Give me the choice between tracking down one person who'd hit an old lady with a frying pan and shoved her down a flight of stairs and serving prison time? I was probably much safer finding the killer. And if I wasn't, well, other than what it would do to Fancy and my grandpa and Jamie and the barkery, I'd rather go out swinging, you know?)

Anyway. We had a very pleasant evening playing Scrabble—I even almost won a game. But then the next day came and I knew I had to do something more than sit around the house waiting for my trial date.

CHAPTER 24

Jamie and I agreed I shouldn't work at the barkery for a few days. It was going to cost us some money to have our assistants work longer hours, but it was better than people staying away because they didn't want to associate with a murderer.

Of course, I should've remembered the lesson I'd learned working at the dropzone. Every time there was a serious accident that made the news we actually had more people show up wanting to jump. You'd think stories about slamming into the ground at terminal velocity would make people reconsider their dangerous life choices, but nope. It somehow drove them to take that risk themselves.

What can I tell you? People are crazy. Especially skydivers.

Even though I wasn't working I did still go into the barkery to meet Greta and hear what her investigator had found. Fancy was thrilled by the chance to get out of the house for a few hours. The last few days had severely disrupted her routine and she just didn't know what to make of it.

There were a few overflow customers from the café sitting on the barkery side and they all eyed me as I walked in, leaning over to whisper to one another.

(Guilty until proven innocent sounds nice and all, but the reality is that the minute someone is charged with a crime all the people in their world assume they're guilty. At least rational people do. Not like the cops go around charging people with murder all willy-nilly. *I* knew I was innocent, but there was no reason anyone else should believe that.)

Don was leaning against the café counter chatting with Jamie as I let Fancy into her cubby.

"Hey, there." Jamie gave me a quick hug. "How are you holding up?"

"As well as can be expected I guess." I told her about how I'd occupied myself the day before and she laughed.

"I bet she gets used to it eventually."

"I hope so. Or else I'm going to have a very crowded closet. Assuming I can fit that thing in there." I sneezed and reached for my bottle of Benadryl. Maybe I really did have seasonal allergies.

Don had been listening in on our conversation. "You could just take it apart again."

"It took me five hours to build that thing. No way am I taking it apart. I will find a use for those stairs if it's the last thing I do."

You know, it's funny. I say things like that a lot. "If it's the last thing I do." But right then it struck me that if I were sent to prison, that that could really be true.

Ugh.

"So, Don, how's your business going?" I asked, trying to be polite.

"Good. Hoping to wrap up in the next week or so and then maybe Jamie can come visit me in Vegas."

"Wouldn't that be fun, Maggie? You could get by without me for a few days, couldn't you?"

"Absolutely." After all of this Jamie was going to deserve a break. She'd been taking way more of the burden running the café than she deserved.

I sat down with Greta and we exchanged a little small talk. Within a few minutes we were surrounded by the overly curious. One woman hadn't even tried to hide it. She'd just picked up her meal that was half-eaten and moved to the table right behind ours. If the table hadn't been bolted into the floor I'm pretty sure she would've moved it closer. As it was she pushed her chair so far back she almost bumped into me.

"You know," I said. "Fancy hasn't had much of a chance to play the last few days. What do you say to us taking the dogs out back while we talk?"

"Yes. This would be good."

We had a large grassy area out back where the dogs could run around, but because you had to go through the kitchens to get there, it was private. Only Lulu and Fancy were normally allowed back there. But I figured Greta was my friend and Hans was one of the most well-behaved dogs I'd ever met, so why not.

Plus, it would give us privacy from all the obnoxious lookie-loos.

Fancy practically tore my arm off as soon as she realized where we were headed. She loved to run around back there. Only reason I didn't let her spend more time out back was because the border on the far end was just a stream, one that Fancy loved to wade in, and I just knew that if I left her alone out there enough that one day she'd run right across that stream and into the woods behind it.

Hans was his normal restrained self until Greta let him off his leash. Even then he sat and watched her like there was nothing else in the world, not even a large barking black Newfoundland who desperately wanted to play, until Greta snapped a word in German.

Hans immediately turned and ran towards Fancy, all restraint and dignity forgotten as they tumbled and wrestled on the ground. I watched them, ready to jump in and save one or the other, but as rough as they were being with each other it was clearly all play. They were hopelessly covered in grass and dirt within moments, but at least they were having fun.

I laughed and relaxed onto the bench we kept out back. "Dogs are the best, aren't they?"

Greta nodded and sat down next to me, a little more reserved in her posture than I was. "Oh yes. I would trade all of my husbands for one Hans. He obeys. He is loyal. He is kind. He will defend me."

I leaned my head against the wall. "It's too bad when men resemble dogs that it's usually all the other qualities they embody." I glanced towards the store. "At least Jamie seems to have moved on from Lucas Dean."

"Mm. This I would not be so sure of."

I sat up straighter. "Are they still seeing each other?"

"I am not certain, but I believe so, yes. This man, this Don, he is fun and they talk. But I believe your friend is still in love with Mr. Dean."

"Ugh." I grabbed her hand. "Do me a favor. Please. Find her a man who is worthy of her. I am so tired of seeing her fall for these schmucks. She is so much better than that."

Greta patted my hand. "I will try. But what the heart wants, the heart takes. The mind cannot control this. Now. What my investigator found."

As Greta pulled a folder from her bag, Fancy plopped down next to me, panting heavily. Her limit on extreme play is about two minutes.

Hans ran at her, clearly wanting to play more, but with one uttered command from Greta he stopped short and went to lay by her side instead.

I shook my head. "You have amazing control over him."

"He was trained well." She patted his head and then handed me the folder. "This is the list of people Janice Fletcher has argued with in the last two years. There may be more, but this is the list my man found."

I scanned the list of people and their businesses. There had to be at least forty names there, and a few looked awfully familiar. "Give me a minute. I think we need Jamie for this. She knows the people around here better than I do."

I grabbed Jamie and brought her out back. The store was pretty dead and we still had two assistants working for the lunch rush. They could handle things for a few minutes.

I handed her the list and pointed at the third entry down. "The pool hall, wasn't that what was here before us?"

Jamie nodded. "Yeah. And that Apple Café was one block down. I interviewed the woman who ran it when we were thinking about this location because I wanted to know why they failed."

"What did she say?" I'd been trying to wrap up my life in DC so hadn't been as involved in the set-up of things as I would've liked.

"She said that sales were great initially, but over time the locals turned against her."

"Why? Because of Janice Fletcher?"

"She didn't say that specifically, but given what happened with us I do wonder."

Greta pointed to another name on the list. "This one was near here as well. I ate there the first time I visited three years ago."

"Can I borrow your laptop?" I asked her.

"Certainly."

"And Jamie, can you grab one of the Baker Valley brochures for me?"

Every business in town had a stack of free brochures on their counter that listed all the local businesses. It included a map of downtown Bakerstown as well as coupons. What I wanted was the map.

I fired up the laptop as Jamie grabbed the brochure.

"What are you thinking?" she asked as she handed it to me.

"That there's a pattern here. Maybe Janice had a deeper purpose. She was a very wealthy woman after all. And, no offense to you Greta, but some people get or keep their wealth by playing pretty dirty."

I looked up each of the people on the list her detective had made and had Jamie make a mark on the map for each one. Turns out they'd all been small business owners. And, more interesting than that, they'd all had businesses that were clustered in a four-block area of Bakerstown that included our café.

"Well, that solves that mystery. It looks to me like Janice Fletcher was trying to ruin the businesses in this area. But now the question is why." I closed Greta's laptop and gave it back to her.

"I think I may know." Greta dialed someone on her phone and proceeded to have a long, detailed conversation in German. When she hung up she nodded. "Yes, I know."

"And?"

She pointed to an area on the map to the right of the four-block section we'd identified. "This area here, Janice Fletcher owns. And this area here," she pointed to an area on the other side, "she also owns. My husband tells me that the two areas she owns are too small for big development. But if she were to own it all, she could build a big resort. Or condos. So she ruins these businesses in hopes that the owner of the land sells."

"Who owns the land?" I asked.

"Mason Realty. This is why Janice Fletcher cannot just buy the land. They will not sell to her. She is a Baker, yes?"

"So she tries to ruin every business instead in the hopes that they'll eventually declare the land worthless and sell, even if it's to her."

Greta nodded. "And she has succeeded very well, yes? Many businesses have failed because of her. My husband says the Masons are very close to wanting to sell this block of land."

"They are?"

"Yes. He has made an offer himself."

I sat back, stunned. "What happens to us if they sell?"

"If someone can acquire enough land to build a resort, your store would be torn down."

Jamie and I stared at each other. What would we do then? I shoved that thought aside. Right now what mattered was finding Janice Fletcher's killer. I'd worry about the destruction of all my hopes and dreams after I was sure I wasn't going to prison.

"So now we know why Janice Fletcher targeted us. And we know who else might have wanted her dead. But which of them would have done it?"

"There are names we must add to this list." Greta took a pen and in a scrawling script she wrote, Mason Maxwell, Deborah Mason, and Melinda Maxwell at the bottom of the list, her m's looking much more like w's.

"Mason Maxwell?"

"He is the sole male Mason heir under the age of eighty-five. I do not picture his grandfather getting out of his wheelchair to kill Janice Fletcher and throw her down the stairs." She crossed out the names of Deborah and Melinda. "The women are both old as well. They could not do this."

"But…Mason's my lawyer."

"And he's nice," Jamie added.

Greta shrugged. "When money is involved, people are not so nice, yes?"

Just when I was starting to like the guy, too. I looked at Jamie. "What do you think? Could Mason have done something like this?

"No. Don't be ridiculous. It was not him." She stepped away from me. "I should really get back to things."

Before I could say anything more she'd fled back into the café.

I stared at the map. "Mason Maxwell. I mean…It kind of fits. He definitely has a reason not to like Janice

Fletcher."

Greta nodded. "One more thing. My husband, he tells me, Mason Realty is no longer considering offers on the property. They are instead looking to buy the land that Janice Fletcher once owned."

"So we're still in danger of being torn down."

"Yes. And…Mason Maxwell has more of a motive than just his business being ruined."

"What?"

"Janice Fletcher would not sell him her properties just like he would not sell her his, but Janice's son does not care about these things."

"He inherited both plots of land? Or at least he will?"

She shook her head. "No. My husband says her nephew, Peter Nielsen, he inherited this plot of land. Her son, Mark Fletcher, he inherited this plot of land." She pointed out each of the plots of land on the map.

"Has the son sold yet?"

"No. I do not believe so. The will was just read today. It was quite the disappointment."

"How so?"

"Ms. Fletcher, she left all of her estate, except for the two plots of land, to her cat, Pookums."

"What?"

"Patsy Blackstone, you know her? She will take care of the cats and live at Ms. Fletcher's home and pay for the expenses from a trust."

"Could someone develop this area with just the one plot of land? Or do they need them both?" If they needed them both then the barkery was still safe.

"They would need both."

"So if I want to protect the barkery, I need to convince

Mark Fletcher to sell to me."

Greta nodded. "This would work, yes. But do you have this money?"

"Not yet. But if he'll sell to me, I'll find it."

First, though, I had to figure out if my lawyer was the killer. As far as I could tell, he had as much motive as I did, if not more.

I squeezed Greta's arm. "You're wonderful, you know that? Thank you so much for your help. If you ever need my help, all you have to do is ask." I stood. "Come on, Fancy. We have plans to make."

CHAPTER 25

I called Mason Maxwell and asked him to meet me at my grandpa's house. I figured even if he was a cold-blooded murderer he still wasn't a match for my grandpa and his shotgun. (Which thankfully was no longer kept in his truck, but was still not secured in a gun safe like I would've liked it to be.)

Plus, I needed to get a look at his shoes. If they had two rounded sections on the bottom, then it was quite possible he really was the murderer. And to think he'd seemed so nice and helpful lately. Well, two could play that game.

"I have some meetings this afternoon," he told me. "Can this wait until tomorrow?"

"We're having tacos for dinner, if you'd like to join us," I told him. "I have a good idea who the killer might be. Or at least, why they killed Janice Fletcher."

There was a long pause on the line.

"Jamie's going to be there, too," I added.

"She is?"

"Yeah, she loves Taco Tuesdays."

That was a lie. She'd never been over for Taco Tuesdays, but he didn't have to know that.

"Okay. Can I bring something? What beer does your grandfather drink?"

Beer? Mason Maxwell was going to bring beer? "He's always happy with Coors."

I wasn't, but I was going to have a hard enough time explaining to my grandpa why I'd invited Mason Maxwell to dinner, I didn't need to make it worse by suggesting some microbrew my grandpa would refuse to drink.

As soon as I hung up from Mason Maxwell, I called Jamie. I knew she'd agree to come to dinner because she was my best friend and best friends sit through awkward dinners together.

"Hey. I need you to come over for dinner tonight."

"Maggie. I have plans."

"With Don?"

She didn't answer.

"Don't tell me you have plans with Luke."

"Okay, fine. I won't."

"Well, cancel them. I need your help. I asked Mason Maxwell to come over for dinner."

"Why?"

"Because I need to get a look at his shoes. If he's the killer, I'll know from his shoes. Also, I want to see how he reacts when I tell him about what Janice Fletcher was trying to do and why. I need to know if he already knew."

"Maggie. Call Matt. Tell him what you suspect. Let him deal with this."

"No. I'm doing this myself. Don't you get it? If I don't find the real murderer, I am going to jail. So, please, help me out here?"

"Fine. See you at six."

"Thank you." I'm pretty sure Jamie didn't even hear

it, she'd already hung up. That's okay. She was going to be there and that's what really mattered.

☙ ☙ ☙

When I pulled into the driveway there was a car I didn't recognize parked there. But I soon found out who it belonged to: Lesley Pope. As you might recall she was the very nice former librarian who was "just friends" with my grandpa but who had quite the history with him and probably would have been more than just friends had their circumstances been different. But Lesley was married. To a very nice man who'd given my grandpa a second chance when he got out of prison. A man she still loved dearly even though he was in the final stages of Parkinson's.

"Lesley. How are you?" I was genuinely pleased to see her. After the news that she and my grandpa had a regular lunch date had made the rounds of town there had been a bit of a rough patch. My grandpa wouldn't say much about it, but it seems some of Lesley's husband's family had been less than pleasant about what they saw as a betrayal of her husband.

It would be nice if the world weren't so judgy judgy, but it is. Fortunately, both my grandpa and Lesley also had the love and respect of a lot of people who had stepped up and defended them, so while there might be some lingering resentment and some whispered comments still, most of the nastiness was past.

"I'm doing well." She squeezed my hands. "It sounds like you've hit a bit of a rough patch, though."

"You can say that again. But I think I know why someone killed Janice Fletcher. And I think I even know who it might be."

I sat down at the kitchen table and showed Lesley and my grandpa the map. "See how everyone she targeted was a small business owner in this little section of town? Greta told me the land there is owned by Mason Realty. But the land on either side was owned by Janice. I figure she was trying to drive us all out of business so she could buy the land up cheap."

My grandpa nodded. "Makes sense. And sounds like something Janice would do. But that doesn't explain who would want to kill her for it."

"Mason Maxwell, of course."

My grandpa snorted. "You think Mason Maxwell is the killer."

"I'll know tonight. Matt said they found a footprint at the scene and it was some sort of men's loafer with two circles on the tread. So when Mason Maxwell comes over for dinner, I'll take a peek at his shoes, and then I can know for sure."

"Maggie May. Mason Maxwell is not a killer. And you are not going to go peeking at his shoes while he's over here for…Why is he going to be over here?"

"Oh, I invited him to dinner. And Jamie, too."

"You what?"

"I wanted to see how he reacted to what I'd found out. And I figured inviting him to dinner would make him let his guard down. Plus, I think he likes Jamie. So he'll be all distracted by her and I can make him slip up and tell me something that confirms that he's the killer."

Lesley patted my grandpa's hand. "Let it go, Lou. She needs to feel like she's doing something to clear her name." She turned to me. "Although, for the record, I will tell you the killer is not Mason Maxwell. I have known him since he was little and he is not a murderer. Especially not for money."

"Well, we'll figure that out tonight, won't we? By the way, do either of you know Mark Fletcher?"

I explained to them why I cared and what I was hoping to accomplish.

My grandpa crossed his arms. "Assuming you convince him to sell, what are you going to pay him with, Maggie May?"

"Well…I do still have my 401(k)."

"That's for retirement. You can't go spending that now. You'll have nothing left when you need it."

"I can make it up later."

My grandpa pinched the bridge of his nose. "Maggie May. You don't understand what it's like to get old. You aren't going to have the same energy you do today. You aren't going to be able to work sixteen hour days without batting an eye. And jobs aren't going to be as easy to come by as you get older. You need to save now to survive later. Your generation doesn't have pensions like mine did. And let me tell you, social security is not all it's cracked up to be. That is if it's even around when you get to my age."

I took a deep, deep breath. I knew he hadn't approved of my quitting my good-paying job and opening the barkery. No one had. But I'd done it and now I was too far in to quit. "Grandpa. I hear what you're saying and I appreciate your concern. But I have come too far with the barkery to quit now, so if some ten thousand dollar investment can save us, I'm going to make it. I'm not saying you're wrong. You're probably absolutely right. But I have to do this."

He pushed away from the table. "I better start on dinner seeing as we're going to have a full house."

Lesley patted my arm once more. "And I best get going. From what I hear Mark hasn't done well since his divorce. He'd probably be happy for the money. But you're going to want to get to him before Mason Maxwell does, because there's no family loyalty in that boy. He'll sell to the highest bidder or the quickest cash."

"Thank you, Lesley. It was good to see you."

I hung back and let my grandpa walk her to the door. They stood close, talking softly for a few moments. I didn't want to spy, but I couldn't help it. Love is so complicated sometimes.

CHAPTER 26

It's an interesting thing, preparing to serve dinner to someone you suspect of murder. Fortunately, tacos don't really require a lot of sharp objects. No steak knives, for example. Not that I could really picture Mason Maxwell jumping up from the table, knife in hand, and brandishing it at us while he talked about his evil plan.

One thing I did know—no way was Fancy going to get me out of this if he did do something like that. He intimidated her far too much. But I still had my grandpa. I'd put the odds at ten to one in his favor with pretty much anyone, especially some country club lawyer.

As I helped my grandpa set the dining room table with my grandma's china, he shook his head. "I really wish I'd known earlier that Mason Maxwell was coming to dinner. I would've fixed something other than tacos."

"I don't know. I'm kind of looking forward to seeing how he handles them."

I've never managed to eat a taco in my life without the shell breaking apart at some point and spilling the insides all over my hand. (We're a hard-shell kind of family. None of that tortillas-as-shells in our household.)

Me, I just lick the greasy juice off and keep going. Mason Maxwell? Well, I guess we'd see.

I wondered if he'd try to eat them with a fork. How would that even work?

I filled a matching set of red, green, and yellow earthenware condiment bowls with all the fixings for tacos—tomatoes, lettuce, store-bought salsa, shredded cheddar cheese, and, my favorite, sour cream—and placed them on the lazy Susan in the center of the table. My grandpa added a plateful of taco shells and we stepped back to survey our preparations.

(We were eating fancy. Normally we'd just leave everything in its container and serve ourselves up in the kitchen and then plop down on the couch with our TV trays.)

Jamie was the first to arrive. She'd brought Lulu with her and I had to chase Fancy and Lulu into the backyard before they took out the entire living room. We stood at the sliding glass doors and watched them tumble one another.

"I can't believe you think Mason could do something like this," she said.

"Well, he does have motive."

"So do you."

"But he also has the shoes."

She scoffed. "Oh, okay. That's a good reason to think a man's a murderer. Because he doesn't wear shoes you like."

I would've argued further but the doorbell rang. I jumped half out of my skin at the sound. No one ever used the bell, they just knocked. "Well, that's the man of the hour. You want to get the door while I grab the taco meat?"

"Sure."

I grabbed the taco meat from the kitchen while Jamie went for the door. Our version of taco meat is basically ground beef cooked up with one of those packets of seasoning you can buy at the store, but don't knock it, it makes for a yummy meal.

Fancy and Lulu almost bowled me over as they raced through the kitchen to see who had arrived. Fancy immediately skidded to a halt when she saw Mason Maxwell. Lulu, not quite aware that she was facing an "alpha" ran right up to him and jumped on his pressed khakis.

"Down." He firmly sat her on her butt and stared her down for a second until she stopped wriggling. "Good dog."

As soon as Mason Maxwell stood back up, Lulu was up and running again, but she at least avoided him.

"Mr. Maxwell. Welcome," I said.

"Mason, please. Remember after that interrogation that we are on a first-name basis now."

"Right. Of course."

He held up a six-pack of Coors bottles towards my grandpa. "Mr. Carver. I brought some beer to go with those tacos. They smell delicious, by the way."

"Call me Lou. And much appreciated."

My grandpa took the beers while I gestured at the table. "Well, have a seat guys. No sense letting the food get cold."

As they took their seats, Fancy wandered closer to the table, still keeping a wary eye on Mason. I'd put myself opposite him and she happily settled in next to me as my grandpa handed around bottles and sat down himself. Lulu, taking her cue from Fancy, sat down next to her.

"Do you feed Lulu people food?" I asked Jamie.

"No."

Well, that was going to make things interesting. I'd just have to be a little sneakier than usual.

Mason paused for just the slightest second when he realized no one was going to give him a glass to pour his beer into, but then he took a swig straight from the bottle and set it on the table. He and Jamie had a little back and forth over who should serve themselves first and I felt a little stab of guilt that I'd invited this man over under false pretenses. He clearly had a thing for my friend. And as much as I wasn't a huge fan of his uptight manner, he was most definitely a better choice for her than Luke. (Assuming he wasn't a murderer, of course.)

As my grandpa served himself, he said, "There's one rule at this table. We don't talk business over dinner. So whatever business you're here to talk about, you save it for after."

"Yes, sir. Lou, sir."

Mason answered, but I knew that comment was directed at me, not him. I've never been a fan of small talk. Although it did give me a chance to get to know more about Mr. Mason Maxwell under the guise of not talking business.

As Mason served himself, I wondered if he'd ever actually eaten tacos before. But then I chided myself for the unfair thought. Just because the guy was rich and dressed like he spent his days at the country club didn't mean he'd never had an adventure or two. Plus, these days the country club probably served the occasional taco just to mix things up. Small-town Colorado wasn't as small-town as it had once been.

"So, Mason," I said." Do you like to travel? What's the best country you've ever been to?"

As I prepared my own tacos and snuck a bite of taco meat to Fancy while distracting Lulu from noticing, he launched into a story about riding a camel through a mountainous region in Northern Africa all by himself.

"Really? You just rented a camel and rode off into the mountains?"

I'd never thought I'd be jealous of Mason Maxwell, but I was. As a single woman traveling alone I could have never pulled off a stunt like that. I mean, I could've tried, but the odds that it would have ended with the delightful story he told about spending a night in a tent in the middle of the desert with a bunch of nomads and drinking some sort of alcohol he couldn't identify until the wee hours of the morning while they told tall tales to one another were pretty darned slim.

That story started us on a round of telling our most outrageous travel adventures including the time Jamie and I went backpacking in New Zealand and found ourselves stranded on a one-lane road in the middle of nowhere with no cell service and a baby cow that had somehow decided our car was its mother.

The dinner passed quickly. By the end of it I was starting to see what Jamie saw in him. He *did* have a sense of humor. He'd even been arrested a couple times in college. It seems I'd mistaken his professional restraint for his personality.

If I hadn't been worried he was a murderer, it would've been a very good meal indeed. (He even managed the tacos with aplomb. When the juice from the first taco started to slide down his hand he'd simply wiped it off and kept going. He'd only resorted to his fork at the end to clean up the last little bits, just like I had.)

But then the meal ended and I was reminded why I'd asked him to come over.

"You play Scrabble, son?" my grandpa asked.

"Actually, Grandpa. I need to show him something first, if you don't mind."

My grandpa eyed me, but all he said was "Fine. Go ahead."

Jamie and I quickly took the plates and dishes to the kitchen and then laid out the map I'd prepared at the barkery.

"What's this?" Mason asked, leaning forward to study the map, his sharp intelligence on full display as he traced an outline of the impacted area.

"Those are the business locations of all the people Janice Fletcher harassed in the past few years."

Mason sat back. "Huh. I'd never put it together."

"I think she was trying to ruin those businesses so you'd sell your land to her."

"And she almost succeeded, too. Last week the bait shop told us they were closing up. We were ready to wash our hands of the whole area. It's not easy to make a profit when no business can stay open for more than a few months at a time."

"But Greta said you changed your mind after Janice Fletcher died?"

He nodded and pointed to the same areas on the map Greta had. "Janice Fletcher owned both of these plots. If we can buy them from her heirs then the whole area can be developed as a resort."

"What happens to us?" Jamie asked.

At least Mason Maxwell had the grace to look abashed. "Well, building the resort would require tearing down all the buildings in the area."

"So after all that work we put into getting the café set up we'd be out on the streets?"

"I…" He glanced at all of us. "It's not personal."

"To hell it isn't." It was one of the few times I'd seen Jamie genuinely angry. Ever. She stood up and grabbed Lulu's leash. "I've gotta go. See you at work tomorrow, Maggie."

Mason stood, too. "Jamie, wait."

She stormed out, leaving an awkward silence behind her.

"Ice cream anyone?" I asked.

Mason shook his head. "I think I'll get going, too."

He couldn't leave. I hadn't figured out if he was the murderer yet. But I couldn't exactly say that, could I?

He'd already stood and was moving towards the door.

"Wait. One more question."

"What?"

"Can I see your shoes? What brand are they? I have a friend who still lives in DC who I think might like a pair. And you did say the other day that they're comfortable."

He lifted one foot, revealing two rounded circles on the sole and rattled off some Italian-sounding name. "I'll send you the link to their website if you want."

"That'd be great. Thanks."

I closed the door behind him and turned to see my grandpa watching me, not looking the least bit amused. "That man is not a killer, Maggie May."

"He has the right shoes. And a motive."

My grandpa went to sit on the couch, turning the volume on the television high enough to make it clear he wasn't going to discuss this absurdity any longer.

I carefully folded up my map. I knew I should share it with Matt. Tell him what I'd found out about Mason's motive and his shoes. But, honestly, I knew there was no point. Not yet. Matt would no more believe Mason Maxwell was the killer than my grandpa or Jamie did.

I needed more.

But first I had to do what I could to save the barkery. I had to track down Mark Fletcher and convince him to sell his property to me instead of Mason Realty.

CHAPTER 27

According to Lesley Pope, Mark Fletcher spent most of his days hanging out at a bar that was creatively named *The Hole*. And, man, did it fit the description. This was a place for serious drinkers. It wasn't even trendy trashy like some places geared towards the college crowd are. It was just a dump.

It was located on the edge of Bakerstown, down a rutted road that hadn't been repaved in a good decade or two. The building itself looked like an old wood cabin that had been abandoned in the 1800s and left to rot. I wouldn't have been surprised to learn that the original owner had put the place together himself with trees he cut down from the nearby forest.

It wasn't a place I would've chosen to go. Ever. It was a place for people at the end to drink themselves to death.

But I had worked too hard to get my business off the ground to let one scary, dilapidated building stop me. I mean, really, some of the people in the valley were odd and strange and maybe not good at showers or talking to strangers, but I couldn't bring myself to believe that I was in danger walking into that place.

(What can I say, sometimes when you're used to the big city and the obvious ways it can be dangerous, you fail to see the subtle dangers. As I've since learned, although not in this particular instance, it only takes one bad person for you to be in a heap-load of danger.)

Anyway. I drove out there first thing in the morning as the sun was coming up. They were actually open twenty-four seven, but I figured I could at least wait until seven in the morning to drop by.

I hesitated outside, wondering what I was doing, but it didn't keep me from eventually opening the creaky metal screen door that served as a barrier to the outside world.

I squinted as I stopped just inside the doorway, noting the numerous animal heads on the wall—mostly bucks with big racks, it was that kind of place. There were three men, each seated alone, as well as a female bartender who looked like the toughest person in there. Not mean, per se, just…tough. Her skin was leathery and she was wiry and muscular in a way that said life had sucked everything out of her it could. The tank top she wore had a Harley Davidson symbol on the front and I wouldn't have been surprised to learn that she was the owner of the Harley outside that was about five times her size.

The only real surprise was her lack of tattoos and her bright blue eyes. "Whatchyou want?" she asked.

"I'm looking for Mark Fletcher. I heard he hangs around here."

She looked me up and down. "If you're looking for money, he ain't got any. And he's not the type of man you want to keep in your life."

I stepped closer. "Actually, I had a business deal for him. I was hoping to give him some money."

"Ha. Doubt that." She looked me up and down. "Nice try. You have his kid or something?"

"What? No." I didn't know much about Mark Fletcher other than the woman who'd given birth to him and the place he chose to drink, but I was pretty sure he wasn't my type. "Look. Is he here?" I glanced at the three men, wondering if any of them could be him.

"Nah. But if you want to sit and wait, he'll probably be here soon."

I hesitated. I had his home address in my pocket. I could just drive over there. But maybe this woman could give me information I could use to convince him to sell to me instead of Mason Maxwell.

"Okay. Whatcha got on tap?" It's a bad habit of mine to pick up the accents and vocabulary of people around me. Someone once told me it's a sign of confidence when you do that, a way to build rapport. For me it's just something I do without even thinking about it. Send me to London and I'll be talking loos and mums within the week.

I pulled a barstool out from the end of the bar and wedged myself into the corner. I must've been a gunslinger in a past life, because I always want to sit in the back corner of a room where I have a good sight line on everyone else. Drives me nuts to sit with my back to people.

Turns out my drinking choices were cheap beer number one and its lighter cousin or cheap beer number two and its lighter cousin. No soda. No water. I could also choose whiskey or vodka if I were so inclined.

I chose cheap beer number one, although, honestly, I'm not sure I would've known the difference between the four choices. The bartender handed me a thirty-two-ounce Styrofoam cup, full to the brim. Last time I'd had beer from a big Styrofoam cup had been at some dive bar in New York City that had a bunch of bras hanging from the ceiling. (Never did know the name of the place. A friend of mine's cousin owned it, so I always knew it as "My Cousin's Bar".)

"Cheers." I toasted her and took a sip. (Yes, it was seven in the morning and I was drinking beer, but that kind of beer hardly qualifies.)

She leaned against the bar near me, showing no interest in cleaning the place even though it could've definitely used it. Then again, given the clientele, I figured the dirt and smell of old beer were all part of what made it appealing.

"So, Mark Fletcher comes here a lot?" I asked.

"Daily."

"What's a rich guy like him doing spending his days drinking cheap beer in a place like this? No offense."

"Eh. When people fall, they all fall to the same place. His mom might've been rich. He isn't. He's just a lousy drunk." Left unsaid was the "just like the rest of them".

I wondered what brought a woman to work in a place like this. Did you just over time become more and more of a certain type so that your choices narrowed in on you until you couldn't escape them? Was life just some gigantic funnel and we were all clinging to our place on the sides trying not to fall to the bottom?

(What can I say? Don't give me beer to drink first thing in the morning or you get bad philosophizing.)

The woman leaned closer. "Wait. I know who you are."

"You do?"

"You're the woman who pushed Mark's mother down a flight of stairs, aren't you?"

"No. I'm the woman *accused* of pushing his mother down a flight of stairs. I didn't do it. Wanted to. Even thought about it for a second, but I didn't do it." I took another sip of beer.

She laughed slightly. "Yeah, you and half the town. And Mark. I doubt there was a person that woman met who didn't want to see her dead at the bottom of a flight of stairs."

I sat up straighter. "Do you think Mark could've done it?"

"Mark? No. He's a pathetic wretch. Weighs one-twenty soaking wet. Plus he's a coward. No way he'd hit her in the head with a frying pan and throw her down a flight of stairs."

"You certainly seem to know all the details."

"Coroner's assistant likes to come in here after work. Chatty fellow."

"Ah." I sipped my beer some more. One of the regulars stood up and sauntered our way, clearly intent on saying hello.

"Turn it around, Jim." The bartender pointed him back towards his spot in the far corner. "This lady has no interest in the likes of you."

"No one should drink alone," he slurred, even though he'd just been doing that exact thing.

"She's not alone. We're talking. Girl talk. Go away."

He swayed in place for a second and then turned back towards his table.

"Wow. He got an early start."

"Jim hasn't been sober in at least a decade." She leaned her elbows on the counter. "So what do you want Mark for anyway?"

"He inherited some land when his mom died. I want to see if he'll sell it to me. Mason Maxwell and his family are looking to buy it and if they do they'll probably tear up my store."

"You better move fast."

"Why?"

"Mark's desperate enough he'll sell to the first person who makes an offer."

"I've heard that a few times now. Why's he so desperate for money? Bar tab?"

"Nah. What he owes here is nothing compared to what he owes his bookie."

"There are bookies in the Baker Valley?"

She laughed. "Of course there are. But this one's a Vegas guy. Plays by Vegas rules." She nodded to the clock. "If Mark isn't here by now, he may not be in today. Some days he doesn't muster the energy. Only lives across that lot, but you know how it is."

"Then I guess I'll swing by and see if he's around." I placed a ten dollar bill on the counter even though the early bird special was just a dollar and scrawled my phone number on a napkin. "You see him, you mind giving me a call?"

She took the money. "Sure, I can do that."

"I'm Maggie, by the way."

"Marla."

We shook hands and I left. Call me crazy, but I kind of liked Marla. She was exactly what she was and that's sometimes really refreshing to see. Not that I was going to go back to her fine employer anytime soon. Definitely not my kind of place.

❀❀❀ 353 ❀❀❀

CHAPTER 28

There was a cluster of mobile homes just across the lot that I assumed included Mark Fletcher's home. It was close enough I figured I could just walk it. I'd get there sooner than driving around the block.

There were six mobile homes total scattered in a sloppy half-circle around a dead-end dirt road. The cars and trucks parked around them had to be at least thirty years old if a day, and I would've bet at least half of them were broken-down. The car I walked past to reach the center of the mobile homes had two flat tires and a busted up windshield. The truck parked behind it was rusted through in a half dozen spots and taped up with duct tape in another dozen.

The sounds of some Sunday morning preacher blared from the mobile home at the far end, but it wasn't the one I was looking for. The one I was looking for was a faded beige mobile home with what had once been white curtains covering the small front window, their edges now brown from years of cigarette smoke.

I glanced around but saw no one. The place was as sad and dying as the bar. Another place people went when they'd slid too far down to come back up.

I should've left right then. I didn't know who else lived there. I didn't know anything about Mark Fletcher other than the name of his mother, the fact that he was a degenerate drunk, and that he had gambling debts.

But I had to get to him before Mason Maxwell did. If he was that desperate for money he wasn't going to hold out for other offers or refuse to sell out of respect for his family feud. I moved towards the metal steps leading up to the front door and froze.

On the ground, right there next to the stairs, was a man's footprint. It had two large circles on the sole. Did it belong to Mark Fletcher? Or had Mason Maxwell already been by?

I knocked on the door but no one answered. Determined, I knocked harder, which set a nearby dog to barking, but still didn't bring an answer. Finally, I knocked a third time and the door popped open. It swung slowly inward to reveal a living room as dingy as the curtains I'd already seen.

(I should note here that some mobile homes are absolutely beautiful inside and my description of Mark Fletcher's should in no way be seen as a general opinion on mobile homes. As a matter of fact we used to live in a very nice double-wide when I was younger that you couldn't have told from a house once you were inside. It's all in how you choose to live under the circumstances you're given. But I digress.)

I was about to grab the door and slam it shut and get out of there, because the place was definitely giving me the creeps, but then I heard a soft moan from the direction of the kitchen. I stepped one foot inside and peered around the door. I couldn't see anyone yet, but what I did see was a pool of blood near the kitchen table.

I should've run. I should've run right back to that bar and called the cops. I mean, I didn't know what had happened there. And my memory of being at Janice's house with a possible killer lurking in the shadows waiting to see what I'd do were still pretty fresh. But clearly the guy was still alive. And the last thing I wanted to do was explain to the cops how I'd heard some guy moaning in his kitchen, seen a pool of blood, and just left. I'd already used up my quota of cold-hearted disinterest, you know?

I took another step into the mobile home and paused, listening for any sound that might indicate I wasn't alone. But the only sound I heard was the soft moaning coming from the kitchen and a loud series of meows from the back of the house. I sneezed as I wondered if Mark had inherited his mother's love for feline companions.

At the edge of the kitchen I saw a bloody footprint with two circles. So Mark wasn't the killer. Or if he was, he wasn't the guy on the floor in the kitchen, moaning.

I pulled my phone out and hit the emergency call option. I figured if there was someone about to attack me then at least they'd get busted for it. Not that I was too keen on dying in a dingy mobile home on the outskirts of Bakerstown, but you know. Only so much control you have over fate.

(I know. You're probably thinking to yourself that if you don't want to die in a dingy mobile home filled with cats in some small town, then you shouldn't go there in the first place. And I'd agree. But I think you probably know by now that I'm not always the brightest about the choices I make.)

I took another step forward. A man was sprawled in the middle of the kitchen floor, his face a bloodied mess. He watched me through eyes that were probably going to swell shut soon and moaned again, waving at me like he wanted me to leave.

But it was too late. The emergency dispatcher answered the phone and I told her where I was and to send an ambulance. The man shook his head and tried to stand, muttering "I'm fine. I'm fine. No need to call…"

I gave him my "are you serious" look. As I hung up, he fell over again. This man was in no shape to do anything other than go to a hospital.

"I'm…fine." He again tried to stand and fell back to the floor.

I shoved the phone back into my purse. "You don't look fine to me. If you don't want to press charges against whoever did this, that's your business. But you need to see a doctor. Because if whoever attacked you hit more than your face you could be in serious trouble right now."

"I'm fine. I just need to clean up. Get a little rest. That's all." He shifted to the side of the fridge and somehow managed to get it open, reaching inside for a can of beer. (Am I the only one that remembers when generic products actually came in white containers with black lettering? Back in the day my grandpa literally drank generic beer that just said BEER on the side of the can. But I digress.)

"Maybe you should hold off on that beer until they've taken a look at you." I knelt down and tried to meet his eyes, but he wasn't quite focusing on anything at that point. I sneezed again and muttered something about cats as he took a long, long sip.

"I'm fine. Call them back. Tell them I'm fine."

"Sorry, but I'm going to leave this one to the professionals if you don't mind. Are you Mark Fletcher?"

He nodded and took another sip.

"Who did this to you? Was it Mason Maxwell?"

He started to laugh but it turned into a racking, hacking cough. "Mason? You think little Maisy boy did this to me?" He grabbed at his chest and winced.

"Well if it wasn't him, who was it?"

"Friend. We had a misunderstanding. It's all good now." He took another long swig of his beer.

I desperately wanted to ask him about the plot of land, but it seemed a little rude given the circumstances. I would've probably still done it if I'd thought he'd remember the conversation later, but it was pretty clear he was barely holding on.

I sneezed again. I could already feel my throat starting to close up but I didn't have any Benadryl and I doubted he did either.

"Who are you?" he asked. "Why are you here?"

I sat down across from him, careful to avoid the pool of blood on the floor. "Take it you don't read the papers much."

He shook his head. "Sports. That's all."

His head started to droop and I clapped my hands in front of his face.

"What? What?" He stared at me, bleary-eyed.

"Concussion. Can't nod off like that." I glanced around. There was a picture of him with a pretty woman and a brown lab held onto the fridge with a magnet from Niagara Falls. "Who's that?"

"My wife. Or was. Divorced me."

"She get the dog in the divorce, too?"

He nodded. "And the house. And the money. Well, what was left." He tried to laugh, but gasped in pain instead.

I sneezed again. I really, really wanted to leave, but I knew I needed to stay there until the ambulance arrived. Fortunately, I heard them pull up outside just then. Right behind them came a fire truck and two police cars. Talk about overkill. But when not much happens I guess you send out everyone you can.

The cops came in first, weapons drawn. The first one pointed his gun at me. "You. Put your hands on your head."

"I'm the one who called you."

"Hands on your head," he shouted again.

Really? Did I look like I'd just beaten a man to a pulp?

"Hands. On. Your. Head."

"Fine." I put my hands on my head. No point getting shot.

The next few minutes involved me being manhandled out the door, shoved up against a police car, *frisked*, and *handcuffed*. They sure knew how to treat a Good Samaritan. But since I was also someone charged with the murder of the mother of the man who was beat up inside and he wasn't going to be much help in clearing my name, I just went along with it.

Although, by the time they were done I was thinking I should've just listened to Mark Fletcher and let him lie there on the kitchen floor until he felt well enough to crawl back into his bedroom and die. Of course then I would've been the suspect in yet another murder and I still hadn't figured out how to clear my name on the first one.

The officers were deep into a debate about whether to take me in or not when a third police car pulled up and Matt stepped out. I'd never been so happy to see anyone in my entire life.

"Maggie May. What on earth are you doing out here?"

"If I told you I was trying to buy a plot of land from Mark Fletcher would you believe me?"

"Mark Fletcher doesn't own a thing besides this beat-up mobile home and that truck there with the three flat tires."

He removed my cuffs and I rubbed at my wrists as I told him about Mark's inheritance and why I wanted to buy the land. "But when I got here someone had beat him up. Look." I walked him over to the front of the mobile home to show him the footprint I'd seen, but it turns out that when two policemen and two paramedics storm into a small mobile home they pretty much obliterate any evidence. Same with the one inside. Someone had knelt on it. It was just a bloody smudge now.

So I told him about what I'd seen. "And…Listen to this. Last night I confirmed that Mason Maxwell wears that kind of shoe."

Matt crossed his arms and stared me down. "So let me see if I've got this straight. You came here to try to buy a plot of land from Mark Fletcher. You found him beat up in his kitchen. You saw a print that might be the same kind of print we found at Janice Fletcher's house.

And, for reasons I'm not quite clear on, you now think it was Mason Maxwell who left those prints. So you now think it was Mason who beat up Mark Fletcher and killed his mother."

"Yes."

"Go home, Maggie."

"But…"

"Go. Home. Let the police do their job."

I shook my head. "Don't you get it? Letting you guys do your job is why I'm now charged with murder. Don't you think I'd love to let you do your job? Don't you think I want nothing more than to hang out at the barkery with Fancy or at home with my grandpa? But you keep arresting the wrong people."

"Well, I'm certainly not going to compound that error by arresting one of the most respected men in this county. Mason Maxwell is not a killer and if I were to even suggest that he was to anyone, anywhere, they would laugh at me. Now, where are you parked?"

I nodded towards the parking lot.

"Allow me to escort you back to your vehicle, Ms. Carver." He took me by the elbow and marched me back to the van. After he'd watched me buckle myself in he leaned close. "Go home, Maggie."

"Only if you promise me you're going to talk to Mark Fletcher about whoever did that to him."

He closed his eyes for a long moment and then looked at me with that piercing gaze of his. "Do you think I'm incompetent?"

"No. I think you're very smart and capable."

"So don't you think that I'm going to ask an assault victim who it was who assaulted him?"

"Well. Yeah. I guess. I just…"
"Enough, Maggie. Go. Home."
Reluctantly, I started the van and drove away.

CHAPTER 29

I knew Matt wanted me to go home. He'd practically ordered me to go home. But I was too wound up for that. What was I going to do? Watch TV? Try to read a book? I mean, Fancy would appreciate it, but other than that, I could see no reason it made sense to go home.

Much better to go into the barkery and take my frustrations out on making some dog biscuits. We were running low on canine crunchies and could probably use another batch of doggie delights, too. And if that wasn't enough to calm me down I'd been working on a few new ideas. Might as well take the time to perfect one.

By the time I pulled up outside the barkery it was the downtime between the breakfast rush and the lunch rush, so there was just one other vehicle in the parking lot—a sleek black Range Rover with Nevada plates. (Jamie lives just a couple blocks away so she walks to work every day.)

I wondered whose it was, but that mystery was solved when I walked in through the café door and saw Don and Jamie sharing a coffee.

Jamie stood, watching me closely. "Hey. I didn't think you'd be in today."

I glanced down, but there was no blood on my clothes. She must've just known something was wrong. Best friends are good that way.

"Yeah, I know. I wasn't planning on it. But I needed something to occupy my mind for a couple hours." I almost told her about Mason and what he'd done that morning, but decided it was a waste of breath. I already knew what she'd say. Instead I said, "I thought I'd get caught up on some baking. After I have a cinnamon roll and Coke, of course. Or maybe two."

"Of the cinnamon rolls? Or the Cokes?"

"Both." I heated up a cinnamon roll, grabbed a Coke, and came back to join them.

I sneezed. Me and cats, I tell you. I'd thought getting away from that trailer would be enough, but I was clearly wrong. I was also too lazy to go grab a Benadryl right then. I wanted to eat my cinnamon roll first.

Jamie grabbed my arm. "What's up? You seem off."

"I don't want to talk about it. Let's just say I had an interesting morning." I took a bite of yummy gooey cinnamon roll and sighed in pleasure.

"Did you talk to Mark Fletcher? Is he going to sell to you?"

"He's a bit indisposed at the moment. I'm not sure he'll be selling to anyone, anytime soon."

Don leaned forward. "He dead?"

"No. Just beat to a pulp. And I'm pretty sure I know who did it." I stabbed another bite of cinnamon roll before I met Jamie's eyes. "You do, too."

Jamie pressed her lips together and shook her head.

"Jamie, I know you don't think the same things about Mason that I do." I glanced at Don. He didn't need to know all our business, but I had to say what I had to say. "But you have to agree with me on this one. He has the motive. And the shoes."

"Why are you so obsessed with those shoes, Maggie? Don has those shoes, too. He's not a killer."

I froze with a bite of cinnamon roll halfway to my mouth, suddenly realizing what I'd been missing about this whole situation. (If you realized it before me, good on you, but it's not like I walk around suspecting everyone of murder. I should. I certainly do more now than I did before I moved to the mountains.)

I forced myself to finish the bite, careful not to look at Don.

"Something wrong?" he asked, his voice flat and deadly in a way it had never been all these days he'd been hanging around.

"No. Nothing's wrong. It's just been a heckuva couple of weeks, you know." I chugged down the last of my Coke and pushed my plate away even though there was most of a cinnamon roll left. "I think I'm going to go get started on that baking."

Before I could stand, Mason Maxwell walked through the door. He smiled at Jamie with the look of a man who is definitely infatuated. "Any chance you still have some cinnamon rolls left?"

Mason glanced at Don, recognizing his competition, but determined to pretend otherwise.

"Absolutely. Let me get one for you." Jamie took my plate and started towards the kitchen, Mason trailing after her.

"Wait. I can get that," I called after her, but she was already halfway to the kitchen.

Don grabbed my wrist before I could stand. "Why don't you let Jamie do it? I'd like to talk to you about something."

We both knew he had absolutely nothing he wanted to talk to me about. He just didn't want me calling the cops. But I'd said he was calculated. If he could find some way to get me out of there and get rid of me without Jamie or Mason being any the wiser, he'd take that opportunity.

So to protect my friend and my lawyer, I had to play it cool, too. But I didn't have to play it stupid.

"Mason, why don't you join us while Jamie's heating that up for you?" I called.

"Okay. Thanks."

Don glared at me, but I ignored him. "Have you met Don before?"

"No. Can't say I have officially."

I sat back and tried to figure out how to get out of this mess as they exchanged banal comments. There was no way Don was going to let me live, not if he realized I'd figured out he was the killer. Which meant I needed to find a way to alert the authorities. But how?

I reached towards my purse but Don stepped on my foot, hard enough to let me know he knew what I was doing. Okay, that was out.

I glanced towards the kitchen. "You okay in there, Jamie? You need my help?"

"Nope. I've got it." She came back carrying a cinnamon roll and coffee.

Great, now another potential hostage was in Don's reach. And things were about to get much, much worse. Because pulling up outside was a police car. With Matt behind the wheel. I glanced towards Don and saw him slowly ease a gun out from the small of his back and place it on his thigh.

Jamie sat down as Matt walked through the door and glared right at me. "Maggie May, I thought I told you to go home."

This was it. This was my chance. "I was going to go home, but then I decided to come in here and do some baking. But I got sidetracked by cinnamon rolls. Hey, by the way, I don't think you're allowed to come in here any longer unless you have the appropriate footwear. You're going to have to buy a pair of fancy Italian shoes like Mason and Don here or you have to go home."

Matt frowned at me for a split second, but then he realized what I was telling him and forced a laugh as he glanced at the two men's shoes. "That's too bad. I'm more a tennies kind of guy myself."

Mason—who still didn't know what was going on—raised his pant leg to show off his shoe. "Every man should own at least one pair of nice shoes, Matt. Look at that fine stitching. And they're comfortable, too."

"I'll have to think about it. Maybe you can send me a link to the site where I can find those?"

"Absolutely."

Now that Matt knew who the killer was, I needed to create a distraction. I met his eyes and he nodded slightly.

I grabbed Don's coffee, threw it in his face, and screamed "Get down!"

As I hit the floor I saw Mason grab Jamie and take her to the ground, shielding her with his body. There were shots. I couldn't tell you how many. I couldn't even tell you who fired them. I was so jacked up on adrenaline that all I knew was there were shots and that I was on the ground with Mason and Jamie right beside me.

And that Matt was still standing, exposed. In danger.

I rolled to the side and looked towards where I'd seen Matt last, but he wasn't there. I looked down, worried he'd been shot, but then I saw him. He was standing over Don who was slumped in his chair. Matt kicked Don's gun away so that it went spinning across the floor and checked his pulse.

I wanted to stand. I wanted to run to Matt's side and tell him I was so glad he'd understood what I was telling him, and that I had never been happier to see someone alive and well in my entire life. But I just sat there and shook instead.

It was Matt who came to me. He knelt down in front of me and took my face in his hands and asked if I was okay. I nodded, not trusting myself to speak.

"Good. I better call this in."

When he stood it took everything I had left not to call him back to me.

🐾 🐾 🐾

After the police and Mason left, Jamie and I sat out back, still trying to recover from our near-death experience.

"How did you know Don was the killer? Was it really just the shoes?" she asked.

"No. It was the stupid cats, believe it or not."

"What?"

"You know how allergic I am, right?"

"Yeah."

"Well. At Janice's house and at Mark's trailer I kept sneezing because of their cats. Usually if I can get away from a cat I'm fine. But there were a couple times here at the barkery that I started to sneeze or my eyes started to water, too. I didn't think anything of it because the first time was the same day I'd been at Janice Fletcher's. But when it happened today…And when I realized I'd seen that footprint at Mark Fletcher's and that Don wears those kinds of shoes, too, it all came together. I'd never even suspected he was the killer. He was just some out-of-town guy hanging around you, why would he want Janice Fletcher dead?"

"Good question. Why did he want her dead?"

"I'm not positive, but I suspect he was Mark Fletcher's bookie here from Vegas to collect on what he was owed. But Mark Fletcher didn't have anything to pay him. Don killed her so that Mark would inherit. But then Janice Fletcher went and left everything to her cat. I figure Don probably beat Mark up when he realized that's what had happened."

"Huh. Wow. Do you think they'll drop the charges against you now?"

I stared at her. "They better. I mean, Don was the real killer."

"Yeah, but can someone prove that?"

I had nothing to say. *Could* someone prove it? It was so obvious to me. But what if they couldn't? Now that the killer was dead, there was certainly no chance for a confession.

"Seriously, Jamie. Don't say things like that to me." I stared at nothing, hoping and praying that Matt would be able to convince whoever needed convincing of my innocence.

CHAPTER 30

Fortunately for me, once Mark Fletcher heard that Don was dead, he told the cops all about what had happened. I was right, Don had killed Janice Fletcher to hasten Mark's inheritance. Seems Mark had talked a good talk about how rich his family was to get Don's boss to extend him a very generous line of credit, one that wasn't going to be paid off by the little plot of land he'd inherited. When Don learned that the money had all gone to the cats, he took his frustrations out on Mark. If we hadn't stopped him, the next victim might have been Patsy Blackstone and who knows who else, because the list of people designated as cat caretakers before Mark Fletcher was a very long one indeed.

We learned all of the details at Taco Tuesday that next week.

Matt was there. So was Mason. And Jamie.

I watched Mason and Jamie laughing and talking back and forth and decided that maybe Mason wasn't such a bad choice for my friend after all. He had risked his life for her. Would Lucas Dean have done the same? I think not.

Plus when he looked at her…Well, his eyes just lit up in this amazing way. I actually found myself rooting for him.

(I know. A few days before I'd thought he was a murderer. What can I say? Sometimes when you misjudge a person initially you overcompensate in the opposite direction after you realize your mistake. I know this from the number of people who've gone from thinking of me as a ditzy dumb blonde to thinking of me as a genius. I'm neither. I'm just Maggie May Carver, barkery owner, Miss Fancypants slave, and adequate but not perfect friend and granddaughter.)

As we ate our tacos and laughed and enjoyed ourselves I realized that was the first night I'd felt truly honestly at home. I really had found the place I wanted to be and the people I wanted to be with.

And as I fell asleep that night—wedged into the far corner of the bed because Fancy had finally bothered to try the steps and decided she liked them and was now taking up 95% of the available space—I told myself everything would be okay. I could finally get on with the business of starting my new life in the Baker Valley and spending quality time with my friends, my grandpa, and my dog.

No more dead bodies. No more arrests. Life was just going to be nice and normal from there on out.

Boy was I wrong.

A BURIED BODY
AND BARKERY BITES

A MAGGIE MAY AND MISS FANCYPANTS MYSTERY

ALEKSA BAXTER

CHAPTER 1

Two weeks after we'd discovered Janice Fletcher's real killer, I was finally starting to feel like things in the Baker Valley were going to plan. As I drove the twenty minutes from my grandpa's house to my shop, The Baker Valley Barkery and Café, I couldn't help but smile.

It was a gorgeous Colorado summer morning, the sky an almost perfect shade of blue, the sun as it rose over the mountains coloring the clouds in brilliant shades of pink and red and purple. I blasted my favorite mix of happy songs and sang along (horribly off-key) at the top of my lungs, my van window rolled down so I could feel the wind blowing through my hair.

The drive to and from the barkery had become my favorite part of the day. I loved running a business with my best friend, Jamie, and living with my grandpa—who still insisted on calling me Maggie May no matter how many times I asked him to just call me Maggie—but that time in the van was mine. If you could ignore Fancy, my three-year-old Newfoundland, snoring away in the back, that is.

It was my time to just be alone and indulge in my thoughts and fantasies about the future. (And sing.

Neither Jamie nor my grandpa would let me sing anywhere near them. It was a wonder Fancy didn't launch into howls each time I started singing, I was that bad.)

That future was looking good, too. The online store was doing surprisingly well, so much so that I'd had to up my orders with our manufacturer. (The online store mostly sold pre-packaged treats that were made by a private label company. Drop shipping is a beautiful thing, let me tell you.)

And I even had my first regulars at the barkery—a German woman named Greta and her Irish wolfhound, Hans, who Greta claimed was named after one of her ex-husbands, but she never could remember which one. (She was a little blurry on the details after husbands one through four, and I think she was up to number ten at that point.)

So life was good.

Life was very good.

Of course, you know what they say about that don't you? When life is good best look over your shoulder for the ninety-mile-an-hour freight train headed your way.

Okay, so no one actually says that. But they should. Because it is most definitely true in my life. Every single time things are starting to look up, along comes a dead body. Or a handsome cop I don't have time for. Or both.

Same thing, really.

So there I was, enjoying the beautiful day, singing along to my favorite song, wind whipping at my hair, the beauty of the Baker Valley making my heart soar, minding my own business, when what should happen but I see a cop car ahead, perched on the side of the road, a speed gun pointed right at me.

I didn't want to just slam on the brakes. Talk about looking guilty. So instead I eased up on the accelerator and let the van coast down to a more reasonable fifty-five. It still wasn't the forty-five the sign said was the speed limit, but at least I was now in range of "not worth pulling over" territory.

Unfortunately, the cop didn't buy it. As soon as I passed him he pulled out and flipped his lights on. Great. Just great. There I was, finally having a good morning, everything was going so well, and then I had to get pulled over for speeding. And probably by someone I knew. Small town life was so…intimate.

I slowed the van and pulled to the shoulder silently praying it was anyone other than Mr. Matthew Allen Barnes, a/k/a Officer Handsome Distraction.

I'd actually done a pretty good job of avoiding him once he'd stopped trying to arrest me and my grandpa for murder. It wasn't that I didn't like him. I did. A lot. But I just didn't need that right then. I was starting a new business and…taking care of Fancy and…other things that meant a relationship was just not a good idea.

Plus, he seemed particularly immune to my charms.

I've been fortunate over the years to be let off of a number of speeding tickets. Not because I tried to deny what I was doing or to talk my way out of it or even to flirt my way out of it. I just get all my papers in order and act real nice. (It helps that I'm somewhat curvy and blonde and most officers are men, I won't deny that, but I do think they also appreciate the not crying on them part.)

But Officer Barnes could see right through me. And he was a stickler for the law from what I'd seen so far. He liked my grandpa. He even credited my grandpa with getting him on the straight and narrow so he didn't end up in prison or dead. But that hadn't stopped him from throwing my grandpa in jail when he thought he was a murderer. Same with me, although I wasn't sure he liked me quite as much as he liked my grandpa.

As I waited to see who'd step out of the cop car, Fancy poked her head out my window, leaving a nice stream of slobber on my shoulder.

"Gee, thanks," I muttered, shoving her back.

I glanced in the side mirror and silently cussed as the tall, gorgeous, dark-haired, blue-eyed man who spent way too much time in my dreams stepped out of the car. It should be a sin to look that good in a cop's uniform.

When he reached my window I flashed him my best smile. "Officer Barnes. What can I do for you today?"

"Maggie May Carver. Do you know how fast you were going?"

Now, that's a tricky question, because I did know. And I don't like to lie. But you can't just tell a cop that yes, you were quite well aware that you were going twenty over the speed limit.

"Not exactly. It's an old van. See? No digital display."

Which was *technically* true.

He leaned closer, drilling me with that intense take-no-prisoners look he's so good at. "Do you have a general idea of how fast you were going? Give or take say five miles an hour?"

I bit my lip trying to figure out how to finagle my way around that one. If I told him yes, then I was going to get a ticket, I just knew it. But if I told him no then I might still get one for being a distracted driver.

Fortunately, Fancy decided that she'd been ignored long enough and started barking her head off right in my ear.

I winced. "Just pet her, please. I promise she'll shut up if you just give her a few ear scratches."

He not only rubbed her ears until she was groaning in pleasure but also gave her a big kiss right on the nose and called her a good girl, leaning so close I could smell his aftershave.

It wasn't fair. Not only was he good-looking and good with dogs, but he smelled good, too.

I leaned away. "So if I promise not to speed again, you think you could let me off with a warning? I mean, I did help you solve three murders after all. And I didn't even get a plaque or anything for all my efforts."

His glare pinned me to my seat. Seems he had a different opinion of events than I did. If I were the type to sweat under pressure I would've been pouring buckets, but I'm not so I just met him glare for glare. I *had* solved those murders.

"You were going twenty-one over the speed limit, Maggie."

"But…?"

He shook his head. "But I'm going to let you off with a warning. For now. But if I catch you speeding through here again, you will get a ticket."

I bit my lip. (Something about that man always has me biting my lip. Another reason to avoid him.)

I knew I shouldn't press my luck, but I had to know, so I said, "Define speeding."

"Going over the speed limit."

"*At all?* I mean, really, would you give me a ticket for going, say, *five* over?"

"Yes."

"What about *one* over? I mean that's gotta be within the margin of error, right? One or two?"

He didn't answer, just stared me down.

"Just asking. Because having to go forty-five through this whole area when there's hardly anyone else around seems really…boring."

(I know. Sometimes I'm my own worst enemy.)

He shook his head and gave Fancy's ears one more scratch. "Speeding is speeding, Maggie. And next time it'll be a ticket. Got it?" He held my gaze until I answered.

"Got it."

"Alright then. Have a nice day."

"You too."

As I watched him walk back to his car—a very pleasing sight if I do say so myself—I wondered whether he really meant it or not. I mean, would he actually give me a ticket for going just three over the speed limit? That seemed hardly worth the paper he'd have to write it on.

But did I really want to test him? Because I was pretty sure Officer Matthew Barnes could go toe to toe with me without flinching. And it would be just like him to give me a ticket for two over the speed limit out of sheer stubborn principle.

Men. Making my life miserable for thirty-six years and counting.

CHAPTER 2

I waited until Officer Barnes had headed off to his little speed trap hideaway and then pulled back onto the highway and drove the last five minutes to the barkery, keeping the odometer right at forty-five the whole way.

It drove me nuts to go that slow, but I did it. Just in case.

It also meant I pulled up in front of the barkery about five minutes late. Still, I took a moment to admire my dream come true before going inside. (Not too long of one, because Fancy and her high-pitched "get me out of this car" bark are not a joke. She's a hundred-and-forty pounds of ear-splitting whine when she wants to be, which is pretty much anytime the car stops moving.)

I had to admit, the sign guy had been right when he told me that script font I wanted to use wasn't easy to read. But I didn't care; I liked the look of our sign. Especially the two little Newfie cartoon heads on either side of the text. They made me smile every time I saw them.

We have two separate entrances in the front. On the left-hand side is the café entrance. On the right-hand side is the barkery entrance. Both sides also have a large picture window that gives customers a great view of the mountain range to the east.

The café side is just a regular old-fashioned café serving the best cinnamon rolls in the world as well as a delicious soup and panini lunch combo. The barkery side, my brainchild, is a bakery for dogs.

(People still don't get the concept and are constantly telling me that there's a typo in our sign—one of the drawbacks to being in a tourist town where there are new people coming through every week.)

On the café side we have cute little tables throughout and a long counter at the back where people can place to-go orders. That side of the place has a full kitchen where Jamie makes her delicious food. There's also a small office.

Right by the to-go counter is an area where you can pass through to the barkery side. I have one of those large glass display cases like you'd see in any good bakery, expect mine has dog treats instead of people treats. There's also an area between the two spaces with a whole collection of kitschy touristy items like mugs with our logo on them and pre-packaged dog treats.

The barkery side has seating, too, but the tables are more sturdy and there's a lot more open space so canine companions can lie next to their owners in comfort. There's also a series of waist-high cubbies along the far wall where people can leave their dogs if they need to run to the restroom or just want their dog to have a more peaceful place to rest while they eat.

Fancy has her own special cubby in the back corner with an extra-large dog bed and food and water bowls.

There's also a small private dog run out back that Jamie and I use for Fancy and for Jamie's golden retriever puppy, Lulu.

I call it a dog run, but it's actually about sixty feet long and fifteen feet deep with six-foot wooden fencing at both ends and a stream on the far side that has a large grove of aspens and evergreens beyond that. It's our little after-work oasis. We have a bench set up against the back wall where we can sit and have a beer at the end of a long day while the dogs run around and play. (For a whole five minutes until they get tired and take a nap—puppies and Newfies are a lot alike in that respect, although Lulu is quickly growing out of her puppy phase.)

All in all, it's perfect. My dream come true. And a heckuva lot better than the steel and concrete office building in downtown DC where I'd spent the last five years of my life. Let me tell you, sprawling mountains make a lot better view than some bricked in alleyway that you can only see through the door of the nearest office. And the sound of birds singing beats the seemingly perpetual sound of sirens as some big shot or other makes their way through town.

At least for me. Power and money were never my thing, so I failed kinda miserably at the whole nine to five, corporate ladder gig.

Running a barely thriving business with my best friend was far better. As long as we could keep that barely thriving part going. We had about six months to get things running in the black or we were going to be having some interesting talks with the bank.

But all my worries were forgotten the minute I walked through the front door and was assailed by the delicious smell of cinnamon rolls. That sweet and spicy combination is the best in the world.

You know they actually did a study once that the sexiest smell for men was cinnamon rolls? Seriously. Men find that smell sexy. (In theory. There was a point in college where I used to wear vanilla lotion and cinnamon oil to test that study out in the real world, but can't say it worked. Instead it led to more than one very confused conversation about smelling cookies baking nearby where that shouldn't have been possible. Live and learn. And don't trust everything you hear on the news. Turns out at the end of the day the scent men really like the most is a pumpkin pie lavender combination. Who knew?)

Anyway.

I was in my happy place. At work with my best friend and my dog, with a fresh-baked cinnamon roll dripping gooey frosting just waiting to be tasted. I grabbed a Coke and proceeded to eat my oh-so-healthy breakfast while Jamie doled out coffee, muffins, and cinnamon rolls to her steady stream of regular early morning customers, her long brown hair braided back from her face and an actual genuine smile on her face the whole time.

I didn't know how she did it, being that nice to that many strangers, but she genuinely didn't seem to mind.

Meanwhile, the barkery side sat empty and bereft of visitors. I tried to tell myself it was early in the morning and you can't expect people to run to the store at that time of day to buy a dog biscuit, but it still hurt nonetheless.

Fortunately, I had a handful of custom orders to process from the website and Abe and Evan, the owners of the Creek Inn, had called in a big order for barkery bites and doggie delights—my two most popular dog treats, both involving liberal amounts of peanut butter—that they planned to pick up later in the day. So I kept busy while Fancy snored away in her cubby, one paw thrust into the air like a salute.

CHAPTER 3

By the time Greta and Hans, my only steady daily customers, arrived around one I was ready to take a break and so was Jamie.

I wasn't quite sure how old Greta was. Older than me (I'm thirty-six), but not by much if I had to guess. Then again, the woman was obscenely rich, so there was a possibility that she'd spent very good money to look as good as she did.

She had light blonde hair that I was pretty sure was her natural color and dressed in trim slacks and bright colored tops. She always had her makeup done, and the diamond on her wedding ring was so large I was surprised it didn't weigh her hand down.

She came to the barkery around one every day with Hans and would usually stay until three or even four when we locked up. If it was a slow enough day we'd sit and chat. On busier days she always had a book or her laptop to occupy her. She liked sitting in the front window with the view of the mountains, which was perfect for us because it attracted customers who saw that we were in fact open and that other people were happy to eat our food.

She had to be one of the most intriguing people I'd ever met. (Any woman who's been married so many times she can't keep track of how many husbands she's had is a woman with some fun stories to tell.)

I suspected from a few things she'd said that her younger days were spent doing things that weren't exactly legal. Especially the one comment she'd made about how she'd figured out at some point that it's far easier to marry a rich man and ask him for the jewelry you want than to sneak into his house in the middle of the night and steal what he chose to buy for himself or his latest wife.

I laughed it off at the time, but I'm pretty sure she meant it. Maybe that's why there aren't a whole lot of female jewel thieves out there…

She doted on Hans, her Irish wolfhound. He was as tall as Fancy, but much, much skinnier. I swear there was nothing to him except that wiry gray hair of his. But I wouldn't mess with him. There was something about him that made me think he could take down a bear if the need arose. He was sweet, don't get me wrong, but there was an iron will hiding behind those soft brown eyes of his.

And he was scarily well-behaved. He'd lie at her feet for hours straight without fidgeting or crying. (Fancy would definitely not do that. She did well enough in her cubby, but every couple of hours she would cry to be let out back or be given a little attention. And if one of her favorite people walked in—like Matt—she barked up a storm until they came to say hi.)

While Greta, Jamie, and I shared a late lunch of panini and soup I filled them both in on my little run-in with Officer Barnes, playing it up for all the laughs I could.

"You've done a pretty good job of avoiding him the last couple weeks," Jamie commented when I was done. "Maybe he decided this was the only way to nail you down long enough to say hi."

I took a sip of my Coke. "There is no reason we need to be saying hi to one another. I am a law-abiding citizen who has no need to interact with a police officer ever again, thank you very much."

"But if you don't say hi to one another you can't fall in love, get married, and have babies."

I almost spit out my Coke. I already knew Jamie's theory that Matt and I were destined to be together, but that was taking it a little bit too far. "You've been watching *Love, Actually* again, haven't you? Stop it. And remember that that particular character ended up desperately alone and not with the hot man."

"I agree with Jamie," Greta said. "You two should get married. Sparks in conversation equal sparks in the bedroom."

Jamie started laughing uncontrollably as I blushed scarlet.

I shook my head and glared at both of them. "No. No, no, no. I have…"

"Better things to do with your life than meet some guy and marry him. Yeah, yeah, yeah. We know." Jamie rolled her eyes at me.

"Well, it's true." I stood up before Greta could start offering me a man from her long list of geriatric billionaires—what she considered suitable *first* husband material—or Jamie could start talking about how I'd been in love with Matt since we were in diapers. "What do you say we close up for a bit and let the dogs have a good run out back? Greta? You think Hans would be up for it?"

"Yes. This would be nice. Lucas has not yet finished the fence at our house. Poor Hans would like a run."

"Good. Come on."

I locked up the front while Jamie and Greta led the dogs out back.

CHAPTER 4

Fancy and Lulu immediately started chasing each other around and rolling in the grass, but Hans stayed at Greta's side until she uttered some command in German. As soon as she did that though, he was all in on playtime. He tore after Fancy and Lulu, turning their little dog pile into a milling mass of legs and tails and yipping barks.

They played like that for about five minutes, but then Fancy was done. She was panting and drooling and covered with slobber from the other two. I expected her to just collapse in place and go to sleep, but I'd forgotten about the stream.

As I mentioned earlier, the yard is bordered on the far edge by a stream. Fancy *loves* that stream. I mean, loves it. It is her happy place.

Of course, I have literally seen Fancy happily burrow her face into a two-inch deep puddle before, so it doesn't take much. She loves all forms of water wherever they may be. (Except the bath tub, of course.) Her love of water, and that stream in particular, is why I'd been taking her out back the last week or so on leash.

Otherwise I knew she'd be in that water in a heartbeat, and a hundred and forty pounds of wet Newfoundland is no joke. Especially when she decides to shake it off on anyone nearby.

And don't even get me started on the muddy paws. I love her, but those paws can hold a lot a lot of mud.

Which meant that that day was the first time she'd been out back without being on a leash in at least a week. Maybe two. And after the initial excitement of getting to play with Lulu and Hans wore off she made a mad dash for that stream.

I shouted at her, but shouting does not work on Fancy, especially when she has her eyes on something she wants. She plunged into the stream, waded to the middle, and laid herself down, happy as a clam while I shouted at her to come back.

I even waved treats her way, but she didn't care. I'd been depriving her for too long and she was going to enjoy every moment of her wallow.

The whole mess attracted Hans and Lulu, too. Luckily, Lulu is still scared of water so she stood on the bank and cried and barked and yipped and threw a general fuss trying to get Fancy to come back.

Hans waded into the stream but then kept going right across and into the trees on the other side. I glanced at Greta to see if she was going to call him back, but she just shrugged a shoulder.

"He is fine. He will be back." She took another sip of her beer and turned away from the whole mess, talking quietly with Jamie about something I couldn't hear.

I glared at Fancy who was staring back at me calmly from the center of the stream. "You're hopeless, you know that?"

She just watched me with those amber eyes of hers, the picture of serenity.

"Come on, Lulu. Heel." I waved a treat under Lulu's nose and led her away to practice her obedience training. (I'd been secretly trying to teach her at least a few basic commands since Jamie was far too nice to do it well. Don't get me wrong, Jamie is one of the most competent people I know. But when it comes to Lulu she's all "oh, it's okay…" no matter what Lulu does.)

Eventually, Fancy made her way out of the stream and shook herself off all over me before collapsing in a spot of shade for a little snooze.

Hans reappeared on the other side of the stream about five minutes later, his paws covered in deep black mud up to the elbows and *something* dangling from his mouth. Fancy scrambled to her feet and ran across the stream trying to get whatever it was, but he easily avoided her.

As they chased happily back and forth and Lulu barked her displeasure at not being able to join in, I stared in horror. Because that thing that was dangling from Hans's mouth look suspiciously like a forearm with the hand still attached.

"Jamie. Greta. Do you guys see this?" I asked. "Is that…?"

Jamie came to join me. "Um…What is that?"

"Let us see." Greta put two fingers into her mouth and whistled. It was an ear-piercing sound, but it worked. Hans immediately ran right through the stream and sat down directly in front of her, the thing still hanging from his mouth as he awaited his next command. I managed to block Fancy with my body before she could lunge at it, but it was not easy.

The smell up close was atrocious, although sadly a smell that I was familiar with thanks to Fancy and her love of all things dead and decaying. I buried my face in my elbow to hide the smell, but I couldn't bring myself to look away as Greta used another German word and Hans dropped the thing on the ground at her feet.

I was still staring at it in morbid fascination when Fancy snuck past me and—you guessed it—peed on the damned thing.

(Pardon the language, but seriously. How many dead bodies can one dog pee on? At least two as it turns out.)

I grabbed Fancy's collar and dragged her away just in time for Lulu to run up and roll on it. At which point Jamie took control.

I think I've mentioned before that there's nothing that rattles Jamie. She could be in a burning building, flames crawling the walls around her, and she wouldn't bat an eye. She'd just get down to the business of saving herself. So within a minute she had the arm covered by a packing crate, Lulu hooked up to her leash and tied to the bench by the back door, Fancy hooked up to her leash and tied up right next to her, and the police dispatcher on the line.

I'm sure the dispatcher was just as disbelieving of this call as she'd been of mine when I found Jack Dunner's body, but Jamie handled it with aplomb.

Hans, of course, didn't need to be tied up. With that one command he was fully back into guard dog mode, sitting calmly at Greta's side, not even glancing at the dead thing on the ground.

I stared at the trees, wondering if there was a whole body over there and hoping we could keep any mention of the barkery out of it. (I know. I should have been thinking about the poor dead man that someone had buried in a shallow grave, but all I could think was "please don't let it ruin my business." What can I say? When you don't know the person…)

"I wonder who it is," I said as Jamie ended her call with the cops and came to join us.

Greta answered, "This I know. It is my ex-husband."

I stared at her. She seemed awfully calm for a woman who'd just seen the severed hand of her ex-husband dropped on the ground at her feet. "Your ex-husband? Which one? And how do you know? Did you…?" I couldn't quite bring myself to ask if she'd killed and buried him, but it did seem to be the most likely explanation.

She pointed her toe at the hand. "The ring. It is custom-made. And the scar on the hand. I gave this to him as well."

Jamie glanced towards the barkery. I knew she probably needed to go wait for the cops, but this was too interesting to miss. "Greta, forgive me for saying this, but you don't seem very upset."

I nodded my agreement.

Greta shrugged one shoulder. "It has been many years. Kristof was my first husband."

"But still…He's dead. And it's…his arm."

"It was bound to happen. Kristof, he makes many enemies."

I shook my head. "But what is he doing here? I thought you married your first husband in Germany?"

She turned to face me. "Are you investigating this murder, Maggie?"

"No."

"Then why these questions?"

"I don't know. I was just curious. I mean, your dog just dropped your ex-husband's hand at your feet. I wanted to understand how that could happen."

Greta turned to Jamie. "I would like a coffee. Is this possible?"

Jamie rushed to join Greta as she walked towards the back door. "Yes. Of course. Here, let me get that door for you." She threw a quick glance and shrug at me before following Greta inside.

I would've probably followed after them and tried another angle to get my answers—because I'm nothing if not relentlessly and annoyingly curious—but then I heard the police sirens. Fancy and Lulu started howling away in accompaniment as I ran through the store, ready to yell at whoever it was. Honestly, couldn't they be quiet about it? The man was clearly dead, did they really need to announce to the world that there was yet another police matter at the barkery?

I stopped dead in the doorway as I saw *who* had pulled up out front. Of course it would be Officer Handsome Distraction. Seriously, I was snake bit when it came to that man.

CHAPTER 5

I forced myself to calmly walk towards Matt's patrol car, a smile plastered on my face. When he rolled the window down I said, "Could you please kill the siren and lights? The man in question is very much dead already."

(I know. You're not supposed to order cops around and, as one bratty little intern once informed me, "You get more flies with honey than vinegar." To which I had an appropriately violent thought I could not express since his father was a VP of something or other and I didn't want to get fired. But really. The dead man did not need sirens and lights and neither did we.)

Matt waited long enough to let me know he'd considered ignoring me before he turned them both off. "Dispatch said you guys found a dead body."

"Well, to be accurate, Greta's dog Hans found a dead body. And it's not really here. It's across the stream. So you know, you could go park your car over there."

I glanced past him and cussed. "Never mind. Too late."

Pulling into the parking lot was the only local reporter we have, Peter Nielsen. He works for the *Baker Valley Gazette*. I recognized him instantly because not only had he insulted me when I asked him to cover our grand opening, he'd then tried to ruin my business with a series of articles insinuating awful things about the barkery and me personally.

Suffice it to say, I was not a big fan.

He jumped out of his slick SUV and immediately started snapping photos like he'd found the story of the century. Someone should inform him that one dead body was not going to win him a Pulitzer.

"Come on," I said. "Let's get inside before that loser reaches us."

I led Matt inside and then slammed the door shut, making all the bells at the top jangle loudly. I flipped the sign to Closed and threw a nasty look at Nielsen while I flipped the lock into place and pulled the blinds down.

"Can I reach the body from here?" Matt asked.

"That depends on whether you want to go wading across a stream or not. But you can at least see the part of the body Hans found."

"The *part* of the body?"

"Mmhm." I opened the door to the back and let him walk through. He paused long enough to say hi to Lulu and Fancy who were not enjoying being tied up out back. But what with the mud and dead body smell there really wasn't another choice. Both pups were going to need to be hosed down before they went anywhere.

(That was going to be fun. Not.)

I stepped up to the crate and gave Matt a small half-bow like some fancy maître d before lifting the crate. "May I present to you hand of a dead man."

Matt took two steps forward and crouched down, studying it. "What is it with you and finding dead bodies?"

"Don't look at me. It was Hans that found this one, not Fancy. Although Fancy did pee on it."

"Again?"

I shrugged my shoulders. "What can I say? She likes to pee on dead things. It's part of the cycle of life, you know."

"You could hold her back."

"Well I'll try to remember that for the next time we find a body, okay?"

As he continued to study the hand, his arm held across his nose to hide the smell, I stepped away. I didn't need to be all up close and personal with that thing for a moment longer than necessary. Or with Officer Barnes for that matter.

Like I said. Dead bodies and cute cops. About the same in my book.

🐾 🐾 🐾

Matt came over to join me after another minute or so. "Where did he find this?"

"Somewhere over there." I waved towards the trees.

"Hopefully the face is in better condition than the hand or else we're going to have a hard time identifying this one."

"Oh, actually, Greta already did."

"What do you mean?"

"Greta said she recognized the ring and the scar on the hand. Said it was her first husband and that she'd given both the ring and the scar to him."

"Really? What was he doing here? Isn't she from Germany?"

I nodded. "You're going to have to figure that one out on your own, I'm afraid. I tried asking questions and she informed me it wasn't really my place to do so."

He glanced towards the café. "Wasn't that her inside having a coffee with Jamie?"

I nodded.

"She seemed very calm for someone who just discovered the severed arm of her ex-husband."

"Well, she has had a number of husbands. That could be part of it."

"How many?"

I shrugged. "I'm not sure she even knowns. Nine or ten."

"Nine or ten! Who marries that many times?"

I shook my head.

"Give me a minute." Matt stepped away and radioed in that the report of a dead body was accurate and to send Sue out with waders because the body wasn't going to be easy to access.

"What now?" I asked.

"Now I guess I talk to Greta about how her dog found the body and what else she can tell me about our victim. But actually, you think I could get something to eat first? I skipped right past lunch today."

I glanced in the direction of the severed arm. He'd just seen that and he wanted to eat lunch? Okay…

CHAPTER 6

As Matt dug into his food, I pursed my lips together and studied him. "So tell me, Officer Barnes, I thought you were on speed trap duty today. Why'd you show up for this little murder mystery?"

He glanced at me, his blue eyes dancing with amusement, but didn't answer until he'd finished his bite of sandwich. "Simple enough explanation. I asked to be called whenever there was an incident involving you, your grandfather, or the café."

"And someone agreed to that?"

"I told them you were very litigious. And prone to getting yourself into trouble."

I gasped. "Excuse me? I am neither one of those things."

He wisely chose to take another bite instead of answer.

"I am not prone to getting myself into trouble."

"No? How many cops do you think would've let you get away with asking for a definition of speeding right after they'd just decided to let you go on a ticket for twenty over?"

"I wouldn't have asked any other cops that question. I only asked because it was you."

He raised an eyebrow.

"So I'm stuck with you am I?"

He nodded "Yep. As long as you're causing more trouble than ten other people combined."

I shook my head. "It's not my fault people keep dying. I'm not killing them."

"Good to know."

"As for that ticket thing. I'll have you know that no other cop would've told me not to speed ever again. They would've said something like 'keep it down' and left it at that knowing that any rational driver is going to speed just a little here or there. You've gotta lighten up a bit."

He shook his head. "You are something else, you know that?"

"Am not." I crossed my arms both resenting and resembling his comment at the same time.

"By the way, are you going to the Mason Foundation event?"

I pressed my lips together at the thought of having to wear heels and a dress and glared in Jamie's direction. "Yes. I couldn't get out of it. One of the drawbacks of having your best friend date the kind of man who throws charity events. Are you going to be there?"

He nodded. "I'm kind of looking forward to it."

"Why?"

"To see you in a dress and having to be polite to a bunch of strangers you'd rather not speak to."

"I'm bound to say something offensive to someone. I always do." I shuddered at the memory of the last charity event I'd attended when I was still in DC. One little comment and I'd gone from making a new friend for life to making an enemy. And all because I'd said the wrong name after drinking a tad bit too much champagne.

Really, I should not be allowed out in public with strangers. At least Mason, Jamie, and Matt were going to be there. I could cling to them and hide away from everyone else.

A car pulled up outside and Matt pushed away from the table. "Probably Sue. Better show her what we have. Thanks for lunch."

"You're welcome."

I frowned as he walked outside. So I was stuck with him anytime anything bad happened, was I? Could be worse, I guess. They could've assigned me Officer Clark. But still. I did not relish the idea of Matt showing up every time I had to call the cops.

Of course, that was easy enough to solve. I just wouldn't do anything that required the cops. Simple as.

Or not.

🐾 🐾 🐾

While Matt and Sue were outside examining the body part, I offered to give Greta Mason Maxwell's number, but she said she didn't need it and informed me that just because she'd known the victim didn't mean she'd had any role in his death.

I knew Mason Maxwell would argue with her about managing expectations and that just because you're innocent doesn't mean the cops won't arrest you—something both my grandpa and I had learned the hard way—but Greta was as stubborn as stubborn could be.

She calmly and quickly told Matt how we'd found the

hand and how she'd recognized it as her first husband's. And then she wrote down a phone number she had for Kristof but said the man had no family to speak of so there was no one to corroborate her identification.

"Why was he here?" Matt asked.

She shrugged him off the same way she'd shrugged me off. "How am I to know? It was many years ago we were married. We have not remained friends."

"But you had his phone number?"

"Yes."

"A U.S. number, so not one he would've had when the two of you were married."

She met his steely blue gaze with one of her own. "When we were married there were not cellphones, so no I did not have this number then."

"So how did you get it?"

"A friend gave it to me."

"When?"

"Why does this matter? Why are you asking me these questions?" She crossed her arms and turned away as if dismissing him.

Matt stepped closer. "Because a body was found and you seem to be the only reason he would've been in town."

She scoffed. "This is absurd. I am not the only reason he would be here."

"No? Why else?"

"It is a beautiful town, no? People come here from everywhere in the world. Why would he not come here for the mountains?"

Matt's eyebrows almost rose through the top of his head. "That's what you want me to believe? That your ex-husband was found buried behind the coffee shop where you eat lunch every single day and that it was just a coincidence that he was here? That this has nothing to do with you?"

She stared him down, doing one of the best "uptight rich person who is tired of being bothered by a minion" looks I've ever seen. "Believe what you will. I must go now. If you need to speak to me again, do so through my attorney."

She handed him a card and walked out of the store, leaving Matt open-mouthed in her wake.

CHAPTER 7

When I got home that night I plopped down on the old worn brown couch next to my grandpa, shifting my weight until the loose spring stopped poking into my thigh. At eighty-two he was still as trim and tough as men half his age, his hair a faded brown, his face not nearly as wrinkled as it should've been. He wore his standard uniform of faded Levi's and a plaid shirt over a white t-shirt. Only time I'd seen him in anything else was the day of my grandma's funeral when he'd worn an ill-fitting suit that looked like it hadn't been worn since the seventies.

Heck, he even coached baseball in his jeans and plaid shirts.

Which was kind of nice when I stopped to think about it. I liked to know that no matter how crazy the world might get, my grandpa was always going to be exactly who he was.

He was watching the Justice Channel so I had to wait until the commercial to tell him about the day's craziness. Fortunately, that channel has some of the longest commercials known to man. Boring ones, too, unless you have severe acne or a hankering for life insurance. (What do the three P's stand for? Price, price, and price. Ugh.)

When I'd finished telling him what had happened, he just shook his head. "You know, Maggie May, some people go an entire lifetime without discovering a single dead body."

"You sound like Matt."

"How is he?" He glanced at me slyly.

"Well enough. But you should know better than I do since he's helping you out with baseball now."

He nodded. "True. He is. But we don't get much time to talk about anything other than the kids and the schedule. Maybe I should invite him over for dinner."

"Well, let me know when you do so I can make myself scarce."

"Maggie May, you can't run from him your whole life. Eventually he'll stop chasing."

Worked for me.

The show came back on and we fell silent until the next commercial. It was one of my favorites called *I Survived*, but honestly you'd think they could find one woman who had survived some horrible experience that didn't involve a man doing awful things to her. They had men on there who'd survived car crashes and boating accidents, why couldn't they put at least one woman on there who'd survived a skydiving accident or something? (I knew at least three who'd qualify. Maybe I should write them a letter about it.)

I couldn't focus on it as much as I wanted, though. My mind kept going back to why Greta's ex-husband's body had been dumped so close to the barkery and what involvement she had in it. If any.

I decided I needed ice cream. And lots of it.

As I walked to the kitchen I repeated the serenity prayer to myself. Well, at least my version.

You can't control everything, Maggie, so no point fretting. Let it go.

Okay, so maybe my version is one part serenity prayer and one part *Frozen* theme song. Same thing.

🐾 🐾 🐾

The next morning the barkery parking lot was full of cop cars and cops working on finding the rest of Greta's ex-husband. It wasn't so bad when we were inside, but the minute I took Fancy out back for her morning constitutional she went nuts, barking her head off until I dragged her back inside.

I have to admit, seeing random people walking through woods when you're not expecting it can be a little disconcerting. I just wish she was a little more stiff-British-upper-lip about things sometimes, you know? Instead she's always frantic-five-year-old.

I dragged her back inside, out the front door, and let her do her business on the little grassy area next to the road instead.

The presence of the cops did improve our business, at least on the café side. I'm pretty sure we had every cop in the county drop by at some point or other. I asked one of the officers I didn't know what they were all doing back there and he said they were looking for other bodies.

I raised an eyebrow at that. I mean, honestly, how likely was it we had a serial killer in small-town Colorado? Especially one that was targeting middle-aged white men? Didn't they watch true crime shows like my grandpa and I did? We could tell you the typical victim of a serial killer, and it was not Greta's ex-husband, not unless he'd made a living in ways that didn't seem likely for where we were.

And even then, he was still probably too old to be a likely choice.

I was well-behaved, though. I just nodded and smiled and didn't tell him they were a bunch of fools. Plus, this way I could rest assured that no other bodies would turn up in our backyard anytime soon. If I was really, really lucky this would be the last random dead body I ever had an involvement with.

🐾 🐾 🐾

At least they were gone by the time Greta came by. She took her place at her usual table as if nothing had happened. I was making a bunch of barkery bites, so it was a good hour before things slowed down enough for me to join her.

I sat down at her table with a reheated cinnamon roll and a Coke. (My third of the day, but who was counting.)

We made small talk for a minute or two, discussing the upcoming charity event and how she was looking forward to the chance to introduce me to some of her husband's friends. (She still firmly believed that my first marriage should be to someone old and obscenely rich. I didn't have the heart to tell her that if I got married it was only going to be once and not for money. There was no amount of money on the planet that could make me fake a relationship.)

To change the subject I asked, "So, have you heard anything else about what happened to your ex-husband? How was he killed? Do the cops want to talk to you again?"

She shrugged, as if the whole thing was completely boring and not worth discussion. "Probably."

"Any idea why someone would kill him? I mean, you knew him better than anyone here. You have to have some idea. Money? Love triangle?"

The way she stared at me I was reminded of how Matt's stare could sometimes drill a hole right through me. "Maggie. This is not your business. I do not come here to talk about these things. Talk to me about dogs or leave me alone."

"Sorry. You know me. I was just curious." I leaned back in my seat. "Dogs is it? You want to hear what Fancy has taken to doing the last week or so?"

She nodded.

"Each morning I let her out back like normal when we get up. She has a dog door that she is perfectly capable of using and has been using just fine since we arrived. But for the last week instead of coming back inside on her own she stands there and barks once to be let back in. It's the most ridiculous thing in the world. I've started calling her my vampire puppy because of it. You know, because she has to be invited inside?"

She laughed. "Why do you think she does this?"

"Honestly?" I winced. "I think it's because I accidentally closed the main door while she was outside a couple weeks ago and when she tried to come in the doggie door she ran right into it. So now she can't be sure that she'll actually be able to go through if she tries."

"Maggie! Why would you do this to her?"

"I didn't mean to. I thought my grandpa had brought her inside. It was late and she'd been barking a lot so I figured it was better to block her in for the night. So I closed the door and turned away and next thing you know, whap, I heard her smack right into the door."

"Poor dear."

"I know. I gave her an extra treat, but, well…Trust with dogs is easy to lose and hard to win back."

(I know. I know. I'm horrible. I swear I did not know she was outside.)

We continued to talk for the next half hour or so, laughing about the craziness that dogs can get up to, but then I had to get back to work. I was dying with curiosity about the whole murdered ex-husband thing, but it seemed I wasn't going to get another word out of Greta.

I wondered if Matt would be able to tell me something. Maybe if my grandpa actually did invite him over for dinner I could drop a question or two into the conversation. After dinner, of course. My grandpa frowned on talking "business" at the dinner table. But once he focused in on the Scrabble board, anything was game.

CHAPTER 8

That night I went over to Jamie's to try on gowns for the charity event. I had one or two in my closet, but nothing terribly exciting, whereas Jamie practically had a boutique's worth of fancy dresses. Living in LA will do that to you.

Her place was just around the corner from the barkery. It was a small one-bedroom apartment with a tiny balcony. Remembering my own days of dog ownership while living in an apartment, I shivered slightly. Fancy was actually a great apartment dog—as she proved by immediately curling up in the corner with Lulu at her side—but it was the weather that made the whole experience miserable.

Me, if it's raining or snowing, I want to get outside, get the business done, and get back in. But Fancy loved being outside, *especially* in wet weather, so she'd plop herself down and stare up at the sky while I shivered next to her, wishing I'd remembered to grab my gloves on the way out the door.

Ah, the good old days. Missed them sometimes, but I was also glad they were in the past.

🐾 🐾 🐾

Even though we spent almost every day at work together, Jamie and I rarely had a chance to just talk about things. There was always some customer coming in or we needed to talk business logistics or were just too tired for chit-chat.

So before we tried on the dresses, we fixed up a meal of tossed green salad with cranberries, walnuts, and blue cheese and grilled salmon. (Jamie is so healthy compared to me it's almost sad.) It was a delicious meal. I don't know why I don't eat that way more often, but there you have it.

As we drank our pinot grigio and dug into our yummy food, I asked, "So, things are really heating up with Mason Maxwell are they?"

"Maggie, you can just call him Mason, you know. You don't have to use his full name every single time."

I grimaced. "I know. I just…I prefer to call him by his full name."

She paused for a long moment, as if trying to decide something. "Please start calling him Mason."

I narrowed my eyes at her. "Why? Is he sticking around?"

She blushed and took a sip of her wine.

"Jamie? Is there something you want to tell me?"

"I don't know. I don't want to ruin it. And you…"

"What?"

She sighed. "You always see the flaws, Maggie. You don't see the good parts."

I pursed my lips. "I'm not saying you're wrong…"

"But you think I'm wrong."

"No." I tried to figure out how to explain it to her.

Finally, I leaned in. "Okay. Look at it this way. Lucas Dean."

"Do you have to use him as the example?"

"Yes. Because I think what he did was criminal."

She rolled her eyes.

"It doesn't matter how great he was to you, assuming he even was great to you, which is debatable. And it doesn't matter how much he gave you butterflies or what a great kisser he was. He was not a good man. Right?"

She glared at me. "He has good qualities, Maggie. He's very funny. And open to adventure. And so complimentary."

"But the bad qualities outweigh all of that. He is a lying, cheating sack of you-know-what. If you only focus on the good you don't see the deal-breakers."

"No one is perfect, Maggie. There will always be a negative. If you look hard enough, you can come up with a reason to say no to anyone."

"You know what he did."

"He's not violent or a killer or…He just made a bad decision, that's all."

"He drove a girl to murder. By putting her in an adult situation she wasn't prepared to handle."

"That wasn't Luke's fault. How was he supposed to know she was unhinged?" She threw her napkin on the table. "Come on. Let's look at the dresses. I have an early morning."

"Jamie…"

"No. I don't want to talk about it anymore."

I did. But I let it go and followed Jamie into the bedroom where she was busy throwing various gowns onto the bed.

She studied the pile of sequins and satins and sorted them again until she had a trio of gorgeous gowns for me to choose from. There was a long, sleek black number that looked like falling water, a white sequined dress with a frilled bottom and V-neck, and a red fitted dress that looked like it would barely cover what needs covering.

"What do you think? Which one appeals the most?"

I did like the look of the black one, but honestly what I really wanted was to spend the evening sitting on the couch with my grandpa while eating potato chips and watching old episodes of *The Closer*. Far better than some snooty charity event where I'd worry about holding my fork wrong. Or how to eat a lobster, for cryin' out loud.

I didn't tell Jamie that, though. Especially not after our little blow-up over Mason Maxwell.

Friendship. A necessity, but not always easy to maintain.

I picked up the black dress and held it against my body as I studied myself in the full-length mirror in the corner of the room. I tried to stretch the fabric, but it was at least an inch smaller than I was. On both sides. And I hadn't even put it on yet.

"Uh, Jamie. What size is this thing?"

"I don't know. A four, maybe? It's a little loose on me."

I laughed as I threw the dress back on the bed. "And the other two?"

"One might be a six. Why? What's so funny?"

"That you thought any of those would come even close to fitting me."

"What? We're about the same size, aren't we? At least try it on."

I laughed again. "Jamie, you crack me up. I am not

even close to a size four. If I tried to put that dress on it wouldn't even make it over my head let alone my hips. So, thank you, but it looks like I'm stuck with the little black dress I have at home."

I threw an arm around her shoulders and steered her back to the living room. "Come on. Let's finish off that wine and you can tell me just how wonderful and fabulous Mason is."

"He really is great, you know," she beamed.

"I'm sure he is."

And even if he wasn't, I wasn't going to say a word to my friend about it. Because she was happy. Happier than I'd seen her in a long time. And—compared to the other men she'd shown an interest in in the past—Mason Maxwell was a heck of a step in the right direction.

CHAPTER 9

Two nights later, Matt came over for dinner (T-bones and grilled asparagus, yum) and I finally had my chance to ask him about the Greta matter, but he and my grandpa were not the least bit cooperative in turning the discussion in that direction.

As we sat around the dining room table eating off of my grandma's fine china they wouldn't stop talking about baseball and who was doing well that season and who wasn't.

Since I was focused on eating my steak, I didn't really care, because who needs the distraction of entertaining company when you're eating a really good meal, but once I'd polished that off I felt like a pot of water about to boil listening to them go on and on and on about every single player in town.

All I wanted to know was, had my new friend Greta killed her ex-husband? And, if so, why?

I set my fork and knife down on my napkin and handed my plate to Fancy for a final polish and then turned on them. "Honestly, I think it's great that you guys volunteer your time to coach these kids, but could we talk about something else please?"

"Such as?" Matt grinned at me and I realized he'd been keeping the conversation away from Greta and the dead body on purpose.

"Greta and the severed hand that Hans dropped at her feet, maybe?"

"You're not a cop, Maggie."

"So? Greta's my friend and I'm curious what's going on. Plus, you arrest her and I'll be back to square one in terms of regular customers. Don't take her away from me, please."

He shook his head. "If she killed him, I won't have a choice."

"Do you think she did?"

"I don't know. We're still working on it. So far she seems to be his only connection to the valley, and where the body was left seems awfully suspicious."

"How so?"

"Well, why bury a body in the middle of town if you don't have to? Unless there's some personal reason to do so. Like wanting to drive by it every day while on the way to the café."

"Oh, that's vicious. I don't think Greta's that kind of person. Do you?"

He shrugged. "Hard to tell. Did you think she was a killer?"

"No."

"Well, then."

"Don't you have any other suspects?"

He frowned at me. "Maybe. Kristof had quite the record."

"Was he a thief?"

"What makes you say that?" Matt leaned forward, that intense interrogator look on his face.

"Nothing. Just…"

"Maggie."

"It was something Greta said. Made me think that before she married her second husband she might've been involved in some not exactly legal ways of procuring jewelry for herself."

"That's one way to put it."

"So I was right?"

He shook his head. "She's your friend, Maggie."

"Yeah, I know. Doesn't mean I can't be curious about what's going on."

"What if I didn't already know that about her? What if you telling me that had just clued me in to something about your friend I never would have known otherwise?"

"Ummm…." I hadn't really thought of it that way. I figured if she really had been a jewel thief that there'd be some sort of record. Then again, not every criminal gets caught, do they?

"See? Maybe it's best you keep out of it this time."

I wanted to fire back with some witty retort, but the fact of the matter was he was probably right. Sure, the murder seemed to involve my friend and the body had been buried awfully close to the barkery, but at the end of the day I was an honest business owner who needed to keep my eye on my own lane and focus on my business.

"Fine. I'll keep out of it. But if I'm going to keep out of it, we're going to play a game tonight that I can actually win instead of letting you both beat me at Scrabble again."

My grandpa frowned at me. "And what game would that be?"

"Cribbage?"

"Three-handed?" He grimaced.

"It's possible." I used to play with him and my grandma in the summers when I'd visit when I was growing up. He'd always seemed to be just fine with it.

Matt looked back and forth between us. "I've never played cribbage before."

"Good. Gives me a chance to win for once. Hope your math isn't as good as your vocabulary."

"Oh, it is. You're not going to beat me that easy."

My grandpa stood and stretched. "I think I might just leave the two of you to it. I have a few more pieces I want to place on my latest miniature before Lesley comes over tomorrow."

I opened my mouth to call him back, but I knew there was no point. He had that glint in his eye. Honestly, grandparents should keep their noses out of their grandkids' love lives…

Matt was watching me closely so I just shrugged it off and grabbed the cribbage board from the hall closet and set it on the table. As he shuffled the card deck I grabbed us each another beer.

"Best not," he said. "I have to drive home, remember?"

"Are you sure? You'll probably be sober by the time we're done. And you're always welcome to crash on the couch if you really need to."

"Thanks, but…" Was Matt blushing? Why? "Best not."

"Alright. Fine. More for me." I took a swig of my beer before walking him through the basics of the game. I also gave him the Hoyle guide with all the rules because I always forget something (like nobs) until it comes up, and I didn't want him to accuse me of making the rules up as I went.

Unfortunately, he was a quick study. We played three games and I won each one, but not by near as much as I should have given the fact that he'd never even played the game before.

You know, I always say I want a man who's my equal, but I gotta tell ya, it's downright annoying sometimes to be around a guy who's as good at things as I am.

(Or, even worse, better than I am.)

I had fun, though. Maybe too much fun. I did not need to be distracted that way. I had…other things to do.

CHAPTER 10

You'd think that spending a night at someone's house having a good meal and good conversation might soften you towards them a bit, right? Yeah, well, not Officer Tightass.

(Language, I know. But…Ugh.)

The next day I headed into work at an hour that should be illegal, and I let my speed creep up just a little bit, you know? Not the twenty over Matt had busted me for previously, but probably ten over.

Can you blame me? It was just me on the road at that hour. (And, yes, I know, there are deer and elk and things to watch out for, too, but I'd swerve if I saw one of them. I didn't need to drive slower than an old granny to do that.)

So, yes, I was speeding. Because I'm human and humans speed just a little.

And I rounded that stupid curve in the road and there the cop car was, waiting, the officer inside pointing a speed gun right at me.

This time I did slam on the brakes, hoping to throw the measurement off. But it did me no good. As soon as

I was past him, he pulled me over.

I glared at Matt as he sauntered up to my window and leaned in.

"Here." I shoved my driver's license, registration, and proof of insurance at him.

"Why, thank you, Miss Carver." He smiled at me but I just glared back at him. If he wanted to give me a ticket, fine. I was not going to play all nice about it, thank you very much.

As he strolled back to his police car I struggled not to cry (I do that when I'm angry). I also silently called him every single name I could think of. What kind of man repays someone's hospitality by giving them a speeding ticket? I mean, really. Weren't speeding tickets in small towns reserved for out-of-towners?

He came back in a few minutes and held my documents out to me. I was under control by then, but just barely. Plus, Fancy was crying up a storm in the back and it was getting on my last nerve. There were only so many treats I could shove in her face to keep her quiet and I'd just run out.

I took the papers without even looking at him.

"Maggie…"

"What?" I snapped.

He held out one more piece of paper and I snatched it away from him with a glare.

He leaned closer. "It's just a warning, Maggie. A written one, yes, but it's not a ticket."

"Good to know. Thanks." I found myself staring into those too-blue eyes of his as he leaned closer so that we were only inches apart.

He held my gaze, enunciating each word slowly.

"Next time, even if you're going only one over the speed limit, I will give you a real ticket. Do not test me on this again, Maggie."

"Fine," I muttered and looked away until he left.

CHAPTER 11

Later that morning I was busy restocking the barkery display case when a man walked through the door. For a split second I thought it was Matt. He was about the same height and build and had the same dark hair, but this man had a certain swagger that Matt doesn't have.

He strutted towards me and as the sun glare faded I saw that he had what my grandma would've called a shit-eating grin.

(I know, awful imagery, but that's what it was—that sort of cat got the canary, devilish sort of look that just spells trouble.)

I swallowed heavily as I watched him come closer because it was like someone had taken Matt and all his tall, dark, and handsome sexiness and mixed it together with a double dose of Lucas Dean's mischievousness.

This man wasn't the type to suggest running off behind the bleachers for a quick kiss like Luke was. No, he was the type to suggest jumping in a car, driving to Vegas, and blowing your life's savings on a single roll of the dice at the craps table. You'd find yourself dead broke, alone in a strange city, and all you'd want was another round with him.

Which is why I promptly walked over to the café counter and asked Betty—our latest shop assistant who had to be at least ninety and was a grandmother of ten—to please help the gentleman who'd just walked through the door.

Me, I kept on walking right past her and into the café kitchen so I could not only keep myself away from that kind of trouble but shield Jamie from it as well. If I was tempted, she'd be sucked right in the minute she saw him.

I know. You're probably wondering why I could easily resist a man like Matt who was by all measures a pretty perfect guy and yet I felt the need to walk away from this random stranger. Well, here's the deal. Most men, Matt included, are safe because most men need a pretty good amount of encouragement to make that final move. Oh, they'll flirt or they'll hang around, but to actually put themselves out there and risk a "No"? Yeah, not gonna happen, not without a good dose of encouragement.

And with the guys like Matt I know exactly where the line is in terms of how much encouragement they need to actually act and I just don't give it to them. Keeps my life simple. But with a guy like the one who'd just walked through the door…

Oh no. There'd be none of that hesitation. He'd ask for what he wanted. And, well, turns out I'm kinda impressed when that happens. And tempted. So I just avoid men like that like the plague. Works pretty well if I may say so myself.

Anyway. I hustled away to hide in the kitchen while Betty went to deal with Mr. Too Hot to Handle.

Jamie frowned at me as she tucked a stray bit of hair behind her ear, leaving a smudge of flour behind. "Maggie, what's up?"

"Just checking in, that's all." I sniffed the air. Jamie was hard at work on yet another batch of cinnamon rolls. I still loved them, don't get me wrong, but I could see the day fast approaching when I was going to have had my fill of them. I leaned against the counter. "So what did you get up to last night?"

She smiled a dreamy sort of smile. "Mason had me over for dinner. He made homemade gnocchi and this amazing pesto cream sauce…And…" She blushed and shook herself a little.

"Wow. You are really crushing on him, aren't you? Do you think he's the one?"

She laughed. "It's too early for that. Isn't it?"

The smile said it all. My friend was head over heels.

I heard the deep rumble of the guy out front's voice as he talked to Betty and her answering giggle.

Oh my. It seemed the man had enough charisma to charm any woman, even a little old granny who'd been happily married for sixty years. This man flirted the way other men breathe. Definitely trouble with a capital T.

"Who's out front?" Jamie asked, moving closer to the doorway.

I shook my head and moved to block her. "No one you want to meet."

No matter how far gone she was over Mason, I wasn't going to risk letting her cross paths with this guy. He'd be like catnip to her. No need to mess with a good thing for some guy who'd probably be gone before the week was out.

The front door jangled and I heard a set of footsteps I wished I didn't recognize. I leaned out the doorway just in time to see Matt walk up to the dangerously gorgeous stranger and pull him into a man hug, both of them thumping one another on the back like long lost…

Brothers.

Of course. The stranger must be the evil half of the Barnes Brothers. My grandpa had convinced Matt to enlist and straighten out his life, but he'd failed with Matt's brother who'd been in and out of jail or criminal mischief since he was fourteen.

Matt caught sight of me before I could duck back into the kitchen. "Maggie. Come over here and meet my brother." He was grinning ear to ear, his arm thrown around his brother's shoulder. I'd never seen him so happy.

Reluctantly, I walked towards them. Fancy was barking up a storm now that Matt was there, but it was his brother who quieted her down by going over to her cubby and shadow boxing with her a bit. She loved it.

I shuddered. Of course he'd have the magic touch with dogs, too.

Jamie trailed me out of the kitchen. "Hey, Matt. Did I hear you say your brother was here? Jack? Is that you?"

Jack turned around, leaning his hip against the edge of Fancy's cubby. "Jamie Green. As I live and breathe."

"You two know each other?" I asked, wanting nothing more than to grab the sexy fool leaning next to my dog and frog march him out the front door before he destroyed everything.

Jack nodded, eyeing Jamie up and down with a sexy appraisal. "We crossed paths a few times back in the day. Unfortunately, Jamie was a bit too young back then for anything else. Not anymore, though." He flashed Jamie a look that almost had *me* swooning at his feet and I wasn't even the target.

I moved between them. "Yeah, well. Bad timing again. Jamie's happily dating Mason Maxwell these days. Aren't you, Jamie?"

She mumbled a yes but her gaze was fixed on Jack and his oh-so-well-formed body.

Deprived of his first choice, he turned his intense blue gaze on me. "And you? Are you dating someone dull and boring, too?" He stepped closer, his eyes never leaving my face.

He had the same blue eyes as Matt and I wondered for just a second if Matt's eyes ever looked like that—full of a deep sexual intensity that could suck you under in a moment.

I knew that with a man like Jack my usual "I have better things to do with my time" line wasn't going to fly. That would be like waving a red cape in front of a bull. And if I mentioned some fictitious out-of-town boyfriend he'd probably follow up with some line about how what my boyfriend didn't know wouldn't hurt him.

So I did something crazy and desperate.

I walked over to Matt and took his hand, squeezing it hard in hopes he'd back up what I was about to say. "Dull and boring? I certainly don't think so. You're not dull and boring, are you, honey?" I gazed up at Matt, willing him to play along.

He pulled me close, draping an arm possessively around my shoulder. "Nope. Not at all." He leaned close so his mouth was almost touching my ear. "What the hell are you doing?"

I just squeezed his hand and kept a fake smile plastered on my face.

His brother narrowed his eyes at us. "So it's like that, is it? My baby bro's finally found himself a woman worth envying. Huh. By the way, I don't think we've met. I'm Jack."

Before I could speak, Matt did. "And this is Maggie May Carver. You remember her, don't you, from when we were little?"

Jack laughed. "The girl who wrote your name on the wall?"

"That's the one. Been in love with me ever since, haven't you, honey?" He nuzzled my ear.

"Don't you know it," I answered, promising myself I'd make him pay for that later.

Jack nodded. "I remember that. Your grandpa was livid. Did he ever manage to remove it?"

"Nope. It's still there to this day. Maybe we'll cut it out of the wall and frame it for our wedding day."

Jack looked at me for a long, long moment. "That's great."

He slapped Matt on his arm. "I'm happy for you, bro. Glad you finally found someone." He looked towards the café side. "You hungry? Let me buy you lunch?"

Matt nodded. "Sure. Why not? Love to hear what brought you to town." He squeezed my shoulder one last time and stepped away. "You ladies mind giving us two of the special?"

"Sure thing," I said. "Coming right up. You guys make yourselves comfortable."

🐾 🐾 🐾

I herded Jamie into the kitchen as the brothers seated

themselves at a table near the front of the café. Before I could deliver my "stay far away from that man" lecture, she turned on me. "You and Matt? Since when? Why didn't you tell me?"

"Oh no. That was just panic. I knew I couldn't tell that guy I was single and get away with not going out for at least a drink with him."

"And what would be so wrong with that?"

I laughed. "It never ends with just a drink with a guy like that."

"And what would be so wrong with *that*? Not like you're in a relationship. Have a little fun every once in a while, Maggie."

"Thanks for the suggestion, but one night in jail was enough for me for a lifetime, thank you very much."

"Jack isn't that bad..." She peered out the door, watching him with a little smile on her face.

"He's worse. Trust me. Stay away."

She pressed her lips together as she studied him. "I bet he'd be fun to have a drink with."

"Jamie...You've got a good thing going with Mason. Don't mess it up for a guy like that."

She turned away with a huff. "I know. But if he'd walked through the door before I met Mason..."

"I would've tackled you and tied you up in the office before I would've let you go out with him."

"He's not that bad is he?" She pulled two sandwiches out of the walk-in and put them in the sandwich press, stealing another glimpse of Jack along the way.

"Oh, Jamie. He's like Lucas Dean on steroids. Can't you see that?"

But, no, of course she couldn't.

I grabbed her by the shoulders. "Trust me on this one. Stay away. Stay far, far away."

She stuck her tongue out at me, but at least she didn't try looking out the door again.

Me, I couldn't help but watch the two sitting together and talking. Matt might look relaxed, but I knew him well enough to know he was tense as tense could be. Jack was trouble. And I'm sure Matt was wondering the same thing I was:

Was he really going to be able to arrest his own brother if (or when) it came to that?

CHAPTER 12

It would've been easier for Jamie (and me) to stay away from Jack if he hadn't decided to hang out at the café after Matt left.

At first I couldn't figure out what he was up to. Was he trying to hone in on Jamie? Was it just a convenient place to access free Wi-Fi and decent coffee? But when Greta showed up at her usual time and Jack casually moved to join her, I realized she must be what had brought him through our door in the first place.

Greta looked him up and down, not the least bit phased by that hunky sexuality of his. As a matter of fact, she matched it with a deadly sensuality of her own. For the first time I got a glimpse of what had made at least nine men, perhaps more, propose. She uncoiled like a jaguar scenting prey and leaned forward, staring him down. I saw her casually wave her wedding ring as she looked him slowly up and down and then dismissed him with a wave.

He hesitated, as if he really was going to leave, but then he leaned closer, whispering something that made her sit up straight and slam her hand on the table.

I started towards them, determined to throw him out the door for harassing her, but before I could get close enough to hear what they were saying Greta glared in my direction. She didn't say anything, but that one cold look told me to butt out and mind my own business.

I retreated to the barkery counter and pretended to be straightening out my receipts, but I kept watching the two of them, trying to figure out exactly what was going on.

Supposedly, most of human communication is actually conveyed via body language, but I gotta tell you, words certainly help clarify things, because what I could gather from their movements wasn't exactly clear.

Jack was clearly confident about something at first, leaning forward and taking up space on the table like he owned it. But whatever it was that was driving that confidence hit Greta and bounced right off. She watched him coldly until he sat back and only then did she say something that made him deflate slightly. He slumped back in his chair as she continued to speak.

There was tension in her shoulders, but it wasn't fear. Anger, perhaps? Affront, maybe? Like she was saying "who are you that you would dare to interrupt my day with this worthless issue?"

He leaned forward again, hissing something at her, but she just shrugged one elegant shoulder as if daring him to carry out whatever threat he'd just made.

And then she leaned forward and flung each word like a dagger. He literally flinched with each one she mouthed so calmly and precisely.

She finished with a dismissive laugh and waved towards the door, inviting him to go to hell.

Or so it seemed to me.

Jack sat there for a moment longer, staring out the picture window at the beautiful view of the mountains across the way. Whatever he'd said and whatever she'd said it hadn't gone the way he'd intended.

He stood and paused for a moment looking down at Greta, his fists resting on the back of the chair, but she'd already dismissed him. She didn't even glance in his direction as she opened her laptop and gestured for me to join her.

Jack paused for another moment and then stormed out the door. If he could've slammed it, I'm sure he would have.

Only when he was gone could I finally breathe normally again. I didn't know what had just happened between them, but it was intense.

"Everything okay?" I asked as I joined her, watching Jack get into a very nice pick-up truck and peel out of the parking lot.

She pressed her lips together. "Yes."

"I'm sorry if that guy harassed you."

She gave me a look that made me wonder if I'd somehow crossed an invisible line I hadn't even known existed, but then it faded away. "It was nothing. Please, join me."

She acted as if the conversation had never happened, telling me instead about the latest renovations at her house. They had crews working seven days a week, sun up to sun down, hoping to finish before the weather turned.

(I swear, Luke was going to be working there well into the next century at the rate it was going. But it wasn't really his fault. Greta and her husband were redoing everything. They should've just bulldozed the property and built from scratch, but I was too polite to say it.)

It was a pleasant enough conversation, but I couldn't help but wonder what exactly Jack had said to her and what she'd said to him.

🐾 🐾 🐾

I drove home that night trying to figure out what the connection between them was. Had she hired him to kill her ex? Would Greta do something like that? Would Jack? And, if not, then what had he known? And how?

As I pulled up in front of my grandpa's house I glanced down the street and saw that Matt was still at work. Acting on impulse, I dialed his number as I leashed up Fancy and led her towards the house.

"Matthew Barnes," he answered.

"Matt. It's Maggie. You have dinner plans?"

"I figured I'd try out one of those microwave meals you've told me so much about. I bought some sort of manly man's beef pot pie."

I winced at the thought of it. "How about you swing by for dinner instead."

"Why, Maggie May, did you actually believe that line you fed my brother earlier today? Are we an item and I didn't even know it?"

"If we were an item, you'd definitely know it."

"I would, would I? And how exactly would I know it?"

Fancy dragged me towards the front door, practically running as she raced toward dinner and my grandpa. "Never mind. Look. Something interesting happened after you left. I thought you might want to know about it. Plus, I owe you one for going along with things earlier today."

🐾🐾 435 🐾🐾

"Jack didn't hit on you after I left did he?" he asked, his voice flat with tension.

"No. Nothing like that. But this could have something to do with the case involving Greta's ex. So, see you at six?"

"Make it six-thirty and you have a deal."

"Done."

CHAPTER 13

My grandpa gave me a sly little look when I told him Matt was coming over for dinner.

"It's not like that, Grandpa," I muttered as I finished placing the last tater tot for tater tot casserole. (So easy to make and sooo good.)

"No?"

"No."

I gave him a brief rundown on Jack's sudden appearance at the store and what I'd done to avoid his attention.

My grandpa snorted. "Maggie May, have you ever thought of just telling a man you're not interested in him? It's very easy, he asks you out and you say no."

"But it's not that easy, not with a guy like Jack who sees a no as a challenge."

He shook his head. "Not true. I knew Jackson Barnes very well. He would never pursue a woman who wasn't interested in him."

"I didn't say he didn't pique my interest."

"Ah…So that's the problem. Do you like him more than Matt?"

"No…"

Fortunately, Matt's knock on the front door saved me from the rest of that discussion.

The food wasn't ready yet, so we sat at the kitchen table as the smell of cooking hamburger, tater tots, and mushroom soup wafted from the oven. I filled Matt in on the conversation between Greta and Jack while my grandpa pretended to do his crossword but really eavesdropped on us.

When I was done, Matt didn't say anything, just looked thoughtful.

"So?" I finally asked. "Do you think maybe their conversation had something to do with Greta's ex? Do you think Jack could be the killer?"

Matt winced. "That's my brother you're talking about."

"I know. But…"

"But Jack may be mixed up in this. I agree. The timing is far too convenient. First thing I did when I returned to the station this afternoon was check for connections between Jack and Kristof."

"And?"

He gave me that look that said I wasn't a cop so it wasn't my business, but he answered anyway. "They did time together. They were cellmates for six months. Probably bonded over a shared love of breaking and entering."

My grandpa grunted. "Pretty big jump to go from breaking and entering to murder."

Matt nodded. "Yeah. But maybe a deal went south. Money's a great motivator."

My grandpa set aside his paper. "I don't see it. I'll bet you dollars for donuts he's right in the middle of this mess, but he's not the killer."

I took a sip of my beer. "If you're right about that, Grandpa, then Jack's in danger."

They both looked at me with the same surprised expression.

"Well, isn't he? I mean, if he was in business with Kristof then there has to be a good chance that whoever killed Kristof might kill Jack, too."

Matt grimaced. "I hadn't thought of that. Give me a minute."

He pulled out his phone and dialed a number. A few seconds later he said, "Hey. You still need a place to crash?" And a few seconds after that he said, "Alright. You know where to find the key," and then "No, I'm having dinner with Maggie and her grandpa."

Matt winced and looked at us, but before I could say anything my grandpa said, "Tell him to come over. He knows where to find us."

So Matt did.

I leaned back in my chair. Just what I needed. Jack and Matt at the same dinner table with my grandpa there to make trouble. I tell ya. Life was far easier when I was over-worked and under-socialized and living alone in DC.

❀ ❀ ❀

I don't know where Jack was when Matt called him, but it must not have been very far away, because he was at our house within five minutes. He actually ducked his head a bit when he said hi to my grandpa. It was interesting to watch such a highly confident man suddenly turn meek and polite.

Then again, my grandpa wasn't exactly the type of man you cross. Fifteen years in prison gives a man a certain "don't mess with me" air that even the most hardened criminal would respond to.

I set the casserole dish on a couple of trivets in the middle of the table and shoved the serving spoon into the corner before running back into the kitchen for the green beans. Matt followed me and brought back four bottles of Coors.

As we settled around the table and started to serve ourselves, I asked Jack, "Did you play for my grandpa?"

"No."

When it was clear he had no intention of saying anything more than that, I asked, "Then how do you two know each other?"

Jack shoved a bite of food into his mouth and then answered, still chewing as he spoke. (My grandma would've pinned him to his seat with her worst glare for that. Since she wasn't there, my grandpa did it for her.) "Work release."

My grandpa added, "Jack worked for me for three months as part of his last jail term around these parts."

"Doing what?" I asked. It wasn't like my grandpa had a company to employ him.

Jack snorted and then ducked his head when my grandpa glared at him.

"He helped out at the baseball field. Built the two dugouts. Tended the field. Fixed the fence."

"And listened to your grandpa lecture me about what a better life that was than going down the wrong path." The sneer in his voice was evident.

My grandpa leveled a glare at Jack that would've burned a hole right through most people. "Seems some people have to learn the hard way. Just hope you don't get killed first, boy."

Jack glared right back at him and I wondered if I was going to have to break up a fist fight between my eighty-two-year-old grandpa and Matt's punk of a brother, but Matt distracted them by patting his leg and calling Fancy to his side. He held a tater tot up until she sat, and we all laughed at the drool that streamed from her mouth as she waited, shuffling closer and closer to him until she was nudging his hand with her nose.

For all her excitement, when he finally gave her the tater tot she took it as delicately as a little mouse.

That turned the conversation to dogs for a while. Matt and Jack exchanged stories of the old lab they'd grown up with who it seemed had been a good hunting dog but not the best house dog.

It was almost a pleasant meal after that. Almost.

As we sat around the table eating ice cream, I casually asked, "So, Jack, how long you sticking around for?"

He shrugged one shoulder. "Don't know. I guess until my business is done."

"What kind of business is that?"

"None of ya."

"Excuse me?"

"It's none of your business." He smirked at me and suddenly I found him a lot less attractive than before.

"Don't talk to Maggie like that," Matt said, his voice soft but firm.

"Oh, yeah. I forgot. You're a thing." He took a swig of his beer. "No accounting for taste."

It wasn't clear whether he meant to insult me for choosing Matt or Matt for choosing me, but it didn't matter to my grandpa. He crumpled his napkin and threw it on the table. "Well, I'd say it's about time you headed out, wouldn't you, Jack?"

Jack glanced at his half-finished ice cream, but just nodded. "I guess so." He shoved his chair back, startling Fancy into a growl.

Matt stood. "Then I guess I better go, too. Get Jack settled in and all."

"You need sheets or pillows or anything?" I asked.

"No, thanks."

"Okay. Um…" I stood but didn't move for the door, not sure what to do. At the last minute Matt came over and kissed my cheek.

"Best keep up appearances," he whispered before turning away and following his brother out the front door.

I tried not to blush, but I'm pretty sure I failed miserably. That's okay. No one saw it but Fancy and she could've cared less. She was too busy eyeing all those half-finished bowls of ice cream.

My grandpa closed the door firmly behind them. "Sooner that boy leaves town, the better."

I nodded agreement. I knew Matt wanted to protect his brother but I did not like the idea of Jack staying with him. Not even for one night.

CHAPTER 14

The next night was the big charity event. I only had two fancy party dresses to choose from. One was a short black number that fit well enough but made me exceedingly uncomfortable because of how well it fit, but the other was a long dress with an unfortunate neckline that was just low enough to flash my bra if I didn't keep constant vigilance. So the fitted little black number it was.

I threw it on and grimaced at how it barely reached mid-thigh. It didn't look bad, but it certainly didn't allow for freedom of movement. No bending over to pick up anything tonight, that was for sure. At least not without far more thought and care than I wanted to give it.

I put on some makeup, threw my hair up in a bun, and figured I was good to go. Unfortunately, Jamie and Mason were giving me a ride to the event and when Jamie saw me she decided I needed a bit of an intervention.

"What's the point in having long hair, Maggie, if all you ever do is pull it back in a braid or throw it up in a bun?" She flashed me a grin as she pushed her long, flowing hair back from her face. "Fortunately, I know you well enough to know exactly what you were going to do, so I brought my tools."

She marched me away to the bathroom to torture me with a hair curler while Mason and my grandpa sat in the living room making awkward small talk about Lulu and Fancy. (My grandpa had, very reluctantly, agreed to watch Lulu while we were away.)

By the time Jamie finished with me my hair cascaded halfway down my back in beautiful, graceful curls that I knew wouldn't last an hour let alone an entire night. I snuck a hair thing into my purse so I could throw my hair back into a bun as soon as she wasn't looking.

"Alright, then," I said. "Let's go." I tried to step past her, but she blocked me.

"Not yet. We haven't done your makeup."

"I put on eyeshadow."

"And that's all you put on. It's a ball, Maggie. Close your eyes."

Arguing with Jamie when she's decided something has to happen is a waste of breath, so I patiently let her give me a smoky eye and long lashes. I even let her force me to switch from the plain rose-colored lipstick I'd chosen to a more brilliant red. But when she told me I wasn't allowed to wear hose with my dress, I balked.

"I am keeping on the hose. This dress is short enough as is without my having naked legs underneath."

"Maggie, no one under fifty wears hose."

"I do."

"Maggie…"

"No. I am wearing hose. Look. I let you tart me up like a streetwalker already. I'm wearing heels, which is something I'd hoped I'd never ever have to do again.

And this dress is so short I'm going to be worried about flashing someone all night. The least you can let me do is keep my hose."

When she hesitated, I knew I had her. I pushed past her into the hallway. "Come on. We're going to be late." I tugged at the dress, trying to pull it down an extra inch.

"Stop that." Jamie smacked my hand. "It looks great."

"It's short."

"Not that short."

"It is when Matt's going to be there tonight."

She gave me her best dimpled smile. "Matt's going to be there, huh? Well, then, I'd say it's not short enough."

I rolled my eyes at her and slipped my feet into the torture devices called four-inch high heels that made my butt and legs look great but would turn me into a hobbled cripple by the end of the night. "Can we just get this over with, please?"

"Oh, Maggie. You're gonna love it. You know you will."

🐾 🐾 🐾

When Jamie, Mason, and I pulled up out front of the Baker Valley Country Club I smiled politely at the young man working valet who opened my door and helped me out with a goggle-eyed look. It was the frickin' hair, I knew it. Men and long hair. I swear.

My hand twitched towards my purse, ready to throw my hair up immediately, but Jamie grabbed it before I could. "You look gorgeous."

"That's the problem," I muttered.

Fortunately, Jamie looked even better than I did. She was wearing a bronze-colored mini dress with a scoop in back that stopped just short of indecent. As long as I stayed in her shadow all night, I'd be fine. But I knew I'd be paying for this for the next month, at least.

I have a theory from my business days that men have this little switch in their brains. They can either see you as a competent colleague who happens to be a woman or they can see you as a woman that they want to, well, let's just say get to know really, really well. Flip that switch to the sexy side and it takes weeks to get them back to the competent side. And tonight I was going to be flipping that switch for every professional man in the county.

And, worse yet, Matt.

Oh well. Maybe it would be good for business. Not like I was trying to convince men to listen to my ideas anymore. Instead I was trying to sell them a product…

Heck, come to think of it, I should've brought business cards. And samples. Give out my treats to everyone who asked. Haha.

Ugh.

I longed desperately to tug at the bottom of my stupid dress, but I settled for smoothing it down my hips instead before Mason offered each of us an arm and led us inside, cameras flashing.

I made an immediate beeline for the nearest bathroom, prepared to hole up for the next hour or two—those kinds of places always have spacious bathrooms with makeup mirrors and sitting areas—but Greta intercepted me.

She looked stunningly elegant in a sleek silver number that showed off her figure just enough but not too much. "Maggie. Come. I will introduce you."

"To whom?"

She laughed. "My husband and his nephew."

I sighed in relief. Good. No geriatric billionaires.

She tucked my hand into the crook of her arm and patted it. "And perhaps a few other men I know who are single."

I tried to pull away at that, but Greta was stronger than she looked. Unless I wanted to make a scene, I was stuck in her clutches until she chose to release me.

Her husband, Friedrich, was a dignified man, probably sixty or so, who looked like he'd been born in a tuxedo. He acknowledged me just long enough to fulfill his social duties and then turned away to focus on some twenty-something woman with flowing dark hair in a low-cut red dress that showed off her more than generous assets.

I glanced at Greta, but she didn't seem the least bit upset with his behavior, so I decided I wouldn't be either. Not all marriages work on the same rules. And from what she'd said previously it was clear to me that love wasn't a top priority in her life.

Wilhelm, the nephew, was…interesting. He was probably my age or thereabouts and wore his tuxedo well enough, but not with the same confidence as his uncle. He was sort of pale and awkward, but not terribly so. Just enough to grate on the nerves a bit.

He stepped closer to me. "Greta tells me you own the dog food place," he smiled down at me and I had the distinct impression he was trying to look down my dress. Fortunately, it wasn't low cut enough to give a good view.

"Uh, the barkery? We don't really do dog food, so much as dog treats. But, yes."

"Oh. Maybe I'll have to come by some time and see it for myself." He put his hand on the small of my back and

I glared death at him for two seconds before I managed to control my expression and step away.

"Of course. New customers are always welcome. Do you have a dog?"

He probably owned a Pomeranian.

(Not that there's anything wrong with that. Calm down.)

"No. But I think I'd like to see you again." He stepped closer.

I looked to Greta for help but she'd been pulled into conversation with some exceedingly old man who I was willing to bet was also obscenely wealthy. If I moved over to join them I'd just be jumping from the frying pan into the fire.

Luckily for me, Matt appeared at my elbow. "Maggie. There you are."

He gave me a polite kiss on the cheek and inserted himself between Wilhelm and me. Wilhelm pulled back, staring at him like he'd never been so offended in his life. I would've laughed if I wasn't so disconcerted by the site of Matt in a tux.

I'd figured he'd look awkward or uncomfortable. He didn't. Not at all. And let me tell you, a man built like he was and in a tuxedo? Well, there's a reason there are so many romance novels about sexy billionaires with dark hair and piercing blue eyes. Took my breath away.

I recovered by introducing Matt to Wilhelm. Wilhelm barely controlled his sneer when he heard that Matt was a cop.

"I didn't realize they were letting all sorts attend this event," he sniffed.

"Neither did I," I said, pulling on Matt's arm. "If you'll excuse us, Wilhelm. It was a pleasure to meet you."

See, I can lie when I need to.

Matt chuckled softly. "Have you met enough wealthy bachelors for the night? Ready to get away for a bit."

"Yes, please. I was going to hide away in the bathroom until Greta intercepted me."

"I can do better than that. Come on." He steered me through the crowd and out a side entrance onto a lovely balcony with a gorgeous view of the mountains and a lake in the distance. The moon was almost full and hovered on the far horizon.

"Ah, now this is more like it," I sighed as soon as the door closed behind us.

"You found our girl," Abe called from a table in the corner where he and Evan lounged like movie stars straight from the set of Casablanca.

I smiled at the sight of my favorite not openly gay but so obviously gay couple. Not only are they some of my best customers, but they also have a fabulous St. Bernard named Lucy Carrots and the juiciest gossip.

I sank into a chair next to Abe and kicked off my shoes. "Oh, this would be perfect if we just had booze and food."

"We do." He patted my hand and winked. "Just wait."

Matt sat down across from me. "I rescued her from Wilhelm VanVeldenstein."

"Oh, you poor dear. That man is atrocious."

"That he is," I agreed. "Greta told me that his uncle believes the development deal he's working on is going to be a huge failure."

"I wouldn't be surprised. He has no idea how to run a business." Abe waved at a waiter who peeked out at us from the main room. A moment later the man reappeared with three other waiters in his wake, each one bearing a tray. One had champagne flutes, one had some sort of lettuce wraps, one had *albondigas* (a fancy way of saying meatballs), and one had some sort of crostini that looked awful but tasted delicious. I figured I didn't actually want to know what was smeared on top.

"Thank you, Gabe. Keep them coming," Abe said, as he took enough of the food to fill our table. The man nodded and left with his waiters trailing behind him.

"How do you have the hookup?"

Abe laughed. "Gabe works at the Inn. I gave him the night off to work this event as long as he agreed to keep us supplied with drinks and food."

I laughed. "Well done you. It pays to know the right people."

Matt nodded. "And those people are not inside that room."

"No. No they are not," I agreed.

🐾 🐾 🐾

We spent the next hour having ourselves a wonderful time. Abe and Even knew all of the gossip since they ran the Creek Inn, so as each person floated past the windows inside they told us some juicy little tidbit.

It seemed Wilhelm, my personal favorite of the night, had been forced to have his date pay for dinner the night before when his credit card was declined.

And the woman in red, she of the oh-so-obvious décolletage that had captured Friedrich's attention, was actually his mistress. Some Chilean woman who'd snared his attention a few months before on a business trip. According to Evan's sources, Friedrich was always on the lookout for a new challenge, but this woman had been almost perfectly crafted to appeal to him from her curvy looks to her fiery attitude.

That one hurt because Greta was my friend and whether it bothered her or not it bothered me to have people talking about it so casually.

I didn't have time to dwell on it, though, because the next little bit of gossip was about Jamie. Well, not Jamie. About Mason Maxwell. It seemed he'd been seen shopping for diamond rings and scouting out wedding locations.

"But they barely know each other," I stammered.

Evan laughed. "My dear, when you know, you know." He cast such a fond look at Abe when he said it that I blushed scarlet at intruding on such an intimate moment.

"That you do," Matt said, looking directly at me.

That was not what I needed right then or at any other time. (Although it did give me a soft glowy feeling. Of course, that could've just been the champagne.)

I looked back to the party where Jamie and Mason were dancing slowly, lost in one another. "Do you think she knows?"

In other words, was my best friend practically engaged and hiding it from me?

"No. He wants it to be a surprise."

"Then how do you know?"

"Because her father came into the Inn this afternoon at two for a shot of whiskey and when I asked him what on earth had brought him in at that hour, he said Mason Maxwell had just asked him for his daughter's hand."

"And what did he say?"

"What would you say if some good-looking millionaire

who'd keep your daughter living nearby and was one of the most upstanding citizens in the valley asked for your daughter's hand?"

"That it was too soon. To wait until they'd been dating a few months at least."

Abe chuckled. "Good thing Mason didn't ask your permission then, isn't it?"

I stared at them again. Was Mason going to propose? Maybe tonight?

They were my ride home. How awkward would that be?

I sunk down in my chair already preparing myself for the inevitable decline in our friendship as I found myself the not unwelcome but definitely awkward third wheel. Again.

Seriously, I needed some friends who were nuns. No running off and getting married. No having kids and losing their minds to exhaustion for five years. Just, good, solid female friends that could be counted on to stay the same and never change.

Of course, nuns don't drink. Darn it.

🐾 🐾 🐾

We'd all sunk into silence and I was debating asking Abe and Evan to give me a ride home (I couldn't ask Matt because of what I was wearing and how he might take that), when Jack appeared from around the corner of the patio and walked inside.

I sat up straight. "Matt, what's Jack doing here?"

He certainly wasn't dressed for the party. He was in a black t-shirt and jeans. How he'd managed to get inside, I didn't know, but inside he was. And making a beeline for Friedrich, Greta, Friedrich's mistress, Lucia, and

Wilhelm who were clustered together at the center of the room.

Matt leapt to his feet and raced inside. I chased after him, not even caring that I'd left my shoes behind.

We arrived just in time to hear Jack say, "Mr. VanVeldenstein. It's very important that I speak to you, sir. I have information you'll want to know."

Matt grabbed Jack by the elbow and tried to drag him backwards, but he shook free.

Friedrich looked Jack up and down. "I doubt that you have any information that I would want, young man."

I looked to Greta who was watching the entire exchange with an odd level of intensity. Then again, so was Wilhelm. And the mistress. It seemed they all had their secrets.

Wilhelm moved between Friedrich and Jack. "You overstep yourself. Where is security?"

Matt pulled Jack back and hissed into his ear. "We're leaving. Now. Unless you want me to arrest you?"

Jack shook free again, but he stayed where he was. "Mr. VanVeldenstein, I assure you, you do want to hear what I have to say. My name's Jack Barnes. I suggest you take my next call. It will be worth your while." He paused long enough to meet the eyes of Wilhelm, Friedrich, Greta, and the mistress before he turned away from Matt and strutted out of the room, downing a glass of champagne on his way.

Matt raced after him as Evan and Abe crowded close behind me. "Oh my," Evan murmured. "He does have a flair for the dramatic doesn't he? Mm."

I had to agree, but my heart ached for Matt. His brother certainly wasn't making things easy.

CHAPTER 15

The next day at the barkery was Jamie's day off, so I didn't get to find out if Mason had proposed. But given the way the party had deteriorated after Jack's little appearance, I suspected not. Abe and Evan had given me a ride home, dropping subtle little comments the whole way about how well Matt and I suited each other.

I swear, everyone is a matchmaker. But they just didn't understand. And I wasn't about to explain it to them because then they'd waste their time and mine trying to convince me I was wrong.

I wasn't.

When Greta arrived that afternoon I couldn't help but watch her, looking for any sign that Jack's little scene had been about her. I'd done some Googling on her ex, but all I'd found was that he was a soccer fanatic.

I know, it wasn't my business.

But it was. Greta was my friend. And the body had been buried right behind my store. Plus, Matt's brother was involved somehow. It kind of made me question my judgement, you know. Was she the victim? Was she the mastermind? Or was she just a slightly crazy woman with bad taste in men? (Who hasn't been there, right?)

After about a half hour, Greta snapped her laptop closed. "Maggie. Come here." She leaned back in her chair and waited for me to join her.

"Yes?"

"Sit."

I sat down, trying to hide my nervousness. I hadn't thought I was being all that obvious about things, but I guess I had been.

She leaned forward, her gaze intense. "I have told you before, this is not your business, yes?"

I nodded.

"But you are my friend and I do not like you looking at me like that, so I will tell you what is not your business."

I squirmed a bit. "You don't have to if you don't want to."

(I said the words, but I so wanted to know anything she was willing to tell me.)

She huffed. "You will not let this rest and we both know it." She nodded towards the back of the store. "Perhaps coffee first, though, yes? And a Coke for you."

I hurried to grab her a coffee and myself a Coke. Now that she was going to tell me what was going on, I didn't want to give her a chance to change her mind, but just to top things off I brought us each back a slice of the lemon cheesecake Jamie had made the day before as an experiment.

(It was sooo good, let me tell you. Heaven. Who needed cinnamon rolls when they could have lemon cheesecake with a graham cracker crust?)

Greta took a bite and nodded. "This is very good." She pushed the plate to the side and cradled her coffee in her hands, staring at it for a long, long moment.

I took a quick sip of Coke so I wouldn't be tempted to start blathering and make her change her mind.

"As you know, Kristof was my first husband. I was young and he was handsome and this was enough for me to marry him. But we were poor. And I wanted pretty things."

She glanced at the diamond bracelet on her hand for a brief moment before continuing. "So we stole them."

I tried not to flinch when she said it, but she smiled slightly anyway.

"I know. This is not something you would do. And it is not what I would do now. But at the time…It made sense."

"Were you ever caught?"

"Me? No. Kristof? Yes. But that was later. We started with little things, but eventually we worked our way to bigger items. Jewelry. Paintings. Some we kept. Some we sold." She fiddled with her wedding ring for a moment. "There was a trio of paintings I fell in love with. I stole the first one from a private collection and bought the second one after I had the money to do so—I was a good thief but not that good of one."

Her lips quirked. "In a sense it was realizing that I couldn't have that second painting that made me stop stealing and think of a new way to achieve what I wanted."

"Is that why you left your first husband?"

"Money? No. I left him because he was too young to be married. Too young to be faithful. I could stand the nights out drinking. I could stand the boasting about jobs he should've kept to himself. But I could not stand him stumbling home the next morning smelling of some other woman."

She shook herself, pushing the memories away. "I met my second husband. He fell in love with me and offered to treat me better than Kristof ever had. So I left."

"And Kristof was okay with that?"

"No. Of course not. What man wants to lose what he thinks is his? But I gave him that ring and I gave him that scar—and another one in an area a little more private—and I left."

I took a long sip of my Coke as she took another bite of the cheesecake.

"So how did he come back into your life?" I asked.

"*Back* into my life? He never left. We had the same friends and our families lived next door to one another. We didn't speak for years, but he was always there. Always within reach." She drummed her perfectly manicured fingernails on the table and I knew she was debating whether to continue.

I took a bite of my cheesecake while I waited. I wanted to know what else there was to the story, but I didn't dare ask.

Finally, she nodded and leaned forward again. "He was always there, but we had not spoken for many years. Until six months ago when I called him."

"You called him? Why?"

She drummed her fingers on the table once more. "The third painting. I wanted him to steal it for me."

"Couldn't you just buy it? I mean, you're richer than God aren't you?"

She smiled slightly. "No. I tried to buy it, but the owner would not sell."

"So you decided to steal it?" I tried to keep the judgement out of my voice, but I'm pretty sure I failed from the way Greta's eyebrow quirked upward. "But I thought…"

"That I'd put that behind me? I had. And, no, I didn't decide to steal it. Not right away." She stared out the window, her eyes unfocused. "I decided I would marry the man who owned it instead."

"Huh?" (I know. I'm not very articulate sometimes. But her response threw me for a loop.)

"Friedrich, my husband, he is the one who owns the painting. He would not sell it, so I married him for it."

I laughed. "You married your husband for a painting?"

"Yes."

"Oh. Okay. So what went wrong?"

(At that point I was feeling a bit like someone who's ventured into the middle of an iced-over lake only to realize that the ice is paper thin and about to crack under them. My new friend had actually married a man for a painting? Who did that kind of thing?)

Greta chuckled like she'd read my mind and found my bourgeois sensibilities amusing. "I could not tell Friedrich I married him for the painting, he would've never given it to me. I thought he would give it to me as a wedding gift because I loved it so much, but he did not. And then as a birthday gift. And then as a Christmas gift. And…You see?"

"So, technically you had a right to the painting as his wife, but you wanted him to give it to you as a gift so that it would be yours no matter what? But he never did?"

"Mm. Not quite. We signed a pre-nup. Very basic. His was his, mine was mine. The painting is his. But I thought he would give me the painting as a gift and then it would be mine." She finished her coffee and set the cup down on the table with a little more force than was absolutely necessary. "But he did not."

"You're still married, though, aren't you? So…"

She shook her head. "You saw his mistress last night. Lucia. She is very bold. She wants more than jewelry. She wants a wedding. He will divorce me soon. I give it six months."

I nodded, not really understanding, but trying to. "Okay. So you married him for the painting. He didn't give it to you. It became clear to you that he was never going to give it to you. And that he was likely to divorce you soon. But because of the pre-nup you couldn't just ask for it in the divorce."

She nodded.

"So then you contacted your first husband, who has a history of stealing things, and…asked him to steal the painting for you?"

"Yes."

"How? When?"

"I had Lucas hire him. It gave him access to the house."

"But he didn't do it."

She shrugged. "I do not know if he tried, but he did not succeed."

I thought about it a moment. "So it's possible that Kristof was killed because he tried to steal the painting?"

"Perhaps. I think Friedrich is not a killer, though. And Kristof was not the best at making choices."

"But someone needs to look into it. Just in case. Did you tell the police?"

She gave me a look that had me feeling like a child asking if the moon was really made of cheese.

I winced. "Sorry. I guess you can't exactly tell the cops you hired a thief to steal a painting and he turned up dead. Especially if you ever want to hire someone else to steal it."

She didn't respond, just smiled a thin-lipped smile. I met her calm gaze, wondering what I'd gotten myself into. "So how does Matt's brother, Jack, fit into all of this?"

"Jack? Who is this?"

"The man who confronted you here the other day. And who showed up at the party last night. Jack Barnes."

"Ah. This man is the brother of your cop?"

"Matt's not *my* cop."

She raised one elegantly sculpted eyebrow until I blushed and looked away.

"Anyway. How does Jack fit into this? What did he say to you?"

She studied her nails for a long moment and I expected she'd tell me it was a private conversation and none of my business, but then she sighed and looked at me once more. "That he was a friend of Kristof's, and he knew I had hired him."

"That's all?"

She nodded.

"No offense, Greta, but that's not what it looked like to me. It looked like he said a heckuva lot more than that."

She sniffed. "Fine. He said he was a friend of Kristof's. He knew that I had hired Kristof to steal the painting. And he threatened to tell my husband. He wanted a considerable amount of money in exchange for his silence. I told him no. And I informed him that my husband would not care."

"That's all? Was there anything else?"

She narrowed her gaze. "Yes. That is all."

"So was he trying to scare you last night? Or expose you?"

"I do not know. What I know is that I will not pay this man to protect my secret. He cannot blackmail me if I do not care."

Made sense. Maybe.

I leaned closer. "Why are you telling me all of this? Earlier you said it was none of my business."

She pursed her lips, looking considerably older than she normally did. "Because you are my friend. And you are smart. And you know the cop. I do not want to lose your friendship. And I also hope to find the reason Kristof is dead."

"But how can I help?"

She smiled and took a bite of cheesecake, waiting for me to figure it out.

"Oh. You want me to tell Matt. You can't tell him because then you'd be confessing to a crime. Or more than one I guess. But if I tell Matt, it's just a rumor he can investigate."

She nodded slightly as she took a final bite of cheesecake.

"Okay." I nodded. "I can do that. Thank you for telling me, Greta."

"Thank you for listening, Maggie."

As I cleared our plates and walked to the back of the store I wondered how much of what she'd told me was actually true. I liked Greta. I considered her a friend.

And normally I'll take anything anyone tells me at face value, at least initially, but there was something about her story that just didn't quite sit right with me.

Maybe it was the fact that she wanted me to believe she'd married a man for his painting. I mean, who does that? I knew she wasn't big on love. And there's certainly been more than one attractive woman who has traded her looks for a comfortable life over the years, but…a painting? Really? When you were already that wealthy?

I shook my head.

Rich people, I swear. They live in a different world from the rest of us.

Well, whatever the truth, the least I could do is tell Matt about my conversation with Greta and let him sort fact from fiction. He was a trained investigator. He'd figure it out.

CHAPTER 16

Half an hour after Greta's grand reveal, Wilhelm walked through the door. He was dressed like a bad Italian pimp in a shiny, skinny suit and smelled even worse, the overdone scent of his cologne clogging up the air.

"Maggie. So this is your little shop." He looked around the place and I could see him struggling not to sneer, especially when he saw the kitschy little tourist area we had between the barkery and café counters.

"Mr. VanVeldenstein. To what do I owe this pleasure?" I answered through gritted teeth, hoping he wasn't there for the reason I thought he was.

Greta set aside her book and watched us with a slight smirk on her face. I had no doubt she was on my side in whatever might happen. She thought her nephew an ineffectual fool.

He leaned against the barkery counter and reached a hand towards my hair which I'd thrown into a messy bun early that morning and not thought about since. I ducked back. The customer may always be right, but the customer who tries to touch me without my permission deserves to lose a limb.

He chuckled in such a patronizing way I wanted to do him physical harm. "Oh, Maggie. You have such potential. Like an uncut diamond. I could take you in hand and make you into something amazing."

He could, could he? A dozen not very nice replies ran through my mind, but I settled for, "Were you looking to buy something for a dog? Because that's what we are, you know. A dog barkery."

"Oh no."

"Well then you should really go to the café counter. Betty can get you a coffee or a cinnamon roll or whatever you need."

"Mm. You want to play it that way, do you?" He stood up and smiled that smarmy smile of his. "That's alright. I like a good challenge."

"I'm not a challenge. Just simply not interested."

"You would prefer that cop?"

Any day of the week, buddy, I thought to myself.

He leaned closer, eyeing my neck. "Every woman has a price. It's just a matter of finding it. What kind of jewels do you like? Sapphires perhaps? Or rubies? Flowers are so passé, don't you think? Far better to be given something of value."

"Really, I'm fine. As you can see, I'm not much for jewelry."

"Ah, you just haven't acquired the taste yet. You will."

I was on the verge of telling him exactly what I thought of him, when the door jangled and Jack walked in. He immediately went to Greta's table and sat down without asking.

I wanted to go tell him to get the heck out of my store and stop harassing my customers, but I didn't dare put myself in reach of Wilhelm. He was the type to think an unwanted kiss was exciting courtship and with enough lawyers on speed dial to get out of any assault charges I might want to file.

Interestingly, though, Wilhelm lost interest in me as soon as Jack walked through the door.

He watched intently as Greta and Jack repeated their conversation of the other day with Jack starting off confident, Greta not caring, and Jack slowly wilting against his chair.

"That man. He threatened my uncle." Wilhelm said, his voice suddenly sharp and in control. "Why would you allow a man like that in here?"

I wanted to answer that I'd rather have a man like Jack Barnes in my store any day of the week than a man like Wilhelm, but I refrained. Instead, I said, "He didn't threaten your uncle. He told him he had information for him. If anything, he was threatening the subject of that information."

Greta? Or perhaps Wilhelm who turned a little pale at my comment.

Once again, Greta dismissed Jack and went back to her book, acting as if he wasn't even there. And once again Jack stormed out of the door. But this time Wilhelm went after him.

I was relieved to have Wilhelm leave, but watched closely as he and Jack had a confrontation in the parking lot. I assumed Wilhelm was telling Jack off for barging into the party and "threatening" his uncle, but of course I couldn't hear anything.

Jack certainly looked puzzled by the man's reaction, but that didn't stop him from getting up in Wilhelm's face. They argued back and forth for a moment and then both men left, peeling tires as they drove away in opposite directions, Wilhelm in a Mercedes I was pretty sure was worth millions and Jack in his truck that was definitely nicer than I would've expected an ex-con to drive.

I turned my attention to Greta after they'd left. "Care to tell me what that was all about?"

"The same as before. He is a persistent man, this Jack Barnes." She shrugged and returned to reading her book.

I stared out the window, wondering if that was really true. And if it was, how Wilhelm fit into it.

CHAPTER 17

I called Matt before I headed home, figuring he could come over for dinner and I'd fill him in on what Greta had told me.

"Maggie May," he answered. I could hear the smile in his voice. "This is starting to become a pattern."

"Yeah, yeah. Don't get used to it."

"What's up?"

"I had an interesting conversation today with Greta. One I'm sure she'll deny if you ask her about it directly. You want to come over for dinner tonight and I'll tell you all about it?"

"How about you come by my place instead?"

"Ahhh…." Somehow going to his place put things in a whole different light. Was this a date?

"Don't worry. You can bring Fancy. The yard is fenced. I'll even put down a sharing plate for her."

"Umm…I don't know. Is Jack gonna be there?"

"You want him to be?" I could hear Matt tense up through the phone.

"No. I didn't say that. It's just that what I have to tell you involves him, too, so it'd be a little awkward if he was there."

Although perhaps better on a personal level…

"He won't be. He just texted and said he was going to the Creek Inn tonight to catch up with some old friends. It'll just be you and me. So? What do you say?"

I frowned at the wall. I try very hard not to get myself into awkward situations. I figure it's always better to not give a guy a chance to make a move you'll have to reject than to body block him when he does. Which means I generally don't let myself be alone with a guy I'd want to body block. (Only exception I make to that rule is when it's a guy I am very, very confident isn't going to try anything. Or one I'm willing to let make that move.)

With Matt…

Well…

Hm.

"Yeah, I'll be there. But please tell me we're not going to be eating Ramen noodles and tuna fish for dinner."

He laughed. "I actually make a pretty mean burger, I'll have you know."

"So you *can* cook. All this time we've been inviting you over for dinner because we were worried you were starving, and you've been perfectly capable of taking care of yourself. Wait until my grandpa hears about this."

He laughed again. "Six-thirty?"

"Six-thirty. See you then."

My hands were shaking as I put my phone away. I didn't know why. It was nothing. Just dinner between some friends. He was not going to try something. He wasn't like that. Matt was the kind of guy who'd literally need a woman to plop down in his lap before he tried something. And even then he'd probably just ask her if she'd fallen and offer to help her stand back up.

But if I was wrong…

No. I wasn't. I knew men and Matt was too respectful for that.

(Unfortunately.)

Still. No use sending him any sort of signals, which is why I was going to resist the strong urge I had to put on a little makeup and brush my hair and teeth before I went over there.

It was a business dinner. Nothing more.

🐾 🐾 🐾

I arrived at Matt's at exactly 6:25. I was still a little early, but not near as early as I'd been before I drove around the block twice. Fancy was thoroughly confused by that, let me tell you, but I didn't want to be rude and show up twenty minutes early like I would have otherwise.

That's a constant struggle for me. I don't like being late so I'm generally too early and then have to find some way to kill that extra ten or fifteen minutes until I can be acceptably early. When I'm anywhere near a bookstore that causes problems. I figure I can sneak in for a just a few minutes and maybe grab a new title to read, but then I get distracted and all of a sudden I go from being twenty-five minutes early to five minutes late. I swear, bookstores are my kryptonite.

But fortunately there were none anywhere near Matt's house (or in the entire county) so I'd just driven around the block until I could arrive early but not so early I accidentally caught him in the shower.

Matt's place was a converted mobile home on the outskirts of town. It looked just like any single-story home to the uninitiated, but I happened to know its history from a few things Matt had said. His parents had brought it to the valley and placed it on a plot of land and then his father had expanded it by building on two more rooms and an extra bathroom.

It wasn't pretty—tan with dark brown trim—but it was well-maintained and on a decent-sized plot. There was even a fenced yard out back. And the view of the mountains was to die for, especially with the sun setting. I paused next to the van to take it in, reminding myself that it was these little moments in life that made the rest of it worthwhile.

Fancy lay down at my feet. I swear, her life philosophy is "why stand when you can lie down."

Jack came out the front door and gave me a funny look as he ran his fingers through his hair, expertly messing it up into that bad boy chic look that fit him so well.

I took a moment to admire his beauty, too, knowing he wouldn't mind or find it strange the way Matt probably would if I ever looked at him that way.

"Maggie May." He winked and looked me over in turn. "No overnight bag? Does that mean there's still hope for me yet?"

"Not a chance."

"Your heart beats only for Matt, huh?" He stepped a little too close and I could smell his sexy aftershave and see that devilish look in his eye. "Such a shame. We could've had fun."

I shivered a bit, but all I said was, "Doubt it. I'm a real buzzkill you know. Frigid even."

"Mmm. I could fix that." He reached out to touch my arm, but I stepped around him, Fancy scrambling to join me.

"No need. But thanks for the offer." I waved goodbye as I moved towards the front door. "Matt?" I called when I reached it.

"Come on in. I'm out back."

I led Fancy into a nice basic living room with well-kept, comfortable-looking couches. The theme of brown continued inside. There were a few framed school photos of Matt and Jack here or there but most of the items on the walls were related to NASCAR.

"You or your dad?" I asked, nodding towards them as Matt took the beer and apple pie I'd brought and put them away in the kitchen.

"My dad. Still haven't figured out what to do with it all. I'm sure someone would pay good money for a few of the pieces he had, but I haven't been motivated to try just yet."

I knew his dad had passed away recently, but we'd never actually talked about it. "How long's he been gone?"

"Six months. Heart attack." Matt crossed his arms and shrugged. "He went fast which was good and bad. He didn't suffer, but he died alone. I was still overseas."

"Were you two close?"

He shook his head. "No. My mom raised us after my parents split. But I was all he had. Well, me and Jack, but who can rely on Jack?"

He moved towards the back door, Fancy trailing behind him, following the smell and sizzle of burgers on the grill. "How do you like your burgers?"

"Medium-well?"

"Perfect. Coming right up."

I grabbed a paper towel and wiped up Fancy's drool trail while Matt carefully shooed her back inside and away from the grill. A moment later he brought back a plate with two juicy burgers and set it next to all the fixings he already had arranged on the counter.

He'd gone all out. There were buns and ketchup and mayo and mustard and lettuce and tomatoes and onions (ew) and even real cheese slices.

"Impressive. Real plates even," I said.

"Your grandpa taught me well." He reached into the cabinet by the fridge and pulled down a smaller plate. "Almost forgot." He bowed towards Fancy. "Your plate, my dear."

He set the plate on the floor near the table and Fancy settled herself down, waiting for us to hurry up and start feeding her.

As I served myself, I realized how easy it would be to get used to something like this. There are worse ways to spend a summer night than with an attractive man and good food. Of course, Fancy spoiled the moment by tearing out the back door after a squirrel. She barked so loud I wouldn't have been surprised if someone said they could hear it a mile away.

I went to the door. "Fancy. Knock it off."

Matt stepped up beside me and I suddenly found myself very aware of just how close he was. "It's alright. She'll settle in a minute." He stepped past me and onto the porch. "Come on, Fancy girl. Food."

At that most magic of words, Fancy immediately stopped barking and came back inside to join us at the table. I sat down across from him, trying very hard not to think about anything at all. I didn't need this mess. I had…

Things to do? Maybe. Sort of. Kind of.

"Cheers." Matt tapped his beer against mine and I forced myself to return his smile and toast. "Cheers."

CHAPTER 18

Matt made me hold off on telling him my news until after dinner. He said my grandpa had the right idea about priorities and enjoying meals. I secretly wondered if he was just angling for an opportunity to keep me around a little bit longer—not that I minded all that much if he was. I love my grandpa, but there are only so many nights of sitting on the couch eating dinner and watching reruns I can take.

(I say that, but left to my own devices that's exactly what I did for years when I lived in DC, with only the occasional good night out mixed in. Of course, I worked a lot longer hours back then, too, so most of my nights were work until seven, get home, eat like a zombie while watching something meaningless on the television, and then go to bed so I could wake up and do it all over again the next day. Good times!)

Over dinner Matt told me about the ridiculous call he'd had to take earlier that day. It seemed Wilhelm had been busy. He'd caught his housekeeper in his home office that morning and fired her on the spot, accusing her of attempted theft. She'd been so mortally offended that he'd even think her capable of something like that that she'd told anyone who would listen about it. And since this was the day each week when she met her extended family of five brothers and sisters and all of their kids for lunch, that turned out to be a very large number of people.

When Wilhelm found out he called the cops and demanded that they arrest her for smearing his good name. Matt had to inform him that it wasn't a police matter and suggest he call a good lawyer instead, which led to Wilhelm almost getting himself arrested when he decided to throw a punch at Matt.

"Why didn't you arrest him?" I asked, relishing the thought of that creepy man sitting behind bars for a few hours.

"Because the satisfaction of putting him in cuffs could never outweigh the headache of dealing with him for the next six months as he sued everyone in sight for the affront to his dignity."

"I don't know…I think I'd be willing to take that hit."

I told him about Wilhelm's creepy visit to the barkery and he shook his head. "Well, now that I know that about him, I'll definitely arrest him next time."

"Good. He needs to be brought down about ten notches." I took a swig of my beer and leaned back. "You still thinking about leaving?"

He paused a moment before answering. "I don't know. I like it here. A lot. I enjoy helping your grandpa out with the t-ball team. I'm starting to settle in more. But being a cop's hard. Especially when my ex-con of a brother waltzes into town. I don't want to have to arrest him. I'm not sure I can if it comes to that."

"You're good at it, though."

He shrugged my compliment off and cleared our plates. As he served up the apple pie and ice cream, I added, "Plus, who knows? Maybe you won't have to arrest Jack. Maybe he'll leave before then."

Matt laughed a mirthless laugh. "Do you believe that?"

"No. Not really."

"Me neither."

We took our bowls into the living room and sat on opposite ends of the couch. Even with the distance between us it might've been an intimate moment if Fancy hadn't decided to jump up and wedge herself into the space between us, drooling all over herself and Matt in anticipation of pie and ice cream.

"Fancy!" I pushed on her butt to make her get down, but she just glared at me.

Matt laughed. "You know, you two are a lot alike."

He grabbed her sharing plate from the kitchen and set it on the floor by the couch, adding a small bite of apple pie and ice cream. She immediately jumped off the couch and scarfed it down and then looked for more.

Matt rumpled her ears and dropped another bite of pie onto her plate. "I miss having a dog."

"They're a lot of work. Don't get me wrong. I love Fancy, but some days...It's like having a perpetual toddler, you know?"

Fancy whacked her plate with her paw and stared me down, demanding more ice cream.

When I ignored her and took another bite, she barked at me.

"Now don't you start with me, young lady. Enough is

enough. It is rude to bark inside. You either lie down and behave or you can go outside."

She harrumphed and put her head down on her paws, still staring at me the whole time like I was some cruel, vicious person who was starving her to death.

I took three more bites to make my point before finally admitting defeat and giving her my almost-empty bowl. "Happy?"

She didn't respond (of course) but she certainly seemed to be happy given the gusto with which she licked the bowl clean.

Matt shook his head as he set his bowl down next to mine. "So. Now that dinner's over, what was it you had to tell me?"

I filled him in on what Greta had said about the painting and Jack's blackmail attempt as well as Jack's visit that afternoon.

"Hm. Blackmail, huh? Interesting. Of course, that doesn't give a motive for Kristof's murder. Unless Friedrich caught him trying to steal the painting and killed him for it. But then why not just call it in to the cops as a burglary gone wrong?"

With the food all gone, Fancy took herself out back, leaving us alone.

I shook my head. "I have to say…I can't see it in him. Friedrich just didn't strike me as the type to kill someone and dump their body. He'd never get his hands dirty like that."

"Agreed. I could see him paying someone else to do it, though."

"Yeah. Fair enough. And whoever did kill Kristof was smart enough to clean up so no one noticed until the body was found. If Hans hadn't gone digging, it might never have been found."

Matt nodded as he took our bowls to the kitchen and grabbed each of us another beer. It was only Coors, but I hesitated as he held mine out to me. "Maybe I shouldn't. I still have to drive home."

"You can always sleep on the couch if you need to."

I turned scarlet even though he was just echoing what I'd said to him the other night. "Pretty sure your brother would have something to say about that given our supposed relationship."

"Mmm. Indeed."

Before he could suggest that I sleep in the same bed with him—platonically, of course—I handed the beer back to him. "Some other time, perhaps."

"Sure." Matt put the beer back in the fridge. "Why does Greta want this painting anyway?"

"I don't know. I don't even know what painting it is, just that's it's the third of a three-painting set."

He paced the kitchen, running his hands through his hair until it was messed up in a boyishly attractive way. Watching him pace like that I wondered how much of Jack's fire he had hiding under the surface.

(What? I'm ruthlessly single, not dead.)

Finally, he stopped and sat back on the couch. "I'm still not seeing it. But thanks for letting me know. It's a good lead. One we didn't have before."

"Just be careful, please. I mean, someone did kill him. I'd hate to see something happen to you."

He grinned at me. "Why, Maggie May Carver, do you actually care about me?"

I levered myself up from the couch and reached for

Fancy's leash. "Oh my. Would you look at the time? I better get going." I shook the leash and Fancy came running.

Matt stood, watching me with a grin much too much like his brother's.

I snapped Fancy's leash on. "I'll let you know if Greta clues me in to any other criminal activities. Thanks for dinner."

He beat me to the door, holding it open but not enough for me to sneak by. "You avoided my question."

I met those gorgeous blue eyes of his for a long moment. So tempting…

But no. I had…priorities.

"Yes, I did." I nudged him back so I could squeeze by. "See ya. Thanks again." I raced to my car, dragging Fancy along behind me, never once looking back.

(I know. I'm a grown woman who should be able to handle a moment like that without fleeing for the nearest exit, but what can I say? There are reasons I'm single. Many, many, many reasons.)

CHAPTER 19

As I drove to work the next morning my mind was preoccupied with the night before. It's so hard to hold back when you like someone, but it was because I liked Matt so much that I *had* to hold back. And unfortunately there was no one in my life who'd understand that one. They'd all just say, "Go for it", without realizing why that was such a horrible, horrible idea for me.

I did manage to accomplish a ton once I got there, though. I cleaned everything in the barkery from top to bottom, updated the online store, and made two batches of barkery bites. All before noon.

Good thing Jamie had taken a second day off or she would've definitely been asking me what was wrong. And, love her to death, but the last thing I wanted to tell her was that I was spending way too much time and energy thinking about Matt and how pleasant it would be to sit on his back porch drinking beers and watching the sun set every night.

I did not have time for that. For the thoughts—that were distracting enough—or for Jamie's well-intentioned but misguided intervention in my love life. I was happy for her and Mason, but that did not mean I needed to go down that path anytime soon, thank you very much.

Fortunately for me, Abe and Evan came in mid-morning to pick up a large order of barkery bites and cinnamon rolls for the Creek Inn and I was able to join them for a quick catch-up while they sampled Jamie's cheesecake.

"So…" I leaned closer. "Tell me, who did Jack Barnes go home with night last night?" (Because I just knew he'd hooked up with someone the way he came on to every single woman in sight.)

Abe frowned at me. "Jack hasn't been to the Inn."

"Are you sure?"

He chuckled. "Trust me, darling, Jack Barnes is the type of man you don't forget. If he'd made it to the Inn at any point since he returned to town I would know."

"But he told Matt that's where he was headed."

"And since when does Jack Barnes tell the truth? Especially to a cop? Must've been headed somewhere he didn't want Matt to know about."

I quickly changed the subject to the latest small town scandal—a local girl who'd had a torrid affair with some Austrian ski instructor over the winter and was now knocked up—but after they left I picked up my phone to call Matt and let him know.

And then I stopped myself. What business was it of mine if Jack hadn't gone to the Creek Inn the night before? He was a grown man and Matt wasn't his keeper. I decided to just let it go. As Jack had said so eloquently when he came over for dinner, it was none of my business.

🐾 🐾 🐾

Our lunch rush was unusually slow that day and I

realized it was because none of Luke's crew, half of whom seemed to eat at the café every day, were there. And Greta's house staff hadn't been there that morning either. She employed two sisters who carpooled into work together and always stopped by for their coffee and a cinnamon roll each morning.

When Greta and Hans didn't arrive at their usual time, I figured maybe Greta had given everyone the day off and had stayed home to enjoy the peace and quiet. But my gut told me it was something else. Unfortunately, I didn't even have Greta's number to call her.

But I did have Luke's.

Cringing at the very thought of talking to him—although it was better now that Jamie had left him behind for Mason—I called his number.

"Maggie. To what do I owe the pleasure?" he purred into the phone.

"Hey, none of your guys came into the café today. You working them to death or what?"

"No. Greta texted me and said to take the next couple of days off."

"The next couple of days? I thought you guys were going to be hard-pressed to finish all your work before the weather turns?"

"We are. Now we probably won't make it at all. But the client speaks and I listen. You should try it sometime."

"Haha. Funny. When did she text you?"

"I don't know. Middle of the night."

"She texted you in the middle of the night and told you not to show up at her house for the next couple of days?"

"Yep."

"Alright. Thanks."

That gut instinct of mine had turned into a cramped feeling of dread.

Not knowing what else to do, I called Matt.

His phone rang forever and I wondered if he was screening my calls, but he finally picked up. "Maggie. What is it?" He sounded distracted, but it was too late to hang up at that point.

"I'm worried about Greta. She didn't come into the barkery today and Luke said she texted him sometime in the middle of the night and told him not to come in for a few days. I'm pretty sure she did the same with her house staff."

"She's probably fine, Maggie."

"Yeah, probably." But I didn't believe it. "Any chance you could swing by and make sure?"

"Sorry. Can't. I'm tied up here. Some guy tried to grab a young girl walking down the highway in Creek but she ran to the police station and he drove off. We're all out trying to find him."

"Oh, yeah, okay. That's definitely gotta be your priority." I picked at a spot on the counter, not knowing what else to say but not really wanting to just let it go either.

"I can ask one of the officers in your area to swing by if you really want me to," he said, but I could hear the strain in his voice. He was tracking a child predator. What was my gut feeling that something wasn't right up against that?

"No, that's alright. Thanks for the offer, but I'm sure it's fine. Hope you find the guy."

"Me, too." The note of steel in his voice made me kind

of hope someone else found the guy instead of Matt. He was a stand-up guy and a good cop, but someone who tries to abduct a kid? That person deserves some rough treatment. And even a good man can cross the line given the right circumstances.

CHAPTER 20

I paced the store for another half hour before I finally decided to run by Greta's house myself. I packed up a slice of Jamie's heavenly lemon cheesecake and a box of cinnamon rolls so I'd have an excuse for dropping by, asked Betty if she minded sticking around for another hour and keeping an eye on Fancy, and then I headed out.

I knew it was probably nothing. And I honestly am not a fan of just dropping in on people—maybe because when I'm home alone I run around barefoot in my pajamas and am never fit to entertain company—but I had to be sure she was okay.

Her house was on the top of a nearby mountain with expansive views of the entire valley. I call it a house, but really it was a full-blown mansion. Two stories with wings of rooms off of a central entryway and a manicured lawn that stretched away in all directions. There was even a fountain in the middle of the arched driveway to complete the look.

(A fountain? Seriously? In Colorado? Someone should remind her that this was not Italy. That thing was going to be frozen solid come winter. And we weren't exactly overflowing with excess water to be wasted on something like that. Rich people, I'm telling ya.)

There were no vehicles anywhere in sight, but there was a six-car (or more) garage off to the side of the house where I assumed Greta and her husband would park. Not necessary in the summer, but good practice for the winter.

I stepped out of my van into the most serene silence. I took a moment and looked towards the valley, letting the complete awe I felt at the beauty of nature overwhelm me. It was glorious with the green valley spreading into the distance, the white puffy clouds in the sky, the mountains rising up on either side with the sunlight lighting their peaks. And all of it beneath an incredibly blue sky.

For one moment I regretted not taking the path of excessive wealth.

But then I reminded myself that this kind of opulence was what my heirs would've enjoyed after I'd slaved for decades in air-conditioned offices and spent my life on trans-continental flights and living in hotel rooms. If I'd taken that path and had a ski home like this, I would've maybe spent ten days a year in it and probably spent each one of those in my office working and ignoring the view.

Or so I told myself.

Because there was always the Greta route. Marry a geriatric billionaire and achieve instant wealth.

Unfortunately, my heart seemed to run more to handsome cops who lived in trailer homes. (Although, Matt's home did have a stunning view as well…So maybe I could have it all still.)

I didn't hear a dog barking, but then again, Hans wasn't exactly the barking type. Or maybe Greta and her husband had just decided to go away for a few days and hadn't wanted anyone around while they were gone. There were no obvious signs of danger or violence from what I could see.

I almost left right then, but there was just something in my gut that told me I had to see this through.

I slowly walked up the three front steps and rang the bell trying to decide whether the ongoing silence was peaceful or ominous.

No one answered.

I tried to look through the glass on either side of the door but it was stained glass and too thick to see through. I put my ear to the window, but couldn't hear anything either.

I paused, trying to figure out what to do next. I was tempted to step into the beautifully manicured bushes next to the entrance and peer through the large window there, but that seemed a little extreme. Instead I followed a path around to the back of the house, thinking maybe someone was out back or…something. I didn't know. I just knew that now that I'd started things, I had to finish them.

I still didn't see anyone or hear anything, just a couple birds singing in the trees behind the house, but I kept going, looking around for a sign of…whatever.

I was busy telling myself what I fool I was for thinking something was wrong when I reached the back door.

It was open. Not by much. Maybe an inch or two. Like someone had tried to pull it closed but hadn't quite managed to do so.

I approached it carefully, trying not to make a sound just in case. I looked around, waiting for someone to jump out of the bushes or run at me from the garage, but nothing happened.

I stopped in front of the door. There. Right on the edge. A dark smudge. One that looked a heckuva lot like blood.

That worried feeling in my stomach solidified into a gut punch.

I'd been right. Something was wrong. Something was very, very wrong.

🐾 🐾 🐾

Now, given the fact that I had recently been in a house with a murderer and not known it, you'd think that at that point I'd step back, call the cops, and let *them* enter the house, right? Seems logical?

And I agree that that would have been the smart choice to make.

But, as you've probably figured out by now, I am not always smart.

In my defense, my friend was missing, there was blood on the back door of her house, and every second could count. So…

I compromised.

I took a picture of the door with my phone—so they'd know what it looked like when I'd arrived—and then…

I went in.

CHAPTER 21

"Greta?" I called as I pushed the door open, almost jumping out of my skin when it banged against the far wall.

No response. Not even the scurry of a cat or a dog.

I closed my eyes for a moment. The lack of response was either a very good sign that she'd already left and was safe…

Or a very bad one.

I shivered as I made my way through the gorgeous kitchen that could've come straight off the pages of any top design magazine and into a large living room with fifteen foot ceilings and wall-to-wall bookcases that were currently empty.

(Such a waste. Think of all the books they could've had on display…)

"Greta?" I called again, but still nothing.

And then I heard it.

A whimper. A soft whine.

I ran towards the sound, not even thinking anymore that someone might be there and might hurt me. All I could think was someone was hurt and needed my help.

I froze when I reached the foyer, stopping just on the threshold of the room. It was…bad.

Bloody.

I had my phone in my hand and was dialing 9-1-1 before I'd even thought to do so.

"9-1-1. What's your emergency?"

"I'm at the VanVeldenstein residence. Send an ambulance. And cops. There's been…Please, just send the cops."

I hung up. I know you're not supposed to. But…

Hans was trying to crawl his way towards me, leaving a streak of blood in his wake, his back legs dragging behind him as he scrambled on the tile floor with his front legs. I couldn't let him do that, the poor thing.

I ran to his side. "It's okay, boy, it's okay." I stroked his head and he licked my hand, whimpering. I felt such rage in that moment. That someone would hurt a poor, innocent creature like that. And that after all that Hans would still try to reach me.

"Where's Greta, boy?" I asked.

But he just licked my hand again and stared at me with his sad brown eyes.

I reached for my phone again.

Matt answered on the second ring. "Maggie. What is it now?" He sounded even more stressed than before, but he was the only one I wanted there.

"I'm at Greta's. Please come." My voice shook with the tears I wasn't ready to shed.

"Why? What's happened?"

I finally let myself look at the rest of the room. "Friedrich. He's dead. And Greta…I don't know where she is. But there's so much blood. And Hans…Please. I need you. Help."

"I'm on my way."

After he hung up I forced myself to push aside what I was seeing and figure out what needed to happen. I took a couple pictures from where I was sitting. I'd already messed things up by running to Hans, but at least I could keep from messing things up more.

Friedrich was obviously dead. No question there. If I had to guess I'd say someone had beat him with the statue lying on the ground next to him. It wasn't…tidy.

But there were also some holes in the wall, like someone had used a gun. I suspected that's what had happened to Hans. No gun in sight, though.

I didn't know when everything had happened, but it definitely wasn't recent. The blood told me that. I stroked Hans's head and murmured to him as I waited for help to arrive. Poor guy, lying there all that time alone, waiting for help to arrive, Greta gone, Friedrich dead.

Whoever had done this had Greta's phone, too. They'd told everyone to stay away. They'd sent those texts.

It made me ill with anger to think how they'd condemned Hans to slowly bleeding out all alone in that room of horrors. I felt the knee of my jeans turn sticky and looked down to see that he'd started bleeding again and the blood was oozing along the floor, bright red.

"Stay." I ran to the kitchen and grabbed a pristine white kitchen towel—my only option—and brought it back to staunch his wound, but before I returned to his side I carefully stepped my way to the front door and opened it. (Might as well make it easy for the cops when they arrived. Whenever that was.)

Hans had tried to follow me when I left him, but whatever had happened to him had damaged his legs, so he'd only managed to drag himself about a foot farther. I knelt by his side and rested my hands on his shoulders. "Shhh. Stay. It's okay."

He panted heavily, his eyes glazed with pain.

"Shh. Shh. It's okay," I told him again even though I didn't believe it myself.

I so desperately did not want to be there, but he needed me. So that's what I focused on. I pressed the towel against his wound and prayed that help would arrive soon.

🐾 🐾 🐾

I tried not to think about anything while I waited. I'd done what I could and now I needed the cavalry to arrive so I could collapse in a corner and cry.

Friedrich's wasn't the first dead body I'd seen, obviously, but something about the level of violence and knowing it had happened inside my friend's home shook me to my core.

(That and the terrified thought that Greta could've been the one who did it. Had I really misjudged her so badly?)

I shivered as I looked around that beautiful home. It reminded me that none of us are ever truly safe. All it takes is someone deciding you should die and…

But no. It wasn't that simple. How many episodes of *I Survived* had I watched? How many times had I seen someone who'd been burned or stabbed or shot and left for dead who was still there to tell their tale? Yeah, we were all vulnerable. If someone wanted to hurt you badly enough they could. But that didn't mean they could kill you.

I had to believe that. For Hans's sake. And Greta's, too.

Hans licked my hand and I stroked his head. "It's okay, boy. We'll get you help soon."

I so wanted to cry, but I held back for his sake.

I know. He was just a dog, what would he care? But I did it anyway. I like to think he appreciated it.

When I finally heard the sirens and the sound of cars screeching to a halt outside I was so happy. Two cops barged through the door, guns drawn. One immediately turned back around and I heard him retching in the bushes. So much for thinking they'd be better equipped to handle things than I was.

The other approached, his gun shaky but pointed right at me. "Ma'am. I need you to put your hands up."

"I can't. He's bleeding. Get me a medic."

"Ma'am."

"Get me a medic!" No way was I taking the pressure off that wound to put my hands in the air. Honestly. Some people.

"Ma'am," he said more harshly than before, "I need you to put your hands up. Now."

"Get me a medic and I will. Don't you have frickin' eyes? Can't you see what I'm doing?"

A medic peeked around the doorframe, her eyes going wide with shock at what she saw.

I fixed my gaze on her, ignoring the stupid cop. "You. Come here. Please. He's been shot or something."

She focused on me. "We don't treat dogs."

"What the…?" (I may have used an inappropriate word or two at that point. Actually, I may have used an entire string of inappropriate words. I mean, seriously, you'd rather huddle in the doorway than save the one victim that can actually be saved because he's a frickin' dog?)

I glared at her. "If you hadn't noticed, that man is dead. You can't do a thing for him. But you could save this dog who was probably injured trying to defend his owner. Get over here and help him. Now!"

I don't know if it was my cussing and screaming or my impeccable logic that got through to her, but she finally made her way to my side, another medic trailing along after her, his brown eyes trying to look anywhere but at the dead man on the floor. I didn't blame him. I'm sure most of his days were spent dealing with heart attacks and altitude sickness, not brutally beaten bodies.

I stayed with Hans while they worked on getting him stabilized. I figured he was probably in enough pain to bite, so I put myself between his head and where they were working and held him in place with a firm hand to the neck.

I've gotta say, he was a champ about the whole thing. He twitched a little, but he kept calm and steady throughout.

Finally, the medics stood up. "That's all we can do for him," the woman said.

"You're not going to take him to the emergency vet?"

She shook her head. "Can't. Sorry. We shouldn't have even done what we did."

I stared at her. What the frick good was it going to do if they'd stabilized him but I couldn't get him to the vet? He'd still die, it would just take more time. Not like I could carry him to my van. Not without reopening his wound. That's if I could carry him at all.

What was wrong with these people?

CHAPTER 22

Thankfully for my arrest record, Matt arrived just then.

"Maggie?"

Seeing the fear in his eyes, I realized how awful I must look, covered in Hans's blood in the midst of that horrible scene.

"Matt. I'm so glad you're here."

"Maggie!" He ran to my side and knelt down, gripping my shoulders. "Are you okay?" He pushed my hair back from my face and looked me over for any sign of injury.

I'm not proud of it, but I burst out crying. We all have our limits and I'd finally hit mine.

There I was, feet away from a brutally beaten man I'd met just a few days before, a gravely injured dog I didn't know how to save at my feet, my friend missing, covered in blood that wasn't mine, looking into the worried eyes of the man I'd fallen in love with but couldn't be with, and I just lost it.

To Matt's credit he pulled me close and held me as I sobbed all over him, giving me the time I needed to get myself back under control.

When I finally wiped away the last tear, he pushed the hair back from my face once more. "Are you okay now?"

I nodded. "But Hans. We have to get him to the vet. And they won't take him. I don't know what to do. I can't…"

The medics were standing off to the side, looking incredibly awkward. Matt waved the man over. "Can you transport the dog?"

"No. Regulations. If we get a call and someone is hurt but we can't go to the call because we're transporting the dog…We'd get sued, man."

I snorted in disgust. It seemed to me Hans deserved more care than some random person who was probably just having a panic attack.

"What about moving the dog to the van outside? Can you do that? Please."

The man hesitated, but then nodded. "Yeah, we can do that. But if a call comes in…"

"Understood. Let's move fast so that doesn't happen."

I leaned against Matt as the medics went to grab their carry board, and he squeezed my shoulders and pulled me closer. I wondered if he was ever going to let me go again. I didn't really want him to. It felt very safe to be held there under his arm, especially in the midst of that horrible, awful scene.

🐾 🐾 🐾

We separated, reluctantly, when the medics returned so I could comfort Hans as they loaded him up and carried him to the back of my van. Thankfully all I have back there is just one giant dog bed, so it was a perfect place to put him.

I was halfway to the driver's side door before Matt stopped me. "You can't drive, Maggie."

"What are you talking about? Of course I can."

He shook his head. "I can't let you."

"Don't be ridiculous. I have to get Hans to the vet."

"And we will." He put his hands on my shoulders. "But I can't let you drive in the state you're in. Not to mention, you were a witness. You need to give a statement."

I might have made a less than appropriate comment about how useless giving a statement was compared to saving Hans's life, but Matt just squeezed my shoulders. "Trust me, please?"

I crossed my arms and frowned, but I waited as he went over to the officer who'd tried to get me to put my hands up. They had a back and forth conversation and then Matt nodded and came back to me. "Give me the keys."

I grudgingly handed them over, still not quite sure what was going to happen next.

As Matt started for the driver's side I continued to watch him, frowning. He paused before he opened the door. "Well, are you coming or what? I told Officer Nelson I'd bring you in for a statement after we got Hans taken care of. And found you a change of clothes."

"Oh. Yeah. Definitely." I ran to the passenger's side of the van and got in before he could change his mind.

🐾 🐾 🐾

The drive to the emergency vet was uneventful. I wish we could've driven faster, but we were driving my van so we couldn't flash lights and sirens or anything like that and, as you know by now, Matt has this annoying belief in obeying the speed limit.

The vet and his staff took Hans back to surgery immediately. I wanted to go with him, but they gently told me to stay out of it, and Matt steered me back to the van. "Alright, Maggie. We better get you home and cleaned up and in for that interview."

"Right. Of course." I let him nudge me into the passenger's seat and fasten the seat belt for me like I was still a little kid.

As he was walking around to the driver's side, my phone rang. It was the barkery. I stared at the display for a long moment, wondering who was calling and why. What did they want? Couldn't the world just leave me alone for a couple hours?

But it was work, so I answered. "Hello?"

"Maggie? It's Betty. Are you going to be back soon? I need to get home. I'm having my son over for dinner tonight."

"Oh, right. Yeah. Go ahead and lock up. You have a key, right?"

There was a slight pause and then she asked, "Maggie, are you okay?"

"Of course. Why do you ask?"

She spoke slowly, enunciating every word. "Because Fancy's still here. You don't want me to just leave her here alone, do you?"

I gasped. Fancy. I'd completely forgotten about her. How do you just completely forget about your…child? (Not that she was my child. I'm not delusional. But she was the closest thing I had to a child and I'd just completely forgotten about her. I felt horrible.)

"Oh gosh. Right. I'm so sorry. Of course. I…I forgot. We'll be right there."

Matt raised an eyebrow in question as I hung up the phone.

"I left Fancy at the barkery with Betty. I completely forgot. How could I do that?"

He squeezed my shoulder. "Don't beat yourself up about it, Maggie. It's been a rough couple of hours. Come on. Let's go get Fancy and get you home."

As Matt drove to the barkery, my mind went into overdrive. The back of the van was a complete mess. Even with the efforts of the medics, Hans's wound had continued to bleed, so the dog bed and blanket were covered in blood. We'd have to swap that out when we reached the barkery. And I'd have to call the vet later to see how Hans was doing. The vet had sounded pretty optimistic, but you never know. I mean, how often do pets get shot? Probably more often in the mountains than in the city, but not often enough for a vet to know how to handle something like that. Did they? And where was Greta? Was she okay? If we didn't find her soon I'd need to arrange for someone to watch Hans. Maybe my grandpa? Would he do that? They had sort of similar personalities, but I wasn't sure that was really a good thing. But maybe it was? And what had happened back there? Was Greta a victim? Or the perpetrator? And, oh my gosh, the way Friedrich had been beaten. Ugh.

"Maggie." Matt shook my arm.

I stared at him. "What?"

"We're here. Come on. Let's get Fancy."

Already? I let him lead me inside, still half-dazed and distracted.

🐾 🐾 🐾

Fancy did not know what to do with me. She cried her

little head off the minute she caught sight of me covered in all that blood. Can't say I blamed her. I was a hot mess. And, her being a dog, she might've even been able to tell who the blood came from. That would freak me out, too.

Even though Matt swapped out the dog bed in the back of the van for the one at the barkery, when I leashed her up and tried to lead her out to the van, she was having none of it.

Not even Matt could get her to budge.

"It's the blood. I have to change," I told him. But there was nothing to change into.

Jamie lived right around the corner, but as I'd learned already she was very unlikely to have anything that even came close to fitting me. Plus, I didn't feel like ruining her day off by showing up on her doorstep covered in blood. Knowing my luck (or Mason's) he'd be over there getting ready to propose and I'd ruin it all.

We rummaged around the kitchen, but there were no good options there either, just your standard washrags and hand towels.

Matt frowned at me. "I have a plan, but you're not going to like it."

"What's your plan?"

He grabbed a trash bag and some hand towels. "Come on. Let's go to the van."

I followed after him, reluctantly. "What are those for?"

He stopped next to the passenger door. "Put your clothes in the bag and then use the hand towels to cover yourself."

I laughed. "Are you serious?"

"The only other option I can see is to have a cop car take you to the station while I drive Fancy home."

I held up one of the hand towels. It was not big enough. Not at all. I mean, yeah, sure, it would cover the basics, but no more than the basics. No way I could wrap it around myself like a normal towel.

"Matt…"

"It'll cover the essentials."

"Barely."

"You could just sit there in your underwear."

"No. I don't think so."

He shrugged. "Your call. You want me to get a patrol car to pick you up?"

"Did they find that guy yet?"

He shook his head.

I looked through the barkery window to where Fancy stood watching us. I didn't want to leave her alone, even with Matt. And I certainly didn't want to ride in the back of a cop car, especially not one that should be out looking for a child molester instead of catering to my fragile ego.

"Fine. Turn around. Just because I have to do this doesn't mean you have to watch."

"Yes, ma'am."

As soon as he turned around I quickly stripped off my jeans and t-shirt and threw them in the trash bag and then settled myself into the passenger seat, one hand holding a dish towel across my chest, the other holding one across my lap. I swear, it was more humiliating than those stupid gowns you have to wear at the doctor's office.

Before I could tell him I was ready, Matt turned back around, bundled the trash bag up, and put it at my feet.

"I didn't tell you I was done."

"No. I could see that you were in the reflection from the store window." He winked at me.

"Matthew Allen Barnes! You peeked." If I hadn't been holding dish towels over the essentials I would've smacked him one.

He just grinned at me and went back to the store for Fancy.

I fumed as I waited for them to return. Although, it did tell me one thing—it seemed Matt wasn't always a rule-following, law-abiding saint. Maybe he had a bit of promise after all…

CHAPTER 23

Before he got into the van Matt took a call that had his face shadowed with worry.

"Who was that?" I asked when he finally buckled up and started the van.

"Officer Clark."

"Everything okay?"

He grimaced as he pulled onto the highway. "I can't talk to you about this, Maggie. I'm sorry."

"Was it about Greta? Have they found her? Is she okay?"

"Maggie…"

"She's my friend, Matt."

He drummed his fingers on the steering wheel, his lips pressed tight together. "Maybe you should reconsider that, Maggie."

"What do you mean?"

"Well, think about it. Her husband was bludgeoned to death last night. In the middle of the night. She's nowhere to be found. Who else is going to be there at that time of day? Not to mention her first husband was killed and dumped in a field right by your store."

"But her dog was shot. You've seen them together. Do you honestly think she could do that?"

"No, I don't. But I do think it's possible that Friedrich tried to defend himself and shot Hans instead of Greta." He glanced at me. "He had gunpowder on his hands, Maggie. He was the one who shot the gun."

I sat back in my seat, stunned. Could it be? Could Greta have bludgeoned her husband to death because he'd found out about the painting and was never going to let her have it?

"Who inherits?" I asked, not really wanting to know.

"We don't know yet. Seems he was notorious for changing his will and he'd been in just yesterday to do so."

Could she have found out and killed him because of it? Was she capable of that kind of rage?

I shook my head. "I don't see it. She's not a rage killer, Matt. I'm telling you. She's my friend."

"That's why I can't talk to you about this, Maggie. I have to see this objectively."

I sighed. "Fine. Change of subject. How's Jack?"

He shrugged one shoulder. "No idea. He didn't come home last night. I figure he made a new friend at the Inn and went home with her instead."

"But he didn't go to the Inn last night."

"What? What are you talking about?" He pulled the van to the side of the road and turned to stare at me.

"Matt, what's wrong? Why did you just react like that?"

"Because Friedrich VanVeldenstein was bludgeoned to death last night, but I figured Jack didn't have any part in it because he was at the Inn getting drunk with his buddies. Now you're telling me he wasn't?"

"Not according to Evan and Abe. They said he never came in."

He slammed his hand against the steering wheel. "Damn him. Why couldn't he have just stayed away?"

He pulled out his phone and called Jack's number, but no one answered.

I wanted to reach out and comfort him, but both of my hands were still busy holding those ridiculous towels in place. "Look. I'm sure it's fine. Maybe he met someone before he made it to the Inn. He hits on anything that walks. He could've stopped to get gas and started chatting up some girl at the pump and changed his plans. You can't go jumping to conclusions."

"Yeah. Right."

He hit the button to check his mail and his phone dinged a moment later. The silence in the car grew heavier and heavier as he thumbed open a message.

And then it shattered as he started cussing his head off.

Forgetting my modesty, I moved my hand from my lap and grabbed his arm. "Matt. What on earth is wrong?"

He glanced at me. "We have to go. Now. I'm sorry. This can't wait."

He handed me his phone and then threw the van into a U-turn and headed back the way we'd just come while I read the message he'd received:

Hey bro. In case things go south tonight, I've set this message to deliver to you tomorrow at noon. I'm meeting Wilhelm at the old hunting cabin at ten tonight. Seems that comment I made at the charity event shook him up. I don't know what he's hiding, but if I can get some cash from him to keep it hidden, why not, right?

If you get this message, something went wrong. Come find me.

"Oh no," I whispered, watching the way Matt's jaw clenched and unclenched as he nudged the van to ten over the speed limit, his eyes fixed on the road.

I wanted to tell him it would be okay, but we'd just left a murder scene. I couldn't lie to him. He wouldn't believe me if I did anyway.

He pulled off the highway onto a rutted road and gunned it. He was speeding so fast down the road I wondered if my shocks were going to survive the journey. Last thing we needed was to hit a particularly nasty hole and lose a tire or something.

"Um, Matt. I understand that you want to get there as soon as possible and check this out, but maybe we should call backup? Or you could drop me and Fancy off first and run by the station?"

"He could be dying. I have to get there. Now."

"Okay. I appreciate that. But, um…" I shrugged my shoulders. "I'm not exactly dressed for a big outing here."

He glanced my way and grimaced. "Sorry about that. You're just going to have to wait in the van."

We wound our way up the side of a mountain, large evergreens blocking out the late day sun.

"I am not going to sit in this van while you go into some remote hunting cabin looking for the body of your brother. That is not happening. I will put back on these bloody clothes before I do that."

I reached towards the bag of bloody clothes at my feet, but as soon as I opened it Fancy started whining and crying her head off.

(I'm sure I was flashing all kinds of interesting things Matt's way at that point, but he honestly did not notice.

He was laser focused on the road and getting to his brother as soon as possible.)

"Matt, seriously. Slow down. Call in backup. Handle this like the police officer you are."

"He's my brother, Maggie. You want to call it in you call it in."

"Fine." I grabbed his phone, but there was no signal. I pulled out mine. Same thing. "I can't call it in. There's no signal. Turn back around."

"No."

"Matt!"

He spared me a quick glance. "Look. I'd rather know what I'm dealing with before I involve anyone else, okay? I mean…What if…What if it isn't Jack we find in that cabin? What if he didn't come home because he's on the run?"

"Okay." I nodded. "But I'm going in there with you."

"In your underwear?"

I raised my chin. "If I have to. Maybe it'll cheer him up some, you know."

He snorted. "Probably would."

He whipped the van down an even more rutted narrow road and then pulled off in front of a small little cabin hidden against the side of the mountain. "My dad used to take us here as kids. Only thing we ever really did together," he said, never taking his eyes off the cabin as he stripped off his uniform shirt and then the t-shirt he had on underneath.

I know it was a serious situation and we were maybe about to find yet another dead body, but…Well, when a very good-looking man is shirtless and two feet away from you, it's a moment to savor.

I got a little distracted.

Matt didn't, though. While my mouth was hanging open and little bits of drool were finding their way down my chin (not really, but close), he tossed me the t-shirt, threw back on his uniform shirt, and rushed for the cabin.

I scrambled into his t-shirt—which fortunately covered about as much as that little black dress of mine had at the party—leashed up Fancy, and followed as fast as I could.

Matt had his gun out as he pushed the cabin door open and stepped inside, so I held back, waiting to see what would happen next. I figured Wilhelm wasn't going to be there, but if Jack was…

Well, I could be there for Matt the way he'd been there for me earlier in the day. But if that wasn't the case, then I needed to stay back and let him do his job.

He was back outside in a moment. "He's not here."

"Does it look like he was?" I asked.

He glanced around. "Yeah. See the tire tracks." He pointed at some tracks hidden by my van as well as another set of tracks. "Those are both recent. And it smells inside. Like bleach."

I let Fancy tug me towards a nearby juniper bush. I don't know why, but she loves to pee on the pokiest, most uncomfortable plants—rose bushes, cactus, pfitzers…

"So two men came up here last night and now they're both gone and there are signs someone cleaned up after. Where's the other vehicle? If Wilhelm did something to Jack, what did he do with Jack's truck? And if Jack did something to Wilhelm, then where's Wilhelm's Mercedes? I can't picture either one bringing along an accomplice. And Wilhelm at least doesn't strike me as the type to have a friend who'd bury a dead body for him."

Matt nodded. "You're right. If it was me, I'd dump the vehicle somewhere nearby before I left." He glanced up the road. "The road dead ends a little ways further. I'll check it out. You stay here."

I was going to listen to him, but as soon as he started walking up the road, Fancy decided she was going, too, and dragged me along after.

Matt glared at us, but instead of lecturing me or telling me to turn back he just shook his head and kept walking, his strides so fast I could barely keep up.

CHAPTER 24

He slowed as we reached the end of the road. We were pretty high up the mountain at that point and I figured the drop off ahead was a pretty big one.

Neither one of us knew what we were going to find. Was it going to be a fancy Mercedes crushed to bits? Or a pretty nice truck?

Given the message Matt had received, I was pretty sure it was going to be Jack's truck, but only one way to know.

"I can check for you," I told him as he paused about five feet from the edge.

He shook his head. "No. I can do this."

We both stepped to the edge at the same time. It was the truck, flipped over on its side a couple hundred feet down a steep drop.

Matt looked ready to scramble down to it, but I grabbed his arm.

"We need to call for help now, Matt. You can't do this alone. If he's down there and he's alive, he's injured. And you're not going to do him a darned bit of good if you get injured trying to reach him. He needs someone who can get him out of there and get him the medical attention he needs. That's not you."

He glared at me. "You go back for help. I'm staying here."

"Promise me you'll stay up here until help arrives."

He set his jaw, but he nodded.

"Okay, then. I'll drive the van back down and call 9-1-1 as soon as I have a signal. Where are we?"

He gave me the information I needed and I jogged Fancy back to the van. (Not an easy feat, by the way. Fancy is NOT a jogger. Not for more than about five feet.)

I didn't get signal until I was almost back to the highway. I'm sure the operator was not thrilled to hear from me for the second time in one day, but she hid it well. She was a consummate professional as always. I figured after this day I was going to owe her a fruit basket or something. Or a beer. Given the number of times we'd chatted at that point, maybe we were meant to become besties.

At least she took me seriously and told me an ambulance, fire truck, and police were on the way. I figured that had as much to do with Matt as anything, though. I wasn't above using his name to get the best emergency response I could for him.

If we were lucky, there'd just be a truck at the bottom of that drop and not Jack. Because I didn't know how someone could've survived that.

🐾 🐾 🐾

It took about ten minutes for the fire truck to arrive. They were the first ones there. I flashed my lights as soon as I saw them and pointed up the road. They drove past without stopping. Same with the ambulance. But the police car that came after, pulled up next to the van and waved for me to come over.

Only when I approached the car window and Officer Clark eyed me up and down with an openly astonished look did I remember that I still wasn't wearing any pants. As he opened his mouth to say something suitably obnoxious, I held up my hand to stop him. "Leave it. I don't have time for it right now. Matt's brother, Jack, went missing last night. Their hunting cabin was his last known location. He's not there, but his truck was driven off the road about a quarter mile past the cabin. I left Matt back there and came down to call it in. He needs you there. Now."

To his credit, Officer Clark nodded and took off towards the cabin immediately.

CHAPTER 25

After I'd directed everyone towards the cabin, I wasn't really sure what to do. I had Fancy to deal with and no pants on, but Matt was back there and had maybe found his brother's body and I still had his phone and…

Finally, I decided that whatever was down there it was going to take a bit of time to find it. With Matt on scene there was no one around to pull me over, so I sped home, dropped off Fancy, threw on some pants and a different shirt, gave my grandpa a quick kiss on the cheek and a promise to explain later, and then raced back.

All told, it took about thirty minutes.

I found Matt standing at the end of the road watching the fire crew working around the truck. He didn't even flinch as I approached him, his entire attention focused on whatever they'd found.

"Matt? You okay?" I touched his arm softly and he twitched like I'd brought him back from some other world.

He eyed me from head to toe. "You went home."

"Yeah, sorry. I figured there wasn't much I could do here until they got the truck sorted and it would be easier if I had some pants on, you know?"

"You took off my shirt."

"Yeah. I..." I blushed. "I figured that would cut off some questions as well."

He glanced back down the road to where I'd had to park the van. "Did you bring it back with you?"

I shook my head. I wasn't about to tell him that I'd wanted to keep it because it smelled like his cologne or aftershave or whatever it was. "I forgot. I'm sorry. I'll wash it and get it back to you later."

He turned away to watch as they flipped the truck over. "That's okay, you can keep it."

I stepped closer and rested a hand on his shoulder. "So what did they find down there? Was it Jack?"

"No. Just the truck."

I frowned. "That doesn't make sense, does it? I mean, if Wilhelm did something to your brother and then ditched the truck, why wouldn't he put your brother inside? That would at least give some chance that someone would think it was a tragic accident. Your brother drives up here at night looking for his old hunting cabin, drives a little too far, and goes over the edge."

He crossed his arms, but he didn't shrug me off. "You're right. I don't know what happened here. None of it makes sense."

"Matt, why don't you let me take you home? There's nothing you can do here right now. They'll get the truck out, but if he's not there, then he's still missing. Standing here watching isn't going to help us find him."

He hesitated a moment but then let me pull him away.

"Where is he?" he muttered as we walked back to the van, kicking at a large rock that had the misfortune to be in the middle of the road.

"Well, what do we know? We're pretty sure he came out here last night to meet Wilhelm who thought he knew something he didn't. Something worth paying to keep quiet from what that email said."

"Right."

"But it looks like it was something worth killing for instead."

"Why do you say that?"

"The ditched truck. You don't do that if you expect the person to walk away later."

We reached the van and he leaned against the passenger door, glaring in the direction of the cabin. "But maybe that wasn't the original intent. Maybe Wilhelm was going to pay Jack to keep it quiet."

"He cleaned the place up. That requires some forethought, don't you think?"

Matt rubbed his hands through his hair in frustration. "Okay. Fine. Let's assume Wilhelm arranged the meet not to pay off Jack, but to kill him. He brought the supplies to clean up after himself. He figured he'd ditch the truck and Jack and no one would be the wiser. Jack's a drifter, maybe he just took off again."

"And if he hadn't sent you that email, that's probably exactly what would've happened. Right?"

He nodded.

"But there's no body in that truck. Wilhelm cleaned something up, but he didn't ditch the body. Why?"

Matt stood up straight and looked around, suddenly tense. "Because Jack ran. Maybe Wilhelm got in a blow or a shot, but he didn't kill him. Jack's alive. Or at least he was last night."

"Good. Okay. So Wilhelm hits him or shoots him and he runs. Where does he go? Why doesn't he take the truck?"

"Can't afford to get into the truck and get it started and back it out. Can't risk having Wilhelm shoot him again." He turned and stared up the mountain. "So he flees into the forest. Wilhelm's not going to follow. He's not a hunter. He's not an outdoorsman. He was probably wearing thousand-dollar loafers and a cashmere coat."

I smiled slightly at the way his description echoed my own personal disdain for people who dress for the city when they're in the mountains. "Okay. So he runs into the woods. Where? Does he go for the road? Does he hide out? What would you do?"

Matt looked up the mountain. "We had a deer stand we used to use. It's not far from here." He raced across the road and started up a narrow path between the trees.

I glanced towards the end of the road where all the emergency vehicles were and then decided I'd better go after Matt instead. If he found Jack he was going to need me. Either to provide comfort or run for help.

I stepped onto the narrow path and pushed aside a tree branch that was hanging too low, praying that Jack was still alive. He was trouble, no doubt about it, but he was also Matt's brother.

CHAPTER 26

As I followed Matt up that narrow path that was halfway grown over with long grass and overshadowed by tree branches, I found myself very glad that I'd gone home and thrown on some jeans. I would've been cut and scratched all over if I hadn't.

We couldn't hear anything as we climbed higher. No shouts for help. No birds in the trees. Nothing. Just the sound of us crashing through the woods.

Matt didn't call out Jack's name. I don't know why. Maybe he didn't want to deal with the lack of an answer. Maybe the fear of what he was going to find was choking his throat so much he could barely speak.

He just plowed ahead, shoving his way forward with a relentlessness that left me behind. I still wasn't up to hiking at that altitude and within a couple minutes was gasping for air as I tried to keep up. But I kept going. Because whatever he found up there, he was going to need me. Even if he found nothing. That would probably be the worst. To still not know where Jack was. To wonder if he was hurt somewhere on the mountain, with no way to find him.

I wondered if the local police even had a search dog for that sort of thing. I knew they had drug dogs. There'd been a big article in the paper the week before, but I was pretty sure drug dogs weren't the same as search dogs. And what about cadaver dogs? Were those yet another type of search dog entirely?

Ugh. Hopefully it didn't come to that.

I paused next to a giant evergreen, no longer able to keep moving forward without stopping to get some air into my lungs. But then I heard Matt cry out ahead of me and I raced forward, pushing myself even though it felt like I was breathing glass instead of air.

Matt was on the ground, kneeling over a body, his shoulders shaking. I fell to the ground next to him and wrapped my arm around his shoulders.

"We found him," he whispered as he leaned into me. "We found him."

"Is he…?" I couldn't ask the question. I didn't know if I could handle the answer. Jack was incredibly pale. And still. And there was blood on his shirt. Dried blood.

I reached out to touch his neck. That's what you do, right? You check for someone's pulse. As I laid my hand against his skin I felt the slightest movement. He moaned and opened his eyes, looking up at me with a dazed expression.

"An angel?" He laughed weakly. "No. That's not where I'm headed. I'm headed to that other place. The one with the fun people."

"You're not dead, Jack. And I'm not an angel."

He closed his eyes again. "You sure?"

"Positive."

I glanced back at Matt. "You want to go for help? Or

you think we should just take him down the path ourselves?"

He stared down at Jack. "I don't want to leave him."

I grimaced. "I'm not sure I can get down and back up here again with too much speed. I'm not in the shape you are."

"Then we take him down with us."

He shook Jack awake. "That the only wound you have?"

Jack grinned at him with a dopey grin. "Hey bro. You found me. You gonna arrest me?"

"Not right now."

Jack closed his eyes again. "Good. I didn't actually blackmail him anyway. He shot me first. Can you believe that? He shot me. And I don't even know why." He laughed and then winced.

I put a hand on his cheek. "Jack, take it easy, okay. Is that the only wound? He shot you once?"

He tried to sit up to look at it, but immediately fell back. "Yeah. Just the once. I knew to run after that. Not going to stick around when someone's trying to kill me." He stared at me again. "You really do look like an angel, you know. With that light behind you."

"Good to know." I glanced at Matt. "You already gave up your shirt, but we need something to bind that wound if we're going to move him."

He tore a couple strips off the bottom of Jack's shirt. (Revealing some killer abs, but who was looking?)

We managed to bind up the wound as much as possible and then get Jack standing. He wasn't with it enough to walk down the mountain on his own, but he at least could take the majority of his own weight when we slung him between us.

It wasn't easy to get back to the road. That trail had been narrow for one to travel down, it certainly wasn't made for three people walking side-by-side, so we took it sideways most of the way, with Matt in the lead, Jack in the middle, and me at the back.

We were lucky that the ambulance hadn't left quite yet. We caught it just as it was driving past.

The medics leapt out of the vehicle as soon as they saw us and took over.

I collapsed on the ground next to the van and watched them work as Matt hovered over them, asking over and over again if Jack was going to be okay.

It took a few minutes for them to get Jack stabilized enough to head out to the hospital. He'd lost a lot of blood already and was bleeding even more after our efforts to bring him down the mountain. But at least it was summertime and there was no hypothermia or anything like that to make it worse.

As they loaded him into the ambulance, Matt came and knelt down in front of me. "Thank you, Maggie."

"Of course." I don't know why I suddenly wanted to cry, but I did.

He glanced back at the ambulance. "Are you going to be okay? If so, I'm going to go with him."

"Yeah. Yeah, I'll be fine. Go. He's your brother. He needs you."

"Okay." He gave me a quick kiss on the cheek before he left.

I sat there for a long while after the ambulance had pulled away. I knew I needed to get home and get a shower and tell my grandpa everything that had happened. But I couldn't bring myself to move. It had been one heck of a day.

At least we knew who the killer was. I wondered if Matt had bothered to tell anyone yet. I thought about waving down Officer Clark and letting him know, but I decided to just let it go. Matt would handle it.

Eventually.

Me, I needed a shower.

CHAPTER 27

I didn't get that shower. Not right away, at least. My grandpa was waiting for me in the living room as soon as I walked in the door, Lesley at his side, holding his hand. She looked perfectly groomed as always with her snow white hair pulled back into a simple but elegant little chignon.

"You look like hell," he said. I would've been insulted if it hadn't been true and if I hadn't heard the shake in his voice that meant I'd scared him with the day's events.

"I feel like it, too. I'm going to have to take some actual hikes on my days off. It turns out walking Fancy around the neighborhood is not good enough exercise."

Fancy must've sensed something was off, too, because as soon as I collapsed onto the goldenrod couch across from my grandpa she jumped up next to me and started climbing all over me and licking at my face.

"I'm fine. Stop that."

But it took her a good minute to settle down and believe me. She still didn't go far, though. She jumped off the couch and lay right at my feet, almost touching me. (Which for Fancy and me was about equivalent to settling down right in my lap.)

I pet her with my foot as my grandpa ran to the kitchen and came back with an almost-frozen can of Coke and a big slice of chocolate cake for me.

"How'd you manage this?" I asked. "You didn't know when I was going to be back."

Lesley smiled up at my grandpa as he went back to join her on the other couch. "He's been putting a new Coke into the freezer every fifteen minutes since you left and taking each one out after forty-five minutes to make sure none explode."

"Ah, Grandpa. You're the best."

Fancy nosed at my plate and I pulled it away from her. "Not for puppies. Sorry. No chocolate for you, little one."

She settled her head back on her paws with a little huff and then rolled over on her side, leaning her head against my foot.

"So." My grandpa leaned forward. "Start at the beginning and tell us everything that happened today."

I did.

🐾 🐾 🐾

"So it was Wilhelm who killed everyone?" my grandpa asked, after I'd told him everything.

"Looks like it. He definitely shot Jack if nothing else."

My grandpa shook his head. "It was smart of Jack to set up that email. Didn't know you could do something like that. That boy. If he ever got his head on straight he could really make something of himself."

"Yeah. Imagine where he could go if he turned his mind to being an investment banker or politician instead of a blackmailing thief."

"Maggie May. You be nice. Not all of us start out on the right path."

I gave him my best innocent expression. "I was being nice. He probably would do very well as a politician. He's got the charm and the looks for it. And the moral flexibility."

Lesley patted my grandpa's knee before he could launch into a debate with me over politicians and crooks and what they might have in common. She shook her head slightly. "I have to admit, I did not like Wilhelm the few times I met him, but I still don't understand why he'd want to murder Kristof, Jack, and Friedrich. And what about Greta? Where is she?"

My grandpa reached for his non-existent cigarettes and frowned when all he found was an empty shirt pocket. "Let's assume this all started with Kristof. He came to steal that painting, but stumbled on something else. Something about Wilhelm. So he tries to blackmail him, just like Jack did."

We both nodded. "Makes sense," I said.

"So Wilhelm kills him and that's the end of it. Until they find the body and Jack strolls into town talking about how he knows a secret that Friedrich needs to hear."

"But that was about Greta."

"Wilhelm doesn't know that. So once more whatever secret he was hiding is about to come out. So he tries to kill Jack."

"Okay. But what about Friedrich and Greta?"

"Maybe he's worried that Friedrich already knows the secret. After he takes care of Jack, he goes over there to find out. One thing leads to another and he bashes Friedrich's head in."

Having seen the result of that particular action, I winced at his graphic description. "And Greta?"

"She stumbles upon what's happened and he kills her and hides the body so there'll be someone else to blame."

"Why not just put it on Jack?"

"Because no one's going to connect those two. Jack skips town, no one thinks another thing about it. Just like no one worried when Kristof went missing. But there's no reason to think that Jack killed Friedrich on his way out of town. There's nothing obvious to tie the two together. Greta on the other hand…"

I sank back against the couch. "So you think she's dead already? He just took her somewhere else to make it look like she'd killed her husband and ran? Well, that sucks."

"Life sometimes does."

I pushed myself off the couch. "Alright. Well. I'm going to go take a long, long very hot shower and try to forget all about this. You two take care."

🐾 🐾 🐾

I slept in Matt's shirt that night. It comforted me to have his smell so close, especially after the miserable day I'd had.

(I know. Don't get started with me. I am not a logical human being and my actions and feelings when it comes to members of the opposite sex are not always normal and rational and sane. I could tell you all about why I am the way I am but then I'd have to kill you. Not really, but, you know. "None of ya" as Jack so eloquently told me about *his* business.)

Anyway.

It was a miserable night. Fancy had me smushed right

up against the headboard for most of the night because she was feeling insecure enough to not jump down and sleep on the floor like she normally does after half an hour. And to add to that, I couldn't get to sleep for hours because every time I closed my eyes I saw that horror scene at Greta's house.

Where was she? What had Wilhelm done with her? Hopefully she was just missing but I had to face facts and admit that she was very likely dead. And how horrible was that?

At least Matt had called me before I'd gone to bed to let me know that they'd arrested Wilhelm and that Jack was in stable condition, so I knew it was going to be taken care of eventually. Wilhelm didn't strike me as the type to hold out under any sort of intense interrogation. (Although he did strike me as the type to lawyer up and hide behind his constitutional rights, which wasn't going to help in finding Greta.)

I just wanted it all to turn out alright. And to forget what I'd seen earlier in the day.

I finally fell asleep at three in the morning out of sheer mental exhaustion. Unfortunately, my late bedtime didn't keep Fancy from wanting to be fed at five thirty.

Love that girl, but there are days…

CHAPTER 28

I was seriously dragging when I walked through the door of the barkery the next morning. I'd considered calling in sick. Jamie had just had two days in a row off, she could give me this one, but I was still making it up to her for all the time I'd taken off between my grandpa's little adventures in being a murder suspect and my own.

Plus, I was already up thanks to Fancy and really didn't want to sit around the house with nothing to do while I worried about what Wilhelm might have done to Greta. I knew I wouldn't be able to get into my latest book—it was by one of my favorite authors, but just didn't grab me enough to distract me from murder and mayhem.

If I'd stayed home all I would've done is paced on the front porch and watched the police station for any sign that Wilhelm had confessed what he'd done with Greta.

So I went to work.

And…

Jamie practically tackled me the minute I walked through the door. She was squealing and jumping up and down. And then she gave me a giant hug before squealing again.

I stared at her like she'd gone crazy. She's always been a positive person, but this was an unheard of level of insane happiness that my couple hours of sleep had not prepared me to handle.

"What on earth is wrong with you?" I asked.

She held her left hand up to show me the very large but very classy diamond ring on her finger. I'm sure it was a princess cut or whatever fancy shape fancy people choose when they get engaged. And I'd bet there were a few carats involved as well, if not more.

My first reaction was to turn around, leave, and go bury my head in my arms somewhere where no one could find me. I was happy for her, don't get me wrong. But on top of murder and near death experiences, I did not need my world upended at whatever unholy hour of the morning it was.

But she was my friend. My best friend. And I'd never seen her glowing this way. And, as rushed engagements go, I had to admit that Mason Maxwell was a darned fine catch. As far as I knew, he'd done nothing that warranted prison time, unlike her last couple of love interests. He'd also shown himself to be a pretty stand-up guy, both as a lawyer and a man.

So, I squealed right back at her. "Oh my gosh! Mason proposed?!" I even jumped around with her a bit. I went all in.

Because, really, how often does one of your best friends get engaged to a man who makes her that happy? Sure, it was probably going to be a catastrophe at some point, but for the time being it was amazing and I needed a little bit of amazing given everything else that was going on.

Her smile was so big and bright it was almost blinding. I couldn't help but match it. "Congratulations!" I hugged her close for a long moment.

She had to pull away to help a couple of customers so I grabbed myself a Coke and a cinnamon roll with an extra serving of frosting. I was going to need all the unhealthy fuel I could get to make it through the day.

As soon as the store was empty, she joined me. "I know. You think it's too soon. You think we don't know each other well enough and that we should wait and…" She burst out laughing. "But I don't want to, Maggie. I love him so much. He's so perfect for me. You don't even know…"

I kept my mouth shut and took a really big bite of cinnamon roll as she rambled on.

"Yes. He's uptight. And he's older. And he doesn't own a single pair of jeans or tennies and he's probably never said a cuss word in his life, but…"

She grabbed my hands and squeezed them, laughing once again. "Oh, I love him so much. And he loves me."

"And that's what counts. I'm happy for you Jamie, because you're happy. And if you tell me he's the man for you, then he's the man for you."

She frowned at me. "But I want you to like him, Maggie. I'm only going to be happy if my friends like my husband." She squealed. "Oh my god, my husband. I'm going to get married!"

I laughed. I couldn't help but feel her joy.

"So? Do you approve? Do you like him?"

I nodded. "Yes. Any man who can bring this much joy to my friend's life is a man I approve of. And, added bonus, I don't even feel the need to threaten his life if he ever causes you pain, because I don't think he will. See? Perfect."

She settled back in her chair, staring off into space with a dopey grin on her face. I gotta tell ya, love is scary the way it can completely demolish a person's rationality. To shake off that thought, I asked, "So, when's the wedding?"

"I don't even know. I don't even care. I'd marry him tomorrow if he wanted me to."

"Tomorrow? Wow." I shuddered at the thought of being swept off my feet that completely, but I hid it from Jamie. I was happy for her. I really was.

She shook herself off. "Enough about me. How was the store yesterday?" she asked. "Anything exciting happen?"

"Um. You know. Things were pretty slow here."

I could've told her about finding Friedrich's body and about Hans getting hurt and Greta being missing and finding Jack and riding around in my van with Matt in only my underwear and a couple hand towels, but I didn't. Let her have her moment. She'd hear about all of it soon enough.

CHAPTER 29

I'd forgotten what life in a small town is like. Within half an hour the lookie loos and gossips started trailing into the barkery to ask about what I'd found at Greta's and about Jack and all the rest of it.

Fortunately for me, the prospect of a fancy schmancy wedding was even more interesting to most of them than what I'd seen at Greta's the day before. So before anyone could really dig in and start asking questions, I just said, "Hey, did you hear? Jamie and Mason Maxwell are engaged. Jamie, show them your ring."

That led to a good five minutes of oohs and aahs and where are you going to have it and where will you go for the honeymoon and do you think you'll have kids? Oh, of course you'll have kids. But better get started right away since you waited so long. How many do you think you'll have?

And then the looks turned to me. But before anyone could start with, "Well, I guess you're the only over the hill old maid left, Maggie, we should really do something about that," I fled. I spent the rest of the morning in the back making more barkery bites than I could probably use in the next six weeks.

None of their business if I was going to be some washed up, dried out old prune with a lonely little Christmas tree that was only two feet high and no presents under it and nowhere to go each holiday because I'd neglected to pop out a family of my own.

(And, trust me, that was not what I had planned if that's how things turned out. They could have their white Christmas with their multiple generations of family gathered around the tree. I'd be on a beach in Barbados somewhere sipping tropical booze and having some young cabana boy give me a foot massage while another fed me grapes. Trust me, if it came to that, I'd be far less stressed on my holiday than they'd be on theirs. But I digress.)

Suffice it to say. I kept to myself for most of the morning.

🐾 🐾 🐾

The vet called around noon and said Hans was ready to pick up, but that he'd need to be kept in his crate as much as possible and only leash walked for the next six weeks or so. The bullet had done some damage near his spine, but they'd managed to remove it without losing either leg, so it was as good an outcome as they could expect.

Since Wilhelm was a murderer and Greta's husband was dead and she was still missing and she didn't really have anyone else to step in, I knew I'd have to take him on until something more permanent could be arranged. (And, honestly, if I could learn a little German and the worst happened and Greta was never found or found dead, I'd probably keep him, because at least he knew me. I hadn't planned on taking on another dog anytime soon, but that's life.)

First, though, I called Matt to see what he knew about Greta.

"Hey Maggie. How are you?" There was a casual tenderness to his voice that hadn't been there before.

I liked it, but at the same time…I did not need that. Only thing keeping me from making a horrible mistake was his unwillingness to push the issue.

I shook it off. "I'm good. You guys break Wilhelm yet? Did he confess to the murders? How's Jack? Have you found Greta?"

"I don't know about Wilhelm or Greta. Sorry."

"You don't? Why not? Are you still with Jack?"

"Uh, no. Jack's just sleeping so no point in my hanging around. They're planning on keeping him under for a few days given all the trauma and blood loss."

"So why aren't you busy interrogating Wilhelm? Or looking for Greta? Or…What are you doing?"

I could hear him grimace through the phone. "I'm on traffic duty."

"What? Why?"

"The Chief wasn't too pleased with how I handled things yesterday. Said it wasn't proper behavior for an officer."

"But Jack's your brother. What else did he expect you to do?" I had half a mind to drive to the police station and give that man a lecture on how to treat his officers.

"Oh, yeah. Well, that was a problem, too. But no. It was…He, um, he didn't think I kept the proper distance with you."

"The proper distance? What does that mean?"

"I drove away from the scene in your van, Maggie."

"Because I wasn't in any shape to drive. And Hans needed to get to the vet."

"There was a dead man whose murder needed to be investigated. *That* was my job."

"Oh that's…" (I said a few words I won't repeat here.)

"Still. Plus, after all of that, I didn't even manage to get a witness statement from you. And don't forget that Officer Clark saw you standing there in my t-shirt and nothing else. I had a lot of explaining to do about that."

"Figures he'd rat you out."

"Maggie…Be nice. He didn't. He just teased me about it this morning and the Chief happened to overhear."

I grabbed another Coke from the fridge and took a long sip. "So, what now? You're off the case? You can't even ask what's going on? Who's handling it?"

"Yes. I'm off the case. I'm on traffic duty for the rest of the week. Ben's handling the interview of Wilhelm, but because Wilhelm is who he is they're having to approach it with a certain amount of delicacy."

I snorted. "Delicacy. Please. Someone needs to take that man out to the woodshed. Greta's still missing, Matt. What if she's alive and he decides to kill her?"

Matt didn't answer.

"Matt?"

"You have to know she probably isn't, Maggie. Or if she is, she was in on it."

"Don't say that."

"It's the truth. You and I both know it."

I glared at the wall as I took another sip of my Coke.

"You didn't have to say it, though. Look, I'm going to pick up Hans and take him to my grandpa's. You, um, you want to come over for dinner tonight?"

"I'd love to. But I better go visit Jack. Even if he won't be awake."

"Okay. Don't give out too many speeding tickets. Be nice."

He chuckled. "Only to you, Maggie, if you push your luck. So keep it down when you drive by. Not even one over."

"Yes, sir, officer, sir."

I hung up.

I figured I could probably call the police station to see if they'd found Greta, but no one there was going to talk to me. Plus, even if they had found her, she wasn't likely to be in a position to take care of Hans right now.

Might as well just pick him up and take him home and worry about the rest of it later.

Problem was, I didn't have a crate for him. I'd tried to crate-train Fancy when she was a puppy, but that had not worked out well.

She was fine sitting in the crate when the door was open, but close that door and she immediately started crying and begging to be let out. As someone who also isn't exactly fond of being caged in, I hadn't fought too hard to make her adjust. Eventually I'd just donated the thing to a local shelter rather than continue to let it take up a third of my living room.

(Dog crates for large dogs are *big*. That thing was supposed to be portable but pbbt. It weighed about thirty pounds and was a good four feet by five feet even when it was collapsed.)

So no crate to use for Hans. And there aren't exactly pet stores in the valley where you can just swing by and buy something like that either. Which left me with a bit of a dilemma.

Because I did know where to find one. I'd seen it at Greta's. That would also give me a chance to pick up whatever food Hans liked as well.

Problem was, no one was there and it was probably still a crime scene. So the only way to get the crate was likely going to be breaking in somehow.

I debated calling Matt back and asking if he could meet me there and escort me inside, but decided that was just silly and would also get him in even more trouble than he already was.

I figured I could just swing by and check things out. Hopefully there'd be an unlocked door or window or a hidden key and I could just sneak in, grab the crate and food, and be out of there in five minutes or less.

At least there weren't any nosy neighbors to call the cops on me this time…

CHAPTER 30

My stomach clenched as I pulled up outside the house. It was still as beautiful as it had been the day before, but now that I knew what had happened inside those doors, there was a sinister edge to all of it. Every little shadow, every bird call, made my skin shiver.

I parked in back, hoping that the kitchen door was still unlocked. I figured that also gave me a little bit of protection should someone drive up while I was there. Maybe they'd come and go and never even see me. I wasn't doing anything wrong per se, but it was best to not have to explain myself at all.

The kitchen door was locked. So was the sliding door on the back porch. And all of the windows. I lifted some rocks and ran my fingers along the top of the doorframe of the back door, but no hide-a-key. (I wasn't terribly surprised, I don't use one either. Talk about an easy way to give a complete stranger access to your house.)

I debated breaking one of the windows in the back, but that seemed a little extreme. Finally, I mustered the courage to try the front door. I really, really hadn't wanted to go inside that way. I was sure that it was still a bloody mess inside and I didn't need to see that again. But if it came down to vandalizing my friend's house or just walking in the front door, walking in the front door seemed the better option.

So I did it. I walked around the house, tried the front door, and it opened right on up. I closed my eyes as I stepped inside, but I realized that wasn't going to do me much good. I needed to be able to see the mess to avoid it. I closed the door and leaned against it, forcing myself to open my eyes and look.

It wasn't as bad as before. No injured dog. No dead man. You could still see the signs that violence had occurred there, but it was muted somehow by all the little bits and pieces the police and medics had left behind.

I was still leaning against the door when I heard a car pull up in front of the house and a door slam.

I froze, not sure what to do. If it was a cop, I was in trouble, because no matter how altruistic my motives might be I was trespassing. But maybe it was Greta. Maybe they'd found her and brought her home.

I stepped into the formal dining room and peeked out the curtain just in time to see Friedrich's mistress, Lucia, walk up the steps. Her long black hair was pulled back into a loose bun and she was wearing some hideously tacky Gucci sweatshirt with a leopard on it. I swear, the things people pay money for.

She barged through the door before I could think what to do. I might've been able to just stand there and be really quiet and have her walk right by, but my phone dinged with a text message.

(I hate text messages. They're always arriving at the most inconvenient times.)

And, of course, because I'm programmed to do so, I immediately looked at my phone to see who had texted me. It was just a stupid notice from my cellphone carrier that they'd processed my payment. Waste of time.

When I looked back up, Lucia was facing me. And she had a gun pointed right at my chest.

"Ah, Lucia, isn't it? You're, um, Friedrich's friend, right? We met at the ball. Remember?"

I kept looking back and forth between her face and the gun, not sure which one was more important to pay attention to. Finally, I settled for her face, figuring if she fired the gun it was too late for me to do anything about it, but if her face twisted up in some weird way that meant she was about to fire it, that I could maybe react to it in time.

"What are you doing here?" she demanded.

"I came to get Hans's crate. You know, Greta's dog? He's, um, done at the vet, but they want him to stay in a crate most of the time for the next few weeks. And I don't have one at home, even though I do have a big dog. I have a Newfie. Um. So I figured I'd come here and I'd pick up the crate I saw off the kitchen last time I was here."

I glanced at the gun again. She hadn't lowered it an inch. "And you?" I asked.

I mean, technically, she was trespassing too, wasn't she? She might have walked in the door like she owned the place, but it was Greta's house, not hers. She probably had some fancy apartment somewhere nearby thanks to Friedrich. But she certainly didn't have a right to barge into my friend's home the way she had.

"I needed to get something."

"You seemed awfully sure no one would be here."

She pointed the gun at my face. "What do you mean by that?"

"I just…I mean, no one knows what happened to Greta. But here you are, just walking into her house like you own it. Why is that?"

(I know. I don't know when to keep my mouth shut. It's a curse.)

"What business is it of yours, you…" (She used some Spanish words there that I'm pretty sure aren't suitable for mixed company. It's been a few years since I was fluent in Spanish, but the cuss words are the last to go. Don't ask me for directions, but if you want to know how to insult someone, I've got you covered. And what she called me was not very nice.)

I narrowed my eyes, really studying her this time. At the party I'd just glossed over her as some cheap bimbo with all her assets on display. But now I really took a moment to assess who I was dealing with.

I didn't like what I saw. She was no soft little thing who depended on men to support her; someone who'd cry if she broke a nail. No. This woman was…gritty. She stood like she almost wanted to put the gun aside and just scratch my eyes out. And she held that gun with far too much comfort. Not to mention how her lip curled towards a sneer, something a well-bred woman would never do.

I glanced again at the foyer. That had been one violent attack. Wilhelm, the smarmy little worm that he was, didn't have it in him to bludgeon a man to death.

But Lucia…

She definitely did.

"Why'd you kill him?" I asked. "And where's Greta?"

I could see her consider shooting me and then deciding against it. She might be violent, but she was also cunning. She knew as well as I did that to shoot me there in that house would raise too many suspicions.

She lowered her arm, but kept the gun in her hand. "He lied to me. He told me he would leave her and marry me."

"That's what she thought, too."

"Well, he changed his mind, the…" (She used another colorful Spanish term to describe him and followed that with an improbable suggestion for what he could do with himself.)

"So you killed him? Why not just find another mark?"

"He didn't even have the guts to end things with me. He sent his man to tell me I had a week to get out or they'd throw me out."

"So you came here to confront him?"

"Yes."

I glanced around the foyer. "He met you at the door?"

"Yes."

"And you started shouting at him. He shouted back?"

"No. He was cold. Like I was nothing. He told me I was just gutter trash. He laughed at the idea that he would ever marry a cheap whore like me."

"So you grabbed the statue and hit him."

"Yes."

"How did Hans get hurt?"

"Hans?"

"The dog. That was shot?" I glared at her and she raised the gun slightly until I toned it down a bit.

"Ah, yes. The dog." She flicked her hand, dismissing

him, and for one split second I felt the same kind of blinding range I'm sure Lucia had felt when Friedrich dismissed her. "Friedrich had a gun. He tried to shoot me. But I hit him again before he could hurt me. The noise brought Greta and her mutt. She ordered it to attack me. I grabbed the gun and shot it."

I swallowed hard, not wanting to ask my next question but knowing I had to. "And Greta? What did you do with her?"

"I took her with me."

"Is she alive? Why did you take her?"

"So they'd have a suspect, of course. If I'd killed them both here, they'd be looking for someone else. But by making her leave with me, they see that her husband was killed in the middle of the night and that her dog was shot and they see that she was the killer."

"Where did you take her?"

"The same place I'm going to take you. Somewhere they'll never find your body." She raised the gun again. "Now. We don't have much time. Over here. Down this hall."

She directed me through the house to Friedrich's private office and then made me open a safe hidden behind a painting. There were stacks of hundred-dollar bills inside, each one banded with a mustard-colored strip that said it was worth ten-thousand dollars. She had me throw the money into a bag. All told it had to be about half a million dollars.

She laughed as she had me close the safe once more. "He thought I didn't know the code. That fool. Only reason I hadn't taken the money before was because of how much more I would've had if he'd married me."

"Well, you're going to be a very wealthy woman. Congratulations."

I thought about throwing the bag in her face and running for it, but I didn't have much faith I was going to get far. Then again, if my other option was letting her drive me to a remote location and kill me…The least I could do is try to escape.

I was just about to do it, when she said, "Where are you parked? You will drive," and a new plan occurred to me. It was a slim hope. But a better one than throwing a bag of money in the face of someone with a gun and hoping I could get away in time.

CHAPTER 31

Now, I've watched enough true crime shows to know it never goes well if you get in a car with a person with a gun and drive to a remote location. Chances are, you're not making it home from that. At least, not without some added lead in your brain.

But…

I had a plan to get out of this. A really bad one, but a plan nonetheless. And that really bad plan required actually letting this crazy woman force me to drive my van out of town.

So I didn't fight her when she had me get into the driver's seat of my van and crawled into the back. (She had a few more choice Spanish cusswords for the fact that there are no seats back there, which made me smile despite the circumstances.)

The next five minutes were some of the scariest of my life as I slowly wound my way down the mountainside towards Bakerstown. My plan depended on my making it to the highway, but if wherever she'd stashed Greta was somewhere off that winding mountain road I was never going to have a chance to implement it.

I could barely breathe and my palms were all sweaty as I waited for her to gesture me to turn down some narrow rutted road or off into the driveway of another remotely-located mansion that was probably empty at that time of year.

"Is Greta still alive?" I asked her, wiping my right palm on my pants for the third time.

"Why do you care?"

"Because she's my friend."

I glanced in the rearview mirror and saw the sly calculation in her eyes. She knew if she told me Greta was dead I'd have no reason to cooperate with her. The fact that she wouldn't answer at all made my skin go cold.

I shivered as I finally reached the highway.

"Go left," she told me, pointing that gun into my back.

But I couldn't go left. That was the wrong direction for my plan. So I turned right.

"What are you doing?" she demanded. "I will shoot you."

"Well, sure, you could. But think about it. You shoot me right now, in the middle of town, you're not getting away with it."

She hissed at me, but I didn't care. I had a plan. And I needed to turn right to make it work.

"Plus," I added. "If I take a left and head towards Denver, anyone who knows me and sees me headed in that direction is going to know something is up. This way I'm just headed home."

She growled something nasty at me in Spanish, but she sat back again and let me continue onward.

I tried not to show my relief. I was hanging by a thread as is, no reason to let her know she'd played into my plan. As we left town and the speed limit bumped up from twenty-five to forty-five, I slowly accelerated until I was going a comfortable fifty-two. (Or thereabouts. Like I'd told Matt, I didn't have a digital display.)

A couple minutes outside of town she gestured towards a small dirt side road that led into a copse of trees about a hundred yards off the road. "Turn here."

I ignored her.

"I told you to turn," she screamed, pressing the gun right against the back of my head.

"Sorry. This thing's an old boat. It doesn't maneuver easy."

I closed my eyes for a brief moment, praying to anyone who would listen to please let my plan work. I was so close. So, so close.

She hissed right in my ear, her spittle hitting my face. "The next time I tell you to turn, you turn or I shoot you."

(I wanted to wipe my face, but I didn't because if my plan failed at least she'd have left behind a bit of DNA for the cops to track her down. Not that I put the odds of that working at more than one in a million.)

I glanced back at her. "You're not even wearing a seat belt. Shoot me, you'll probably die, too."

She smacked me on the shoulder with the butt of the gun as she unleashed a string of creative Spanish cusswords that not only accused me of a profession I've never engaged in, but also suggested some very creative ways to perform said profession.

I clung to the steering wheel with all my might, scanning the road ahead of me for any sign of help I could find.

Just when I thought I'd made a very serious mistake, there it was. A police car, nestled into place on the side of the road.

She saw it, too.

"Slow down," she hissed.

I eased up on the accelerator, but made sure to stay two over.

Now it was all in fate's hands. If the officer in the police car was Matt and if he kept his word and pulled me over, then I'd be saved. But if it wasn't him. Or if he decided to let me go because of his new-found tenderness towards me, then that was it. Game over. My body would be found down some remote mountain road someday.

I didn't dare look. Lucia had crouched down and was pointing that gun right at my head. I flicked a glance at the odometer to make sure I was still over the speed limit and held my breath as we cruised past him.

I hadn't even cleared his car before he flipped on his lights. He whipped out behind us, sirens blaring, and I finally allowed myself a moment of hope.

"Don't stop," Lucia demanded, shoving that gun back against my neck once more.

"You want me to run from the cops now? How do you think that ends? You think they'll just let us go because we decided we didn't want to be bothered with a ticket today?" I pulled the van onto the shoulder. "Sit back out of sight, would you? Unless you want to get in a shootout with the cops?"

She glared at me, but moved to the back corner of the van where she was mostly hidden from view.

Now came the moment of truth. I had a crazy woman with a gun in my van, Matt getting out of his car to give me a ticket, and I had to somehow let him know what was going on without getting myself shot in the process.

Or him shot.

Yikes. That was the last thing I wanted.

I took a deep breath. Now or never.

CHAPTER 32

I decided to run for it before Matt reached my door.

Lucia wasn't some law enforcement professional with lightning instincts. She was just a street thug with a gun. And she was busy watching Matt approach the van. This was my one and only chance to get away.

I flung my door open, rolled to the ground, and shouted, "She has a gun."

Matt stared at me open-mouthed for what felt like forever, his hand going to his gun out of sheer instinct, but still standing there, a giant target if she decided to shoot.

"Get down," I shouted as I scrambled towards him, staying crouched below the line of the windows.

He finally caught up to the fact that this wasn't going to be some flirty little traffic stop and ducked behind the rear bumper of the van.

Just in time, too, as she shot out the back side window. If he'd hesitated ten seconds longer, she would've had him. He grabbed my arm and yanked me back towards the patrol car, shielding me with his body.

I tensed, waiting for the sound of another shot to echo through the air. If he got shot because I'd put him in danger, I'd never forgive myself.

But we made it safe.

Only because that wasn't her goal. The van spun out onto the highway, leaving a long black tire mark behind. I should've taken the darned keys with me, but I hadn't been thinking that clearly.

Matt fired one shot, but missed. (I was kind of glad, honestly. It was going to be a pain enough to replace that back side window. Those things are not cheap. I didn't even want to think about what I'd have to do if he shot out a tire or something.)

"Maggie, what the hell just happened? Who was that?"

I gave him the ten second version of what was going on, glossing over the fact that Lucia had caught me breaking and entering at Greta's house. (Didn't actually fool him for one minute. He knew darned well that even if I hadn't entered the house yet according to my story, I'd been up there fully intending to do so.)

"And you're not hurt?" he asked.

"No, I'm fine."

"Good. Stay here." He moved me out of the way, got back in his car, and sped off after her.

🐾 🐾 🐾

Part of me kind of wished he'd taken me along for the pursuit. It would've been fun to be in a police car going a hundred miles an hour, chasing down some murder suspect.

But the more rational part of me was just glad to be out of it. And hoping that I'd get my van back in one piece. It might be old and ugly, but Fancy loved it.

I saw three more police cars speed by while I was standing there trying to figure out what to do next. Lucia had taken my cellphone so I couldn't call for a ride, which meant I could either hitch a ride back into town, walk there myself, or hope that Matt remembered that he'd left me on the side of the road once it was all over.

I wasn't willing to bet on Matt's memory, so I crossed the road and started walking back the way I'd come. Fortunately, Darryl, one of the café regulars who leads hunting trips during deer hunting season and generally hangs around talking to people the rest of the year, drove by not long after and offered me a ride to the barkery.

🐾 🐾 🐾

"You coming in?" I asked as he pulled up outside. "You just saved me a hot, dusty walk to town. I figure you earned a cinnamon roll or a sandwich or a coffee or whatever you want."

"Nah. Rain check."

"Done." As I walked inside he pulled out, his truck making a banging sound loud enough to wake the dead.

Jamie frowned at me. "Why'd Joe just drop you off? What happened to your van? Are you okay? Come on. Sit down."

She set me up with an ice cold Coke and a chocolate croissant (something new she'd been working on that was absolutely heavenly).

"Now spill. What happened to your van?"

"Wait. First we need to make a couple calls." I called the vet and told him I'd be a bit longer picking up Hans. He was absolutely fine with it, thankfully. Then I called Matt and left him a message so he'd know I was at the barkery. I also asked him to retrieve my phone.

(I know. He was probably in the midst of a high-speed chase right about then, but I figured it was better to call his cellphone than to call the police station and let it get around that I'd been involved in yet another police matter. Not that it wasn't going to be obvious since she was in my van. But, well, you know.)

Jamie stared me down from across the table. "Alright, missy. I've heard enough today to know that a lot happened while I was off yesterday. And that you didn't bother to tell me about it. Why not?"

"I didn't want to ruin your good news."

"Maggie. You're my friend. If something serious happens to you, I want to know about it."

"Okay. Fine. So I guess I'll start with finding Friedrich's body."

"What?"

"I thought you said you'd heard some of what happened yesterday."

"Yeah, obviously not as much as I thought I had."

I spent the next half hour filling her in. When I was finally done she sat back and stared at me. "It was only twenty-four hours, Maggie. How do you do that?"

I shrugged. "A special skill, I guess."

One I'd gladly exchange for being good at botany or flower arranging or something a little more peaceful.

🐾 🐾 🐾

Matt arrived shortly after that and I jumped up. "You got her? You got Lucia?"

He nodded. "We got her. Good thing about that van of yours. It doesn't really do more than seventy, does it?"

"No. You get it to seventy-five and the whole steering wheel starts to shake like it's gonna come apart." I grabbed his arm. "Did you find Greta? Is she…" I searched his eyes for signs of the worst.

"Not yet. But we will."

"Then why are you here? Why aren't you out there looking for her? Did you check Lucia's car? Her GPS?"

"Officer Clark is taking care of it."

"I don't want him to find her. I want you to."

Matt smiled. "I'm glad you have such faith in me, Maggie, but it seems I have a few witness statements I need to collect. Starting with yesterday at Greta's house."

I muttered something not very polite as I threw myself into a chair. "Fine. Let's get this out of the way so you can go do what actually matters."

Jamie squeezed my shoulder. "Be nice, Maggie. Here." She handed me another Coke and Matt a coffee. "Have you eaten lunch today? Either one of you?"

Matt grinned at her. "I'd love a panini and soup, if you don't mind."

I just shook my head. "How can you two be talking about lunch when Greta is out there, who knows where, maybe still alive?"

Jamie wisely left Matt to answer. He leaned across the table and held my gaze. "Maggie. You can't do everything. Officer Clark will find her, wherever she is. And he'll let me know as soon as he does. Now, please, be cooperative?"

I rolled my eyes, but I answered all of his questions. If helping him do his silly paperwork helped put Lucia away, I'd do all the paperwork in the world. But someone somewhere better be working on finding Greta.

CHAPTER 33

We were just finishing up with my last witness statement when Matt's phone rang. I gripped his arm without even thinking about what I was doing. "Who is it?"

He pried my fingers loose with a gentle smile. "Officer Clark. But I can't tell you what he has to say if you don't let me answer."

I leaned in as he answered, trying to overhear the conversation. Matt stood up and walked away, mostly listening. To give myself something to do other than yank the phone out of his hand and ask if they'd found Greta, I went over to see Fancy.

She was snoring away in her cubby, making little snuffling noises as her feet jerked in a puppy dream. I almost woke her, but she doesn't do well when she's startled out of a deep sleep, so I just stared down at her and smiled, wondering once more at how lucky I was to have her in my life and thinking how much she'd changed everything.

Before her I'd been a happy little workaholic. But after? As soon as I realized this wide-eyed little puppy was looking to me to protect her, I'd had to change things. No more long hours. No more weeks on end of travel. She was too precious to suffer through that.

One little puppy had flipped my life end over end.

I glanced across the room to where Matt had just hung up the phone. If one puppy had changed my life that much, what would being with him do?

I squashed the thought.

"So?" I asked. "Did they find her? Can I see her?"

He didn't answer, just walked over to me.

"Matt. Please…"

He nodded. "They found her."

"And? You're not doing me any favors here. Just tell me what they found."

"She's alive."

My knees almost gave out. I leaned against the edge of Fancy's cubby. "Oh, thank you."

He rested his hands on my shoulders. "But."

"But?"

"She's in pretty rough shape. It's…gonna be touch and go for a while."

"Why? What did that vile woman do to her?"

"Greta tried to escape. To get back to Hans. She knew he needed help."

"What did she do to her?" I clenched my fists, ready to go track that woman down and do her serious harm for hurting my friend.

"Shot her. Twice. At least one of the wounds is infected."

I moved towards the door without even realizing it, but Matt grabbed and pulled me close. "Remember, Maggie. The most important thing is that she's still alive. Greta's a force. She'll make it through this. You know she will."

"I'd like to see her."

"Not today. Today we need to go get that kennel for Hans and get him settled in at your place and then get Fancy home. There'll be time to see Greta later. I promise."

"Okay, fine."

I wanted to argue, but I knew he was right.

CHAPTER 34

A week later I stopped by the hospital with a cinnamon roll and coffee for Greta. She was finally doing well enough to receive visitors. According to Matt she wasn't the least bit coherent the first couple of days and she'd let slip a few pieces of information that would've led to a criminal investigation or two if the cops had been so inclined.

Fortunately, they weren't. What happened in Germany could stay in Germany as far as they were concerned.

As I approached her door I saw a man in a very expensive suit walk out. He gave me a small nod as we passed in the hall.

"Who was that that just left?" I asked as I set the cinnamon roll and coffee on her tray table.

"Estate lawyer. He came to tell me the terms of Friedrich's will."

"Oh. Right. I thought you guys had a pre-nup?"

She patted my hand. "Ah, Maggie. You are so sweet sometimes."

(I'm pretty sure that was code for naively stupid, but I let her have it.)

She carefully sat up, wincing with the effort. Lucia had shot her once in the shoulder and once in the lower back. Fortunately, neither shot had done long-term damage, but they definitely caused some short-term pain.

"Friedrich left me almost everything in his will."

"Including the painting?" I asked as I helped her slice the cinnamon roll into bite-sized pieces.

She chuckled. "No."

"No?"

"He amended the will right before he died." She handed me a packet of papers sitting next to her bed. "Read the first page."

I skimmed the text that covered all the legal basics. When I reached the part about what he'd left her, I almost choked.

"Six hundred and twenty-five million. Not bad." Especially for a man she'd married for a painting. I figured maybe I should reconsider my extreme stance against random marriages.

But it was the next paragraph that was the real brow-raiser. I glanced at her. "I assume this is referring to the painting you wanted?"

She nodded.

"Wow. He sure knew how to twist a knife, didn't he?"

He'd left her everything. An estate valued at approximately six hundred and twenty-five million. But he had very explicitly not left her the painting. He'd bequeathed it to a museum in Germany on the condition that while Greta was alive it never be leant to any private collection and never be allowed to leave the museum premises.

"At least you can go see it if you want, right?"

She shook her head. "No. I have not been back to Germany since my second husband died. I am not welcome there."

I handed her back the papers. "This was no accident. He knew why you married him."

"It would seem so."

"Can you challenge it?"

"No."

"Ouch."

"Yes, ouch. Such a tragedy, don't you think, that my husband had bought a forged painting and never knew it?"

It took me a few seconds to understand what she was saying. "Greta."

"What? These things happen in the art world, yes? Things are not always what they seem." She took a sip of her coffee. "Now, tell me how my Hans is? Is he doing okay?"

I spent the next twenty minutes filling her in on Hans and everything that had happened over the last week, including Lucia's arrest and Wilhelm's failed attempt to flee to a country that didn't have an extradition agreement with the United States. (Unfortunately for him, his pilots hated him as much as anyone and they'd turned him into the authorities for the reward money.)

"Will you stay now that Friedrich and Wilhelm are gone?" I asked, hoping the answer was yes. She might be an art thief, but she was also my friend and my only on-site customer.

"Yes. I believe I will. I like it here."

"Oh, good. I'm so glad to hear that. And you let me know if you need anything. But right now I have to run. It's Mason and Jamie's engagement party."

"Send them my congratulations." She grabbed my arm before I could leave. "And, Maggie, I know it was fast, but he'll make a good husband for her. Trust me on this."

I nodded, not trusting myself to answer.

I hoped she was right.

☙ ☙ ☙

The engagement party was at the barkery. It was just a small one. Mason had plans for an even bigger one at the country club in a few weeks, but this was for Jamie's family and friends, some of whom would've stuck out like a sore thumb in a country club setting. (Including yours truly even though I knew I'd be forced to pretty up and attend the other one, too.)

Jamie had insisted on making the cakes even though it was her party which meant that I was probably going to gain a good five pounds before the day was out.

(She'd already told Mason she was making the wedding cake, too, so he better get used to it. He'd looked to me for support in suggesting that wasn't the best of ideas, but I knew Jamie. If she wanted to have an eight-hundred-person wedding and make the cake for it, too, she would and it would be a flawless masterpiece.)

Mason was the first person I saw when I walked through the door. He was grinning with such delirious happiness I almost didn't recognize him.

I stopped and stared at him for a long moment.

He laughed. "Like the jeans? They were Jamie's engagement gift to me. She said they would make you like me more."

"You know…She's kind of right. I hate to be so shallow, but I do like you more in jeans. Makes you more…approachable." Sort of. I glanced at the thousand dollar loafers. Someday we'd get him into tennis shoes. But, you know, baby steps.

I wished him luck and fled to the corner where Matt and Jack were, Jack surrounded by pretty much every single woman in the place.

"Good to see you out of the hospital, Jack."

"Thanks, Maggie. I appreciate you helping my brother save my life. Heard I missed an interesting adventure. Something about you in nothing more than my brother's t-shirt?"

I glanced at Matt who held his hands up. "I didn't tell him anything other than that you helped me carry him down the mountain."

I shrugged. "I don't know what you're talking about, Jack."

"Hmm." He glanced back and forth between me and Matt as some pretty young thing snuck over to offer him a slice of coconut cake. "Thank you, sweetie." The girl blushed and ran away.

"You need to learn how to use that power for good, you know that?"

He winked at me. "Maybe I'll use it on you when I'm better."

I pointed at Matt. "I'm pretty sure your brother might have something to say about that."

Jack took a bite of cake. "I'm pretty sure I know my brother well enough to know when he's actually in a relationship and when he's just helping out a friend." He glanced up at Matt. "So if you don't want competition, brother, I'd suggest you act before I'm able to walk again."

As they stared each other down, I stepped away. "Alrighty then. I think that's my cue to go find a Coke or beer or something. Glad you're better, Jack."

I fled, trying not to think of how easily Matt had wormed his way past my defenses. I'd only had one defense left: that he didn't know he'd done it and was too scared to push and find out. Something his brother had just handily taken away.

Maybe.

Because I wasn't the only one hesitating. There was something holding Matt back as well. I was pretty sure he liked me, but I hadn't forgotten those comments about not being sure he wanted to stay a cop. Or about re-enlisting. Or moving away.

His feet weren't very firmly planted just yet. I could wake up the next day and he'd be gone.

A thought that didn't sit very well with me. But not one I was going to act on either.

I caught sight of Jamie on the other side of the room, glowing with such happiness it was almost blinding. I was happy for her, I really was. But I wondered what that meant for the café. And for our friendship. Not that we'd ever stop being friends, but you know, marriage, babies. They change things.

Ah well. Whichever way things went, I had a feeling the next couple of months were going to be far more interesting than I'd actually wanted them to be. But it'd be okay, because I was where I wanted to be and with the people I wanted to be with.

For now.

🐾 🐾 🐾

A Buried Body and Barkery Bites

To read about Maggie May's and Miss Fancypants's next adventure, check out **A Missing Mom and Mutt Munchies**.

ABOUT THE AUTHOR

When Aleksa Baxter decided to write what she loves it was a no-brainer to write a cozy mystery set in the mountains of Colorado where she grew up and starring a Newfie, Miss Fancypants, that is very much like her own Newfie, in both the good ways and the bad.

You can reach her at aleksabaxterwriter@gmail.com or on her website aleksabaxter.com.